the

EVENING
SPIDER

Emily Arsenault

wm

WILLIAM MORROW
An Imprint of HarperCollins*Publishers*

P.S.™ is a trademark of HarperCollins Publishers.

HarperCollins books may be purchased for educational, business, or sales promotional use. For information please e-mail the Special Markets Department at SPsales@harpercollins.com.

FIRST EDITION

Designed by Diahann Sturge

Chapter opener art copyright © by saki80 via Shutterstock, Inc.

Library of Congress Cataloging-in-Publication Data has been applied for.

ISBN 978-0-06-237931-3

16 17 18 19 20   OV/RRD   10 9 8 7 6 5 4 3 2

In memory of
Elizabeth Stannard Rastelli
and
Anna Carbonneau Arsenault

the

EVENING
SPIDER

Chapter 1

A YOUNG WOMAN'S RUIN AND DEATH.

MARY STANNARD'S DEAD BODY FOUND AT DURHAM,
CONN.-THE MANNER OF HER DEATH UNEXPLAINED-
A STATEMENT IMPLICATING A CLERGYMAN.

Special Dispatch to the *New-York Times*.

HARTFORD, Sept. 5, 1878-The dead body of Mary E.
Stannard, 22 years old, was found at Durham, near the
border of Madison, on Tuesday night. She had been living
with her father, and on Tuesday left home to go, as she
said, into the woods half a mile away after berries. As
she did not return, a search was made and she was found
dead in the woods, lying in a by-path on her back, with
her hands folded across her breast. On the left side of
her neck was a puncture wound, apparently made by a
pointed knife, which had severed the carotid artery and
jugular vein and larynx. There was also a hole through
her scalp, and a severe contusion on the back of her right
hand. At a Coroner's inquest a sister of the girl told this
story:

"Mary returned from Guilford Sunday last, bringing
with her her 2-year-old illegitimate child-the cause of

her having to leave the house where she had been at service. She was very low-spirited, and said she was pregnant, and that Rev. H. H. Hayden, who lives in Rockland and preaches in the Methodist Church in Madison, was the father of the unborn child. She said further that she had informed the clergyman of her condition, and he had promised to stand by her. He called at the house at 11 o'clock on that day, and made an appointment to meet her at a large rock, where the body was found. The deceased left at the time appointed to fulfill the engagement with him."

The post-mortem examination disclosed the fact that she was not in the condition alleged. Nor was there any evidence that her person had been violated, the latter fact being important in connection with a theory that she might have been outraged by a tramp and then murdered. The testimony of a woman who was passing by the woods where the body was found and heard shrieks seems to indicate an assault. The story of the sister implicating the clergyman looks like an invention, and possibly was told by the deceased while in a distracted state of mind. It is said that insanity runs in the family, and the mother died insane.

A special dispatch from Madison tonight says that Rev. Mr. Hayden's name has not been reproachfully mentioned there, and that nothing has been heard of any movement to arrest him. The scene of the tragedy is remote from thickly settled places, away from railroads and telegraph, and much that is heard comes by rumor.

Chapter 2

Rowan College
Rowan, Vermont
February 20, 1998

A ll of the doors in Davidson Hall had a distinct creak—
like a dog groaning in his sleep, and then waking with an
excited, rasping half yawn.

UUUUUURRRII—eeep!

A friendly old dog awakening upon your arrival.

*It wasn't a ghostly sound, exactly, but more one of old-timey
warmth. Revered building. Strong wood. Strong doors. Old hinges.*

Welcome home.

*That's how I felt about every corner of this campus. More like
home than any place I'd ever been. But Davidson Hall most of
all. It was the oldest dorm—maybe the oldest building—in the
entire school. I loved its musty stairwells and its clinking, steam-
ing radiators.*

*My stomach growled as I climbed the stairs to the second floor.
I couldn't get Bon Jovi's "Bad Medicine" out of my mind. I'd just
gotten an A on a political science paper and whenever I had little
victories, my head wanted to play through its favorite songs from
when I was ten. Pop metal was apparently hardwired into the pleasure centers of my brain.*

Two doors from the stairwell. Number 202. My chunky-heeled loafers were pinching my feet and I couldn't wait to get out of them. I turned the loose doorknob and pressed against the Einstein-with-his-tongue-out poster that hung above it.

UUUUUURRRHH—eeep.

After the sound of the door, I noticed a silence in place of the sluggish "Oh . . . Hullo" that usually greeted me at that time of day.

The silence was not coming from an absence, however. It was coming from the figure on the bed—with the familiarly pale and knobby knee poking out from beneath the lilac afghan.

I approached the bed and touched the knee. Despite its cold, I was able to swallow the sensation of horror because this could not be real. This only happened in movies, and not to regular girls like me and certainly not to drippy girls like her.

After I jostled her arm and saw her face, that horror came back up my throat as a scream that I could not stop.

Chapter 3

Haverton, Connecticut
December 1, 2014

Shhhhh.

The sound followed so immediately after my daughter's cry that I didn't even open my eyes. Lucy was doing her saddest cry—the jagged, choking one that normally sent me flying into her room. Tonight, though, I could remain in bed, warm under the down comforter. Even over the fuzzy secondhand baby monitor we'd been using, the shushing sound was distinct and assured. Chad had apparently heard her first as I'd slept uncharacteristically deeply. A welcome role reversal, if only for a night.

Sweet, I thought.

Shhhhh.

I smiled, wondering if Chad had picked up Lucy or was trying to settle her with just patting and reassuring from the side of the crib. It was a fool's errand with our live-wire daughter, but we still tried sometimes—in hopes that she'd one day learn how to fall asleep somewhere besides our arms or a car seat.

Shhhhh.

I tossed from my right side to my left. Upon landing on my

elbow, my gaze met the familiar hill of my husband's back. He was clad in his robe—probably because there were no clean pajamas. Lately, I'd been better about doing Lucy's laundry than our own. The thought *I need to pop in a load of shirts and underwear one of these days* somehow registered in my brain just before this more alarming one: *If Chad is here in bed with me, who is in there shushing Lucy?*

Shhhhh.

I wasn't dreaming.

I threw off the covers.

"What? What is it? Wantmetogo?" Chad mumbled.

I jumped out of bed and raced down the hall—a hall whose blue-lit carpet and wall seemed endless and unfamiliar as I ran toward the sound of my pulse and my daughter's cries.

When I reached into her crib, I swiftly snatched her up. I heard a *thunk* as I did it, but a few seconds later, after my heart stopped pounding, it felt like the sound had been a product of my nervous imagination. Lucy was in my arms now. That was all that mattered.

Chapter 4

Northampton Lunatic Hospital
Northampton, Massachusetts
December 20, 1885

Five years. That's how long it's taken you to come see me. Did you forget about me, dear brother? Or did you think—do you still think—they would not—and will not—ever let me out? Did you not want to hear my side of things, for fear I would be too persuasive?

Fear not. I barely know why I am even here—though over the years I have developed some theories. Don't I always have theories? Yet none of those theories quite explains your absence or your silence until now.

Were you afraid you might find me bald and naked in a cage? Certainly it happens here, somewhere in the back halls of this monstrous brick building—far behind the grand front rotunda and these front parlor rooms. I hear the screams, but I tend not to put pictures to them in my mind lest I begin screaming myself and end up back there with them, joining their terrible chorus. If one can manage not to rage and wail, one stands a chance of a sedate existence. Did the nurse tell you that I occasionally work in the greenhouse? It is my favorite time, if it is possible to have a favorite of anything in this life. Many of the nurses have remarked on my delicate touch with the seedlings.

Surely, though, you did not come to hear about that.

You wish to know my side, truly?

Very well, then. Since you have taken so long to come and find me, I think it best to tell the whole story. I shouldn't want to leave anything out, since perhaps you won't return for another five years? Ten? For eternity? I have been waiting some time to tell it to you, so if you'll indulge me, I shall go back to the very beginning.

Chapter 5

In the light of morning—even a dreary, rainy morning like this one—and accompanied by the invigorating whir of the coffee grinder, the night's drama seemed silly, and its explanation obvious.

We had an iPod playing water sounds in Lucy's room all night long. There were four tracks on the album—waterfall, rain storm, babbling brook, and ocean waves. We'd used this recording since Lucy's very first night home from the hospital. The waves one in particular had an undertone of *shush . . . swish . . . shush* to it.

"You know what it probably was, *really*?" Chad shouted at me over the grinding of his fancy beans. He still allowed himself an espresso twice a week when his Crohn's wasn't threatening to flare.

"What's that?" I shouted back, dumping baby oatmeal into a purple plastic bowl.

"Wishful thinking," he yelled as the grinding stopped. "Your subconscious is telling you what a better husband would have been doing in that moment."

I snorted. "Yeah. My subconscious is a real ballbuster, I guess."

I stepped out of the kitchen for a moment to squeeze some breast milk into the bowl. Chad doesn't know that I do this, and I'm sure it would wig him out if he did. But I am always engorged in the morning and it's such a pain to sterilize the manual pump for just an ounce or so for Lucy's cereal. Interestingly, Chad never seemed to notice that I occasionally came back into the kitchen with wet cereal when I'd left with dry. Too busy with the espresso ritual. For the best, really.

I fed Lucy her baby oatmeal, which she gobbled happily. I'd heard of babies rejecting solid food at first, but this had never been the case with our Lucy. At the first taste of it two weeks ago, her eyes had lit up at the novelty of it—and had been lighting up with each spoonful since. It was quite different from her approach to nursing—sucking in a scowling, workmanlike fashion from the very first day.

"She's got something on her nose," I said, watching her brow crinkle with concern for the proximity of her next spoonful. One side of the top of her nose looked sore and red. "A kind of . . . ding."

"Maybe she rolled hard into one of the crib slats," Chad said, pouring my cappuccino foam. "She's going a little crazy with the rolling, I've noticed. She's got some WWE moves lately."

"Yeah." I glanced out the window at our driveway, where the puddles were dimpling with rain. Most likely there would be no walking with Lucy today.

"If she wakes up tonight, why don't you nudge me?" Chad said. "It's my turn."

Tonight seemed so far away. Two more solid meals. Two naps for Lucy—probably on my chest. Nursing. Board books ad nauseam. *Feel the fluffy yellow chick. The pig is PINK. The strawberry is RED*. Straining—straining so hard—not to turn on the television to speed up the long midafternoon hours. The evils of secondhand television, after all. As bad for the tiny brain as secondhand smoke is for the lungs, they say. *There is no such thing as educational programming for children under three*. It was more difficult now that the weather was getting chillier, and walks were growing unappealing and sometimes ill-advised. Annoyingly, it had been a particularly cold and rainy autumn so far.

"Okay?" Chad said.

"Okay," I said, then gulped my coffee greedily as Chad pulled on his coat. It seemed that once Chad was gone, I always forgot to drink what was left in my cup.

Lucy was writhing in her chair, already bored with sitting. I knocked a spoon rhythmically against her tray table. She seemed mesmerized by it for a few moments—not nearly as long as I was. I was easily mesmerized these days.

"Maybe it was Florabelle," Chad said.

"Who? What?" I said, looking up.

"Shushing Lucy, I mean."

"Oh." I pushed the spoon to Lucy.

Florabelle was what we called the dressmaker's dummy we'd found in the deepest depths of our house's storage space. We'd made the discovery a couple of months before Lucy was born, when we were storing stuff from the "guest room" (really the junk room, with the old futon on the floor) we'd cleared out for her nursery. It had been a funny moment—through the wall I'd heard a shout of surprise, then Chad laughing. *Abby, I want you to see this.*

Ultimately, we'd decided it wasn't worth my trying to hunch my giant pregnant body into the space just to look at an old dummy. It was a tight, dusty space with a slanted ceiling, running all along one side of the upstairs hall of the house. You had to stay hunched down quite low to walk the length of it, and if you accidentally pulled yourself up, you risked bonking your head or jabbing your shoulder on a rusty nail. Chad took a picture on his iPhone for me to see. Chad left her right where he'd found her, putting all of our old boxes at her feet. We named her Florabelle and spoke of her affectionately until Lucy was born. Then we promptly forgot about her.

I smiled. "Florabelle doesn't have a head, my dear. What would she shush with, exactly?"

"Hmm," Chad said, twisting his mouth into a feigned look of puzzlement.

Then he picked up his travel mug, messenger bag, and plastic tub of loose pennies. For the past couple of months, he'd been doing something he called "coin roll hunting." He bought one or two hundred dollars' worth of one coin or another, examined them for old collectibles, silver dimes or quarters, minting errors, or other oddities that made them worth more than their face value. Then he returned the remaining coins for his money back, saving the occasional special one to eventually sell on eBay.

"Back to the bank with your pennies?" I said.

"I think I'll just go ahead and trade them in for dimes."

"Live dangerously, dear."

"I always do," he said and kissed Lucy and me good-bye.

Chapter 6

It begins when we were children, doesn't it?

It begins with the assumption that I was, like Clara, to take after Mother and you after Father. I was to be gentle and affectionate, and you bookish and systematic.

Perhaps it didn't work out that way since we were twins. In the womb, you got some of the substance intended for me, and vice versa. Gestational medicine—is that the term for it?—has never been one of my interests, but is it not possible that things get mixed up in there and improperly distributed?

Remember when Father brought home the old microscope for you to try? It was for your—our—twelfth birthday. I received a beautiful blue dress and was appropriately grateful for it, I hope. I still remember it well—the lace collar and the mother-of-pearl buttons. Thankfully, though, you were perfectly willing to share *your* treasure—more than I could mine.

At first, I was only allowed to fetch tree bark and feathers outdoors and dead moths from the cupboards, bringing them to you as we imagined Father's lab assistant would.

Within a week you grew bored of the game, the microscope,

and my constant company in its presence. You returned to your friends and to kicking a ball up and down the street in the afternoons.

I became my own assistant. The first thing I looked at was a dandelion pappus. Yes, the pappus is the fluffy crown—I have a good memory for these things. Its tufts are a hundred times more beautiful up close—each one a radiant sun. Not every object I found was so brilliant as a dandelion's pappus, of course. But nearly everything seemed to offer a hidden, if subtle, surprise. How I adored my stolen time at your desk.

Mother allowed it as long as she thought I was looking at things beautiful and delicate—flower petals and blades of grass. She didn't know how I loved to look at scabs and fingernails and the wings of dead flies. Even Father did not know that. Even you.

You did not know how beastly your sister was, did you?

Chapter 7

L ucy had been sleeping for nearly two hours.

I'd had a shower and taken care of the dishes and done the laundry. The triple crown of naptime. So rare that one got to accomplish all three. But I had done it, and now I was staring up our narrow staircase, wondering if there was something wrong.

Lucy never slept this long in the afternoon.

But *why bite a gift horse in the mouth*, as my malaprop-prone grandmother used to say. If I crept up the stairs, they'd squeak and grunt and probably wake her.

I palmed the spherical wooden knob at the bottom of our banister and tried to identify what, exactly, I'd been longing to do the last time I'd wished Lucy would take longer naps. Wasn't there a book I'd been meaning to read? A friend I'd been meaning to call?

Surely Lucy would be waking any moment now, so perhaps it was best to simply embrace the quiet. I'd been better at that when Lucy was a newborn. Now that she was a bit older, and now that the beginning of the school year had come and gone without me, quiet seemed a bit less tender, a bit less precious. More like something that had to be filled and endured.

When we'd learned last year that I was due in June, it had never been a question that I'd take the following school year off. The administration at Brigham Girls' Academy did not seem particularly broken up about losing me for a year. I'd been there only two years, and I believe they found me serviceable but replaceable—though they'd promised to hold my position, giving my eager substitute only a one-year contract. I wondered what she was teaching the AP girls today. Thomas Paine? No. Already too late in the year for that. The Federalists? I supposed I was glad to miss that today.

I slipped my phone out of my pocket and looked at the time. It had been more than two hours now. And what of that *thunk* I'd heard in the night as I lifted Lucy out of the crib? A hard hit on the head. Shaken baby. *Don't let the baby sleep after a bump on the head.* I'd seen it all over the mom forums online. My heart jumped, and I started up the stairs. How had I forgotten that?

I took the final steps two at a time, leaping toward Lucy's room, stretching my hand toward her door.

The door felt heavy for a moment—as if there was someone behind it, pushing it in the opposite direction. The sensation sent a chill down my arm and through my fingers. I tried to grip the doorknob tighter, but my hand felt paralyzed.

Taking my hand off the knob, I pressed the door with my shoulder. I wasn't sure if it was me or the door that grunted as it swung open, popping abruptly against the naked metal doorstop. We'd taken the rubber parts of the doorstop off before Lucy was born because they were a choking hazard. Why not childproof what you can, when you can?

Lucy sighed in response to the noise. I caught my breath and then held it. Her arms were flung out in both directions—as if she were making snow angels against the fitted white sheet.

I stared at Lucy's turned head, admiring the clockwise swirl of her delicate blond-brown hair. Lighter than mine, but darker than her dad's. The friendly woman who used to sit near me at the Mommies and Babies group at the library—the tall one named Sara, with the completely bald baby girl—had complimented its color.

This was the first week I'd skipped the group since the summer. I'd grown bored of it—all of us nursing and sipping cold decafs and pretending we weren't already secretly judging each other. I'd thought I'd make a few friends among the other mothers there, but it hadn't happened. Sara had been nice, but we hadn't really clicked. I didn't think I'd go again.

I *did* need to think of a way to get out more. Maybe I should at least sign up for a moms and babies swimming class. Something like that. Was Lucy old enough for that? Even if she was, I'd have to order a one-piece bathing suit for sure. My stomach had not fared well during the pregnancy. My navel, now misshapen and framed with wrinkles, felt more like a vile and private orifice than anything deserving of a cute label like "belly button."

For a week or so I'd attempted calling it "the dowager countess," to remind myself that something wrinkled could still be cool and dignified, but I didn't manage to convince myself. Nor did I particularly wish to become the sort of person who named her body parts.

Lucy turned her face toward me but didn't open her eyes. I knelt down on the floor next to the crib, wincing as the floorboards creaked.

The mark on her face had more definition now, circling the outside of her nose and the inner part of her right cheekbone. It also appeared to be turning purple. Maybe it was just the dull light of her room. I had lowered her shades for naptime.

Lucy's water sounds were playing on repeat. Sitting cross-legged now on her floor with nothing better to do, I had a chance to see if I was correct about the "waves" track. When it came around, I closed my eyes and listened carefully. The waves were thunderous on their way in but hissed softly on their way out. *Ssssssss*. Sometimes more like *swish swish*. Maybe, when one was sleepy, one wanted to hear *shhhhh*. So that was how I'd heard it through the monitor the previous night.

As I waited for Lucy to wake up, I listened to all four tracks a couple of times and rated them from my first to least favorite: rain storm, babbling brook, ocean waves, waterfall. Or maybe babbling brook first. But waterfall was definitely last.

Chapter 8

Northampton Lunatic Hospital
Northampton, Massachusetts
December 20, 1885

My point, Harry, is that I perhaps appreciate the world's tiny mechanisms better than I do the more significant hows and whys.

The why of our Lord taking Father from us when he did, for sad example.

When Father died, a fog settled over all of us. It seemed, after some months, that it lifted for you and Clara and even Mother. Not for me, though. Do you remember? You all mourned so efficiently, so neatly—at least, compared to me. You all simply turned back to your everyday affairs. I, however, did not have everyday affairs as such. I was between one stage and another. No school as you had. No husband as Clara had. My days were occupied cooking and cleaning for Mother, and occasionally practicing the piano. Of course, I read whenever Mother allowed. My selections most often came from Father's library—usually about plants and anatomy and microscopy. Stories never appealed to me. At least not made-up ones.

How I dragged about the house for months. I was Mother's rag doll. I knew that our circumstances required me to be especially dutiful. Yet I could not rouse myself beyond the minimal chores and affections.

Mother did, however, find me most useful in her Saturday baking. Baking was, of all the chores, the most like Father's science, with its measurements and proportions and chemical reactions. I took notes on the results and improved the product each week. It was a childish endeavor, but it kept me earnestly occupied.

My condition improved by small degrees. Still, home was never the same, was it? Without Father's good cheer and Father's curiosities? That is not to say Mother did not provide us with as much comfort as she was able. Frankly, though, I missed the way Father indulged me. Specifically, the way he would talk of my future, my education. All of that talk died with him.

When he was alive, Father spoke highly of a women's college in Massachusetts that he thought would be suitable for me. Now that we were being educated on Uncle John's generosity, however, there was little possibility of anything so frivolous. We were lucky that your plans for Yale were so fully realized.

I digress. I bring up the changed atmosphere of home by way of explanation. You never did understand why I was so agreeable to Matthew's courtship, and so eager to accept his proposal. You hinted I ought to wait for someone closer in age, someone more similar in disposition.

My disposition would have been a tricky match, though, don't you think? And Matthew had such an air of tidy optimism, did he not?

Of *course* you know what that means, Harry. Don't be silly.

Haven't I ever told you about the first time he brought me a gift? It was perhaps his third call to the house, and he gave me a tiny figurine of a kitten. I have never much liked kittens, but I was nonetheless flattered that Matthew had so quickly elevated our courtship to that level.

To accompany the gift, Matthew had a charming story of how it came into his possession.

"I was on my way to the train in Boston when I got drawn into this queer little shop not far from the station."

"Is it pleasing to you, traveling by train?" I asked. *"My father didn't care much for it, but I have never tried it."*

"I've done it so much in recent years, I hardly think about it."

I did not know how to reply. I looked away because I found myself, as often, inappropriately transfixed by the curious part in his hair, so wide and so far to one side. I wondered if, were we ever married, it would be impertinent to suggest moving it a half-inch back toward the middle.

"When you first started, then, did you enjoy it?" I inquired. *"Or did you find it very jarring, very noisy, the first time or two?"*

"Not so very much," Matthew answered before scooting forward in his chair, balancing himself quite eagerly at its very edge. *"Now, about this kitten. The man had wares from all over the world. I believe this little treasure was from China. So entranced was I by it that I forgot my train for some time. Perhaps I'd have stood there looking at it for some time more had the train not blasted its horn. So startled was I that I dropped the little creature. The shopkeeper was incensed and rushed at me. When I bent to pick it up, I saw, to my astonishment, that it had survived the fall intact! Not a scratch. Now my time for making my selections was clearly over. And this cat had proven itself to be a very special find indeed. I*

decided he was fated for me. I have had him for a year or two now, but I had always intended him to be a gift for someone."

The tiny figurine was pink. I considered asking him, to be witty, if cats were pink in China. I bit my tongue, however, for fear of appearing ungrateful.

"Eight lives left on him," I said. "Or perhaps fewer, for all we know."

What's that, Harry? Pardon me. Was I drifting for a moment? The nurses tell me I do that often—even in the middle of our conversations, such as they are. Or in the sewing room, when my progress has stalled and my quota of curtains or shirts is not filled. They think me mad, I suppose. Silly me! Why would they think me anything else? In my defense, I believe there is something about this place that enlivens one's memory. On some days, as I fall asleep to white walls and other women's groans and snores, all I can remember of my day—aside from the consoling light of the greenhouse—is the experience of remembering something else.

Ah, but returning to Matthew—all other things aside, waiting for someone closer in age would mean waiting for years upon years. That's what I told you, wasn't it? I was only twenty. All the young men my age had to finish their schooling and establish themselves. Was I to wait that long, sweeping the kitchen floor in the afternoons, stirring Mother's tiresome pots of peas, pulling endless—though perfected—cider loaves from that oppressive oven?

Matthew was already a lawyer. He already had a house to his name. Yes, the house was in Haverton—a few miles away from our New Haven home, and from Mother. But that wouldn't be such a bad thing, would it? A new place? I would be closer to Clara. And my old friend Louise was in Haverton, caring for her aunt Dorothy. I would not be so terribly lonely then.

Things would surely be different if I was the woman of the house? With Matthew's means, I'd even have a maid to assist me. There would be time for reading and explorations. There would be trips on mighty, bellowing trains.

Chapter 9

Chad was going to be home late, so it was a good time to catch up on his least favorite entertainments. He didn't understand my taste for stand-up and late-night comedy. I clicked on a old Louis C.K. special, pulled the laptop up close to my pillow, and pulled up the duvet.

CLING!

I heard the sound of something small and metallic falling out of the bed and onto our wood floor. Probably a penny. Chad brought the occasional penny roll to bed—to examine under a reading lamp while I dozed off early. Sometimes I'd peer over to his side of the bed and feel a twinge of guilt at what my postpartum period had done to him. It had turned him into a nerd.

But it was payback, in a way. Chad didn't know that my stand-up habit started in the second year of our marriage. That was the year that his dog Bartleby—who had predated me by several years—had to be put down. Then Chad's Crohn's—mild up till that point—flared up worse than it ever had. Chad grew frighteningly thin and had to go to the hospital for an IV a couple of times, then take a few weeks off from his job. I'd make him a special gluten-free, dairy-free dinner every night, then sit up with him, correcting papers while we watched his sci-fi shows. When that was all over, I'd tune in to my Conan or my Jimmy or whoever else was available. Or if the timing was off, I'd get on YouTube and watch old clips of George Carlin, Chris Rock, or Bill Hicks. Sometimes till two A.M. Then I'd get up at five-thirty in the morning to go teach—all yawns and private giggles.

That was five years ago. But to this day, I dreaded our cat Monty ever getting sick. I watched his eating habits with great care. I took him to the vet religiously. Maybe the timing of Bartleby's death and Chad's flare-up was partially coincidental. There was a lot of stress involved in Chad's job—marketing consultation—that never seemed to affect him at all. But it was all a bloodless sort of stress—petty client needs and tedious business travel. It made perfect sense that Chad's weak spot was for cute, furry little animals.

Now Louis C.K. was talking about his little daughter and her idea of "secrets." I'd seen it several times before, of course, but I heard it differently now that I had Lucy. Lucy would tell me secrets someday. And then someday, she wouldn't. My eyelids started to droop, and Louis C.K.'s words started to lose their meaning, dissolving into the beginning of a dream about a squirrel in a bloated diaper. I couldn't get the squirrel to sit still to change it, and the diaper was way too big.

When a cry awoke me, the comedy was still playing, but the clock at the corner of the computer said 9:12. I nestled my head in my pillow and waited a moment. Occasionally she got herself back to sleep when she awoke so early in the night. Very occasionally, but it was possible. There was a silence, and I allowed myself to drift off a bit.

After what felt like a minute or two, there was another cry, and then a *shhhhh*.

Right. Chad *had* said he'd be getting in around nine.

He must've just come in the door and heard Lucy crying. He'd gone straight to her room to tend to her—before even coming to me.

Shhhhh, he whispered.

I closed my eyes again. But I hadn't heard the car in the driveway at all. Nor had I heard the side door open.

Shhhhh.

My eyes snapped open. I sprang up and staggered into the hallway. When I reached Lucy's door, I grabbed the doorknob and pushed.

The door felt heavy.

I pushed harder. There was a stickiness to the doorframe.

Turning the knob, I put my full weight against the door and it flew open with an *OOOOOAAHHHHR* sound.

I rushed to Lucy's crib but paused before picking her up. I needed to lift her out carefully this time. In my hesitation, I noticed that she had suddenly stopped crying. Her eyes were wide open, and she was staring at me with a half smile on her face.

"Come here, my little night owl," I whispered, trying to control the wobbling sensation in my mouth.

Once Lucy was nestled against my chest, I whispered in her ear, "Who? Who? Who?"

Lucy giggled. I was about to congratulate myself for my spontaneous inventiveness, but I noticed that Lucy wasn't looking at me at all. Her eyes were fixed on the doorway.

Could it have been the sound of the door that had stopped her crying? Lucy had only laughed a few times in her life so far, and each time it had been at something enigmatically unfunny from an adult perspective: the fluttering of a plastic bag to the floor, the sound of Chad flipping through a pile of bills, the sudden appearance of George Stephanopoulos on television.

"What is it, honey?" I said. "The door?"

I carried Lucy to the door and gently pushed it halfway closed and then open again.

OOOOOAAHHHHR. I glanced at Lucy. She seemed interested, but not particularly amused.

I opened the door again, wider this time.

OOOOOAAHHHHR-eeee.

Lucy cracked a smile at the squeaky finish.

I did it again. And again. Still no laugh.

OOOOOAAHHHHR-eeee.

Lucy nestled her head into my chest and closed her eyes.

I opened and closed the door again. And again. It didn't sound quite right. Something about that sound was just not at all right for a baby girl's room.

OOOOOAAHHHHR-eeee.

And again and again. Some illogical part of me thought that if I opened and closed it enough times, the sound would either wear itself out or morph into a slightly different—if not a slightly more pleasant—sound.

OOOOOAAHHHHR eeee. OOOOOAAHIIIIIIR-eeee.

"What're you two up to?"

I jumped. Chad was at the bottom of the stairs, looking up at me.

"Oh. When did you get home?"

"Just now. You guys are up late."

"Lucy likes the door sound."

"Really," said Chad, tiptoeing up the stairs to meet me.

I looked down at Lucy, who was dozing on my arm. Her mouth was open, her lower lip mushed against my flannel pajamas. Chad took my arms in his so we were both cradling Lucy at the same time.

"Wow," he said, studying Lucy's face. "That bruise looks kinda nasty."

I stared at Lucy's face. He was right. It had turned a blue-purple. It looked bigger than it had earlier in the day—though perhaps it was just its two-toned quality that made it seem so.

"Huh. I guess we need to be more careful," he said, shrugging. "Do we even know how she got that?"

I was pretty sure I knew *when* she'd gotten it. The first night I'd heard the shushing sound over the monitor. But *how*—I wasn't so sure of that. Had it been when I lifted her out of the crib so hastily? Or had the bump happened before I arrived? And was that why she'd been crying in the first place? And what was this *we* Chad was using, when he couldn't have meant anything but *you*?

"No," I murmured. "No, we don't."

Chapter 10

Yes, yes. You are correct. There were no mighty, bellowing trains. I got nothing more than a whistling teakettle in my Haverton kitchen.

I understand that you were skeptical, Harry. You must nonetheless admit that early married life suited me better than wasting away in Mother's home? Granting, of course, that I have adjusted my conception of what *wasting* really means in more recent years—

Yes. *Early* married life suited me well. I have already made that stipulation. You needn't interrupt.

I *did* enjoy being the mistress of a household—at least more than being a dutiful daughter. Our maid, Tessa, took up most of the more tedious housework, and I got to focus on the fancier cooking and hostessing tasks.

Matthew would come home and tell me about his work. When we were first married, he tried and won an embezzlement case. I'd look forward to hearing the details over dinner, but those conversations were often disappointing.

*The secretary wasn't recording the funds correctly in the ac-
counting books and was taking the difference for himself.*

He's a revolting little fellow, really. That's what it boils down to.

Oh, I don't remember the exact numbers, darling.

*The lesson is, Frances, that we all ought to be careful about
whom we trust.*

For a time, I felt that if I spent half the day in the kitchen
working to serve his dinner hot, at the appointed time, and with
the most precisely pleasing flavors, Matthew would in return
serve up a decent and detailed story of his day's endeavors. That
is not how marriage and housekeeping operates, I soon learned.
Matthew never explained his work as vividly as you always did
your studies.

Perhaps it was the age difference between Matthew and me
that made him speak of things so simply. Or perhaps you always
spoiled me with information since I'm your sister.

*That is fascinating, Harry. I do wonder if the human brain is
similarly organized? But how, specifically, did Fritsch and Hitzig
access that part of dogs' brains while they were still alive?*

Do you really want to know, Frances?

Why wouldn't I want to know?

Very well, then . . .

Matthew, however, thought I would not understand. It didn't
bother me a great deal with that embezzlement case. But then,
about six months into our marriage, he helped take on a more
important case: the McFarlene murder, which occurred right
there in our Haverton! Suddenly the details—the ones I could
get out of him—were more enticing. A Wiggins Hill drunkard
named John McFarlene had beaten Walter Beck, his brother-
in-law, to death, they said. He had apparently dragged the body

to the woods in hopes it wouldn't be discovered. But a dog had found it the very next day, and barked and barked till his master came and saw it, too.

It was around that time, however, that I started to feel unsteady on my feet, and nauseous at kitchen smells. Not long after, Dr. Graham confirmed my pregnancy. My interest in nearly everything around me—and Matthew's work was no exception—wore thin as I became consumed with worries about the future.

I'd always enjoyed compliments on my small and delicate frame. Now those qualities felt like a death sentence. Surely I would not survive the birth of a child? And if I did survive? What then? I had never thought of myself as a mother. Why hadn't I?

Matthew was entirely occupied with his work and perhaps did not notice his wife's mortal fear. And then—rather quickly—his case was won. Of course Matthew was the younger, assisting prosecutor. Nonetheless, it was quite an impressive and celebrated win for such a young attorney. Do you remember? McFarlene was hanged in New Haven. Matthew was even present for the execution—can you imagine? Despite—or perhaps because of—my own (I presumed) imminent death, I longed to hear the details.

Was there a look of dread or a look of peace on McFarlene's face as he walked his final steps? Did he have any last words? Did his neck make a snapping noise after the trap was sprung? Is it true that the eyes bulge out in the terminal moments? Is it a purely physical response to the rope's constriction, or is it perhaps a final begging sort of gesture—begging to see just one more moment of life on Earth?

I suppose Matthew would not have been able to answer about the eyes since the convict's face is always covered. In any case, he would not have wished to answer any such questions. He surely would have been troubled to hear them out of the mouth of his sweet young bride. Besides, my condition made him regard me with even more delicacy than before.

Once the "unpleasant business" (as Matthew often called the execution) was over, Matthew was entrusted with ever more important cases. We enjoyed a respectable, even enviable, position in New Haven society.

We were the model of a happy young family, poised for even more auspicious times. At least, I believe that is how we *appeared*. There was a darkness growing inside me by then, however. I hid it well, but I pictured it often as a black tulip—like the ones I used to see with Father at his friend Mr. Cogdill's grand greenhouse.

Strong and pointed foliage unfurling. Petals with all the beauty of a crow's plumage.

Chapter 11

Haverton, Connecticut
December 5, 2014

The wind was freezing, but the sun was shining. And we needed paper towels. At least, as much as you could really *need* paper towels. It was a decent enough excuse to walk to the nearby convenience store. Lucy was usually pretty happy rolling around in her covered stroller, and I was usually happy if there was a coffee in its cupholder—even if it was convenience store coffee.

I made my way back slowly, pushing the stroller one-handed as I sipped. As I took the corner to our street, the stroller's plastic wheels groaned painfully over the gravel on the sidewalk and refused to straighten. I had to put down the coffee for a moment and use both hands to reorient the stroller in the right direction. Coffee splattered out of the cup's little sip-hole, and I muttered a couple of curse words under my breath.

As I picked up the cup and continued toward home, I saw that our neighbor was watching me from her driveway.

Patty, I had to remind myself. She looked so uncannily like Liza Minnelli that *L* names always came to my head first when I grasped for her name.

"Tiiiii-naaaaaah" Patty called when she saw me looking back at her. Patty seemed to keep her cat on a tight meal schedule. "Time for breakfast!" "Time for lunch!" "Time for din-din!" she called consistently at eight, one, and six o'clock. Chad had recently claimed that he'd heard her calling "Tina, time for your bath!" Patty—who was divorced, in her sixties, and, in her words, "still waiting for grandbabies"—always seemed eager to interact with Lucy.

"Hi there," I called as we approached her driveway.

"Hello," Patty said. "I saw you walk by when you left. I hope you two didn't go too far in this windy weather."

"Just to SmartMart."

Patty nodded. "Can I say hi to the little one?"

I pulled the hood of the stroller open slightly and peeked in. "She's asleep," I said.

"The movement puts them to sleep real good, huh?"

"Yeah," I agreed. "She's in la-la land."

I considered my house for a moment, trying to take in its antique charm as I had the first time I'd laid eyes on it: its unusually steep roof, its cozy blue solidity as it perched on its high stone steps. When you faced it from the street, it had perfect square symmetry—like a child's drawing of a house. There was a single black shuttered window on each side of its perky evergreen door.

"Patty . . ." I said slowly, "you've lived here in this neighborhood quite a few years, haven't you?"

"Almost twenty, yes."

"You knew the previous owner of my house pretty well?"

"Janelle? No. She only lived here a year or so. I don't think it was ever her plan to stay very long. Just to fix it up nice and flip it."

"Oh, I didn't mean her. I meant before that."

"Shirley, you mean? The Barnetts? You know, before Janelle, the Barnetts owned this house going *way* way back. Like, more than a hundred years, I think."

"I know." The real estate agent told us the basic story. The house had been in the Barnett family for generations. Shirley Barnett—a Barnett by marriage—had been in her eighties, living in the place alone, when she'd broken her hip and her family had decided to move her out and sell the place. Shirley had died in a nursing home soon after that. "Lately, I've just been curious about the house's history."

Patty nodded knowingly. "You're a history teacher, aren't you?"

"Yeah," I said. If I blamed it on that, this conversation didn't have to be creepy at all. "I'm a history nerd."

Patty looked offended on my behalf. "You don't need to be a nerd to be interested in history. Like, I'm all into Marie Antoinette. Or at least, I was at one time. Do you know much about her?"

"Uh . . . just the basics," I admitted.

"Anyway," Patty waved the subject away. "You were talking about your house. Yeah, Shirley and Eddie were real proud the house had been in his family so long. Shame no one in the family wanted it when she had to move out. But she had just the niece and nephew left. Nephew has a house . . . in Southington, I think. And the niece . . . not sure about her. Just didn't want it. They split the money from the sale, I guess. I don't know the details."

Patty shook her head, then tugged thoughtfully at a thick tuft of dark hair by her ear.

"It was a shame," she said, "how they had to move Shirley out of here like they did. She didn't want to leave. But it was obvious she couldn't take care of herself anymore. It was the hip that did it, finally. But even before that I think there was a little dementia setting in, or something. Her nephew Gerard was telling me, the day they moved her out, she was crying, 'Please don't take me away! Who is going to take care of the baby?' She never even had kids. So figure that one out. Poor thing!"

"Umm." I stared at my hands as they tightened around the stroller handle. They'd grown bright pink from the cold. "Maybe she was talking about a pet, or something?"

"I don't think so. I'm pretty sure Shirley disliked cats, and I'm certain she didn't have a dog."

"Maybe she meant the house," I suggested. "Maybe she thought of the house as her baby."

Patty scrunched up her sculpted eyebrows. "You know, I never thought of it that way before. Not sure that makes it any less sad. Huh. But hey—speaking of her nephew Gerard, you might want to talk to him. He's the one who did most of the cleaning of the house when they had to move her out. I know he found some pretty old stuff. Old books, old pictures, I think. The family had been in the place for so long, see, no one knew how *old* some of the stuff was that was packed away in there. He told me he got a few hundred dollars selling some of the old books. But since you're interested in history, like you say, maybe you want to take a look? I can give you his number if you want. If I can find it. It's been a few years."

"Sure. That would be great. Thank you."

As I said this, a happy little warble came from under the hooded stroller.

"Oh!" Patty clapped her hands. "I was hoping she'd wake up!"

I pulled open the hood, and Patty peered in. "How are you, Little Miss? Ooh, look at your little lamb fleece! What a doll!"

"She seems pretty well rested," I said. "Or she'd be crying."

"Hey, honey." Patty leaned closer to Lucy, who seemed to narrow her eyes at her. "Oh! Dear. What happened, honey? What happened to your sweet little face? Did you take a tumble? You've got almost like a shiner there."

"She . . ." I started to explain that we weren't sure what happened, but realized that sounded worse than almost anything else I could say. *In fact, we don't watch her at all. Could've been a sharp corner, could've been a falling whiskey tumbler. What can you do? Can't watch 'em every minute.*

"She bumped the side of her crib. When she was sleeping."

"Huh. Kind of an interesting shape, that bruise. Almost perfectly round." Patty sighed and looked up at me. "Isn't that what those baby bumpers are for? My niece, she had some real pretty ones for her daughter. They had pink and orange polka dots. The whole room was pink and orange. Real bright. It was gorgeous. But you can get bumpers to match whatever you've got going on in her room, you know?"

"They say bumpers are a safety hazard now," I said. "Babies get their heads caught under them sometimes and suffocate."

Patty made a face. "Huh. I bet it doesn't happen very often, though. One person doesn't tie on their bumpers right and one kid has a freak accident and then that's the end of the baby bumper business. That's how it goes these days, huh?"

I hesitated. I wasn't sure I wished to extend this conversation.

As much as I was dreading the wordless monotony that awaited me inside the house, this was probably worse. It was a toss-up.

"I know, right?" I said.

Lucy popped her hand in her mouth and started sucking on it enthusiastically.

"She's hungry," Patty said. "She says, 'Mama, feed me.'"

"We'd better go in and do that, then," I said.

Chapter 12

Are you listening to me? What are you squinting at? Yes, that is indeed a wire screen up there around that beautiful balustrade. They installed that a couple of months after my arrival here. A woman had jumped and died. Not the first, apparently. It's remarkable that this hospital had been functioning for decades before someone thought of that, isn't it? Progress! It seems to me a more obviously efficient preventative move than denying almost all of us forks at meals, but I am not a medical doctor, so perhaps it is not for me to say.

Now. Where was I? I believe I was about to tell you about Martha's birth. I have never told you the story of her birth till now since, while a man of science, you are still a man. Nonetheless, *now* you are a man sitting before a madwoman, so you will have to endure the details.

You see, dear brother—I was convinced, even months before the event, that I was to die. The fact that no one else ever broached the subject made me ever more certain. I felt I saw Mother and Clara giving me sad, sideways glances that hinted their knowledge of my fate. I was too terrified at the time to realize that in Clara's instance it was probably jealousy, and in Mother's a parent's natural worry—not premonitions. Still, I was not readying myself for motherhood but simply Death. Late at night, after Matthew had fallen asleep, I prayed to God to be kind to me in the final moments and to do with the child what He felt was best for its little soul. Matthew, meanwhile, happily tended to nursery preparations and gave my fate not a single thought as far as I could discern.

The pains began on a Thursday afternoon, while Matthew was still working. I believe he was at the courthouse that day, so there was no telling when he would return. At first it was just a bothersome stomach cramp, but I experienced it as a solemn bell tolling. My time on this Earth had come to an end.

Our little maid, Tessa, sensed the time had come.

Do you wish to lie down, ma'am?

No, Tessa. That makes it worse.

Do you want someone to sit with you, ma'am? Can I tell you a story to take your mind off the pain?

If you wish, Tessa.

She told me the story of the Ugly Duckling. Of course I had heard it before, but she told it with a surprising passion, nearly weeping when the duckling decides he would rather die than endure any more scorn.

And I think the lesson is not that we can all grow to be beautiful, but there is a place of love and comfort for all of us, somewhere, somehow, if we endure for long enough to find it. Don't you think, ma'am?

I don't know, Tessa. To me, the cruelty is more memorable than the rare and lucky fate of the ending.

I'd barely choked out my answer when another pain overtook

me. Pain nagged at me for a full day and did not become dire until Friday night. At that time, Matthew sent for Dr. Graham. He needn't have bothered as the labors went on for another full day. Martha did not arrive until sundown on Saturday night. I recall the final hours as a series of painful freezing sensations. In between the sustained impressions of exhausted madness were the short glimpses of Clara—her tight raven hair and eager eyes—and Dr. Graham—his dreadfully long mustache. Tessa dashed in and out, breathless and shaking and crying by the end—in her young mind, perhaps promising against marriage and motherhood for what she saw. As those hours drove on, I surrendered to God, asking for forgiveness for my girlish pettiness through the years, and for my lack of fortitude now. I did my best, in the short moments between those of agony, to thank Him for the blessings I had received until then.

I recall nothing of the moment of Martha's actual birth— only that once she was born, she seemed to me just a squalling mass of pinkish-purple limbs. In my delusional state I thought I might have given birth to an octopus. Only Clara's cry of delight indicated to me otherwise. Oh, but I was too exhausted to care either way in that particular moment.

Frances, would you like to hold your precious girl? Frances!

Let me go, Clara. Please, just let me go.

My bed felt excessively soft, and then immaterial, and then cold. When I opened my eyes, I found myself in a clearing in a wood. I lifted the upper half of my body to discover that I was lying in snow. It was still falling, but gently. Surrounding me were towering evergreens, all of them layered with white.

Have you ever seen such beauty, Frances?

I turned to find the owner of the voice that said those words.

But the voice eluded me. I turned and turned and turned in circles, until I slipped and fell backwards into the snow.

Someone appeared over me with deep and searching green eyes. I was dizzy, I could see only their color, and little of the shape of the face around them.

"Father?" I murmured, and blinked.

But when I blinked, I saw that the eyes looking at me were *like* his—but belonged to a stranger. A small stranger was being held up to me.

Eyes like emeralds, reflecting a question back at me.

I blinked again.

Father?

"No," I whispered back. "Never in all of my days."

I was allowed to sleep—for how long, I do not know. An hour? A day? More? When I awoke to my bedroom, its details felt imprecise somehow. The bed felt to be a different height, the windows not quite rectangular, the tick of the clock distant and desultory. Was this an illusion of my room? A death-dream? Or was this life a cruel bit of trickery? The birth had come and gone, and still I was here on this Earth? How was this possible? Did I not belong with Father, in the hush of the snow?

Chapter 13

> **Possible causes of easy bruising in children:**
> *Hemophilia*
> *Von Willebrand Disease*
> *Leukemia*

My Google search had brought me here. Didn't I know better than to type symptoms into Google and expect to be reassured? And yet—I hadn't been able to help myself. When I had changed Lucy for bed, I found a small pink-purple discoloration by her elbow.

> **When to seek medical help:**
> *If your baby has multiple bruises that you can't account for*
> *If bruising is accompanied by a fever*
> *If a bruise is not healing*
> *If your baby appears to be in pain*

I stared at the phrase "that you can't account for." Did we fall into that category? Or had I, on that night she got the other bruise, gripped her so tightly on the arm that I'd made a mark there, too?

Bruises that you can't account for.

I closed my computer as I heard Chad coming down the hall. He'd been resettling Lucy, who'd awoken just as we'd started to undress for bed.

"She just needed her pacifier," Chad said, climbing into bed. "She'd dropped it."

"Oh," I said, pushing my laptop away and giving him a grateful squeeze on the arm. "Thanks."

"Abby?"

"Yeah?"

"Where's the iPod and player I set up for Lucy?"

"I took them out of her room."

"When?"

"This morning."

"Umm . . . Why?" Chad's tone had the slightest hint of annoyance.

"I decided we shouldn't have her listening to those water sounds all night. I mean, it was okay when she was a newborn. But what, is she going to have to listen to a babbling brook in order to fall asleep every night for the rest of her life? Do we really want to set her up for that?"

"Oh." Chad considered this gravely. This was officially a *parenting decision.*

"You disagree?" I said, intentionally adding a trace of indignation to my own voice. As the parent who did only about fifteen percent of the napping and nighttime duties, did he really have a case?

"No. I was just curious. What about all of those lullaby albums we put on there?"

"I never use those. Do you?"

"No."

"So we have an extra iPod now," I added cheerfully. "I was thinking I should start listening to audiobooks or something."

I had no intention of doing any such thing. But it had an air of "Mommy's treating herself," to which Chad would find it difficult to object. More importantly, it sounded more level-headed than *I'm sick of the phantom shushing sounds in the dark.*

"Sure," Chad said. "Okay. That sounds good."

Chad nestled closer to me and put his face against mine. As he leaned into me for a kiss, his heft annoyed me vaguely. It had for months now. My brain had recently undergone a subtle semantic shift with regard to Chad's physical presence. I used to think of him as *manly*. Now I thought of him as *burly*. *Burly* wasn't offensive, but it still felt like an entirely different thing somehow.

"Maybe I'll listen to *All the Presidents' Men*," I said. "I've always wanted to read that. Do you think it would be hard to get an audio version?"

I honestly thought this quandary would distract him long enough for me to think of a polite way to decline. I wasn't feeling flirtatious in the least.

"I don't know," Chad murmured before kissing my neck.

"Chad?" I pulled away slightly.

"Yes?"

"Do you ever wonder about the people who lived in this house before us?"

Chad crossed his arms and scratched his shoulders absently.

"What do you mean? That Janelle lady who sold it to us?"

"I mean before her. Do you ever wonder about all the people

who slept in this room before us? Or slept in Lucy's room? I mean, a house this old . . ."

We knew from the deed that it was built in 1867.

"I thought that was what you loved most about it," Chad said. "Its . . . classical appeal."

Had it been? *Antique charm* was how the real estate agent had put it.

"Sure. But 1867. People did things pretty differently then. Probably babies were born here. Probably . . ." I hesitated. "Probably some people died here."

Chad considered this. "Probably. Yeah."

"Don't you ever want to know a little more, then?"

Chad leaned in for another kiss. "I don't think so. Sometimes it's better not to know details. Maybe that's just me."

I was slightly annoyed with him for putting off this conversation so decisively. But after so many months, I felt I owed him something.

"Maybe," I said, and returned his kiss.

I felt myself gasp, then sat up.

"NO!" I heard myself shout.

I stared into the blackness of our bedroom, focusing on the tiny green light that indicated that the baby monitor was on. I strained to hear a sound but heard nothing.

I waited for my pulse to slow down, and it did, steadily, for about a minute. Chad didn't stir. I tried to remember what had wakened me. Was it something from the monitor, something from Lucy's room?

No, I determined. It was not. It was a dream. And in the dream, Lucy had been at the bottom of the stairwell while I was on a middle step. Lucy was screaming. Clearly I'd tripped and dropped her on my way down. As I rushed down the final steps to pick her up, I saw that her face was not hers. The face was familiar to me, but it wasn't Lucy's.

I stared into the little green monitor light now, terrified that I'd hear a *shhhhh*.

But all was quiet in Lucy's room. So quiet. I missed the gentle, reassuring gurgle of her babbling brook track. I lay down on my back, caught my breath, and tried to remember where I'd seen that face before.

Chapter 14

Northampton Lunatic Hospital
Northampton, Massachusetts
December 20, 1885

The injuries from the birth were significant. I suppose you needn't know those details, but I could not stand and walk for some weeks. I nursed the baby but Clara did everything else—until I recovered.

The evening spider made its visit some time later—when Martha was almost five months old.

I *know* Matthew saw that spider. I know it was not a product of my diseased imagination. You know the night to which I am referring, don't you? The night that Martha had her fall? I understand that it was much discussed out of my presence in the weeks and months that followed. You needn't pretend that wasn't the case.

While I was physically recovered, I still allowed Clara—when she was about—and Tessa to take on more of the maternal responsibilities than was necessary or perhaps appropriate.

It felt so much easier to take on the simpler duties—the peeling of potatoes or the washing of clothes. Care of the baby, by contrast, seemed to require so many decisions—significant ones. Such a tiny and incommunicative creature—I didn't trust myself to know *always* when she was hungry, when her aches and cries were typical, and when they required more serious attention or medical advice. It seemed best to let those judgments fall occasionally upon others—not solely on the abilities of my meek and recovering mind. The child's chances seemed better that way. Any child's chances would be better that way, would they not?

On the night of the terrible incident, however, Martha was in my care alone. Unless one counts Matthew, and I don't think one should. He was downstairs, reading his newspaper. He never played any part in Martha's bedtime.

I was feeling fatigued that evening—more than usual. All day Martha had had some sort of stomach complaint, and nothing seemed to soothe her. After a simple supper, I retired to our bedroom with her. Under normal circumstances I would have nursed her and then laid her down in her cradle. I was so tired, though, and she was so unsettled, that I nursed her on our bed. She fell asleep more promptly than I expected, but I was not in a rush to get her into her cradle. I waited some minutes, dozing and daydreaming and waiting for her to fall into a deeper sleep, so my transporting her wouldn't rouse her. As I lay there, I saw a small but thick-legged spider crawling across the ceiling, just above us.

In general, I am quite fond of spiders. I admire their industry—and at times their efficient savagery. Yet I do not wish to share a bed with one. I had a vision of the spider falling into my hair—or onto Martha's bald head—at night. I also took a notion to seeing the creature up close. I believe you know this about me—and knew it even then—that when I'm fatigued or nervous, I find my brain focuses more easily on small things. In that moment, the spider seemed like a small gift from Providence—like finding a flower on a gloomy day, or coming across an old letter from a loved one at a moment when its kind words are most needed. (I have never received any letters here, by the way, Harry. But I still know the feeling of needing—or hoping for—small mercies.)

I picked up Matthew's Bible and stood very gingerly on the edge of the bed, careful not to step near Martha. Using the Bible, I plucked the spider more easily from the ceiling than I'd anticipated. Perhaps the creature knew my intentions were benevolent? Surprised, I jumped off the bed rather hastily, and rushed my tiny passenger to the window. Thinking about it later, I believe it was my haste that jostled little Martha's position on the bed. At the time, though, I was eager to get the creature to the window. I pulled at the window but had great difficulty opening it with one hand. I paused to watch the spider, as it had stopped moving. It looked stunned. I wondered if it was watching me, if it trusted me—if it *should* trust me. Its legs moved slightly, then stopped, as if it was contemplating bolting, then decided against it.

In that moment I heard the terrible thump, and then the screams. Martha had rolled off the bed. I cried out and flung the Bible to the floor. When I rushed to her, there was already blood streaming from a gash by her eyebrow. She had apparently hit her poor little face on the bedside table on her way down.

As I applied my sleeve to it, I saw the spider crawl across my palm and onto Martha's nightdress. I shouted and swiped it away just as Matthew appeared in the doorframe.

"What was that dreadful noise! My God, Frances! She's bleeding!"

"There was a spider!" I screamed, wiping Martha's face frantically. "A spider!"

"And you dropped Martha?" Matthew demanded.

"No. She tumbled off the bed."

"Tumbled off the bed! How is that possible? Give her to me." Matthew took the baby from my arms.

The child continued to scream, and the sound of it threatened to break my heart in two. I reached for her, but Matthew pulled away.

"I must take her to Dr. Graham at once. This wound almost certainly needs stitching, and he should examine her."

"I will get dressed."

"No. Stay here. Try to sleep."

"Please let me hold her. It's just the short walk down the road."

"You obviously need some rest, Frances."

I followed him to the front door, begging and sobbing. He handed Martha back to me briefly while he put on his coat and shoes but then snatched her back.

"Please let me go with you!" I cried as he opened the front door. "Or else send for Dr. Graham, rather than taking the poor baby out like this."

As soon as I said it I wondered why he had not suggested this earlier.

"You are not well enough to accompany me," he said, pressing his handkerchief to Martha's head. "Try to get some rest."

I cried until Matthew returned. I knew that he had gone to Dr. Graham's home—rather than sending for him—because he did not wish for the doctor to see me in my fragile state. I cried not only for *this incident but for the last. Matthew was right to be concerned about Dr. Graham.*

Dr. Graham was the only one who knew of the goblet incident— the time I'd dropped a goblet when I was with child, and the pieces had cut Matthew's leg. Dr. Graham had surely understood that that had been an accident, but what might he think now? How many accidents can one sound-minded woman have?

Matthew returned after an hour and tucked Martha into her cradle without a word.

"How is she?"

"She is asleep. Don't disturb her. She is fine, but there may very well be a scar. Fortunately it is far to the side of her face."

"Did Dr. Graham—"

"What, Frances?"

"Did he ask about the details of the accident?"

"Only those that he needed to know."

When I awoke, I found Tessa tending to Martha downstairs in the kitchen. Matthew had evidently sent for her in the early-morning hours. He sent for Clara later that day.

I was not certain, at the time, how many details of that evening Matthew had shared, and with whom. Clara treated me gently, but she always had, in her elder-sisterly way. You were lost in your studies, I believe. And when I saw Dr. Graham thereafter, I was afraid to meet his eye.

Chapter 15

Haverton, Connecticut
December 9, 2014

I woke up a little before five—relieved that I'd gotten a few hours of sleep, but vaguely annoyed that my early waking had no apparent purpose. Lucy was not crying. What, then, had wakened me?

Shut up, please.

Yes. That was it. Those words had drifted into my head as I slept—a vestige of a dream that would otherwise have slipped back into my subconscious unnoticed—and woken me up.

Shut up, please.

I stared into the morning gloom, avoiding looking at the little green light of Lucy's monitor. I'd never been great at getting back to sleep in the morning. By six o'clock, I gave up trying. Lucy was likely to be up within a half hour, so if I was successful, it would only end in frustration. After briefly poking my head into Lucy's room to watch her chest rise and fall, I tiptoed down the stairs. In the kitchen, I started up some coffee.

While the coffee machine grunted, I sat in our cold kitchen and thought about Wendy. Wendy, my freshman roommate in college. Wendy, about whom I'd dreamt last night.

Shut up, please.

Wendy used to say that to me while I was sleeping sometimes—usually in a small and pleading tone. Probably she said it only two or three times, but my friend Kristin and I had such a great time making fun of it, it felt like more often.

The first time or two that it happened, I thought I imagined it—an almost elfin voice in my dreams asking me to kindly shut up.

The next time, I recognized Wendy's voice through the haze and asked her about it the following morning.

Well, Wendy had said, blushing bright beneath her half-grown-out bangs. *You kind of snore.*

And telling me to shut up . . . does that help? Does it make me stop?

Sometimes, yeah.

Those bangs drove me crazy. I knew that Wendy showered pretty frequently, and yet her hair always seemed wilted with oil. Maybe it was because she always fingered her hair so much, knotting and unknotting it while she studied or talked on the phone.

Do you want me to say something more polite? Wendy sat up in her bed and pulled her skinny knees to her chest.

No, I mumbled. *By all means, do what works.*

Wendy promptly stopped. She never spoke to me again in my sleep—to my knowledge, anyway.

Still, my friend Kristin and I got a kick out of telling each other to *shut up, please*—and combining other polite turns of phrase with rude ones.

Go to hell, ma'am.

Pardon me, bitch.

You're so fucking welcome.

Kristin and I were such idiots.

But maybe *that* was what I was hearing in my head at night. The beginning of a *shut up, please.* Starting with the *shhhhh*, but never fully forming.

I poured a cup of coffee and opened my laptop. Closing the site about baby bruises that I'd searched the previous night, I opened a new tab and typed *Hoey.*

That had been Wendy's last name.

Hoey.

I remembered it well because when I first saw Wendy's name on my room assignment—all those years ago—I'd thought it looked like "hooey." *Wendy Hooey? That's funny. Oh. No. Wendy* Hoey.

And her mother's name? Wendy had sometimes used her mother's first name when addressing her exasperatedly over the phone. It was something a bit unusual for her generation— Selena or Serena or something like that.

I heard Chad shuffling down the stairs. When I looked up, he was standing in the kitchen doorway with Lucy in his arms. He looked like a zombie, but Lucy was bright-eyed and ready for action. She squealed at the sight of me—a habit of hers that I still found disconcerting. *No one has ever thought I was all that great, ever,* I thought sometimes. *What's wrong with Lucy, that she isn't as discerning as the rest of the world?*

"Hey, sweetie," I said.

As I got up and took out a box of baby oatmeal, I realized that I hadn't greeted Chad at all. Maybe "sweetie" could cover him, if he wanted to read it that way.

"Hi, hon," I added.

"Hey." He yawned. "Here comes bruiser baby. Black eye and all."

"It's not a black eye," I snapped.

"I was just kidding. It really doesn't look that bad. I mean, the yellowish part is a little gross, but I think it's healing."

"Yeah," I stared at my computer screen. *Selena? Serena?* "You said you wanted to be more involved in Lucy's meals once she started on solid food. Remember that?"

"Oh. Yeah."

"Well, here you are," I said, sweeping my hand over the oatmeal box before settling back into my kitchen chair.

"What do you usually mix it with?"

I took a patient sip of my coffee. "A couple of ounces of Red Bull."

"Pumped milk from the freezer?" Chad asked.

"Water's fine this time," I said "She gets plenty of milk."

"Are you okay?" Chad asked, mixing the oatmeal.

"Yeah," I murmured. "I just had a bad dream."

"You seem tired."

Lucy gurgled at me, and I fluttered my fingernails against her high chair table in response.

"Well, I *am* tired. I couldn't go back to sleep."

Returning my hands to the keys, I Googled Selena Hoey and Serena Hoey. I found no Selena Hoey, but a couple of Serena Hoeys. One in Ireland. One in Rhode Island. Wendy had been from Massachusetts, but of course her parents might have moved in the past decade and a half.

"Was I in it?" Chad asked.

"In what?"

Chad sat across from Lucy and began to feed her. "Your dream, Abby."

"No," I said, staring at the computer screen. So I knew where Serena Hoey lived now. What exactly did I think I was going to do with this information?

"Do I snore?" I asked.

"Maaaaah!" Lucy squealed in wild anticipation.

Chad fed her a large spoonful of oatmeal. A blob of it stuck to her cheek. "Not generally. Why? Are you trying to tell me that *I* snore?"

"No."

"You getting enough sleep, you think?"

"Actually . . . yeah. Since Lucy doesn't wake up at night as much as she used to."

This was another reason I'd felt uncomfortable at that mothers' group at the library. I was the only one who didn't nurse at night anymore. Sure, Lucy still had her occasional two A.M. wakeups. But usually she only required a replaced pacifier and a bit of rocking. She was a healthy weight and was learning the basic human skill of surviving a night without a meal. Why mess with that? Of course, I'd never say that to the other mothers.

She doesn't eat at night anymore? That mom Sara had asked me that. The red-eyed but perfectly coiffed one. The one with the very bald baby—so bald that her head practically sparkled. *Are you worried about losing your supply?*

No, I'd said, vaguely unsettled by the word "supply." *Should I be?*

"I'm not sure I should admit this," Chad said. "But I dreamt about pennies."

I smiled. "Filthy, Chad."

"I had this armor . . . like chain mail. It was all pennies."

I laughed, looking up. "You didn't dream that. You made that up."

Chad shrugged and fed Lucy another oversized scoop of oatmeal. "Maybe I did, yeah. But at least I made you laugh. Hey—I forgot I was going to ask you about something."

He flipped through the mail on the counter and handed me a folded piece of plain white computer paper.

"This was in with the mail," he said as I opened it. It said *Gerard Barnett* in blue ink. Following that was a phone number.

"Oh!" I said. "Patty must've left this. Patty our neighbor. She and I were talking about the Barnetts, who used to own this house, and . . . anyway, she thought I might want to call him. He's got some old genealogical stuff about the family, or something like that."

Chad bobbled his head back and forth, considering this. "Huh. You know, you might enjoy a history project right now. That might be good for you."

I clicked on a White Pages site. The Hoeys lived on a street named Willow Road. Well, wasn't that memorable? Since Wendy and Willow were alliterative? And since Willow was so very close to *weeping*?

"What do you mean, good for me?" I said.

"I just meant, since you're not teaching this year. Something that's not baby related."

"A history project," I said, closing my laptop. "Sure."
Wendy. Willow. Weeping.

Unfortunately, I'm unemployed at the moment, Gerard Barnett had told me over the phone. *I can meet pretty much whenever you want.*

Gerard suggested we meet at an Arby's near his house. I told him that was perfect. I didn't imagine that very many people dined in at Arby's at two in the afternoon, and anyone who did wouldn't likely be offended at the presence of a potentially screaming baby.

We met at the side door, as we'd agreed. Gerard was about fifty, with a very pink face, a receding hairline of close-cut blond-white hair, and a firm but sweaty handshake.

"You getting anything?" he asked after we went inside and selected a table by the windows. "Cuz I'm not."

I felt one of us had to order something, so I got a coffee—plus a plastic spoon for Lucy to hold. By the time I returned to the table, Gerard had shed his jacket to reveal a Bruins T-shirt that was slightly too small for his blush biceps.

"Cute kid," Gerard said, a smile spreading across his fleshy cheeks. Up close, I saw that his face wasn't a robust sunburn sort of pink. Rather, his skin seemed thin and delicate, with a surprising rosiness bursting through. In general, he had sort of a football coach way about him. I wondered what his job had been before he'd lost it.

"Thanks." I lifted Lucy out of her car carrier and positioned her to face Gerard.

So," he said. "Give me an idea of what you're looking for

here. Old-timey history, or like when was the last time Ed and Shirley replaced the roof?"

"Most of the structural stuff we know about from the sale documents."

"Uh huh. So you're wondering about . . . *what* part of the house, exactly?"

"Well," I said hurriedly. "I don't know if Patty told you in her text that I'm a history teacher. So maybe it's just a personal quirk of mine. But when a building is that old, I just start to wonder about everyone who passed through there. A lot of the time you wonder but you're not going to get to find out. But in this case . . . well, Patty told me you found some very old materials relating to your family as you were cleaning the house out."

Gerard nodded. "Yeah. There was a little trunk in the storage space behind the wall."

"Didn't you find a whole bunch of old letters, or something?"

"Old letters? No. Books. Mostly old law books. They belonged to a guy named Matthew Barnett—who lived in the house in the late 1800s. I remember my grandfather talking about him—he was a pretty well-known lawyer, I guess. His name was in some of them. Anyway, I got a few hundred dollars for them, total, on eBay. I think that's what I mentioned to Patty."

"Didn't you want to keep them?"

"I kept *one*. One with his name in it. They didn't all have it. Just the one in case I get sentimental in my old age. I'm not a big reader, and I don't have a kid to pass this kind of stuff along to."

"Oh." I said. I tried to hide my disappointment. I'd hoped Gerard would have a stash of letters and photographs he'd let me look through—as Patty had implied.

Lucy pumped her plastic spoon up and down like a drunken drum majorette. Gerard watched her for a moment and chuckled before speaking again.

"Now, I have *one* thing I thought you might like to have, though. Thought of it right away when Patty texted me. Stacked in with all those law books I found this one thing . . . this little book of handwritten recipes, baking notes, stuff like that. I've got it in the trunk of my car."

"Who wrote it?" I asked. "When?"

"Lady named Frances. Frances Flinch Barnett. She wrote her name on the inside cover. She dated some of the recipes. Eighteen seventy-eight, mostly."

"Well." I hesitated. "That sounds cool."

"Doesn't it? Recipes of a real lady who lived in *your* house. You and your daughter could cook some of that stuff together."

"Yeah, maybe. I'm kind of a crappy cook, but—"

"In the same kitchen," Gerard interrupted. "Think of that, huh? It'd be a real experience for you."

I realized in that moment that I had walked into a sales pitch. Uncertain how I wanted to handle it, I shifted the subject.

"Did you ever spend much time in the house?" I asked.

"My aunt and uncle's house?" Gerard puckered his lips, considering the question. "No. Just holidays. My parents usually had Christmas at our house. Thanksgiving was at my uncle Eddie and aunt Shirley's, though."

"Did you ever stay overnight?"

"No. My folks lived in Hamden then. Close. No reason to sleep over."

"Never?"

"No. Never. My sister lived in the house for a little while when we were teenagers. Stephanie had a little falling-out with our parents and stayed with Eddie and Shirley for a couple of months."

"Oh," I said. Lucy dropped her spoon, and I reached down to pick it up.

A falling-out with our parents. These words made my arms stiffen, and my fingers seize up. Lucy would be a teenager someday. Maybe she'd find me intolerable then. Maybe she'd want to move in with my brother. Maybe, in fact, my head would explode.

"They were real nice to my sister, Eddie and Shirley were."

"Your sister . . . you said her name was Stephanie?"

"Yeah." Gerard watched Lucy mouth the plastic spoon. I tried not to be self-conscious about letting her suck on something that had been on the floor. She did it all the time at home. With all of its health department codes, Arby's probably kept its floor cleaner than I did mine.

"Maybe she'd want that little cookbook?" I asked.

Gerard scratched at his hairline. "I guess Patty didn't tell you much about my sister. She's, uh, not a sentimental person either. If I gave her the book, she'd probably sell it herself."

"But do you want to ask her first?"

"Listen." Gerard slapped both of his hands on the table between us. "I was going to tell you I'd give it to you for, say, thirty bucks. Stephanie doesn't know it exists because she couldn't be bothered to help me clean out our aunt's place when she needed our help."

I hesitated. "Your sister . . . she still lives close to here?"

"Yeah. East Haven right now. And still she couldn't come by to help. Let me do it all myself. Me and my wife."

"I'm sorry. Sounds really difficult. Does your sister have kids? A daughter? Who'd maybe want it?"

Gerard shook his head. "Neither of us have kids. We're the dead end on this Barnett family branch."

Gerard's face seemed even pinker than it had when he'd first sat down. There was an eagerness to his expression that made me think he could really use thirty dollars at this moment in his life. A year ago I probably would've told him to get lost. Now, though, I didn't feel I was up to it. I was one of the nurturers now—not out of righteousness but out of irritating instinct. I saw naked and defenseless babies everywhere.

"Why don't you bring that cookbook in here?" I said. "It sounds kind of interesting."

"Sure thing." Gerard started to get up.

"But before you do," I hurried to say. "Can you answer one question for me? I know it might sound odd."

"Okay?" Gerard said.

"Has anyone ever died in the house? That you know of?"

Gerard took in a breath and then released it slowly. "Oooh. So this is one of *those* kinds of conversations. Why? You got a poltergeist coming through the TV or something? I promise the house isn't built on a cemetery or whatever. At least—not that I know of."

"You mention poltergeists." I hesitated. "Did your aunt ever complain about anything like that?"

Gerard shook his head. "No. But if you've got something spooky going on, maybe it's just Aunt Shirley paying a visit. She *didn't* want to leave the place, I've gotta be honest about that."

I stared down at the swirl of Lucy's hair, considering this

answer. "You didn't say whether or not anyone ever died in the house."

Gerard shrugged. "Not that I know of. Uncle Eddie had a massive heart attack at work. I think my grandparents both died in hospitals. I don't know about anyone before that. Suppose it's possible since people died at home more often back then, right? But there were never any stories. Like of axe murderers or whatever. If that's what you're getting at."

"And no one besides Shirley ever talked about any . . . odd experiences in the house?"

Gerard watched Lucy for a moment more. I wondered if he might report this conversation back to Patty. And then Patty could get on the phone to DCF to report the crazy mommy on her street.

"Just my sister," he said slowly. "She said something to me once. But my sister, when she stayed with Eddie and Shirley, she had a lot of problems. She did a lot of drugs. If she saw a ghost, it was probably an acid flashback."

"Did she say she saw a ghost?"

"No. She just said that their house creeped her out. Stopped showing up for holidays there and gave that as an excuse. But she has a lot of excuses for things." Gerard got up. "I probably sound like a real jerk, saying this stuff about my sister. I should shut up now because I'm sure you don't want to hear it. You want to look at the cookbook or not?"

I nodded. "Yeah. But can you give me your sister's number?"

"If you want. I can't promise you'll get her, though. She's on-again, off-again with her phone plan. She and I don't talk that much."

Gerard went outside and returned with a brown leather

book with a red and gold binding. It was small—the size of Gerard's hand—and clearly old—worn down at the bottom of the spine and the hinge of the front cover. *Frances Flinch Barnett* was indeed written on its marbled front endpaper.

Gerard let me hold it in my hands and open it up to its first yellowed page. A tidy but exaggeratedly slanting handwriting said in black ink: *Mother's Cider Loaves.* A recipe was scrawled beneath it.

"Cool," I whispered, and meant it.

A few minutes later, as he tucked his thirty dollars into his wallet, Gerard said to me, "You know, I'm glad you got my aunt's house. You seem like a nice young lady. You deserve it."

Chapter 16

Northampton Lunatic Hospital
Northampton, Massachusetts
December 20, 1885

I needn't have worried about Dr. Graham's opinion of me. I should have known that Matthew was too prideful to share his concerns about me with a local doctor of such esteem. To discuss his wife's hysterical difficulties, he turned to the services of someone whose practice was some distance away—in Hartford—and who could therefore be trusted not to turn Matthew's troubles into local gossip.

This doctor—a Dr. Stayer—had a specific treatment in mind for me. He had observed this treatment at a clinic in Philadelphia—practiced by a renowned neurologist there. I believe Matthew had spoken to Dr. Stayer in secret before the evening of the spider and then discussed this treatment more seriously thereafter. From what I gather, there was some talk of sending me to Philadelphia, but either Matthew didn't quite have the means, or Dr. Stayer was eager to try his own version of the method.

I do not know how much Matthew would've told you of this "rest cure" before he decided to take Dr. Stayer's advice and go forward with it. Nothing? Well. You were so caught up in your laboratory studies, after all.

Approximately a week after Martha's injury, Matthew presented it to me thusly:

He was concerned about my health, so he had arranged one month—perhaps more—of restful treatment for me. He had hired a nurse to help me, and he had enlisted Clara's help for Martha's care. For the entire month, Martha would stay with her and Jonathan.

You cannot be serious, Matthew. A month away from her mother? How can that be good for either of us?

How much nurturing is the child getting with you, Frances? How many evenings have I come home and found you staring into your bubbling stewpots, with Martha squalling in her cradle, or with Tessa trying to comfort her?

Oh, it had happened but once or twice! He was exaggerating.

No matter. Matthew had made up his mind and there would be no changing it.

Dr. Stayer and the hired nurse set up a bed for me in the small room at the top of the stairs. They removed everything from the room except for that bed, a chair, a table, and a tray. The bed was for me, the chair for the nurse.

And what was I to do for a month in this room?

Why, *rest*, of course, Matthew explained. Simply lie on the bed and rest. I was to sit up occasionally to eat rich meals and drink copious amounts of milk. I was to be fattened like a heifer, as apparently I'd grown thin since Martha's birth.

There would be no books, no music, no going outdoors, and no visitors. Matthew would of course drop in to check on me, and Dr. Stayer would come weekly to check my progress and massage my muscles. The nurse—a sturdy young woman with an incessantly foolish smile—also did this to some degree.

Did you ever think of me, during that month? Did you miss me? Did you know I nearly went mad in the first three days?

I was saved from madness, however, by the incompetence of the hired nurse. It was clear to me, from the early days, that she was instructed not to leave my side unless I was sleeping. It was easy enough to feign sleep to get rid of her. The first few times, I wasn't sure what to do with myself. All I could do was sit up in bed and stretch—I feared she would hear me if I stepped onto the floorboards. The first time or two, I amused myself practicing different fancy plaits on my hair. Of course, I couldn't see the result because I had no mirror, but it kept my hands occupied. When I'd hear the nurse's footsteps, I'd rush to undo my work and slip back onto my pillow. Sometimes the window was open, but from my position on the bed, I could see only the sky. When clouds were visible, I fancied them animals, and whispered stories about them, pretending Martha was with me to hear them. This endeavor became too painful, however, so I ceased. Thinking of Martha made the void of that room ever more vast. Sometimes it was easiest to forget she existed at all.

After a few days in that little room, I would often hear my nurse chattering with Tessa downstairs. Her absences lengthened as their friendship developed.

Twice I stood and plucked tiny yellow moth larvae from the ceiling—cautiously and shakily, as I knew such endeavors had caused this very ordeal. Then I would watch their inching movements atop my hand, or across the hills and valleys of my quilt. I longed to find two at once, so I could race them, but I was never so fortunate.

I listened for birdcalls and attempted to identify the different types, as Father used to do. No matter that I knew nothing of bird species. Their twitterings were most welcome, and I learned to distinguish between the songs of the three types of birds that appeared to frequent the trees surrounding our house.

Two particular birds seemed to call out most often. I named them Archibald and Mercy. They did not have the prettiest songs, but they had the most consistent. Nor did they seem to be calling to each other. I decided they were singing for me, reporting the existence of the world and the day outside the narrowing white of that room.

To this very day, I still often return to thoughts of Archibald and Mercy. After six hours of silent sewing, I close my eyes and listen for their calls coming through the maddening void. Or on a night when sleep eludes me—when the youngest of my three roommates will not stop weeping, or the eldest won't stop sitting up and whispering about the proof of the pudding and the devil in the darkness (her two indecipherably favorite topics, poor exasperating thing)—I put my palms to my ears and listen for those birds singing somewhere beyond the room.

And in that way, in the hollow of night, my mind often still occupies that upstairs room on Miller Avenue. Not because it was a place of comfort, but because it was a time and place whose desolation I survived. That time came to an end. So perhaps this one will yet, as well.

Of course, we'll leave aside the question of the wisdom of attempting to maintain one's sanity with imagined birdsong.

Chapter 17

Mother's Cider Loaves
Molasses Biscuits
Saturday Spice Cake
Sponge Cake 1
Sponge Cake 2

November 10, 1878
   I believe I've solved the problem of my sponge cakes. Clara has given me an education on the subject. This may not be how Harry intended me to use this book when he selected it for my birthday gift, but I'm recording Clara's recipe here for now and will transcribe it when I have the opportunity, back home. The eggs should be beaten for much longer than I had done on my first attempt, for more air. Sponge cake is something Mother never much cared for, so I'd never tried it before.

1 cup sugar
1 cup flour
1 tsp. baking soda
3 eggs
3 tbs. water—warmed

November 13, 1878

My sponge cake endeavors have made me reconsider the number and quality of eggs in all of my cakes, particularly the more festive ones. There is a fair amount of variation in size of eggs between hens. I wonder if I weighed the contents of the eggs—if Harry could provide me with a quality scale—I might improve the proportion of egg more precisely?

November 16, 1878

What should a young wife think about when her husband is so engaged?

Surely it isn't too early to be thinking of the Christmas niceties, if one wishes them to be truly remarkable. Of course there will be plum pudding for Christmas Eve, but Christmas Day allows for a bit more variety. Gingerbread is too common—too simple. Clara has suggested gateau, but I was hoping to try something very different from last year.

After the first few pages of recipes, the cookbook relaxed into a more personal style—a cooking journal, just as Gerard had promised. Lucy was tired from our outing, which gave me a chance to settle at the kitchen table and read several pages while she napped. All of this baking business was making me hungry for sweets. I started a cup of coffee and rummaged in the cabinets until I found a bag of stale gluten-free ginger snaps.

December 19, 1878

Today I attempted a carrot pie, fashioned after Mother's pumpkin pie, with the same custard. I boiled and mashed the carrots to a similar soft consistency as baked pumpkin. The results were disappointing. I believe that with sweeter carrots—or, more easily, more molasses—it would have been successful. Matthew disliked it so robustly, however, that I probably won't attempt it again till he's forgotten this one. I should like to try again, however, because it is such a pleasant pie and I so often have an overabundance of carrots. We haven't so very much pumpkin now that that Frederick fellow does not come to the house anymore.

I forgot to write last week that our girl has left us. I think that Vicky thought me strange, anyhow. Matthew has already found a new girl. Her name is Tessa Ripley, and I'm finding her quite agreeable. She's tall and reaches for the tins on my highest shelves for me without making me feel particularly small.

I smiled at this entry, feeling a little sense of satisfaction at seeing something about Frances's life outside of cooking. I skipped a chunk of pages and read ahead.

March 14, 1879

I was foolish last night, attempting the roast from so late an hour. I should have foreseen that it would be too difficult to manage with Martha's fussing. Matthew tried to stay in good humor about it, but the meat was not served until nearly nine o'clock. Tessa was positively frantic, but it wasn't her fault. This afternoon I shall cook soup—and start early to make certain there will be no delay! I am too tired to write more. Martha's troubles are the same. I hope for more sun and more warmth tomorrow. It has rained for three days. Four, perhaps. I have lost count. I suppose I have lost count in more than one respect.

My pulse jumped a bit. Still a little less about cooking—and more about life in general. Had Gerard Barnett even read this far? Or had he just assumed this whole thing was about recipes? And of what, exactly, had Frances lost count?

I skipped forward again and read this:

October 14, 1879

Professor Johnson is to testify soon. On our walk yesterday, Harry answered all of the questions I had about his colleague's experiments and their place in the trial. It was a pleasure to have my brother all to myself. Matthew is, of late, so intent on cushioning my mind from anything so interesting.

This is my understanding of the significance of the experimental stomachs. It is to show that the poor girl's stomach was not tampered with unlawfully after her death! There was no denying that her stomach had poison in it, but what is likely to be argued by the defense is that the arsenic was deposited there by someone on the prosecutor's side—someone intent on convicting Rev. Mr. Hayden.

The Stannard girl's stomach had, as a result of the arsenic, enlarged blood vessels in the postmortem examination. Under the direction of Professor Johnson, Harry and his colleagues obtained two stomachs for experimentation, and applied a similar amount of arsenic to them. After some time sitting in jars in the lab, with the arsenic inside of them, it was found that they did not have the same enlarged condition of blood vessels as the girl's stomach. These results will make it more difficult for the defense to make their accusation regarding the arsenic's introduction after the death, rather than before.

I gather that the physical evidence will be much more complex than what I've described here, but this explains Harry's part. I inquired whether he would be taking the stand, but he said no. Dr. Johnson will be speaking for his own work, including this part in which Harry assisted. It would be exciting if he testified! Mother would be beside herself, however, so perhaps it is best he has a quieter role.

Arsenic?

"Whoa," I whispered.

I reread the entry, then turned the page. The next entry was short, about cold weather and something called "Baked Apple Pudding." It sounded good, but Frances only fretted over the egg to milk ratio and didn't actually record a recipe.

Then I took out my laptop.

When I Googled "Hayden" and "Stannard," quite a few articles and pages came up. The trial to which Frances Flinch Barnett referred was in late 1879 and evidently quite famous—though I'd never heard of it.

Herbert Hayden, a minister, was accused of murdering a young woman named Mary Stannard, who had occasionally worked for him and his wife—helping around the house and looking after their children. Mary thought she was pregnant with Herbert's child at the time of her murder. She'd asked him for his help—she wanted an abortion—and ended up dead of arsenic poisoning and *simultaneous* throat slitting, it appeared. According to his accusers, Hayden had met her in the woods of Rockland, Connecticut, promising to bring her an abortion tonic. What he gave her instead was arsenic. She'd drunk it, and when she'd begun screaming in pain, he'd hit her with a rock and slit her throat.

One of the more general online articles made reference to the trial's sensationalistic coverage in the *New York Times*, so I went to their site and looked in the archives. I was surprised at the number of articles that came up.

A long one—that appeared right before the trial started—summarized the events that had led up to Herbert Hayden's being tried.

MARY STANNARD'S MURDER
WHAT CAUSED THE ARREST OF REV. MR. HAYDEN.

HIS TRIAL TO BEGIN TO-DAY—A HISTORY OF THE PROCEEDINGS IN THE CASE—THE CLERGYMAN ARRESTED, ACQUITTED, AGAIN ARRESTED, AND THEN INDICTED—SUBSTANCE OF THE TESTIMONY THAT WILL BE PRESENTED

NEW-HAVEN, Oct. 6—The Township of Madison, which lies 20 miles East of this city, is long and narrow. Its southern boundary is the Sound, and the land in its southern half is level and comparatively fertile. But at its northern end lies one of the wildest districts in the State, inhabited by a few hard-working families who earn a living by cultivating the stony soil and making charcoal. In this district, not inaptly called Rockland, a horrible and mysterious murder was committed on the afternoon of Tuesday, Sept. 3, 1878, and to-morrow afternoon, in this city, the trial of Rev. Herbert H. Hayden, for having committed that murder, will begin in the Superior Court. Charles S. Stannard, a middle-aged widower, had lived for some years in an isolated house in Rockland. He is an example of the "poor white" of New England, an inoffensive man, with nothing criminal or vicious in his character, so far as is known. He is working for neighboring farmers, and his housekeeper was Susan S. Hawley, his wife's daughter by a former marriage. Mary E. Stannard, his daughter, an attractive young woman, 22 years old, had become the mother of an illegitimate child two years before the murder; but she had seemed so penitent, and conducted herself so properly afterward, that the honest farmers of Rockland admitted her to their families as a domestic, and forgot her deviation from the paths of virtue. She had frequently worked in the house of Rev. Mr. Hayden, a Methodist preacher, and in September she was employed by a family by the name of Studley, in the neighboring town of Guilford. On Sunday, Sept. 1, she came home from Guilford. Soon after she reached home a letter arrived which she had sent to her sister, Susan, and which had been delayed. It inclosed a letter addressed to the Rev. Mr. Hayden, and it instructed Susan to give this to him with great secrecy. The inclosed letter, being then of no use, was burned by Mary, but the letter to Susan is in existence. Susan says that Mary told her she had come home because she thought she was about to become a mother. The person with whom she had been criminally intimate, she said, was the Rev. Mr. Hayden, and she hoped he could aid her in some way. Mrs. Studley says that on Aug. 29 Mary made a similar confession to her, and told her that the letter sent to Hayden through her sister contained a request that he should do something to remove her anxiety. Mr. Studley, who carried the girl home, says he told her on the way that he would see Hayden and ask him to take care of her; but when he reached Rockland Hayden was in South Madison, where he preached, and he had to return to Guilford without having seen him. Hayden's house is on the same road, and not far south of Mr. Stannard's. On Monday Mary went to his house two or three times on errands. Late in the day she went in that direction, and upon her return her sister says that she told her that Hayden had met her, and told her to keep up her courage, for he would go to the City of Middletown in the morning and get something which would remove the cause of her anxiety. On Tuesday morning Hayden told his wife he was going to Durham to buy some oats. He passed Durham and went to Middletown, and on his way home he stopped at the Stannard house, about noon, and got a glass of water. The water was warm, and Mary volunteered to go to a spring which was on the road to his house, and get some that was cool. At the spring she dipped up a pail of water, and he drank of it; Susan says that when Mary returned she said to her that Hayden while at the spring had told her that he had procured some medicine, and had asked her to meet him in an hour in the woods opposite the Stannard house, near a rock known as Big Rock. Soon afterward Mary went in the direction of the rock, with a tin pail in her hand, saying she was going to pick blackberries. Her friends never saw her again alive. Late in the afternoon her father became anxious about her, and went into the woods to find her. His first search failed, and he returned. By the advice of Susan, who had kept to herself the story about Hayden, he went again, and this time he found his daughter's dead body. It seemed plain that her murderer had knocked her down with a blood-stained stone which was lying near her, and had then stabbed her in the throat with a sharp and narrow knife-blade. She lay as one prepared for burial; her arms had been folded on her breast, and her sun-bonnet had been placed under her head. Her empty tin-pail stood near the body, but no weapon could be found . . .

The article went on to describe a knife of Herbert Hayden's that was taken into evidence and examined under a microscope:

In the little notch for the thumb-nail on one sharp and narrow blade were found 15 or 20 corpuscles, which were pronounced corpuscles of human blood. But Hayden's wife testified that when he went to his wood-lot that day he and his wife agreed that with this blade he had recently cut one of his fingers.

The article included some details of the whereabouts of the reverend on the day of Mary's death—including this one:

Mr. Hayden said that in Middletown, Tuesday, he had
bought some arsenic with which to kill rats, and had
hidden it in his barn, to keep it away from his children.

Herbert Hayden was arrested, and there was a hearing. He
denied ever having an affair with Mary Stannard, and his wife
provided supportive testimony. His lawyers managed to keep
Mary's half-sister's statements out of the hearing, and he was
eventually released. But more evidence against him was found
after that initial hearing. Most compellingly, sixty grains of arsenic were found in Mary Stannard's stomach when her body
was exhumed and reexamined. She wasn't pregnant, they
found—but she had a mass in her uterus that likely would have
mimicked the symptoms of pregnancy. Herbert Hayden was
arrested again and put on trial in October of 1879.

The article concluded with the names of all of the many lawyers who would be trying and defending the case. I looked for
Matthew Barnett's name, since Gerard had mentioned he was a
lawyer. But his name wasn't there.

The brutality of the murder was horrific even to my modern
sensibilities, so it was curious to me that Little Miss Muffin
Minutes could be so matter-of-fact about the gory details of
the trial. But then, perhaps by the time she'd gotten around to
writing of her acquaintance's—her brother's?—involvement in
the testimony, she'd grown used to some of the more shocking
details being bandied about.

I skimmed some of the subsequent pages of the journal, looking for more references to Harry, Professor Johnson, Herbert
Hayden, and the trial. It appeared there were several.

Then I looked over a few more *New York Times* articles. It

was getting late, and I was too tired to digest all of the details, but one fact became clear as I read: Mary Stannard's body had been exhumed three times at various points in the investigation. I wasn't sure why, but that part chilled me nearly as much as the murder itself. Her various organs and body parts were kept in jars and examined by experts—many of them from Yale—and discussed in the courtroom.

Said the *New York Times* on October 18:

> Prof. Samuel W. Johnson, a most important expert in this case, is a small man who dresses in an unassuming way, and wears spectacles. He looks like a German *savant*. For 23 years he has been an instructor in the Yale Scientific School, for 15 years in the Chair of Analytical Chemistry, and for the remainder of the time as Professor of Theoretical and Agricultural Chemistry.

As I was reading this, I thought I heard a slight squeak. The receiving end of the baby monitor was upstairs, so I had to stop what I was doing and listen carefully.

Silence.

I read on, finding the early portions of the professor's testimony:

> "Dr. White brought to me, Oct. 4, 1878, what he said were her stomach and liver, in a large glass bottle; he brought to me Oct. 8 what he said was her brain; Dr. Hotchkiss brought to me, March 7, 1879, what he said were portions of her diaphragm, gullet, intestines and lungs, and one kidney."

"What did you do with the stomach?"

"No incisions had been made in it. I opened it, and found in it about two tablespoons full of liquid, and partly-digested food. There were some little lumps, which were probably white of egg, and some seeds of pulp of blackberries. Beside the food there was about a teaspoonful of a heavy, gritty white powder—a powder which when exposed to the sunlight and moved, reflected light like a crystalline substance. Under the microscope this substance was found to consist mainly of regular crystals; some of it was in opaque white lumps. This gritty powder I found to be ordinary white arsenic, mingled with flakes of yellow arsenic. Or arsenic sulphide; on the inner membrane of the stomach were stains of a canary-yellow color; these I scraped off, and found to be arsenious sulphide; this substance is produced when hydrogen sulphide gas generated by putrefaction comes in contact with white arsenic."

Then I heard Lucy's little cry. Not a loud or desperate cry, but still I needed to check it out. I felt calm as I climbed the stairs, but as I reached the final step, I heard the cry change tone and become more impatient. I felt my stomach drop a little.

The door was open a crack. I put my hand up to it to push it open.

It wouldn't go.

It wouldn't open.

"Lucy!" I cried and kicked at the door, which promptly swung open.

OOOOOAAAHHHR-eeeee.

I stepped past the door and to the crib, then lifted Lucy up to my shoulder. She put her hand on my shoulder and made a little noise that sounded almost like "AHA!"

"Just wanted to make sure I was still here?" I whispered, taking a deep breath.

Lucy gurgled and pushed her face into my neck. My pulse stopped racing

"Don't you want to sleep a little more?" I asked.

Don't you want to sleep a little more so Mama can read more about arsenic and disembodied stomachs?

Another contented gurgle.

"No? You want to play?"

I sat in the rocker and grabbed a board book from the floor. *The Touch and Feel Farm* was the title.

"Oooh. Just what I need. The touchy-feely farm," I said, and chuckled at my own joke.

Lucy smiled at me just slightly—as if trying to understand my laughter, or trying to humor me. Her face crinkled a little bit, bringing her bruise into focus. Patty had been right that it was "almost perfectly round." And there seemed to be a perfect spiral of yellow forming inside the purple.

Lucy stopped smiling, apparently bored or perplexed by my silence. The bruise seemed to fade back into formlessness.

I opened the book. I took another deep breath.

"The cow says moo," I announced.

Chapter 18

Northampton Lunatic Hospital
Northampton, Massachusetts
December 20, 1885

During that time that I was made to rest in that little upstairs room, I didn't have enough physical activity in the day to allow me to sleep soundly at night. At night, my mind was often in chaos.

On the worst of those nights, a particular memory troubled me—an incident that had occurred approximately a year earlier—in the summer of 1878.

A goblet had broken at Matthew's feet, and a shard had cut him in the leg. It *had* been an accident, had it not? Lying half-mad in that bed for days on end, however, I no longer felt certain of anything.

He had been reading and asked me to pour him some water. As I'd approached him with it, I'd felt a bit light-headed. I know now—and knew soon afterward—that it was the pregnancy. For a moment, the air in front of me speckled pink and orange, and my stomach was gripped with a sudden pain. The crash of the goblet swept away the pink and orange spots, and I managed to grip the wall to keep from falling.

Ahhh! Frances! What in God's name . . .

Oh, Matthew! Oh, I'm so sorry! Let me have a look . . .

And what made me lie awake now, worrying over a cut that had long since healed? (Should I not be thinking of Martha's, which hadn't yet?) Had Matthew perhaps suspected some wicked intention in my clumsiness, that time and this more recent one with poor Martha?

I troubled over this for the rest of the night, and by daylight my mind was numb with the thought. That was the day I might have gone mad, completely and forever.

But that very day, fate left me a gift—a distraction. The nurse—whose name I cannot recall, and don't wish to—left her book on her chair when she had gone to procure my lunch from the kitchen. I snatched it up and jammed it under my mattress without looking at the title. She was, for the hour after that, so occupied with the feeding of her patient— buttered bread and then two monstrously tall glasses of milk —that she seemed not to notice the absence of her book. Later that afternoon, I saw her peering under the table, under the bed. Since I played so passive when she was present, it apparently didn't occur to her that I could've taken it. Perhaps she was simply afraid to cause a stir by accusing me and thus alerting Matthew to the length and frequency of her absences from the room.

I looked at the book before suppertime, when the nurse was downstairs, occupied with the preparation of my next meal. It was a small green book, not much bigger than my hand, with a pretty gold design on its spine. Its title was *The Sunny Side*, and it was published by an organization called the American

Sunday-School Union. It was a simply written little book, about the trials and tribulations of the wife of a minister.

At first, I was rather annoyed with the milquetoast little nurse for her tame taste in stories. Why couldn't she have been a devious sort of girl who'd bring to her work a novel with a bit of scandal or crime? Or at least a touch of romance? After many days with that book as my only entertainment, however, Emily, the wife, and Henry, the minister—and their family—became dear friends to me. I rationed the little book's twenty-six chapters (yes, I remember exactly), allowing myself one chapter per day, and occasionally more if I was feeling particularly lonely or desperate and the nurse absented herself at length. The faithful and hardworking Emily had seven children, which the couple struggled to feed and clothe and educate on Henry's meager earnings. Two chapters were devoted to finding the means to buy their son an appropriate cloak for college. One child died, one daughter married, and then another. The remaining sons eventually entered successful careers. Emily died, and then Henry followed her on the book's final page.

When I reached this ending, I wept—not because I found the story particularly compelling, or even because Emily and Henry were dead, as they both lived long and pious lives and had happy, successful progeny to show for it—but because I'd have nothing new to read, or to anticipate reading. Still, I turned back to the beginning during my next reading opportunity. I was five chapters into my second reading when Dr. Stayer declared the end of my treatment.

I was given two days to move about the house and re-acclimate myself to the household duties before I was to see

Martha again. At my earliest opportunity, I tossed *The Sunny Side* into the oven coals. I didn't want any evidence to remain of my rebellion against the treatment. Nor did I wish to ever think about Emily and Henry again. The mere thought of them left a terrible taste of milk in my mouth.

Chapter 19

January 3, 1879

This will probably be my last entry. I tried, at Christmas, to have special, private words with everyone dear to me—Mother, Clara, Matthew, and most of all Harry—to let them know how much I love them. Affection is not my strongest quality, but I tried my best.

I made the mistake, with Matthew, of saying something about my "final Christmas," and he looked positively stunned. Poor dear. He'll look even more stunned when the day comes and he sees how right I was.

Blessed Lord, I am in your hands.

February 2, 1879

The birth was long and difficult, and my recovery has been slow. Clara has been assisting me a great deal. Martha Elizabeth Barnett was born on January 10, late in the evening.

February 5, 1879

Clara's help continues to be invaluable. I am finally up and about the house more, although I am not yet as efficient in the kitchen as I was. Both Clara and Tessa have rushed me back to bed on more than one occasion, saying I don't look well.

Sometimes I think Clara wishes to keep Martha mostly to herself. I do not blame her. Martha is an enchanting little creature when she isn't crying. Her eyes have the same shape and glimmer as Father's. A deep and complex color, like twilight approaching.

I am too tired to write more tonight.

February 9, 1879

Mother came to visit us again. I find it surprising that she never remarks on Martha's resemblance to Father. In any case, she held and rocked her for nearly two hours while Tessa helped me to organize the pantry and other downstairs rooms after such a long period of neglect. On Saturday, I hope to make cider loaves. I believe that making such a familiar recipe will help me feel at ease in the kitchen again. I hope that the familiar taste will have a curative effect as well.

February 19, 1879

Another snow today. It seems light at the moment, but as we know from last week, what can appear a delightful flurry can quickly turn furious and unending. I pray we don't get a storm like last week's.

Matthew was assisting with a prosecution in Hartford, and I expected him home on Wednesday. He had warned me many times this winter that if there is ever treacherous weather while he is in Hartford, he will stay an extra day or two with his cousin. Still, as evening approached and Martha grew more agitated, I began to dread the nights alone with her. Matthew is not skilled with infants or Martha in particular. His presence, however, makes me more efficient in my motherly duties. It has the opposite effect of Clara's or Tessa's presence.

I had not been alone with Martha for any significant length of time. I found, in Matthew's absence, I could forgo any supper and simply focus on Martha's nursing and sleeping. All was fine until she awoke around midnight. In her cries I thought I heard despair—despair at the dark, despair at the late hour, despair, primarily, at the sense that she was alone with me.

I nursed her back down as I've done nearly every night, and she was quiet again.

My heart was, for a sleepless night, nonetheless filled with blackness at hearing her despair.

And that is why I wish for it not to snow so heavily again—this week particularly, as Matthew's trial continues.

February 25, 1879

I had so long forgotten the simple pleasures of snow! I was too eager to outgrow it, when I was a girl. Now I am eager for Martha to be old enough to play in it with me.

Today, light flakes were falling, but the temperature was surprisingly mild.

I bundled myself and Martha and went out walking. Such big, fluffy flakes landed on my coat. I stayed out as long as I could, to preserve their beauty.

We stayed out till Tessa came looking for us. She had a soup waiting on the stove, she said. And Matthew had told her to insist that I eat.

March 1, 1879

An unusually warm day for the season, and much of the snow is turning to mush.

How odd to have a glimpse of this spring I did not think myself meant to see.

I am sewing Martha a blue sun bonnet with a lacey trim.

March 14, 1879

I was foolish last night, attempting the roast from so late an hour. I should have foreseen that it would be too difficult to manage with Martha's fussing. Matthew tried to stay in good humor about it, but supper was not served until nearly nine o'clock. Tessa was positively frantic, but it wasn't her fault. This afternoon I shall cook soup—and start early to make certain there will be no delay! I am too tired to write more. Martha's troubles are the same. I hope for more sun and more warmth tomorrow. It has rained for three days. Four, perhaps. I have lost count. I suppose I have lost count in more than one respect.

March 22, 1879

The wind was strong today, and the air as cold as any winter day's, but Martha and I took the carriage on its maiden voyage nonetheless. When we were on Winston Street, near the church, there was such a violent gust that I gripped the handle and said a little prayer. Martha's eyes fluttered but she didn't wake. Still, in that moment, I wondered what had possessed me to go out in this weather. I suppose I am simply too eager for spring to come, to cast its healing light and warmth on me.

I believe I shall be a better wife and mother in the spring, when Nature can lend a hand. Until then, is all of the light to come from me?

April 14, 1879

I finished sewing for Matthew the white shirt. He seemed quite delighted by the surprise, tried it on for me late in the evening after Martha had gone to sleep. The shoulders were, disappointingly, a bit large—I had thought I'd measured correctly against his other shirts. Still, he was very complimentary about it. (Despite mentioning that he hoped I had not "given up more enjoyable pursuits" to complete it.)

As he undressed for bed, I caught a glimpse of the scar on his calf. I occurs to me I hadn't seen the poor leg in some time. It is bigger than I remember it—angrier than I'd have imagined it. It is half-purple, half-red, with a jagged downward turn, frowning at me. I had to look away.

I should be glad Matthew did not see me looking.

Perhaps I should make him another shirt. Or perhaps challenge myself with a pair of trousers.

April 25, 1879

I could not sleep the other night, for I was still thinking about Matthew's scar.

I wished to see it again—to examine it more thoroughly. He was conveniently positioned on his stomach, with his right leg angling almost out of the bed. I loosened the covers by degrees. There was enough moonlight to get a fair glimpse, I thought. When I finally managed to push up his hem, however, I found its shape and color obscured in the darkness. I lowered my face close to the leg and looked for the frown I'd seen the other night. As I did so, Matthew grunted and flipped himself round.

"What is the matter?" he mumbled sleepily. "Is Martha crying?"

"No," I said. "I believe you were dreaming of wolves again."

Matthew often dreams of wolves and awakens with a start. I shouldn't have deceived him, but I didn't wish to explain my desire to examine the scar. He would think it too strange.

May 2, 1879

Yesterday was May Day, and some of the ladies held festivities on the green. Mrs. Lawton invited me along, but I was not in the right spirit.

I have completed a sewing project this week and begun a new one. Martha's new nightdress is not perfect—the button holes are uneven. Hardly anyone will see her in it, however, and I'm eager to try a different shirt design for Matthew. I'm disappointed that I miscalculated the shoulders on the last one. He has worn it once, and quite happily, but to my eye he didn't look as sharp as he could. I hope he doesn't announce too exuberantly that it is his wife's handiwork.

Chapter 20

Haverton, Connecticut
December 10, 2014

I closed the journal pages. My eyelids were feeling heavy, and I needed a break.

Since Lucy was still napping, I tried Stephanie Barnett's number for the second time. The first time I'd left a message, explaining who I was and that her brother had given me her number.

This time it rang three times, and then a woman picked up with an exasperated-sounding "Hello?"

"Oh!" I said. "Stephanie?"

"Yeah?"

"My name is Abby Olson Bernacki. I called you earlier and—"

"Yup. I recognized your number this time. You're in the Miller Avenue house, huh?"

"Yes. Can you talk right now?"

"I'm taking a smoke break at work."

I wasn't sure if that was a yes or a no.

"Oh. Where do you work?" I asked, trying for a little small talk.

"I cut hair at GreatCuts. I've got a couple minutes. What's this about? I'm curious."

"Well." I took a breath. "I guess I'll get right to the point. I've been having odd experiences in the house. I implied as much to your brother, and he said that you had, too."

"Odd experiences," Stephanie repeated quietly.

Was she going to make me come out and say it?

"Creepy, like," I said, using the same word her brother had used.

"Oh." Stephanie didn't sound particularly surprised. "Like what?"

As Stephanie asked this, I heard a little cough and a sputter. A tiny sneeze, and then a cry. Lucy was awake.

"Hold on just a second?" I said, making my way quickly down the hall.

Lucy's door was wide open, as I'd left it. When I reached for her, she made a cute little squeak and stopped crying.

"Sorry," I said, sinking into the rocker so I could put the phone back to my ear. "Stephanie?"

"You . . . have a baby?" Stephanie asked.

"Yeah," I said.

"Oh."

Stephanie was silent for a moment, but I could hear her breathing.

"Are you still there?" I asked.

"Um. Yeah. How old's the baby? Do you have any other kids?"

"Just her. She's five months old."

More silence.

"Stephanie?"

"Yeah. Sorry. Which room is the baby's room?"

"The little one upstairs. Right at the top of the stairs."

Stephanie didn't reply. I heard her exhale—perhaps letting out a puff of cigarette smoke.

"Hello?" I said.

Lucy reached up and tapped the side of my face, saying "Oh! Oh!" in surprisingly imitative fashion.

"Hello?" I repeated.

"Oooohh!" Lucy gasped, her mouth forming a precocious little "o."

"Hi. I . . . sorry." Stephanie sounded hurried now. "I don't think I can talk about this right now. I'll . . . call you back. Bye."

"But could we—"

I was going to say *Could we set up a time to talk*, but a moment later my phone was beeping gently. The screen said, "Call ended."

I tried calling Stephanie back but got her voice mail.

"Shit," I muttered, and scowled at the phone.

Lucy slapped my chin and laughed.

Chapter 21

The day Clara brought Martha back home to me was a hot and muggy one. I recall mopping my face with cold water as I waited by the window, struggling to appear cool and natural. Despite the obvious intensity of the heat, I feared looking anxious.

When Clara finally arrived—clutching the bonneted Martha—I sprang up from my chair. I wasn't sure, though, if I should run outside to greet her. Again, would that be natural? Would that be correct?

I do not know why I worried so, as Martha's and my separation had been so unnatural that surely nothing I did could top it. Still, I worried how carefully my behavior was being watched and analyzed. Matthew was not present, but my tedious nurse was, and I knew she reported the details of my behavior (that is, the ones that didn't make her look incompetent) directly to Dr. Stayer.

Dear Clara thankfully took things in hand.

"Frances and her girl should have a chance to reunite in private, don't you think?" she asked the nurse in a manner that clearly communicated that she wasn't really *asking* at all. "I'm parched. Let's have a drink out back under that beautiful maple tree."

"I will bring some water right out to you ladies," Tessa added.

Clara thrust Martha into my arms, hustling the nurse out before she could protest.

The nurse was to leave on the following day—unless she and Dr. Stayer dreamt up some reason for her to stay and keep drawing a wage from Matthew.

The ladies' voices faded from me as Clara drew the nurse toward the maple tree. For a glorious moment, Harry, it was all Martha's eyes again. They'd fluttered open from Clara's sudden movement, and there they were—like two secret gems kept from me the entire time I'd been "resting." As familiar now as ever. And as beautiful.

I'd have stared into them all that afternoon had Martha not begun to fuss just then. I panicked, wondering if she'd forgotten my face. And as I lifted her to my shoulder, whispering my love to her, her weight felt unfamiliar to me. I stretched out my arms to look at her again. I panicked. Her face seemed wider than my Martha's—her ears slightly pointier. I could not remember—had Martha's ears really been this pointy?

"My girl," I said, perhaps trying to convince myself. "My sweet girl."

She quieted more quickly than I expected, and I was relieved to think she had not forgotten me after all. I feared, however, that I'd forgotten something fundamental about her. What that was precisely, I couldn't determine.

I carried Martha up the stairs and looked at her and myself in the mirror. The sight of us together strengthened me and pushed back the doubt. There were her eyes again, confirming a truth larger than that doubt: We belonged together, Martha and I. She'd still been in this world a shorter time than she'd been inside of me. This felt significant to me, even if the people and circumstances around us did not acknowledge its significance.

I whispered to our reflection, "I shall try again, my dear girl."

I felt every word of that phrase, and feel it even now. *My dear girl.*

Forward and backward.

My. Dear. Girl.

Girl. Dear. Mine.

For I felt in that moment the sad importance of her being female. And she was indeed dear to me. More dear than anything had ever been before. And she was mine. *That* everyone seemed to have forgotten in the month that had separated us. She was *my* daughter. *Mine.*

Chapter 22

May 7, 1879

I haven't sewn a stitch since my last entry. Yesterday was such a brilliant sunny day that Martha and I walked all the way to Beebe's store, where I was delighted to find a new selection of fabrics. There will be more summer dresses and bonnets for Martha, as I purchased a yard of each of the three prettiest.

As we arrived back home from Beebe's, I noticed the beginnings of the tulips peeking out from beneath last autumn's leaves—the patch by the side of the door, which Mrs. Lawton helped me plant when I was a new bride. Because Martha was sleeping contentedly in her carriage, I busied myself clearing away the old leaves and pulled up two tiny saplings that were trying to establish themselves among them. And as Martha was still sleeping after that, I fetched my old sketchbook—with some effort, as I hadn't seen it in many months—and attempted to draw the charming little plants. There is something about that flower's first unfurling that is most beguiling. I could not capture it with my pencil. My drawings looked like soiled fingers with ragged nails, reaching up from the dirt. ("They look a bit frightful, ma'am," Tessa admitted when I showed her my work. "But wasn't that how you intended it?")

My attempt today was considerably better, and dear Martha slept through all of my sketching, but the effort delayed my supper plans by an hour or two. I had to serve Matthew bread before the soup was ready, as his stomach was growling so viciously.

May 12, 1879

Clara made an unexpected visit yesterday. I was surprised to see she had her carpet bag with her—bulging with clothes for several nights. It appears Matthew wrote Jonathan and suggested I'd appreciate a visit. I certainly am enjoying the company, but it is out of character for Matthew to forget to tell me something like this. I would have done some special baking for my sister. Now that she is here, we are baking cider loaves together. She so enjoys holding Martha and singing to her. Her voice is so much lovelier than mine. I wonder if Martha notices the difference. I sing to her when I am certain nobody else can hear. Soon she will understand the distinction between a sweet voice and an unmelodic one. I like to think, however, that in the earliest days, her mother's was nonetheless her favorite.

May 14, 1879

I have tucked in here my last attempt I made at drawing the early tulip leaves. I drew it on the first day Clara was here. She held Martha while I went outdoors after Matthew had gone. This will be the last drawing until next year, as they have all bloomed now. I don't have as strong a desire to draw the actual blooms. They are perhaps too ostentatious. The early leaves, just emerging, are like impish little secrets, every one. That is what I most wanted to capture. I don't know if I've done so very successfully, but I'll save the attempt until next year and compare the two.

Clara asked, when she saw what I had done, if I had recently taken up botany more seriously. I told her no and tried to explain to her the singular attraction of the early tulip leaves, rolled up so coyly. She replied with a doubtful smile, as if I'd said that I expected winged fairies to crop up from the soil.

I did not show her my drawings. I don't begrudge her her older-sisterly airs—I simply wish my drawing skills matched her musical ones.

October 14, 1879

Professor Johnson is to testify soon. On our walk yesterday, Harry answered all of my questions about his colleague's experiments and their place in the trial. It was a pleasure to have my brother all to myself. Matthew is, of late, so intent on cushioning my mind from anything so interesting.

This is my understanding of the significance of the experimental stomachs. It is to show that the poor girl's stomach was not tampered with unlawfully after her death! There was no denying that her stomach had poison in it, but what is likely to be argued by the defense is that it

*was deposited there by someone on the prosecutor's side—
someone intent on convicting Rev. Mr. Hayden.*

*The Stannard girl's stomach had, as a result of the ar-
senic, enlarged blood vessels in the postmortem examination. Under the direction of Professor Johnson, Harry and
his colleagues obtained two stomachs for experimentation,
and applied a similar amount of arsenic to them. After
some time sitting in jars in the lab, with the arsenic inside
of them, it was found that the stomachs did not have the
same enlarged condition of blood vessels as the girl's stomach. These results will make it more difficult for the defense
to make their accusation regarding the arsenic's introduction after the death, rather than before.*

*I gather that the physical evidence will be much more
complex than what I've described here, but this explains
Harry's part. I inquired whether he would be taking the
stand, but he said no. Dr. Johnson will be speaking for his
own work, including this part in which Harry assisted.
It would be exciting if Harry testified! Mother would be
beside herself, however, so perhaps it is best he has a quieter role.*

October 18, 1879

*Harry has fulfilled his promise of late. He finally came
to visit me at home—spent an hour with Martha on his
knee and gave me more than a week's worth of New
Haven newspapers. I'd have liked to have read them right
away and asked him questions about what he's seen and
heard, as he was present in the courtroom for one day of*

Dr. Johnson's testimony! I stashed them in my chest in the bedroom, however, while he and Matthew were chatting.

It was altogether a clandestine affair. Harry brought the newspapers in a basket of sweet breads made and sent, he said, by Mother. Harry had given me a tiny wink as he'd said this, and when I brought them to the kitchen, I saw the newspapers stuffed beneath them.

I have only managed to read two so far. They involve the selection of the jury and Herbert Hayden's plea of not guilty.

I gather, from peeking, that the further articles involve the details of Dr. Johnson's testimony. I am saving those for tomorrow—when Matthew won't be present, and I won't be so tired.

Chapter 23

I bolted up as soon as I heard it. The little journal tumbled to the floor.

Shhhhh.

I must have dozed off while reading—and Chad must have switched off my lamp when he came upstairs. My eyes took a moment to focus on the little green light of the baby monitor.

Shhhhh.

There were no water sounds to muddle it now. I'd taken the iPod player out of Lucy's room altogether.

"Chad!" I snapped. "Wake up! Do you hear that?"

Chad rolled over and mumbled, "Hear . . . whuh?"

I ran down the hall and threw open the door, shouting, "Stop it!"

I approached Lucy's bed, and her eyes flew open. She fussed a little but didn't scream. Still, I had to pick her up.

We rocked for about a half hour until I could put her down again. After I did, I knew I wouldn't be able to sleep. Instead, I went downstairs to find my laptop and a blanket, and then came back up and settled by her doorway—curling up on the floor beneath the blanket.

I had no idea how I was going to distract myself into

sleepiness. Maybe it was time to research baby monitors? A brand new, highly rated audio monitor would cost well over a hundred dollars, but I suspected it wouldn't solve my problems. Maybe our monitor was picking up some kind of radio static, and a new, expensive one wasn't the solution.

A video monitor was a possibility, however. It would cost twice as much at least. Chad and I had promised each other, when we opted for me to take a year's leave, that we'd avoid extravagant purchases. That was how we'd ended up with a decade-old secondhand monitor in the first place. We'd bought nearly all of Lucy's things secondhand. But this, I decided, had been an error. An investment in my sleep and my sanity was entirely different from fancy baby dresses or weekly meals out for Indian food or steak.

When I opened my computer, I found a new message in my inbox.

Hi Abby,

It's Sara, from the baby play group. We'd talked a little about maybe getting the girls together sometime. Since you haven't been to the last few meetings, I did a little detective work on Facebook! (You mentioned that you worked at Brigham Girls' Academy, and it was pretty easy from there.) Would a playdate still interest you? Wendy naps at around ten and around three. (Never for very long, sadly.) We could get take-out sandwiches and do lunchtime, if that works for Lucy's schedule.

Hope to hear from you!
Sara

I hesitated, staring at the name *Wendy*.

Of course. That baby's name had been Wendy.

The last time I'd gone to the group, Sara had put her nose against her bald baby's, rubbed it back and forth in a gentle Eskimo kiss, and sang *WEN-dy, WEN-dy, WEN-dy!* Up until then she'd referred to her daughter as Gwendolyn. The nickname shouldn't have startled me—and yet, it had.

I had not wished to go back to the group after that. I'd not wished to see that baby's sweet bald head again. Nor her blue eyes, so much like her mother's.

I closed the e-mail and then Googled the name of an online baby store. Settling quickly on a middle-range video monitor, I clicked hastily through to the checkout. When I was finished, I got up, crept into the bedroom, and yanked the monitor's cord out of its socket. I carried it downstairs, flipping on all the lights in my path. When I reached the kitchen, I set the receiving end of the old monitor on the counter and stared at it. Innocent white plastic, with a silver-gray circle framing that little green light—now cloudy in its unplugged, inactive state. A cheerful red Fisher-Price label was blazoned across the little gray speaker below the light.

I pulled out my French rolling pin and gave the monitor two swift and efficient whacks—enough to break it into several plastic pieces. I didn't worry about Chad waking, because apparently he never heard anything much in this house at night.

The new monitor would be here in a few days. In the meantime, Chad and I would just have to keep our ears and our bedroom door open.

There could easily be a story about fumbling around in the

dark, the monitor breaking on our hardwood floor. I could justify the new one more easily with the old one broken.

I put away my laptop, tiptoed upstairs, grabbed my pillow from the bedroom, and crawled back under the blanket by Lucy's door.

Every time I felt my eyelids droop, the words *Shut up, please* crept out from somewhere deep in my head. When I tried to block them out, *You deserve it* would slip out instead. I must have fallen asleep eventually. The next thing I knew, Lucy was up with the first morning light.

Chapter 24

Northampton Lunatic Hospital
Northampton, Massachusetts
December 20, 1885

It was the summer of bonnets.

In the first days of my return to mothering, I wondered if there was a tonic or dietary regimen that might make Martha's hair grow faster. I was, you see, eager for her scar to be disguised. Because Mother always said we were, all three of us, especially bald infants for an especially long time, I decided bonnets were a more promising solution.

I sewed dear Martha nearly a dozen bonnets and purchased a few more. White ones and blue ones, mostly. Simple ones and fussy ones. Some with lacy rims, some with large ruffles that made Martha look like a daisy. She grew used to wearing them all the time—even in the house. I removed the bonnets only while she slept at night. Matthew accepted this, assuming I was so proud of my handiwork that I was reluctant to remove them from her head.

I did not return to the old sewing projects I'd attempted before my rest, however—with the exception of a single dress for Martha, which I worked on in a leisurely way. Bonnets were relatively simple—simple enough not to distract me from my day-to-day duties—regular mealtimes, keeping the kitchen and drawing room tidy, directing and aiding Tessa with the laundry.

I tried not to get lost in the veins of maple leaves or the pattern of ants parading the kitchen floor. And I believe I performed rather well.

One August day, I was afflicted with a peculiar urgency to finish the dress for Martha. It was a summer dress, and the days of summer were dwindling. I'd intended it to be a dress for Sundays, and now I would be lucky if I could use it for a single Sunday. I decided I'd walk with Martha to see Louise, and use her sewing machine.

The urgency of the dress was perhaps exacerbated by my growing loneliness. I missed Louise's company and sensed a separation between us since my marriage and particularly since my period of rest.

There was great surprise on her face when she saw me arrive with Martha's carriage—and with rivulets of sweat running down both my temples.

Oh, my dear! Frances! What a pleasant surprise! But is something the matter?

I thought I might use your Singer?

Of course, but for what? On a day like today?

I'm sewing Martha a special dress with a matching bonnet. For Sundays.

For Sundays?

Louise looked perplexed. How could something for Sundays be a matter of such urgency that I'd bring my delicate child out in this heat? What she didn't understand was how Sundays troubled me. How I could feel other ladies' eyes on me—and on my Martha—in church. How desperately I needed for Martha to be the most beautifully outfitted, most supple-skinned, most rosy-cheeked child in the room to distract those women from any gossip they may have heard.

Louise's dear aunt Dorothy joined her in the drawing room, and together they played with Martha while I sewed. As I attached the sleeves to the bodice of Martha's dress, I considered how I could separate Louise from Dorothy and have a private conversation.

I was not certain what I wished to discuss with my old friend. That feeling of urgency—the urgency I'd awoken with, and which I'd associated with Martha's summer dress—had not left me.

I looked down at the little dress and found I'd sewn on one arm upside-down. To wear it, little Martha would have to keep her arm up in a permanent salute. I scanned the room for a sewing box, for a seam ripper. Seeing no such thing, I nearly burst into tears. Instead, I called out for Louise to help me. When she came in, I whispered to her that I'd like to step outside with her for a little chat. She extracted us from the house expertly, saying she wanted to show me some bugs on the lettuce in the garden, and claiming my entomological expertise.

As we bent over the lettuce heads, a desperate rush of words came out—words that felt necessary to prevent more tears.

Louise, do you think some of the ladies in town regard me as an inept mother?

Louise's response was slower than I'd have liked. *Frances. Pardon me?*

Do you think some of the . . .

Why are you troubling yourself in this way? Did someone say something unkind to you?

*No. It isn't about words. It's about looks. Hard looks and cen-
suring eyes.*

Who?

There were women in church. I know I wasn't imagining it.

*Who? I know Haverton's characters better than you, Frances,
and—*

*One of them had red hair. But Louise, my feelings are not
about any one woman. There is truth to any criticism one could
apply to me.*

Oh, Frances . . . Red hair. Might that be John McFarlene's sister?

It was possible. Louise, however, did not seem to understand
what I was truly asking of her. I changed my approach.

*Louise. Do you remember the time we walked by the stream
behind the Wilsons' barn, and it was so muddy I started to fall
in? Do you remember how I grabbed you and pulled you down
with me?*

When we were girls?

*And do you remember how that broken stick cut you so terribly
on the back of your leg?*

Yes?

*Did you ever think that I had done it deliberately? Pulled you
down?*

Frances? We were twelve years old.

And do you still have the scar?

*No. I don't believe so. It was on the back of the thigh, so I don't
really often see . . .*

So perhaps you still have it.

I don't think so. If I do, it is quite faint.

Might I look and see?

Frances . . . no. You're being very silly. I'm not going to lift my skirt out here in the garden for you. Or anywhere else, for that matter.

Louise pulled a head of lettuce from the ground, stood up, and placed it in my hands.

I've missed you, my friend. I thought I should visit you more this summer.

Why didn't you?

Your brother said that the doctor said you should have only necessary guests. That you weren't to be excited without good reason.

Excited?

Is that the correct word?

I think so. But Louise, what I meant to ask, about that fall you had, about the scar—

Louise had moved farther down the line of lettuces, and I wondered if she could hear me. As I caught up with her, I considered what I'd been about to ask her next—about whether the scar now or ever had a distinct shape. I considered how this question might sound, even to an old friend. It would, of course, sound mad.

Therefore I did my best to forget the question. I took a deep breath and asked a different one.

What is the interesting news around town, Louise?

Louise hesitated before answering.

Have you been following the story in the papers, about the Madison minister accused of murder? It is about to be tried in New Haven. Surely Matthew has talked about it?

Surely. But not with me.

I believe that is how I first got wind of that case. The Mary Stannard case. *The Great Case.* Do they still call it that, or has a greater, more gruesome, more complex case replaced it since?

A minister had killed the girl Mary in the woods because she was pregnant with his child. Others had been talking about it for some time, apparently. I, of course, had had other concerns in the preceding months. I didn't read the papers, and Matthew sheltered me from such unpleasant matters.

It occurred to me later that Louise was asking because she already knew of your involvement in some of the anatomical testimony that was being prepared at Yale.

You were secretly courting her by then, weren't you? If I hadn't been so busy with my endeavor to appear as happy and maternal as possible, I probably would have known that by then. In those days, however, I hadn't had time for visiting with either of you. And you were, of course, hiding yourself in that lab a great deal.

In any case, you'd already spoken to her about it—surely with great excitement. Perhaps not in gruesome detail, gentleman that you are and delicate flower that she appears to be. Maybe you know now that she is not that at all. I hope I don't offend you by saying so. I might be a lunatic, but I know as well as anyone who has experienced marriage that there are usually limits to one's capacity to pretend.

But I digress. I was probably relieved to have my troubles nudged gently back into the dark and to have the lurid troubles of a stranger to discuss instead.

They dug her up three times. Louise was so breathless about this fact that you'd have thought she herself had done some of the toilsome digging. *The second time, they chopped her head off.*

Of course Louise would use the word "chop" in this context. Wasn't that just like her? Wasn't that the sort of irreverent peculiarity I'd missed about her company?

Where did you hear that?

It's been in the papers. But hasn't Harry spoken to you about it?

I've not seen Harry for two months.

I see.

How dreadful for her family. What on earth do they need her head for?

Something about arsenic traveling up to the brain. I believe her head was nearly severed off anyway, with how deep the cut of her throat was.

The cut of her throat? So she wasn't poisoned?

This is what's so terrible. Poisoned, throat slit, bludgeoned with a rock.

Do they have a great deal of evidence against the minister?

Apparently their strongest evidence has to do with the poison. Apparently they are doing a number of experiments at Yale. With her stomach, I believe. Several professors will be testifying.

Oh? How interesting. I wonder if Harry's mentor will be among them.

Louise was silent for a moment.

You ought to ask him.

I will. I would like to see him soon.

He has missed you, too, I would imagine.

I like to think you had, Harry. All the way home, my thoughts were of you. Of how I missed you, and perhaps more so, of how lucky you were.

Chapter 25

October 19, 1879

I've spent the day reading, when Martha has allowed.

First, the known and provable facts:

There is no question that Herbert Hayden purchased arsenic on the day that Mary Stannard was murdered. He purchased it at Tyler's drugstore in Middletown. He admits it himself, and there are witnesses and records from the drugstore.

What is suspicious about this arsenic, however, is how long it took for investigators to find it. Prosecutors' men went to look for it in his barn (where he said he'd hidden it out of his children's reach) as soon as he admitted to purchasing it. But it couldn't be found! It was not until after his first acquittal and second arrest—weeks later—that a friend of Rev. Hayden's found it in the barn. This friend had searched the barn at the request of Rev. Hayden's defense lawyers.

Whatever is the story with that batch of arsenic, there is no question that arsenic was found in Mary Stannard's body. I will summarize the evidence of that further along.

What the defense is of course calling into question is whether the arsenic that Rev. Hayden purchased is in fact the arsenic that ended up in Mary Stannard's body. A full ounce was found in his barn—and that is the amount Rev. Hayden purchased.

Also, the defense is very much pressing the possibility that arsenic was deviously introduced into the body after Mary's death, by someone intent on pinning the murder on Rev. Herbert Hayden. (Who, exactly, would have done this, the defense never says. Nonetheless, it appears to me that their strategy is to show errors in the doctors' and scientists' procedures, to show the many places where it could have happened. Though they appear to be hinting that Mary's half-sister Susan may have had reason or opportunity to do it.) This appears to be the strategy that they have been relying on most heavily over the past couple of days of testimony.

For example, a Dr. White was the one who first cut organs out of Mary's body—as her body lay on a board in front of her father's house, eight days after her death. He cut out her liver and her stomach and put them in glass jars. The defense made much of asking if the jars were clean, and how Dr. White was certain they were. Also of great concern was who might have had access to the keys of the strongbox into which those jars were subsequently stored.

Similar questions were posed to the doctor who later took out Mary's kidney (only one, as the other appears to have decomposed by then) and several other organs.

Harry's mentor, Dr. Johnson, took the stand after all of these experts. It was to him that all of Mary's organs were delivered for experimentation. He found arsenic in her stomach, liver, and brain.

The newspaper accounts ended there.

I have begun my plans to stay with Mother in New Haven, and to attend the trial with Harry next week.

October 22, 1879

I write this from New Haven. Tomorrow, I shall accompany Harry to the courtroom, where he has been viewing the murder trial with his colleagues for several days. I regret that I missed the first day of Dr. Edward Salisbury Dana's testimony, but I could not come to New Haven earlier. Matthew and Clara think I am here only to visit Mother, and Clara knows how the ladies' church group keeps Mother busy early in the week.

Harry says that during Dr. Johnson's testimony, before Dr. Dana took the stand, there was a fair amount of arsenic lying about the courtroom, from various packages brought into evidence. Dr. Johnson was explaining about different samples he'd procured from different stores, and how they were packaged. The defense attorney, Mr. Watrous, joked that the jury should "respectfully" refrain from inhaling the arsenic, "at least until you are through with this case."

According to Harry, this Watrous thinks he is very entertaining. I can tell that Harry is very frustrated with him, as he has tried to trip up Dr. Johnson at every opportunity.

Harry gave me the details of today's testimony, and this is my understanding of it.

Dr. Dana spent all of July and August of this year trav-

eling to England and back, to strengthen his testimony. The purpose of his trip was to study the manufacture of arsenic. There are two manufacturers of arsenic there, from which most of the arsenic in the U.S. comes. He wanted to see if, due to specific conditions of the grinding process, arsenic prepared at different factories—or even in different batches from the same factory, ground at different times—could have visible differences when examined under a microscope.

He spoke of a very small crystal called an octahedron— eight-sided and 1/1,000 to 1/2,000 of an inch, even and brilliant under the microscope. They generally are too small to be affected by the grinding process. Under some manufacturing conditions, however, the arsenic has lumps before it is ground—and those lumps are crushed, producing irregular, jagged fragments that look very distinct from the octahedron.

Dr. Dana said that he'd collected samples of arsenic ground at different times from both factories. His testimony ended there and will continue tomorrow.

I am feeling very nervous, but I hope we get a seat in the courtroom! Harry will be coming by quite early to fetch me. Clara believes he is taking me on a tour of his lab, and then for a meal together.

October 23, 1879

We managed to get into the courtroom, and the testimony was riveting!

I had worried I would be one of very few women, and

therefore quite conspicuous, but I was not. There were many ladies in the courtroom. I felt less like an imposter for that reason, even though it wasn't clear to me how many of them had significant connection to the victim or the accused.

Dr. Dana was on the stand all day. He is so young, but so confident and engaging.

Later I teased Harry that he ought to be so accomplished by the time he is twenty-nine. He replied that all of the students in his circle secretly envy Edward Dana. He is like the little prince of Yale, son of Professor Wallace Dwight Dana and grandson—on the other side—of the famous Professor Silliman, about whom Father once spoke quite admiringly. Harry tells me that Edward's success is, despite his family connections, very much deserved. He has already written a textbook on mineralogy.

The testimony began with Dr. Dana explaining that he'd gotten several arsenic samples from one factory—from various batches produced between 1870 and August of this year.

He made a study of all of the samples and discovered that he could distinguish very easily between the batches. Depending on where and how and when the arsenic is ground, there is a large variation in the proportion of polished octahedrons to jagged fragments. The proportional differences were what made them so easy to distinguish.

When asked to explain why the batches were so proportionally different in distribution of octahedrons to fragments, Dr. Dana admitted that he did not know—that he

*would have to study the factory conditions for a year or so
to propose a theory.*

*To that, Mr. Watrous objected, saying that Dr. Dana
should not waste the court's time with "theories," as a
man's life hangs on the case. The judge overruled him. It
seemed, in any case, simply a way to put stress on the word
"theory," to taint all of Dr. Dana's findings with it. Dr.
Dana, however, did not seem rattled! I am starting to understand Harry's frustration with Watrous. He does seem
something of a windbag.*

*But I am getting to the most exciting part now, as from
there Dr. Dana's testimony soon moved to the arsenic samples more directly related to the murder.*

*Dr. Dana was given 110 portions of arsenic by Dr.
Johnson, Dr. White, and a few others. Some were of Rev.
Hayden's "barn arsenic," some of a Mr. Colegrove's arsenic (Colegrove bought arsenic at Tyler's drugstore in
Middletown the same day as Hayden did), some of the
arsenic found in Mary's stomach, and some from a Mr.
McKee—a druggist across the street from Tyler's, from
whom Mr. Tyler had gotten the arsenic he sold on that day.
There were other samples among these, as well as repeated
portions of some of the important ones—numbered but not
labeled for Dr. Dana, to provide "checks" to his work. He
correctly catalogued all of the samples, grouping together
those that had come from the same source.*

*He then said that he carefully examined the Colegrove
samples against Rev. Hayden's barn arsenic and found
them quite distinct.*

"I have no hesitation," he said, "in saying that it is impossible that they should have come from the same source, or been manufactured at the same time."

Oh, my goodness! I believe most everyone in that room understood what his words meant. The arsenic found in Rev. Hayden's barn was not the arsenic he bought the day of Mary Stannard's murder! What happened to THAT arsenic?

The lawyers had a little tussle after that, but I was so stunned that I do not recall what it was about. Dr. Dana went on to explain that the barn arsenic had a much higher percentage of the octahedron crystals.

Soon after, Dr. Dana was asked about his comparison of the Colegrove arsenic with that in Mary Stannard's stomach. He found them to match, except for some markings on the crystals that he attributed to exposure to solvents in the decomposition process. He described an experiment he did with some of the McKee arsenic—exposing it to water over the course of three weeks—and found similar marks. He showed diagrams of his findings, and then the court was adjourned shortly thereafter.

As Harry walked me back to Mother's house, we talked about that moment of revelation about the barn arsenic's dissimilarity to the Colegrove arsenic. He said that he was not surprised. Why wouldn't Herbert Hayden attempt to cover his crime? What surprised Harry was that it seemed likely that his lawyers had planted the replacement arsenic, not him. Sometimes I think Harry a bit naïve for a man of his age and intellectual ability.

Clara was cross with both of us when we arrived, saying

she had expected us hours earlier. We had no choice but to confess our whereabouts, as I had designs on going the next day to see Dr. Dana's testimony through. She was still irritated with us, but I could tell she was riveted by our report. She reluctantly agreed to take charge of Martha's care tomorrow if I promised to stay with Martha and Mother all of Saturday, so she could have a day in the city to do some errands.

October 24, 1879

It was somewhat tiresome, sitting in that courtroom all day today. Mr. Watrous, of course, tried to take down Dr. Dana's science. I am not sure if he succeeded, but I did witness some foggy expressions on the faces of a couple of jurors. He succeeded, perhaps, in muddling the science. He asked very many questions about the furnaces and their proximity to the condensing chambers at the arsenic factories. I found myself nodding off during this portion, and wouldn't be surprised if I saw a juror doing the same. When I managed to wake myself up, Mr. Watrous was presenting Dr. Dana with a scenario in which a laborer at the factory put a shovelful of fine crystals into the mill, bottled the arsenic, and then put in a shovelful consisting of bigger crystals and bottled that. Wouldn't there be significant differences between those two samples? Wouldn't they appear to be from different mills, when in fact they were not? Dr. Dana said no—that the differences between the different factories' products were consistent.

Throughout these sorts of questions, Dr. Dana maintained

that when samples contained significant differences, he could say "with perfect confidence" that they came from different sources.

His cross-examination will continue on Tuesday, but Clara and I are set to return to Haverton on Monday. Clara is eager to return to Jonathan.

Chapter 26

Haverton, Connecticut
December 11, 2014

"H ello?"

"Good afternoon. Is this Abby Olson Bernacki?"

"Yes."

"Great. My name is Regina Gaylord. I'm one of the nurses at Haverton Pediatrics, returning your call about Lucy. Our secretary tells me you wanted to talk with one of us, and that you were considering bringing her in to have us look at a bruise? Is that correct?"

"Yes. She has a bruise that doesn't seem to be healing very well."

"Okay. When did she get this bruise?"

"Um . . . about a week and a half ago."

"Okay. Is it a very large bruise? How did she get it?"

"I guess it's the size of a nickel, but . . . bigger. Not as big as a quarter, though. It's between her eye and her nose."

"Has it changed color?"

"Yeah, it started out red and purple, and now it's yellow and brown. Yellow swirled with a line of brown. Like a snail shell."

"Well, that's pretty normal. That kind of color change.

Bruises tend to look more brown and yellow when they heal, as you probably know."

"Yes," I said.

"Is it just the one bruise?"

"No, it's . . ." I examined Lucy's arm, looking for the red-purple spot I'd found the other day. I couldn't find it. "Well . . . there was one other, but it's gone now."

"No other bruising? Did you say where the bruise near her nose came from?"

"We're not a hundred percent sure. We think it was from when we accidentally took her out of the crib too fast, and maybe hit her nose that way. But it doesn't seem like that would be enough to get a bruise that bad. I'm . . . we're . . . worried that it wasn't that, that did it, but it was maybe actually . . . something else."

"Something else?"

I breathed into the phone, catching my breath after talking so fast. I couldn't quite explain because I wasn't sure why I had said that. Had I meant *someone else?*

"Ms. Olson? Or . . . . um, Ms. Bernacki? Are you still there?"

"Yes. So, the bottom line is that I'm concerned about her bruising easily."

"But you said it's just the one bruise?"

"Yeah. Well, there was one tiny bruise before, but . . ."

"Okay. Well, bruises often do take two weeks—and sometimes more—to heal completely, and it sounds like it is healing. And at her age—I'm looking at her file—they're often getting around better, and more quickly than we expect. She may have rolled herself into something. Now, if you're worried about frequent or easy bruising, I'd be on the lookout for more bruises than the one. And call us if she gets any more."

"Do you think you want me to bring her in?"

"Um . . . not at this point, no. Let's save you the trip in. But certainly get in touch if there are additional bruises."

"Well . . . okay. Thank you."

Chapter 27

Northampton Lunatic Hospital
Northampton, Massachusetts
December 20, 1885

S o it was dear Louise, not you, who first told me of the infamous Mary Stannard murder. You needn't worry about that.

That is, in part, why you are here, I imagine. You wish to know about the arsenic, do you not? I mention the Mary Stannard murder—or should I call it the Herbert Hayden murder?—because that's where my interest in arsenic began in earnest. You have my word—I'll get round to the arsenic.

In any event, after my visit with Louise, I was quite curious about the murder. That evening, after sweet Martha was in bed. I worked up the courage to ask Matthew about it.

He didn't seem startled that I'd heard of the case—rather, he was startled that I hadn't heard of it until that point.

"Do you know any of the lawyers involved?" I asked.

"Not well. But I am an admirer of Waller's oratory style."

"Waller?"

"Thomas Waller. He has recently joined the state's team."

"And do you believe that he's on the right side?"

"Do I believe the minister is guilty, you're asking?"

"I suppose."

"I'm not familiar enough with the evidence to make a judgment. It appears, however, that there is significant evidence against the minister. The scientists say Mary Stannard had arsenic in her body. And it's been confirmed that Hayden purchased arsenic that very day at a store in Middletown. I don't know the details, but apparently the state is working on something regarding the nature of the arsenic in her stomach."

"The nature of it?"

"Something to prove that that very arsenic matches up somehow with the arsenic from the store."

"Is not all arsenic essentially the same?" I asked.

"Not under a microscope, apparently," Matthew answered.

"Oh my."

"It shall be interesting to see if this argument will work for them. Apparently it's going to be the first of its kind.

"Of course, this isn't their only evidence. The young woman, Mary, was seen at the minister's house earlier that day, and Mary's half-sister claims that she and the minister had planned a secret meeting in the woods in the very place her body was found. Only the minister didn't realize that Mary shared the plan with her half-sister. Of course, that is simply one girl's word against the minister's.

"Quite a thing. The girl's own father is the one who found her in the woods. Poor fellow. I've heard he's something of a drunkard, but no one deserves that. And then the minister was one of the party of men who carried her body out of the woods."

"But that isn't evidence of anything one way or another, is it?"

Matthew chuckled at me. "Of course not. I simply thought it was an interesting detail. That is what you're after, is it not? Details?"

"What was used to cut her throat? A knife, I imagine? Did they find a knife?"

"When did you become so interested in such grisly matters?"

"I was simply thinking about your McFarlene case. The blood on the firewood in that case, specifically."

"Oh. Well. Yes, there is some question about a knife of the minister's in this instance. There was no knife left on the scene, but from what I gather there is a knife of the minister's that is going to be presented into evidence."

"With blood on it?"

I was remembering about the blood in the McFarlene trial. That in that trial, too, they'd used microscopy. Something about the blood cells, and how the scientists involved could tell if blood was likely human blood. In the McFarlene case, they'd determined that the blood on the logs and shirt found in John McFarlene's woodpile was human. And there had been a great deal of it. That evidence had helped build the prosecutor's case.

"I'm not certain. I gather the arsenic testimony is what is going to be most compelling."

"Well. We shall have to wait and see."

"I wouldn't trouble yourself with it, Frances. It is going to be an ugly business. That's already obvious. I don't know what good it will do you to fill your mind with such unpleasantness."

"It seems to me you and your colleagues will be following it—have been following it—quite closely."

"Oh, but I have to—we have to—for professional reasons. I would, if I could, erase my mind of the whole vile affair. You have that privilege, Frances. Now. Didn't you say you have a bit of that spice cake left?"

Of course, Matthew's admonitions left me all the more curi-

ous of the matter. It was then, after the spice cake, that I resolved to see you as soon as possible.

Whatever your role was in the "vile affair," it sounded most
exciting, and I wanted you to share a bit of it with me, as you
had your first microscope. You knew this about me—that
I'd never be afraid of a little blood. Why do some gentlemen
assume this about ladies? Does it make sense to you? It never
has to me.

Chapter 28

November 1, 1879

Harry has kept his promise to visit more frequently. We had tea cake while he chatted with Matthew and me this afternoon. He was sour on the subject of the Great Trial, and he failed to bring me any newspapers. You see, yesterday was to be the testimony about the stomach experiment on which Harry assisted. And yesterday, the whole business was withdrawn! The difficulty arose when Mr. Watrous insisted upon knowing from whom the sample stomachs came. Dr. Johnson was unwilling to announce those names in open court, as donations of that sort are usually done with the solemn promise of discretion.

Matthew, for once, allowed Harry to speak freely in front of me about these matters—perhaps because he sensed Harry's disappointment. I tried to cheer Harry, saying that the results of the experiment were still useful generally, for the knowledge of poisons and how they affect the organs in different situations. He grumbled in response to this. Matthew gave him a sympathetic slap on the back and told him that Watrous was "impossibly tricky" and that it wasn't a scientist's job to find his way around people like him. It was upon the State's lawyers to do that—and how unfortunate that they weren't able to find a way. He repeated the sentiment even after Harry took his leave.

I feel sympathy for Harry, but I think it seems he is moping more for himself than for poor Mary Stannard.

November 8, 1879

Today was a long baking day. Squash pie and the usual cider loaves. I walked to Louise to give her a loaf, although she likely didn't need it, given her own baking endeavors of late. There were such strong gusts, it feels winter is already upon us. I am glad I insisted on the walk as it felt a rare opportunity now that the weather has turned so soon. I hope for a gentler winter this year.

November 15, 1879

Harry has come again. There was time only for niceties between the three of us, and then he was off to visit Louise. They are indeed courting, it seems.

This time Harry did remember to bring me two newspapers. I was especially interested in the description of the testimony of a Dr. Treadwell, who informed the court of the science of blood corpuscles—in particular, how human ones are distinguished from those of animals. It is important to this case as blood was found on Herbert Hayden's knife. I suppose the motivation behind this testimony is to rule out any arguments of the knife being used for animal slaughter?

A human blood corpuscle falls within the range of

1/2,700 and 1/3,800 of an inch. (A dog or a pig's blood can sometimes fall into that range, too, but most other animals do not.) The blood corpuscles on Rev. Hayden's knife were all in that range.

The defense made sure it was known by the jury that Rev. Hayden's young son had a habit of taking his father's knife and playing with it. And of course, such a young boy was likely to cut himself accidentally.

I remember similar blood corpuscle testimony being used in the McFarlene trial. There it was perhaps more relevant, as John McFarlene actually said that the blood splattered across his woodpile—and on the shirt hidden in a crevice of that woodpile—were from a chicken his wife had slaughtered. The blood corpuscle testimony showed he was lying. In this case, it seems the defense has several routes around the testimony, no matter how certain they might be that the blood is human. I suppose every small bit of evidence helps the prosecutorial endeavor, even if the defense attempts to explain most of it away. The overall effect perhaps still convinces the jury.

November 16, 1879

I awoke last night with a fright.

I believe I'd been dreaming of Martha's fall. I dreamt it was not a fall at all, but something more deliberate. I had a strong desire to go to her, to wake her, to examine her, to assure myself that her scar had healed efficiently.

She awoke with a smile on her face early this morning, a full hour before Matthew rose. I adore these early private *moments between us. It feels like we have so many word-less secrets, Martha and I.*

It is unfortunate that by nighttime, when I am tired and eager for her to fall asleep, it feels those delicious secrets have faded into burdens.

November 17, 1879

I awoke abruptly again—terrified again. This time it was not in the dead of night, but as the sun was rising. Matthew's leg was buried deep beneath the blankets. I removed them, one at a time, till I could see what was left of the old wound. It was still quite purple in tone. Not a single, neat slice, but a wide mass of scar, with several prongs outward.

It was such an angry scar. Surely I'd done it deliberately. I'd thrown that heavy goblet at him. Something had possessed me. Something Matthew did not wish to acknowledge—not in the light of day, or in my presence. And yet he'd acknowledged it silently when he'd had me take my long rest in the early summer.

Now that I consider it again, I realize the scar's shape. It is a spider. God forgive me, it is a spider. They are all connected—the wounds I have created.

Now Martha is up and crying.

November 27, 1879

Thanksgiving Day. Matthew and Martha are asleep. I am tired but too troubled for sleep.

The feast was at Clara's, but I did my best to help. I baked two pies and cornbread, arrived early this morning to assist with the turkey and the oyster stuffing. I believe Clara was grateful for the company, at the very least.

I did not have an opportunity to speak with Harry privately until nearly dusk, after I'd helped Mother and Clara and her girl with most of the cleaning. On my insistence, we took a walk down to Kingsley's Orchard and back.

Harry was morose when I asked him for news of the trial. He has been bitter about the whole business since they decided to throw away the stomach experiment.

He said he had not been attending much of late since his Yale colleagues were finished with their testimony. He told me he heard a terrible story from yesterday's trial, that he heard from a friend. Dr. Treadwell—the very man who testified about the blood corpuscles—was on the stand again to talk about Mary Stannard's face. His claim was that some marks on her face were potentially made by a boot heel. He'd presented diagrams of the location of the markings on the face and those of the nails of Rev. Hayden's boot heel and showed how they matched.

The face had been removed from Mary's skull and preserved in a jar of alcohol. He'd had to re-drape it over her skull in a lab to make these observations. The defense eventually insisted that if these claims were to be made, the face itself would need to be shown in court! The face and skull were sent for, and after much quibbling between the lawyers, the prosecution decided to throw out this argu-

ment rather than present these materials in court. Harry is not certain if the lawyers were hesitant to make such a grisly spectacle of the dead girl, or simply weren't sure if the whole show would, in the end, be scientifically sound. Likely they would've risked the former if they were confident of the latter.

"That should demonstrate to you what a circus that trial has become," Harry grumbled.

When I asked if he was becoming rather like Matthew in his treatment of me, he said no. He reminded me that Matthew would never have told me about something so grotesque. And perhaps for that Matthew was a better man than himself

"It is not about your femininity," Harry said. "It is about humanity. That trial is becoming an insult to humanity."

He did not wish to say anything more about it.

December 5, 1879

I must put more effort into planning the Christmas festivities. As I look backward in these pages, I see that I had grand plans last year. This year they ought to be even more so, as I can anticipate the sparkle in Martha's eye at the sight of her first decorated tree, or her first taste of fancy plum pudding. I have notions, too, of going to New Haven for a rocking horse. Martha is too small for one now, but will not be for very long!

Matthew will likely agree that another visit to Mother is appropriate.

December 10, 1879

I went to the courthouse today and saw Mrs. Hayden on the stand.

Am I a strong wife and mother? Is she?

Am I asking the most pertinent question?

December 13, 1879

We have a tree cut down from Wiggins Hill. I've spent most of the day stringing popcorn and berries. It seems a somewhat silly endeavor, but I suppose it is a restful activity compared to some. Perhaps repetition is good for the soundness of the mind. Corn corn corn berry berry corn corn corn. As long as one doesn't allow too many stray thoughts to interrupt the pattern. And yet—the thoughts keep flooding in, despite my efforts to dam them. After hours of stringing, Tessa asked me if I was feeling well. She has noticed, perhaps, all of the housework that is being sacrificed for this decorative endeavor.

December 17, 1879

Reviewing the articles from Harry. Perplexing that Hayden might have given that girl so much arsenic at once. Surely he knew he didn't need nearly so much to kill her?

How much would be enough for someone significantly smaller than Mary Stannard? A mere dusting? Perhaps an amount so small the doctors and scientists would not be able to find it?

Chapter 29

The Haverton Historical Society was tucked behind the Congregational church on the Haverton green, in a severe brown saltbox house with a cranberry-colored door. I parked in its tight, maple-canopied lot and nursed Lucy briefly in the backseat, draping us with a receiving blanket. While I waited for her to finish, I tried Stephanie Barnett's number again. The call went straight to voice mail.

As I straightened my shirt and wiped Lucy's mouth, I thought I saw movement in one of the long, narrow windows of the brown house and hoped I hadn't flashed a nip.

I hadn't heard of this place until yesterday. That was when I'd called the Haverton Library to ask how far back their *Haverton Heralds* went, and the librarian told me the paper had only been around since 1951.

"Then how did Havertonians get their news . . . uh, say, in the late 1800s?" I had asked.

"Can you tell me exactly what you're looking for?" the librarian had replied.

I wasn't sure what I was looking for. I knew that Frances

Flinch Barnett's journal had left me with an uneasy feeling, and I wondered if I could find something more about her or her family in old newspapers or other historical documents.

"I'm actually a history teacher," I'd said, hoping this would gloss things over nicely as it had with Patty.

"Wonderful," the librarian said. "Now, what we *do* have is a compendium of all of the mentions of Haverton or Haverton news in other Connecticut papers from 1720 through 1960. Some folks doing genealogy research have found that quite useful. We have a copy here as well as one at the Haverton Historical Society. Are you familiar with the historical society? Have you contacted them at all? In addition to looking at that newspaper source, you may wish to speak with Wallace Bradley, the curator. He grew up in Haverton. Knows its history quite well. He's a little gruff at first, but when he hears you're interested in nineteenth-century Haverton, I'm sure he'll warm right up. He's quite a treasure. Worked at the Beinecke at Yale for many years. Volunteers at the historical society now that he's retired. Shall I give you his e-mail address?"

I approached the maroon door and wondered what "gruff at first" meant, exactly. Or how Mr. Beinecke-at-Yale would respond to an infant entering his historical space unannounced. I hadn't mentioned, in our brief e-mail exchange, that I'd be bringing Lucy along. I knew this was borderline Obnoxious Parenting, but I was too desperate to risk having to postpone until I could find a babysitter. I'd barely slept since I'd read the final entry of the journal. Besides, Lucy would probably be content and quiet in her Björn if I kept the trip short.

I wasn't sure if I should knock or walk right in, as there was no sign on the door. It had large black hinges and an old-fashioned latch. As I reached to unlatch it, the door opened slightly, and an eager brown eye peered out at me.

"Abby?"

"Yes. Mr. Bradley?"

"Please." He pulled the door open wide and stepped backward to let us in. He was so tall that he didn't fit into the doorframe. "Wallace. And . . . who is this?"

"This?" I said stupidly, pointing to Lucy's head.

"This. Yes. Indeed." Wallace Bradley stepped to my side to get a view of Lucy's face. His thin legs were so long that he had to bend down awkwardly to attempt to meet her gaze. "Hello . . . you. Your mother hasn't told me your name yet."

"Lucy," I said, praying she wouldn't scream at the sheer oddity of his body language.

"You two have the same eyes," he said to Lucy. I held my breath, expecting him to say something about Lucy's seashell bruise.

"Come in," he said.

I followed Wallace into the house. The first room was cream white with olive wainscoting. The low ceiling made Wallace look like a giant as he led me to a table with narrow wooden chairs. The room's wide old floorboards—like the ones in my own living room—creaked as we moved.

"I'm sorry I don't have a more comfortable setup for you two," Wallace said. "We like to keep things colonial, you see."

"No problem." The wicker seat of my chair squealed under my weight. Lucy's eyes widened at the sound but relaxed again as I patted her back through her carrier.

"So you said in your e-mail that you teach at Brigham? The girls' school, correct?"

I studied Wallace for a moment before answering. He had a craggy face, tempered by sedate oval eyeglasses with nearly invisible wire frames. His gray hair was longish in the back, but thinning slightly on top. Intentional hippie style choice? Or forgot-to-get-a-haircut of the absent-minded-professor variety? I couldn't tell.

"Um . . . yes," I said. "Not this year. I took a leave of absence."

"So you're researching for . . . graduate work?"

"No . . . this really is just a personal interest. I live in an old house in town, and I've grown kind of curious about the house's history. The house belonged to the Barnett family—I guess they've been—or were—in town for over a century."

Wallace nodded. "The Barnetts. Yes. Which house? They owned several properties."

"On Miller Avenue."

"Oh. Yes! Shirley and Ed Barnett lived there."

"You knew them?"

"Shirley and my mother were roughly the same age, growing up in Haverton. They were . . . acquaintances, let's say. I don't know if either would say they were friends. But I know of the family, and I believe I know the house."

"Well, when I started asking Shirley's niece and nephew about the house . . . Do you know them?"

Wallace shook his head. I started to explain to him about the journal.

Wallace took in a breath and curled a forefinger over his lips. As he did this, I noticed a thin scar—or maybe it was just a very deep wrinkle—running from his nostril to his mouth. "Interesting . . . Did you bring it with you?"

I patted my big black diaper bag. The journal was in the very middle, wrapped in paper and cushioned by Pampers.

"Yes . . . I wanted to show it to you and see if you could direct me to any information about the woman who wrote it. Her husband's name was Matthew."

"Matthew Barnett! Of course. I've come across Matthew Barnett's name in a few contexts—mostly legal. Particularly when I prepared a display about the McFarlene murder trial of 1878 . . . that involved a man stabbing his brother-in-law . . . well, this is exciting. I'm quite eager to see this diary."

I bounced Lucy on one hip while I dug for the journal.

"And I'm eager for someone else to see it, actually," I said. "First of all, there's the authenticity issue. I don't think Shirley Barnett's nephew would have any reason to mislead me about this thing. But beyond that, I'm really curious about some things this woman wrote. She was *very* interested in a particular murder trial."

"The McFarlene murder? Here in Haverton?"

I shook my head. "No . . . I've never heard of that. This was a big case in New Haven. A young woman named Mary Stannard was murdered. A minister was accused. His name was . . ." I paused. Something like *Humbert Humbert*, wasn't it?

"Herbert Hayden," I said, unwrapping the journal and placing it on Wallace's desk.

"Ah," said Wallace. "I believe I've heard of that trial. Was Matthew Barnett one of the lawyers?"

Wallace's knobby hand crept toward Frances's journal.

"I don't think so. I looked that up, and his name is never mentioned in any of the articles about it."

"Hmm." Wallace's hand was on the journal now. "May I?"

"Sure. Flip past the recipes on the first few pages."

Wallace opened the journal in the middle and began to read.

"I . . . um . . . became a little concerned with this lady when I got to the end of the journal," I confessed. "It ends abruptly, and she's kind of preoccupied with arsenic."

"Arsenic?" Wallace's head snapped up and a flap of his gray hair fell into his face.

"The Mary Stannard murder trial had a lot of testimony about arsenic, and this Frances lady . . . she got pretty into it."

An ache crept up my chest as I spoke. Frances had written somewhat obsessively about arsenic and then stopped writing altogether. What had happened after that last entry?

"Oh." Tidying his hair, Wallace looked at me, then back at the journal, and then at me again. I could tell he sensed that I was unsettled, but he desperately wanted to binge-read the words of a nineteenth-century Havertonian.

"Do you have a bathroom?" I asked, hearing a slight whimper in my voice.

"Certainly. Through that room and then to the right."

The privacy of the spare little bathroom eased the urgency of my nausea somewhat. I stared at the white toilet and wondered how difficult it would be to puke over Lucy's head. The toilet seemed unusually low to the ground—perhaps to accommodate the small dimensions of this room? Or else the town custodian had an extra toilet lying around that had originally been intended for the elementary school and installed it here due to budget constraints. I imagined Wallace perched on it, his long legs folded up like a grasshopper's.

Stop that, I hissed to myself. I was a mother now and presumably should avoid immature thoughts of that nature. And yet I was here because of one big, fat immature thought, wasn't I?

Ghosts.

Lucy cooed, bringing my attention back to her. She seemed to be studying my expression in the bathroom mirror. I smiled.

"Hey there, cutie," I said.

I took a deep breath and headed back to the main room.

"This is extraordinary," Wallace declared as I approached his table. "What a find! You've read the whole thing, I assume."

"Yes. Unlike the Barnett fellow who gave it to me, I think."

"I'm so glad you brought this in," Wallace said, still hunched over the journal.

"Well . . . sure. But I'm wondering about this lady . . . this Frances Barnett. I don't quite know what to think of her. And the journal stops rather suddenly. You'll see."

Wallace kept reading.

"There are spots," I said slowly, "where she disturbs me."

Wallace looked up. "Disturbs you?"

"I mean . . ." I wondered if I was being too dramatic. "I just would like to know what happened to her. Because of some of the things she wrote."

Wallace leaned back in his chair for a moment and then said, "Frances Barnett."

He squinted at me and repeated the name under his breath before pushing back his chair and walking over to bookcases at the back of the room. He ran his hand along a series of black books with gold bindings, then pulled one out and muttered, "Hm, 1870 to 1875. No."

He replaced that book on the shelf and pulled out the next one.

Returning to the table, he said, "Why don't you sit down?"

"I'll try," I said, shifting Lucy's position on my chest. "She doesn't really like it when I sit."

Wallace nodded, then began flipping through the book. "You see, we're lucky here in Haverton to have this series of journals . . . well, not really *journals*. Logs of patients and ailments of a Dr. Graham, who treated most everyone in Haverton at that time. I've really only skimmed through it—it's quite long, and rather dry reading, as he was very meticulous and treated patients here for nearly thirty years."

Wallace continued flipping pages, muttering to himself. "Jonathan. Wheelock. Nathaniel. Barrows. Caldwell. Mary. No."

He looked back up at me. "There are names in those logs that don't come up anywhere else. So they're a great resource for helping us learn who actually lived in Haverton and what everyday life was like. Especially when cross-referenced with other resources. I haven't read every single page of his log, but I've read through quite a bit of it."

"I see," I said.

"There are of course a few surnames that come up over and over. Porter. Caldwell. Barnett. Dr. Graham treated many of these families' illnesses and naturally delivered a lot of babies. So that gives us a good idea of who was married to whom. There are the vital records as well, of course, but sometimes there are holes there. Now, leaving that aside for a moment, there are some notes in Dr. Graham's journal that can be cryptic. There is one particular thing that comes to mind now that you . . . Ah! There it is. Right here. Do you see that?"

I leaned forward to read the entry, gently holding Lucy's head at an angle that would not allow her to drool on the elegantly handwritten page.

22 December 1879. Frances Barnett. No improvement in condition. Dispatched to Northampton.

"Frances," I murmured.

"Yes. Frances Barnett. Dr. Graham's notes were, as I said, very dry. So there's not a great deal that's memorable. But *this* note was, the first time I read it."

"Why's that?" I asked.

Wallace sniffled and gripped his nose, closing his nostrils between his thumb and forefinger. He seemed to be deliberating what he was going to say next. "Well, you know there is no Northampton in Connecticut, don't you? But there is one in Massachusetts."

"Right. Where Smith College is."

"Yes . . . But of course, that is not where this patient would be going. There was, for well over a century, another institution in that community."

"Uh oh," I murmured, resenting Wallace slightly for keeping me in suspense.

"The state hospital. Now, they certainly had euphemisms in the nineteenth century, but not so much for mental illness. In Matthew and Frances Barnett's time, they called it the *Northampton Lunatic Hospital.*"

"Oh my God," I said. "Can I see that?"

"Certainly." He pushed the doctor's journal over to me, and I gazed down at the handwritten words. Dr. Graham liked to give his T's long, sweeping crosses, giving the words a grim sort of drama.

"Are his notes so minimalistic that he never says what was wrong with her?"

"As I recall, there was one other note that referred to this patient. I believe it was a few pages back."

Wallace slid the journal back and turned pages backwards.

"Okay. That's right. Frances Barnett. A few days earlier."

Wallace pointed to an entry that said:

18 December 1879. Frances Barnett. Hysterical symptoms. Possibly suicidal in nature.

"Oh," I said. My hand, which had been idly stroking Lucy's hair, froze. "Jesus."

"I recall that there is no other mention of her in the few months prior to this. I believe I checked when I first came across this."

Wallace tapped the bridge of his glasses, pushing it tighter against his nose. "Perhaps it was going on for some time before her family turned to a doctor for help. No group therapy or holistic healing in nineteenth-century Haverton, I'm afraid."

I smiled, trying not to look impatient. "I know, I know. But . . ."

"I noticed from the pages I just read that Mrs. Barnett had a baby. Let's see, now. A whole year before she was sent away. Seems rather late for postpartum to have been the main issue, no?"

I glanced down at Lucy's head. "Uh . . . I'm not sure."

"Unless there was another baby in between?"

I shook my head. "No. No second baby in the journal."

Wallace shrugged. "Because that was common, then. One after another. Anyway, postpartum or no, it was easier for a woman to find herself in a hospital like that than a man."

Wallace made an apologetic face, as if he were responsible for this injustice.

"Naturally," I nudged.

"A husband could put away a wife at his discretion. The populations of those hospitals were often more female than male."

"Right," I said. "Makes sense. But weren't there similar hospitals in Connecticut?"

"Yes, there were. Interesting that they chose to have her travel all that way. I wondered about that the first time I saw that note. But I've read a thing or two about the Northampton state hospital. It was considered state-of-the-art, at the time. They relied more on 'work therapy' than restraint or seclusion or some of the more barbaric methods of the time. Still not a place I'd have wanted to hang out, but . . ."

I nodded in spite of the sick feeling ballooning in my stomach again. Frances Flinch Barnett was sent to Northampton *five days* after she'd mused in her journal about the amount of arsenic necessary to kill someone "significantly smaller" than Mary Stannard.

Lucy whimpered and wriggled against my chest, throwing a fist against my chin.

"So perhaps the Northampton hospital was a place they felt she'd fare better, or have a better chance of recovery." Wallace shrugged, then took off his glasses. "Would you by any chance like a coffee? We have a machine in the other room."

"Better not," I said. This conversation was already making me pretty jittery. "I think I'm going to have to get going soon. My daughter needs a nap, I think. But thank you."

"Well, now." Wallace shifted his weight, pulled his foot up to his knee and gripped his sturdy brown shoe. "I suppose now you know a little something more about Frances Barnett than when you walked in. Maybe not the something you wished to find out."

"Yeah. Maybe not." I got up and bounced Lucy gently.

Wallace's eyebrows twitched hopefully. "I imagine you want to find out more?"

"If I can."

"Would you mind if I kept Mrs. Barnett's journal for a couple of days, until I can read it through?"

"Not at all," I said. It was a relief to think of Frances Flinch Barnett's words in someone else's hands for a little while.

"I'm not sure how much more we can find out," Wallace admitted. "But I can't tell you how eager I am to keep reading, and then maybe after that we could set up an appointment to share some ideas about that? We might see if her death certificate is on file here in Haverton. If she died here, then we'd at least know she got out of the asylum. If not, perhaps you could pursue the death records in Northampton, Massachusetts? I believe if she died at the hospital, the record would've been filed in that town."

Lucy, who'd apparently had enough, threw her head back and wailed.

"That would be nice," I said, bouncing away from Wallace. "Why don't you e-mail me when you're done reading? In the meantime I'll see if I can find her death record at the town vital records. . . . in the meantime, we're going to get out of your hair now."

"You weren't in my hair," Wallace said but nonetheless got up hastily and opened the maroon door for me.

Chapter 30

Northampton Lunatic Hospital
Northampton, Massachusetts
December 20, 1885

O f course, it was not *blood* that attracted me to the Mary Stannard affair—not at first. It was not the violence or even the scandal. It was the way all of the minute elements of it promised to affect the outcome. It was that lovely notion that if you broke the event and its objects into enough tiny parts, and examined them thoroughly enough, you could arrive at the truth. And it was, perhaps more than you realize, your involvement that attracted me to it. I missed you—and I missed our long conversations about your studies. Perhaps I was a bit jealous that you'd begun to share those details with Louise instead of with me.

Do you remember that I sent you a few letters? *Dear brother, come visit me! Little Martha's grown so much, you'll scarcely recognize her.* I was trying to appeal to your avuncular side.

Surely you remember that I finally had to make a trip to New Haven to see you—under the pretense of visiting Mother for a few nights. It took some planning, and some convincing Matthew. In the end, though, Dr. Stayer encouraged Matthew to have me take a holiday.

It was such a perfect autumn day that we strolled back and forth over the New Haven green, talking of the stomachs and the poison under the bright blue sky. You told me of Mary Stannard's brain and stomach and liver and womb—all in different jars and different labs at Yale. Despite the gravity of our chosen topic, I took such pleasure in our reconnection—and in the hours away from Martha, while Mother tended to her.

If Johnson is nervous, he doesn't show it. But when he steps up in that courtroom, it's not just the ears actually in the room that will hear his words. Reporters from all around are attending, ready to scribble down every word.

What do you think makes this trial so special, Harry? Is it the science? Or the brutality?

Probably both. Either way, I intend to be in the gallery when Dr. Johnson testifies. He's not the only Yale professor who will be on the stand. I plan to hear as much of the scientific testimony as I can.

I wish I could join you.

Perhaps, Frances . . .

What is it, Harry?

Perhaps you can.

I stopped walking to stare at you, and was warmed by a familiar twinkle in your eye.

You found Mother lonely on this visit, did you not? You think she will be needing another visit from her daughter and granddaughter quite soon. Kindly old Matthew couldn't possibly argue with that.

I laughed and felt some of the years of separation lift from us—your years of study, mine of wifely duties and new motherhood. You still knew my mind, after all.

Ah . . . we shall see. But would I be the only woman in attendance?

Surely you wouldn't. Many women seem quite compelled by this case.

Of course they are, Harry. I'm not sure how it is for a man. Maybe a man could not ever see himself in that girl's stead—while a woman would more easily do so, and be much troubled by it.

A man can be equally troubled by such evil, don't you think?

I suppose so.

Perhaps the science is easier to consider than the brutality.

How do you mean?

All you bespectacled men of Yale . . . separating the girl's parts into jars and obsessing over them. Does it perhaps allow you to forget the girl herself? The whole girl? Who had thoughts and emotions just like ours, right up until the final moment?

It does nothing of the kind. It only gives us power to give her— and her family—justice. We wouldn't care to do that if we cared nothing for her humanity.

I'm not certain of that.

Are you trying to argue that your gender makes your interest in the case more noble somehow?

Of course not. Oh, but the poor Stannard girl. Who was she, and how did she stumble into such great misfortune? What were her exact steps that day? How was it that she found herself alone with a murderer in the wood that afternoon, and was there any moment when she could have turned and found her way back unscathed? I would have recognized that moment, wouldn't I have, had it been me? Wouldn't we all like to convince ourselves of that? What made the girl so trusting, and so unlucky? Even if you all examined every cell in her body, you wouldn't have found answers to those questions.

You were silent then. Perhaps you thought my questions had

ceased to be interesting and had become too flighty. Perhaps I embarrassed you in some way. I didn't care. I kept talking because I had been so long starved for meaningful conversation.

Shame we do not have the opportunity to study the cells of the murderer. Wouldn't you like to have the chance to do that as well? Is there something inherent about him—about the specifics of his makeup or the sum of his parts—that makes him capable of such a thing? Or are both of these people—murderer and victim—fundamentally like us, but for a few missteps?

Do you remember how you replied, Harry? No?

Father used to say that you were more ambitious than me, Frances, you said. *I think, in a sense, that might be true.*

Chapter 31

Haverton, Connecticut
December 12, 2014

I wasn't ready to go home. Not alone. Or rather—alone with Lucy. I was too rattled by what I'd just learned about Frances. I wasn't sure what to make of her sad story, or its potential connection to my experience in the house. If Frances had died in an asylum, I'd think she'd want to haunt *that* building instead of mine. Wasn't that how these things were supposed to work?

I drove about a mile from the historical society and then turned into the Stop & Shop parking lot. Though I wanted to go in and buy a few things and clear my head, Lucy was already blissing out with her pacifier, eyes closed. It wouldn't be smart to bring her into the bright light and bustle of a grocery store.

Popping a lullaby CD out of the car's player, I turned the volume down low and hit *scan* on the radio. Maybe I could find some news, at least, and feel like a woman of the world for a moment. As the radio spat out blurbs from different stations—a car sale ad, a male country singer with an expertly macho whine, some Taylor Swift—I wondered who listened to the radio regularly anymore. My parents did until they retired to Santa Fe two years ago. Until then my mother had always listened to the same obnoxious morning show on her way to work. Did she miss those aging DJs now, I wondered, or had it always just been a way to survive the daily monotony?

My thought was interrupted by the loud gurgle and pop of a distant radio station. Before I had a chance to turn it down, the radio scan had moved on to its next station.

"Bring it to me . . . Bring it on home to me . . ."

I jumped.

Then the scanner moved on to another station, feeding me a line of German sung by a baritone on public radio.

"Wendy?" I whispered.

I reached out and started pressing buttons madly, trying to scan backward, which the radio wouldn't allow. What had the station been? Ninety-three point something? I moved up and down that range, trying to find the song again. After about a minute, I gave up.

It was that old Sam Cooke song. The one Wendy loved.

Wendy had introduced me to Sam Cooke. Not on purpose, exactly. She was always studying with her headphones on, listening to a little portable CD player. One time, while I was trying to write a paper, she was sprawled on her bed, writing a letter to her ex-boyfriend on seashell stationary, picking at her lilac afghan, and whispering to herself "Yeah . . . yeah . . . yeah." She must've had the song on repeat, because she kept "Yeah-ing" for about a half hour until I slammed my copy of Thomas Paine's *Rights of Man* down on my desk and shouted, "What are you *doing*, Wendy?"

Wordlessly, Wendy had taken her CD out of her player and put it in my stereo. She played the song for me so I could hear for myself Sam Cooke singing "Yeah" with a backup singer echoing "Yeah." Wendy hummed along until it was over and then said, "Isn't this an awesome song? I love it."

And I didn't think the song was half bad.

Wendy then told me a little bit about Sam Cooke—about all of his early success and his violent death. She played me "A Change Is Gonna Come" and I had to admit that one was pretty damn good, too.

"I listen to music from the sixties, mostly," Wendy had admitted. And then she looked at me as if expecting some sort of judgment. "And not the cool part of the sixties. I know it's really weird."

"Oh, I don't know," I'd said, returning to my work. "It's not that weird."

My response was kind on its surface. But I'd had a feeling, at the time, that Wendy wanted to be weirder than she was, and I had not particularly wanted to indulge her.

Now I glanced into the backseat mirror above Lucy's seat. The pacifier had fallen out of her mouth, and her head had fallen to the side. Unbuckling my seat belt, I leaned into the backseat and nudged her shoulder. She shifted and sighed. I returned to my seat and closed my eyes.

No, I hadn't ever been willing to indulge Wendy. Not in the least. Not even on the very last morning.

You'll actually feel better if you get up and get your ass to class. Or at least take a shower and have a little breakfast, and see how you feel.

I had barely looked at her as I slipped out of the room. She was facedown, surely pouting into her pillow, her half-grown bangs hanging over her wrist, which was mashed against her forehead. Her knee poking out from beneath the twisted sheets, her toe tangled in that light purple afghan.

UUUUUURRRH—eeep! Bang!

That was how I'd left her.

That afghan. Washed nearly to a dull gray, pilled and dirty at the corners and with such wide holes that often Wendy's bare foot would emerge from it while she was sleeping. Her mother had crocheted it when she was a baby, she'd told me once.

"No," I whispered and curled my fingers so tight that my nails dug hard into my palms. "Shut up."

Lucy sighed in her sleep and made a slurping noise—sucking on her now-imaginary pacifier.

We needed a destination—so she could sleep longer and so I could think about something else. I picked up my phone and tried Stephanie Barnett's number for the third time since our conversation had ended abruptly the other night. I got her voice mail again.

I typed in "GreatCuts" and found there was only one in this part of the state. It would be a twenty-minute trip. I didn't know what I'd do when I got there, but I didn't care. For the moment, anywhere was better than home.

Chapter 32

Northampton Lunatic Hospital
Northampton, Massachusetts
December 20, 1885

How grateful I was, after my trip to New Haven, that you promised to come see me more frequently. And to supply me with the newspapers to satisfy my curiosity about the complexities of the trial and your related experiments.

The more I learned about the topic, the more, at times, I had difficulty keeping my mind on my household tasks.

I'd gaze upon the jars in my kitchen and wonder which would be large enough for my stomach, and which for my brain.

I would see a rope in the shed and think of Reverend Hayden's probable fate. How does the world look to a person about to hang, I would wonder. Is it brighter or more beautiful in those last moments of regret? Or cold and frozen with the fear of anticipated pain? And why should I care how a killer felt in his last moments? Did I sympathize with men of such dark impulses?

I worried about this question as I lay sleepless in the dark.

In the light of day, I preferred to consider it thusly: that a world that could allow such evil and such suffering did not seem the right and true place for my Martha. But this new science had the potential to put me at ease. Science could prevail over evil. Martha would become a woman in a world with a different, more assured justice. Perhaps I believed all of the newspaper editorials that said this was a revolutionary case. Perhaps I thought this was the first courtroom case in which the truth would definitively and undeniably be revealed. That promise had such power.

I convinced myself—quite thoroughly—of the nobility of my motivations. And so I conspired, as you suggested, to return to New Haven as quickly as possible. I spoke to Matthew of Mother's loneliness and her physical complaints. Your letter—to the same effect—helped immensely. Oh, couldn't Matthew spare me and Martha for another visit soon? We all worried about Mother so. Matthew asked if Clara could not visit Mother instead—and wondered if having an infant around would increase Mother's burden rather than lessen it. I then begged Clara to accompany us to Mother's for a few days. She was perplexed by my urgency, but agreed. She was quite willing to be wherever Martha was.

And so I was stepping back into the world. I felt great exhilaration at the thought of being around so many people, in the heart of my home city, witnessing this great spectacle.

The first day I attended that trial was terribly exciting. I admit, I no longer remember the name of that talented young professor who kept an entire courtroom full of people enthralled for several days. I do remember, however, the excitement in the air—especially among your colleagues, with whom I had the privilege to sit.

I recall that the young professor crossed the Atlantic Ocean to complete his experiments. Imagine—crossing a whole ocean to gain insights into something so tiny. A whole ocean for a few granules under a microscope.

Which brings us to the arsenic. I told you I would get to it, didn't I?

Harry, I will tell you that at that time—the time you so kindly escorted me to that courtroom on that glorious fall day—I was happier than I had been in many months.

I was not happy to be away from my daughter so much as to have my mind engaged in a different way—a way familiar to me, from my days as a girl with Father, walking in the woods and observing ants and tree bark and fungi. The world was so large in its number of small things to be discovered.

That scientist had crossed an ocean to learn about a granule—an octahedron?—and had done so successfully. And I was among the first to hear of it.

Yes, a girl had been murdered, and yet—

And yet, here was the world wide open with the wonderment of learning new things. Large and small, and for the betterment of all.

The darkness that had plagued me as a young wife—and in the earliest days of motherhood—receded. Perhaps shamefully so, as my happiness developed in the shadows of a young girl's murder. Perhaps it was my penance that when the darkness returned, it was more sinister than it had been before.

Chapter 33

East Haven, Connecticut
December 12, 2014

S tephanie? She's just finishing up a cut right now," said the
girl with the two-toned hair—red in the front and blond
in the back. She threw the angular red bangs out of her
eyes. "But I'm free. Is the cut for you or the little one?"

I looked down at Lucy, whom I was carrying at my hip. "Uh.
Neither of us. I just wanted to talk to Stephanie for a minute."

"Okay . . ." the girl said reluctantly. "Stephanie!"

A raven-haired but familiarly pink-looking woman looked up
from the curly gray head she'd been pruning.

"Yeah?"

"This lady wants to see you when you're done."

Stephanie nodded, unsurprised. After she'd cashed out her
customer, she said, "I'm sorry, have we met before? You want to
make an appointment?"

I stuck my hand out. "We spoke on the phone. My name is
Abby Bernacki."

Stephanie hesitated, then shook my hand. "I've been kind of
swamped. Or I'd have called you back."

"Can you talk for a minute?" I asked.

"Is it too cold outside for the kid?" Stephanie glanced at her coworker.

"Not at all."

Stephanie called to the motley-headed girl that she was taking a smoke break. We walked a few paces away from the GreatCuts storefront until Stephanie stopped in front the drugstore next door.

"I'm sorry to surprise you at work," I said as Stephanie lit a cigarette.

Stephanie was expressionless as she smoked. She was at least fifteen years older than me but had a youthful style that made me feel like a slob. Jeans and a nursing camisole—covered with an old-man cardigan—had become my autumn uniform. Stephanie was wearing tailored black trousers and a drapey beige blouse with a subtle braid of ribbons across the top of the chest. Her hair was inky-black, so stark against her pale pink skin that it had to be dyed. It was arranged in a wispy pixie cut that brought out her dark gray eyes and, less flatteringly, her bulbous pink nose.

After a few silent moments, Stephanie stepped away from me and waved her arms around.

"Geez. What am I thinking? Secondhand smoke."

"Oh," I said. I hadn't even thought of that. While I didn't want carcinogens blowing in Lucy's face, I didn't think it appropriate to tell Stephanie not to smoke—given how polite she was being about me stalking her.

"Okay, so you live in Eddie and Shirley's old house." Stephanie lowered her cigarette and flicked it. "That's where we left it on the phone, huh? And what was it you wanted to know?"

Since we probably didn't have a lot of time, I decided not to worry too much about looking like a weirdo.

"Your brother said you mentioned you had some kind of a creepy experience in the house," I reminded her.

"Yeah." Stephanie took a quick puff off her cigarette and then took another step away from Lucy and me. "But . . . It was a long time ago."

"Can you tell me about it?" I asked.

Stephanie puckered her lips and swished them from one side to the other.

"Listen. It was so long ago, my memory is fuzzy and I'm not even sure it really happened anymore. My brother shouldn't have mentioned it to you, and I don't want to make you feel bad about your new house."

"You won't."

"I don't know . . ." Stephanie started to bring her cigarette to her mouth but glanced at Lucy and flicked it instead.

"I'm a history teacher," I said.

"So?" Stephanie curled her lip at me skeptically. "What the hell does that have to do with it?"

Lucy perked up at Stephanie's change of expression and grinned.

"I know, right?" Stephanie said to her.

"What room did you stay in, when you stayed with your aunt and uncle?" I asked.

"The little one upstairs." Stephanie glanced into the window of the drugstore, tidying her bangs. "The one that looks out to the street."

I nodded. "Yeah . . . I thought so."

Stephanie continued to stare at her reflection.

"All right, then," she said softly. "Who's gonna go first, hon?"

My throat felt tight, but I tried to speak.

"There's . . ."

"What?" Stephanie turned to face me, her eyes either eager or impatient. I couldn't tell which. Either way, I could feel my heart pounding.

"There's a voice that goes *Shhhhh*," I whispered.

Stephanie's cigarette fell out of her hand. Then she stepped on it—maybe to make it look like it wasn't an accident. All of the pink drained out of her face. She was silent for a couple of minutes.

"What's *your* story?" I asked softly.

"I was a teenager." Stephanie finally allowed her gaze to meet mine. "I had a lot of issues. And I liked to dramatize things, I'm afraid."

"But . . . the room—"

"I had something like that happen in that room, too. Yes. Once or twice. A feeling like someone was in there with me."

"Did they . . . it . . . say anything?"

Stephanie looked toward the GreatCuts entrance. "No."

"No . . . *shhhhh*?"

"Well . . . maybe once. But something so subtle, it's hard to know if it's your imagination. And when I was that age . . ." Stephanie trailed off and shook her head.

My hands prickled. "And did weird stuff happen with the doors?"

"The doors?" Stephanie repeated.

"Like, they made funny noises, and you couldn't open them very easily?"

"No. Nothing like that."

"Okay. But you felt a presence in the room."

"That's what I remember, yes."

"What do you think it was?"

Stephanie glanced at her flattened cigarette on the pavement. "You really want to know?"

"Yes."

Stephanie sighed and shrugged. "All right, then. I think it's the crazy lady who used to live there."

"Crazy lady." My forearms went cold and then prickled with goose bumps. "Umm . . . Someone you knew?"

"No." Stephanie shook her head. "A hundred years ago. Well—let's see—way more than a hundred years ago now. I forget how very old I am sometimes."

"What do you know about this crazy lady?" I demanded. "Do you know what her name was?"

"No. This is the family lore, anyway. There was this pretty well-known Barnett guy who was a lawyer."

"Matthew Barnett," I offered.

"Yeah." Stephanie whipped her head up. "That's right. You've been doing research?"

"A little. Your brother mentioned it."

"I'm surprised he even knew that, or remembered it."

I was debating whether to mention the law books or Frances's journal—but Stephanie continued.

"Yeah, so he was a lawyer. Some up-and-coming lawyer when he was young. On his way to being famous. A real great career ahead of him, trying criminal cases. Real big, famous cases he was involved with. But unfortunately he had a very sick young wife. A real nut job, apparently. She did something so terrible, so unspeakable, that she had to be thrown into jail herself. It broke his heart so bad that he wasn't ever able to practice criminal law again. He couldn't stomach it. He became an estates lawyer, or something like that. Lived the rest of his days as a bachelor."

Lucy was starting to make hungry noises. I stuck my thumb in her mouth.

"But . . . What did she do?" I asked.

"I don't know. Uncle Eddie always said that his father—my grandfather—said it was 'unspeakable.' I guess he meant it because Eddie always claimed he really, truly never found out."

I considered this answer for a moment. "Did your uncle tell you this story before or after you had the weird experience in that room?"

Stephanie gazed at Lucy, then shook her head. "I actually never told my uncle that I thought I felt a ghost in that room. But I think it was before."

"Your brother didn't tell me any of this," I said.

Stephanie shrugged. "I wouldn't be surprised if my brother never knew it. My brother was never all that close to Uncle Eddie and Aunt Shirley. Not like I was. Not when we were younger anyway. And he's not—how shall I put this?—he's not, um, intellectually curious. That's what my dad used to say about him. He's not into . . . talking. Talking about the past. Talking about much besides the last Red Sox game and how rare he wants his meat cooked."

"Mmmm," Lucy said, as if commiserating.

Stephanie looked startled and studied Lucy for a moment. "Didn't you tell me the baby stays in that room? The little one right at the top of the stairs?"

"Yeah."

Stephanie took out another cigarette and lit it. "How'd she get that bruise?"

I studied Lucy's bruise for perhaps the hundredth time. Its yellow part seemed to be growing more prominent, its spiral growing more defined within the circle of purple-brown.

"I wish I knew exactly," I said.

I looked up at Stephanie, feeling my chin wobble. I could almost hear myself saying it to her. *She got it on the first night I heard the shushing.*

"I'm thinking I don't want her sleeping in that room anymore," I confessed.

Stephanie took a long drag on her cigarette. "Oh, Christ."

"Christ . . . what?"

Stephanie shook her head. "What did you say your name was?"

"Abby."

"Abby. You're not a Barnett. So I wouldn't worry about the house. I think it's all about us dysfunctional Barnetts. I did pot and LSD—and even worse, a few times—when I was kid, staying with my aunt and uncle. Did my brother tell you that?"

I sucked in a breath and tried to formulate an answer quickly—but wasn't quick enough.

"I see," Stephanie said sharply. "So you ought to have the sense to forget this whole thing and enjoy your sweet little house."

Lucy hiccupped in agreement, then squirmed in my arms. Stephanie drew on her cigarette one more time, then dropped it and mashed it with the pointy black toe of her boot.

"I believe you about what you felt in the house," I hurried to say. "That's why I came here to talk to you about it."

"Not sure why you'd believe me if I'm not sure *I* do," Stephanie said, turning toward the GreatCuts door. "I'm sorry. But I have to get back to work."

If Lucy had not been growing restless, I'd have gone after Stephanie. But I had already begun to doubt the wisdom of interrupting her work. Before she reached for the door to go back inside, I saw her pause, take a deep breath, and twist her nervous hands together. All the way home, I worried that the next person who popped into GreatCuts for a quick trim was likely to lose an earlobe. And it would probably be my fault.

Chapter 34

Northampton Lunatic Hospital
Northampton, Massachusetts
December 20, 1885

And that, my dear Harry, brings me to the arsenic.

Yes. I purchased arsenic. It wasn't long after I returned from hearing that young professor's testimony. About the octahedrons!

I confess: I wished to see them myself.

Martha was with me when I bought my ounce of arsenic at Fuller's General Store—along with ten buttons and a pound of butter.

Ma'am, it's customary for me to inquire why you are making this purchase, said the gentleman behind the apothecary counter.

I recall keeping my eyes down while I explained.

My kitchen is overrun with mice, sir. And I don't like having cats about. I think they're bad luck to me.

Safer than this, though, ma'am. Is your baby crawling yet?

Not yet. I wouldn't buy it if she was, sir.

Very well. One ounce?

Yes, sir.

He packaged it twice and labeled it with big, commanding letters: *POISON*.

I tucked the package into my coat and felt the terrible power of it all the way home. That evening, I put it in my oak box with the lock, and then inside my hope chest, beneath my wedding dress. So you see, it was safely stowed where it could not harm anyone. And I would like to tell you what else was in that oak box. There was a small square of white silk, a dead fly, a stick of pussy willow, and a collection of dried citrus rinds. Each was wrapped in its own paper package. I believe you, of all people, Harry, can guess what each of these items had in common? Each was something I wished to see up close, when I had the opportunity. I wasn't sure when that opportunity would arrive, but I was hopeful that it would. You had long since given away that old primitive microscope of our childhood. Nonetheless, life is long, and I had a brother in the biology department at Yale. Surely I'd have a chance to look more closely at these things—and others—sometime. That was the purpose of my queer little collection. I understood its oddity, and that is why I kept it a secret.

Chapter 35

Haverton, Connecticut
December 12, 2014

It was dark when I pulled into the driveway. Chad approached the car as I turned off the engine.

"Where were you guys?" he asked, opening my door. "I was worried."

"I just needed to get out for a while," I said. "Since you said you wouldn't be home in time for supper, we ended up eating at the food court at the mall and just people watching."

Chad peered into the backseat, where Lucy was dozing. "She ate food court food?"

"Uhh . . . no." This question gave me pause, wondering if Chad was picturing me placating our tiny daughter with a Cinnabon. "She had breast milk and organic squash and pear baby food."

"Did you know it's almost eight?" Chad whispered.

"Oh!" I feigned surprise.

"It's okay," Chad said, unhooking Lucy's carrier from the car-seat base. "I have a surprise for you and Lucy."

Chad led me to the living room, where a plump Christmas tree was set up in the corner. Our boxes of ornaments were shoved underneath. Chad set down Lucy's car seat by the couch.

"Oh." I took off my jacket. "How sweet."

"I put on the lights but wasn't going to plug them in till you got here. Figured we'd do the ornaments together."

"Tonight?" I asked.

"Why not? And I got pfeffernuesse."

"But you can't eat that."

"Who cares?" Chad replied, and plugged in the Christmas lights. "I get to say pfeffernuesse."

I glanced at Lucy, still asleep in her carrier.

"Are we doing this now?"

"Why not? Lucy seems pretty comfortable there. We can put her in the crib when we're done."

Chad put on some Haydn string quartets because he knows I don't like Christmas music. I started to pull the boxes of decorations into the middle of the carpet.

"Sit with me for a minute before we start," Chad said. "I need to tell you something."

I nodded and took one of the boxes with me, opening it as I sat down next to Chad.

"Phil needs me to go to Chicago with him again for a few days."

"Oh," I said, unsurprised. I lifted up one of the ornaments from the box—a tiny knitted Santa hat with a jingle bell at its tip.

"It'll just be next week. I'll be home before Christmas. The twenty-first or twenty-second. But that's why I got this tree on the way home. I thought it might be nice to do this early, so we wouldn't be rushing and you and Lucy could at least enjoy a little Christmas spirit while I'm gone."

He was talking fast. Maybe he thought I was going to chew

him out—even though we both knew this was beyond his control. This was his second business trip since Lucy's birth.

"It's okay," I said, but I felt my chin wobbling.

I knew now that I would not—for some time, or possibly forever—be telling him all that I had learned about the house today. I had showed him Frances's journal the day I'd gotten it from Gerard, but I had not told him about some of the more worrying later entries as I'd read them. And now definitely wasn't the right time.

"We could ask your mother to come out and help," he said.

Monty hopped up onto the couch and crept into Chad's lap.

I closed my eyes for a moment. "My parents already have their tickets for Christmas. They're coming on the twenty-third and leaving on the twenty-seventh. It would be stupid to have her do an additional trip."

"It probably wouldn't cost her that much to change her ticket."

Chad was now giving Monty such a deep, luxurious head scratching that Monty's head was tipped back blissfully, his eyes closed. Monty never came to me for petting anymore. He'd decided he hated me the day we came home with Lucy.

"I don't want to ask her to do that. Don't worry about it. I'll be fine."

"Or my mother could come for part of it."

I did my best not to give Chad a skeptical look. Chad's mom clearly thought breastfeeding was a weird hippie practice—and also seemed disappointed that I didn't bathe Lucy nightly. I loved Chad's mom on holidays and after two glasses of wine—anything beyond that was pushing it, and Chad knew it.

"I'll be okay. Really," I said.

Chad's suggestion annoyed me, setting off a familiar sensation that I'd been fighting for five months.

It started the morning after Lucy was born. After everything was cleaned up and sewn up and we'd had a few hours of rest, Chad had gone down to the cafeteria for a cup of coffee and to make a few more phone calls. While he was gone, Lucy stirred in her little plastic bed, so I hobbled over to her to pick her up. Her eyes fluttered open and stunned me.

I had the overwhelming sensation that I *recognized* her. Ignoring the searing pain in the lower half of my body, I picked her up and held her close to me. Her eyelids drooped again, and I stood there for several moments willing them to open again, swaying blissfully in anticipation.

Chad opened the door to the room, paper coffee cup in hand.

I got you a bagel 'cuz I bet the hospital breakfast sucks, he was saying.

When I looked up, Chad seemed unfamiliar to me—his eyes as unrecognizable as Lucy's were the opposite. He could be any man in the world with his casual coffee and his talk of things sucking or not sucking.

Go away, whispered a voice deep in my head.

The birth was still vivid in my head—the suffocating breathlessness of it, the graphically Sisyphean moments at the very end, and Chad's slack-mouthed horror in the corner of my eye.

GO AWAY.

The sentiment had revisited me several times in subsequent months, with fluctuating intensity and varying degrees of accompanying guilt.

Now the thought was confusing me, battling with an entirely different one:

Please don't leave me alone in this house.

"Abby?" Chad was saying now. "Are you crying?"

"No." I sniffled and blinked and met his gaze. "I'm just a little tired."

No, I wasn't going to worry him. The last thing we needed was for his insides to flare up again—to render him skinny and sad and unable to work. I was playing homemaker for just one year—as he was the sole breadwinner for just one year. Surely I could deal, on my own, with all of the home's little problems— the spoiled leftovers and unexpected guests.

"And hungry," I added, hanging a tiny Santa hat over his ear and attempting a playful smile. "Feed me a pfeffernuss, darling."

Chapter 36

Northampton Lunatic Hospital
Northampton, Massachusetts
December 20, 1885

For a time, I forgot about my secret in the hope chest.

As the last delightful days of autumn left us, and November settled in, my girlish secrets faded into insignificance, and a heaviness came upon me. It was a familiar feeling—and one I did not wish to recognize. There was a nagging pull at my core, and distracting thoughts of blood.

With Matthew I tried to stay in exuberant spirits—to disguise my troubled state.

One time, I could not restrain myself. Over a roast chicken—a chicken I'd plucked myself, as Tessa had been engaged with the laundry—I began talking about Dr. Treadwell's corpuscles.

Matthew smiled gently at my use of such a technical word.

I do wish I could see one myself, under a microscope.

Oh, my dear Frances. Why would you wish to see such a thing?

To see up close this substance on which so much of life depends? Why would one not wish to see it?

I suppose . . . And yet I suppose I can appreciate something without the need to see it myself.

And yet you had the opportunity to see it yourself. So you have the luxury of speaking of it so casually. Did they not bring slides of the corpuscles into the courtroom for the McFarlene trial?

Yes. Indeed. We used those resources as part of our evidence.

I wonder why John McFarlene did not create a better story to explain why there had been human blood on that wood and his shirt. Didn't he say it was probably from his wife slaughtering a chicken near the woodpile? Might he have at least said he accidentally cut himself?

There was too much blood for that to be a believable claim. Not without a significant wound to his person. Besides, he did not know that a scientist could tell the difference between chicken blood and human blood. He probably did not even know what a microscope was. Until it was too late to change his story.

Dr. Tipley's results were revealed rather late in the investigation, as I recall. Because Frederick Baines did not find that first blood-stained log till rather the last minute. Now, what has become of Frederick these days, Matthew? Does he no longer sell pumpkins? I haven't seen him in an age.

Perhaps he did not grow any this year. But yes. By the time Tipley gave his scientific testimony, McFarlene had already told the story of the chicken many times over.

The corpuscles told the true story.

Yes, darling. The corpuscles.

It often surprises me how unskilled people can be at hiding evil intentions.

It surprises you? Why?

Perhaps I've always paired deviance with cleverness?

That is folly, Frances.

I suppose you are right.

I suppose I am.

Chapter 37

Haverton, Connecticut
December 14, 2014

L ucy was crying—though not desperately, nor particularly loudly. She had a casual cry sometimes. More of
a whine building on a sob, slow to cross over—though
it always did, eventually. I slid reluctantly out of bed and lum-
bered down the hall.

I'd neglected to fully close the blinds the previous night,
so she was awake with the morning light—sitting up in her
crib, which I didn't realize she could do on her own. It was
exhilarating—and admittedly, a bit unsettling—to see her that
way, puffed up with such confidence in her own agency.

She was smiling a big, well-rested-baby smile. It wasn't until
I was right next to her crib that I wondered, *Wasn't she just
crying a moment ago?*

And then I heard her cry again. Again that whining half-cry.
But it wasn't coming from her mouth. It wasn't even coming
from this room.

The baby in the crib was still smiling, her mouth unmoving.
The baby in the crib, in fact, was not Lucy at all.

The next cry was more urgent. But where was it coming
from? Not this beaming bald baby. The cry was, in fact, coming

from somewhere in the walls. The storage space where Flora-belle lived, perhaps? Or somewhere else? With each cry, the location of its source seemed to switch.

Where *was* Lucy?

"Lucy!"

I woke up to an accelerated heartbeat and the sound of Lucy still crying. Chad was lying on his back, hands folded across his stomach.

"You really don't hear that, Sleeping Beauty?" I demanded.

"Monty?" he mumbled, moving a slow hand up and down his chest. "You're mad at me, Monty?"

"Jesus," I hissed, slid out of bed, and stumbled to Lucy's room.

Lucy was lying on her back as I'd left her. The sun was coming up. I picked her up and settled into the rocking chair. She closed her eyes almost immediately. I breathed in her sweet warmth, which made the dream feel hazy and distant. We dozed together until Chad's alarm went off down the hall.

Chapter 38

Northampton Lunatic Hospital
Northampton, Massachusetts
December 20, 1885

I could not cease thinking about Mary Stannard's face, detached from her head and floating in a jar at Yale. I began to wonder what it would have been like if they'd brought it into court as the defense had requested. Her face would have been nothing more than a putrid flap by then—draped over a skull.

And I considered my own mask—equally removable, and equally grotesque. Did I not deserve to have mine torn off as well? Did I not deserve it more—much more—than that poor innocent?

You see, I was becoming more certain that I was not what I appeared to be. Even the pages of my journal revealed a false character—a fantasy.

I don't care much for sewing, for one. And truly, I've never gotten excitable, in my heart, for a plum pudding or a spice cake—except when I was a child and did not have to cook it myself.

There were days when I cursed both duties. And now, in one

way I have gotten my wish. In another, I've gotten the absolute opposite.

For now I sew all day, on most days.

While I rarely work in the hospital kitchen, I *do* sew all winter long. I am allowed the privilege of helping in the greenhouse from time to time, but the majority of my days are spent in the Sewing Room. Mr. Pliny Earl, the director of the hospital, sets quotas for us, with incentives. More meat and fruit for those who meet the expectations, and less desirable accommodations for those who refuse to produce.

Mostly I've sewn shirts, but I've sewn two straitjackets as well. I wonder if there is some calculation to the assignment of sewing a straitjacket. Is one given the job because of one's precision with the needle, or as a perceived need for a reminder of where, exactly, one resides?

Have I worn one? Yes, Harry. But only in the earliest of my days here. When I'd throw myself about and scream my Martha's name. On the last and longest night so restrained, I felt an itching up my chest and was convinced a spider had crawled inside the terrible garment. I was so hoarse then that my claims of the spider went unheard. My screams became whimpers, and then nothing at all. As dawn came, I thought of my two lovely birds. They'd helped numb me of Martha's memory once—and so they did it again. And thereafter, the nurses found they did not need to restrain me any longer. Archibald and Mercy keep me quiet and still enough that my body can be put to work, and my mind, at night, to sleep.

Chapter 39

Haverton, Connecticut
December 15, 2014

To: *Abby Olson Bernacki*
From: *Wallace Bradley*
Subject: *Frances Barnett*

Hello Abby,

I hope this finds you and Lucy and the rest of your family well.

I have finished reading Frances Barnett's diary, and I would like to discuss it with you. Let me know if there would be a convenient time and place for you to meet—I realize that the HHS house is not the most accommodating place for you and Lucy.

Many thanks.

Kind regards,
Wallace Bradley

Wallace agreed to come to my house during Lucy's morning nap. We left the time open, and when Lucy was finally down, I called Wallace at the historical society, and he drove over.

As we settled at the kitchen table, I propped the video monitor on a nearby windowsill so I could spy on Lucy as she slept. Wallace watched me as I adjusted the monitor's volume and brightness but didn't comment.

"Since finishing reading," he said, "I've been doing a bit of research on Frances Barnett and some of the people she mentions in the journal. I gather from your response to my e-mail that you've been doing the same."

I nodded. "I looked up all three Barnetts—Matthew, Frances, and Martha—on a Connecticut vital records database. I could only find Matthew. He died here in Haverton in 1912. Of course, the basic death record doesn't say if he died at home or not."

Wallace glanced around my kitchen for a moment, taking in the hastily wiped countertops, the neon plastic baby bowls, and perhaps the slight whiff of diaper coming from the garbage can.

"Does that matter?" he said in a stage whisper.

"It's just one of those things that would be nice to know," I said. "Anyway, I couldn't find Frances on either the Connecticut one or the Massachusetts one. I tried Frances Flinch and Frances Barnett. There was a Frances Barnett who died in 1864 in Framingham, but of course that's not her."

Wallace nodded. "Those databases are, of course, missing information from the nineteenth century. You can often get lucky and find something you're looking for, but you can't count on someone being there."

"I called the vital records office here in Haverton, too. They couldn't locate a Frances Flinch Barnett or any variation on that name. Martha, either. There is a record of her birth, but not her death."

"There's a reason you didn't find Martha," Wallace said. "I

figured out that she went by the last name Barnett for only one year of her life."

"What? How?"

"I also tried vital records," Wallace explained. "I couldn't find a marriage or a death record for her at first. But then I recalled something—again, Dr. Graham's notes. There is a little girl named Martha Wooley whom Graham visited in 1885. She had the measles. As did her mother, Clara. Clara had a really terrible case, apparently. Clara Flinch Wooley. Kind of cozy name, huh? Wooley."

"Clara, Frances's sister, then?"

"Yes. I believe so. It appears that Clara and her husband, Jonathan, raised Martha as their own after Frances was sent to Northampton. Makes sense, doesn't it? Frances's journal—if it is to be believed—indicates that Clara often cared for Martha even in her infancy. Perhaps Matthew Barnett—perhaps everyone involved—felt that it would be most kind to the child to be raised by her aunt rather than some hired nanny. I mean, I can only speculate as to the reason."

"Did they both make it through?" I felt my chest tightening. "The measles, I mean?"

"Yes. They did."

I let out a sigh of relief.

"I'm sorry," I said, after a moment. "I just realized I didn't even offer you anything to drink. Tea, maybe?"

"I'll have a tea if you're having one. But don't make it just for me, please. I'm sure you spend a fair amount of time catering to someone else's needs. I don't want to . . ."

Wallace stopped speaking as I filled a teakettle with water and plopped a basket of assorted teabags in front of him.

Catering. I hadn't thought of it that way before. I was a *caterer* this year. That was so much more respectable than a *cow.*

Wallace selected a plain English tea, and I pulled out chai spice.

"Do you wish to hear more about Martha?"

"There's more?"

"Yes. I went back to the vital records and found a marriage certificate for Martha Wooley of Haverton who married an Alexander Soloway in 1903. I didn't find her death certificate. But I've had some luck, quite often, sniffing out people in the old census records that are available through the state library system. I found a Martha Soloway showing up several times living with Alexander Soloway in Cheshire, with seven children. She showed up there consistently until 1940. The census records aren't accessible after that. But still. If someone who was born in 1879 made it at least until 1940, I'd say she did pretty well. If we're talking about quantity and not quality, of course. There's that."

"You did a lot of work," I said. "Thank you."

"It only took a few minutes, actually. I access those sorts of records all the time when people want a little help with genealogy projects and the like."

"It's a relief," I admitted. "After the tone of Frances's last few journal entries . . . I was worried about Martha."

"I sensed you were, yes. Now you know that she was probably okay. I gathered from the journal—as I'm sure you did—that her aunt Clara doted on her."

"Yes . . ." I said.

The teakettle's metal bottom began to squeak softly as it

heated, as if voicing the unease that was settling back upon me as quickly as it had lifted.

"But then . . . Martha never lived in this house again, after that," I pointed out. "Probably. So while it's a relief to know she survived her mother's difficulties and lived a long life . . . it doesn't really answer any of my concerns about Frances."

The crag near Wallace's nose deepened. "Your concerns?"

"She was crazy, right? So . . . knowing what happened to Martha doesn't help me to know what Frances did. What Frances did in *my house*."

I watched Wallace carefully as he reacted to this. He didn't seem to know what to do with his face. He grimaced and bit his lip.

"Well, it was Frances's house first, let's remember," he said.

The teakettle was rumbling to life. I picked it up rather than waiting for it to whistle, and poured.

"Exactly," I said. "That's exactly it. I'm starting to wonder . . . maybe it still *is* her house, in a sense."

I sat across from Wallace, sliding his tea to him. He fiddled with his teabag tag, then dipped the bag up and down.

"Still *is* her house?" Wallace repeated.

"Like she's still here. Or like there's something of hers that was left."

I heard my own voice go low as I said these words.

"Something?" Wallace said, smiling uncertainly, as if trying to detect if I was joking.

As I stared at the steam rising from my tea, my neighbor Patty's words came back to me: *She was crying, "Please don't take me away! Who is going to take care of the baby?"*

Wallace stared at me, lifting his mug to his lips. He took a swallow, then gasped at its heat and put the cup down.

"GAH!" he said, and flicked his tongue, apparently trying to cool it off.

"Would you like some water?"

"Please."

I handed him a glass from the tap, and after he'd taken a long sip, he said, "I'm sorry. Of course I should've let it cool off. Your expression . . . distracted me."

"I'm sorry," I said softly.

I seized the video monitor and turned up the volume.

"Are you all right?" Wallace asked.

"Yeah. I just thought I heard her waking."

"That really is a nifty thing. I wish they'd had them when my sons were growing up."

"Sons? How many?" I asked.

"Three. Trouble is . . . when do you shut it off?"

"What do you mean?"

"I mean exactly that. *When* do you shut that thing off? When they're three? Four? I wonder if I'd still be watching my sons while they sleep, if I could." Wallace paused and massaged his chin between his thumb and forefinger. "I mean, if the technology had been available to me."

"Well, I think I'll turn it off when she's not as likely to hurt herself. Like, when she's old enough not to strangle herself in a tangled blanket."

"Not as likely to hurt herself," Wallace repeated, shrugged slightly, and took a sip of tea. "You realize, of course, that they never become any less likely to hurt themselves? It's just the conceivable manner in which they'll do it that changes."

"Of course." I sighed. I wondered why older parents so often felt the need to piss on the parade—to remind you of how mouthy or pimply or drug addled your baby might soon be. "I just meant hurt herself in her sleep. When they're a little older, they at least learn to pull things off their faces. Untangle themselves from blankets. That sort of—"

I stopped talking. *Untangle themselves from blankets.* The lilac afghan. With holes so big her elbows and feet sometimes poked right through.

"Abby?" Wallace prompted.

"Look," I said. "Can I find Frances Flinch Barnett on the census records, you think?"

Wallace shook his head. "I tried already. Frances Barnett and Frances Flinch, but I didn't find anything relevant. The national census records for 1890 were destroyed in a fire in 1921. So that certainly doesn't help—as that would be the decade I'd think she'd be most likely to show up if she ever got out of the asylum. I fear she may have died in Northampton. A next step would be to check Northampton's death records—which might require a trip up there. But I suspect that deaths in that institution might not have been meticulously documented. Just a hunch."

Wallace blew on his tea, puckering his lips delicately. For such a dapper older gentleman, he seemed to have a slightly exhibitionist way with his mouth.

"Now . . . can we get back to your previous comment? About what Frances may have left in the house? Now, did you mean that literally? Figuratively?" Wallace hesitated. "Supernaturally?"

I looked up, startled. Wallace was watching me with eyebrows raised and a sheepish little smile—as if he half expected me to slap him. He also looked slightly weary. It took me a moment to identify what made me think so. The skin beneath his eyes formed two thin little pouches. Was he tired today? Or just old? I couldn't remember if they'd been so prominent on the day I'd met him.

Just old, I decided. He had three grown children. He'd heard it all before. Surely he'd met crazier people than me. For all I knew, he was one.

"The last one," I admitted and then sat back in my chair and finally took a sip of my own tea.

"Okay," Wallace said and nodded just slightly. "Do you wish to say more about that?"

"I'm not sure," I answered, glancing at the monitor again.

"All right," Wallace said. "Fair enough. Thank you for answering the initial question, though."

"Suffice it to say, I'm concerned specifically about what happened to precipitate Frances's being dragged off to an insane asylum. Because whatever that was—and I'm assuming it had to be pretty bad—probably happened *here*."

Wallace stretched and massaged the back of his neck. "Dr. Graham's note said she was suicidal."

"Yes. But he doesn't say what she actually *did*. And she didn't write about suicide."

"But she wrote about arsenic. That's close, in a way, isn't it?"

"Not for someone who actually seemed pretty interested in forensics. Not for someone who didn't sound suicidal in her diary even a few days earlier."

"Didn't she?"

Wallace picked up the caramel-colored briefcase at his feet and pulled out Frances's journal and a stack of photocopies.

"I copied the pages so I could give the original back to you. And so we could both use copies if we want to reread, and prevent wear and tear on the original," Wallace flipped through his pages and read, " 'Perhaps repetition is good for the soundness of the mind. Corn corn corn berry berry corn corn corn. As long as one doesn't allow too many stray thoughts to interrupt the pattern.' "

"That sounds suicidal to you?"

"Well . . . no. But it sounds like someone who might be struggling to keep herself in a certain frame of mind . . . or out of a certain frame of mind. Don't you think?"

I shrugged. "Certainly possible. I guess we're not ever going to know what actually happened. Like, if there was an actual suicide attempt or not. Or if it was just a theory on the part of her husband and doctor."

"Does it matter terribly if there was an actual attempt? We know what the outcome was. Attempt or no, she was sent to the hospital in Northampton. And likely never came back to Haverton."

"It might just be useful to know how . . ." I hesitated. "Well, how dark things got."

"Useful?" Wallace repeated. "Are you sure of that?"

"She wants to know how much arsenic it would take to kill someone smaller than Mary Stannard," I reminded Wallace.

"And she was apparently a very small woman," Wallace said. "She mentions in the diary not being able to reach things in the kitchen."

"So I wonder if she actually tried to ingest some arsenic."

"Often people who attempted to take arsenic vomited it all up if they took too much."

"But would that happen to someone so concerned about taking the *minimal* amount to be noticed?" I asked. "The right amount to kill you efficiently?"

"I'm sure it could. It might have more to do with the relative strength of your stomach than how much, exactly, you chose to take. Or, just—luck."

"So maybe she tried to take some and threw up."

"Maybe . . . or maybe there was some other attempt altogether . . . or maybe she just mentioned to a friend or relative what she was considering . . . or something like that. I would think if there was a real attempt and therefore a real medical emergency, Dr. Graham would've written about it. But how much do you really want to know about this? There is potentially a lot to be learned about Frances and her family, but this very incident? I'm afraid you might not have much luck. Putting a family member in a hospital like that was generally a hush-hush affair. Maybe that was even why they went to great lengths to take her all the way up to Northampton. Far away, out of sight, out of mind. It's quite possible the details of that story were between Frances and her husband and the doctor and never went any further."

"Oh, it went further," I said. "In a general way."

Wallace took a noisy sip of tea. "What does that mean?"

I started to tell Wallace about Stephanie Barnett, leaving out the issue of the ghostly presence and just telling him about the unspeakable thing that Matthew Barnett's wife had apparently done, breaking his heart and rendering him unable to practice criminal law.

"Which leads me to believe that she maybe did something

criminal," I said. "Rather than something suicidal. Something really, really horrifying."

Wallace was quiet for a moment, absently running his forefinger along his lower lip.

"*And* it makes me wonder who this 'significantly smaller' person is she's writing about in that last entry," I said.

"It makes *me* wonder if that family is full of shit," Wallace said.

"*What?*" I sputtered, startled to hear Wallace use that particular turn of phrase.

"I know that can't be true, what this Stephanie person told you. I know that I've seen Matthew Barnett's name in accounts of other criminal cases after 1879. At least one or two. Although it's true that he didn't really live up to the potential he showed in those early cases like the McFarlene case."

"Maybe it took a few years for his heart to break?" I said.

"Maybe the family needed to blame his ultimately lackluster career on someone, and the poor crazy wife in the asylum was an easy target. Perhaps she was a little off, or maybe even a little suicidal. And over the years, that became the 'unspeakable' of the Barnett family legend. You know, off the top of my head, I can think of at least one later case Matthew Barnett was involved in that contradicts this dramatically vague family story. I'm going to dig it up for you."

"Oh . . . you know . . . you've already done so much work on this for me . . . you don't need to do that."

"Nonsense," said Wallace. "And I hope you realize that I'm not being entirely unselfish, researching the various names and stories that come up in Frances's writings. It has already helped to fill one or two holes in that era of Haverton's history. Most notable for me is the mention of Matthew and Clara's hired girl, Tessa Ripley. I didn't know she once worked for Matthew Barnett. She later married Edward Cowan. Now, I had to check that, because I wasn't sure if it was indeed the same Tessa. Edward Cowan was one of the luckiest guys in Haverton history, in my opinion. The Barnett family—specifically Daniel Barnett, Matthew's father—or Old Man Barnett, as he came to be known—sold Edward a small plot of land on Maple Avenue—with a little house on it—for next to nothing in 1885 or so. Edward Cowan ran a fairly successful tavern there for several years. It made him enough money to start a more respectable business in town later—a general store he ran with Tessa—that ended up doing quite well and then extended down the block as an added clothing store. *And* he ended up somehow investing in a textile mill in the eastern part of the state, and did quite well from there. And from that point on, they were fairly influential in town, both economically and politically."

I stared at Lucy in the monitor screen. Did I see her arm twitch? Or did I just *want* to see her arm twitch so I'd have an excuse to stop Wallace's verbal overflow of names and dates?

"Anyway . . . *anyway*. Excuse my going on and on. It's just that—that initial transaction between Daniel Barnett and Edward Cowan—it's always been a mystery to me. Tessa's working for Matthew Barnett doesn't explain it completely, but it's an interesting tidbit. She went from being his maid to rising up the town's ranks to being his near equal socially and economically. I'm sorry to drone on. It's just one of several things I found interesting about Frances's account. A minor thing to you, perhaps."

"Oh, I don't know," I murmured.

"A couple of Edward Cowan's descendants still live here. Do you know of Ralph Greer, in town?"

"No," I admitted.

"Of course. What am I thinking? You probably haven't lived here long enough yet. Ralph grew up here. He's a bit younger than me. His mother was a Cowan. Ralph was a day trader for a while, and then after all of that worldly New York stuff he retired back here. No place like home, I guess. For all his money, he goes to the town library and reads their copy of the *Wall Street Journal.* Then he spends the rest of the morning at the Dunkin' Donuts, gossiping with the other townies. Anyway. Why am I telling you this? Because he and I get along quite well. He has all of the old family papers and pictures that his grandfather kept, and he's let me peruse them on several occasions, for this historical display or that."

No, Lucy wasn't awakening after all. I put down the monitor. "Uh huh?"

"I was thinking yesterday that he'd be *very* interested to know about this Tessa connection," Wallace said. "He always jokes about that original land deal. That maybe Edward Cowan had something on Old Man Barnett. Caught him smooching on one of his sheep or something . . ." Wallace shook his head and cleared his throat. "Ralph can be a bit crass sometimes, but in any case . . . Well. Maybe, with Tessa working for Matthew and—who knows, possibly other Barnetts—maybe old Daniel Barnett had a soft spot for her. Wanted to give her and her husband a good, prosperous start in their new married life together."

"That sounds a little . . . romantic."

"Yes. Old Ralph will surely prefer his bestiality jokes, but nonetheless . . ."

"Umm . . ." I looked into my teacup, hoping a segue was about to present itself.

"But I'd like for Ralph to be able to see a copy of the journal. Would you mind terribly much if I showed it to him?"

"Not at all."

"Maybe you'd like to come along? We'd probably meet at the library. Sometime in the next few days, if he answers his phone. Would you be comfortable bringing Lucy into the library?"

"Sure," I said.

"Good. Ralph's quite knowledgeable about some aspects of Haverton history himself, and he might have some insights about Frances or some of the other Barnetts."

"Hey—Wallace? While we're all sharing Frances's journal, I was wondering if I could see that doctor's log myself? I'd like to look through it in more detail."

I had been thinking about the doctor's records since Wallace had shown them to me at the historical society. I couldn't quite believe there were *no* other hints of Frances's mental condition beyond the two terse entries Wallace had shown me. I wanted to believe there was some insight that Wallace had missed. He had never said he'd gone over it thoroughly—through the years preceding the hospitalization—with that question in mind. Nor did I consider it appropriate to ask him to do something so time consuming for me.

Wallace paused, then drained the last of his tea. "It's in several volumes."

"I know. But I wonder if I could start just by borrowing the one you showed me that mentions Frances going to Northampton. It's difficult for me to get out to the historical society—comfortably, I mean—for any good chunk of reading time."

"I'm sure we can make some arrangement." Wallace set down his mug. "I'll bring the relevant volumes when we meet with Ralph."

"Thank you."

"Well." Wallace clapped his palms and rubbed them together for a moment. "I imagine you don't get a lot of time for yourself, so I'm going to leave you to it. Give Lucy my best, will you?"

I nodded, stifling a giggle as Wallace got up. I imagined myself propping a drooling, hand-sucking Lucy on my knee and informing her, *Wallace sends his best.*

"Of course," I said.

Chapter 40

Northampton Lunatic Hospital
Northampton, Massachusetts
December 20, 1885

For a time, I did try to take your advice, Harry. I *did* try to put the murder and the trial out of my mind. I did a thorough cleaning of the house—of the sort one usually does only in spring—baked sweet breads and pies and knitted Martha three winter hats. And yet, the harder I worked, the thicker and more grotesque I felt my mask became.

Corpuscles. Corpuscles! I'd say to myself often as I toiled in the kitchen or at the needle. I tried not to do it in front of Matthew, but sometimes the word seemed to simply spit itself out of my mouth without my permission.

Corpuscles!

Pardon me, Frances?

Oh, fussy! Martha was so fussy today.

Perhaps I preferred the word to *blood*. *Blood* was a frightening word. *Corpuscle* felt relatively innocuous, perhaps, in its scientific way.

I was trying not to think of blood.

And yet I was. Increasingly, and always.

Blood in the kitchen. Blood in my best cake pan.

Was it easier to think of *corpuscles* in my best cake pan?

These were not the kinds of questions I could share with Matthew. With you. With Louise. With anyone.

Chapter 41

How much would be enough for someone significantly smaller than Mary Stannard? A mere dusting? Perhaps an amount so small the doctors and scientists would not be able to find it?

I gazed at the journal copy Wallace had made me, whispering the words "significantly smaller" and "mere dusting" to myself a few times. They seemed the most important words in that entry. They had an oddity to them that unsettled me. The more I repeated the words, the slower I pronounced them, as if their true meaning would leak out between their syllables.

Lucy was asleep—looking eerily white in the night-cam mode of the baby monitor, sprawled out on her back, both fists raised above her head.

I took out the original journal, flipped to that final page, and stared at it. I put it close to my face, then held it at arm's length. As I repositioned my fingers to hold it at a normal range, I felt something slightly rough between that final entry and the previous page. In a move that probably would've given Wallace a coronary, I bent both sides of the page backward to examine closely in between the pages.

There was paper in between the pages—a jagged but extremely thin flap of paper, about half an inch long. It was only discernible if you bent the pages wide open. It looked as if someone had torn a page out—or maybe several pages—and missed one tiny spot where they'd cleared off the remains of the paper.

"Were you hiding something, Frances?" I whispered. I flipped the book over, pages hanging downward, and shook it. "Something suicidal, or something else?"

As I said it, I glanced again at Lucy's monitor. In that very moment, Lucy's eyes popped open, pupils glowing white on my screen.

I screamed. Tossing the monitor onto the floor, I hopped off the bed and ran down the hall. I found her door shut. I knew I hadn't shut it completely. I'd *always* left the door open a crack—but especially lately.

I stood there for a moment, unsure if I really wished to open it. Half-terrified that I'd find a demonic white-pupiled baby behind it. Half-terrified of something else altogether.

Had I heard the door slamming shut? Had I heard it, somewhere beyond my own voice, in the moment I screamed? I reached for the doorknob but dropped it quickly. I reached for it again.

OOOOOAAHHHHR-eeeee.

Lucy was awake, but she wasn't crying. She was kicking her legs and making conversational noises at her mobile.

I stepped into the room and closed the door, then opened it again.

OOOOOAAHHHHR-eeeee.

And again.

Since Lucy seemed content enough, I crept downstairs to the front hall, where we kept the toolbox.

I heard the front door just as I was removing the third hinge pin. I was surprised at how quickly I'd managed to finish the job.

When Chad appeared at the bottom of the stairs, I called down to him softly. "Hey—why don't you come up and help me with this?"

Chad pulled off his shoes and padded up the stairs. "What are we doing?"

"Moving the door. We'll store it along the side wall of the bedroom for now."

"Why?" he whispered. "Isn't this going to wake up Lucy?"

I shook my head. "She watched me for a little while as I took off the hinge caps, but she fell back to sleep."

"But why are we doing this?"

"The door needs new hinges. They make too much noise. They wake her up."

"But tonight?"

"That way I don't have to deal with the door at all while you're gone."

Chad held one side of the door, following me into the bedroom with it.

Once we'd positioned it against the wall, Chad said, "I was chatting with Ben Trask this morning. His daughter is definitely looking for babysitting jobs. Maybe you want to have her come over while I'm away. Give yourself a little break? You wouldn't have to leave the house if that would worry you too much. Just give yourself a little time to read or watch a movie or something."

"You have her number?"

"Yeah."

"Okay. Leave it with me, and I'll call if I get desperate."

"Well, you shouldn't have to wait until you're *desperate*."

"When's your flight, anyway?"

"Quarter after six," Chad said, yanking his carry-on out from under the bed. "And I still need to pack."

Please don't leave me alone in this house.

"Don't forget your medication," I said.

Chapter 42

Northampton Lunatic Hospital
Northampton, Massachusetts
December 20, 1885

Accompanying my grim thoughts was a familiar physical sensation—but not comfortingly familiar. It should have been recognizable to me immediately, but it was not. I denied its familiarity for days—perhaps even weeks. It was a hunger combined, frustratingly, with nausea. An unease at being on one's feet, followed by an unease with sitting. For a time, I thought my body was simply attempting to chase away my mind's troubling thoughts.

One cold night—after Thanksgiving but before Christmas—when Matthew was sleeping, I lay awake and faced the hard truth. My body was not fighting with my mind. My body was doing something familiar and functional. Without my mind's permission. Without any regard for whether my mind could endure it. My body was a cruel and demanding master.

I could not sleep. I tried not to weep but could not stop myself. I did so as quietly as I could—swallowing my sobs and soaking my pillow. The only thing that comforted me, finally, was my resolve to go see Louise on the following day. Whatever the weather, I'd go see her. I might not confess every detail of my predicament. I'd decide how much to say when I arrived. Regardless, I'd draw comfort from seeing her. The anticipation of that comfort—however small, however brief—helped me endure my worries until dawn.

Chapter 43

Haverton, Connecticut
December 16, 2014

I was nursing Lucy when my e-mail dinged.

From: Wallace Bradley
Subject: Clocks, Coins, Broken Hearts

Hi Abby,

Can you meet with me and Ralph Greer at the public library tomorrow at 11 A.M.? It might be possible to adjust the time if it doesn't work for you. We will meet by the periodicals.

As promised, here is some information about a criminal case Matthew Barnett tried in 1885. The Connecticut library system gives access to some, though not all, historical CT newspapers from the late 18th century to the present. I've included a link to a relevant article from a short-lived New Haven weekly.

It was a simple case of theft at first, but a little bit of sex

*and scandal apparently caught the attention of some of
the newspapers near the end of the trial.*

*I couldn't find any more mentions of Matthew Barnett
trying criminal cases after this one, so maybe there is a
grain of truth to Stephanie Barnett's family story.*

Kind regards,
Wallace

I switched Lucy to my other side and read the link.

STUNNING FINAL EVIDENCE IN HAVERTON'S "CLOCK AND COIN" THEFT CASE

ANDREW PARSONS ACQUITTED

Oct. 29, 1885—A promising case for the prosecution
turned sour yesterday in the trial of Andrew Parsons, accused of stealing the savings of a Haverton widow.

A box of legal tender amounting to $1,300, a collection
of silver coins, as well as a century-old clock of significant
value, were taken from the home of Anna Darlington on
the evening of September fourth, while Mrs. Darlington
was visiting a friend for supper. These items were the life
savings of the elderly widow. Her neighbor, Andrew Parsons, whom Anna occasionally employed for home repair
projects, was said to be one of the few people—aside from
Anna's three children—who knew of the savings kept in a
locked dresser drawer in the widow's bedroom.

Last week, prosecutor Matthew Barnett presented the jury with a letter penned by Parsons, and sent to an acquaintance, Robert Maddox, also of Haverton, to whom Parsons owed a debt. The letter claimed that he had recently "come into money" and suggested arranging a clandestine meeting for payment to occur. Maddox turned the letter over to the constable soon after Parsons had come under suspicion. The letter provided the prosecution with some tangible evidence in a difficult case—for the stolen items have never been found.

Two surprise witnesses for the defense testified on the final day of proceedings. The first was an alibi for Parsons—not on the evening of the theft, but on the day of the postmark of the letter. Gregory Hadley of Hamden, who occasionally employed Parsons, testified that Parsons was with him for nearly the entire first week of September, picking peaches in his orchard. Parsons, he said, lodged in his barn. He testified that he did not believe Parsons could have posted the damning letter.

The second witness was Charles Whitehead, who admitted to having unlawful relations with Parsons's wife, Roberta. A collective gasp echoed through the courtroom as Whitehead confessed that Roberta had often expressed her wish to "be done with" her husband and marry anew.

In his final argument, defense lawyer William Boyd posited that Roberta had likely forged the letter in hopes of framing her husband for the theft.

The jury apparently found that to be a plausible possibility. They deliberated for two hours before issuing a verdict of not guilty.

I clicked *reply* on Wallace's e-mail, positioning my arms over Lucy as she continued to nuzzle and gurgle against my chest.

Hi Wallace,

> *Eleven works fine for me. Looking forward to it.*
> *Thanks for the article. Interesting. Maybe the wires got crossed, and this was the thing that "broke Matthew's heart"? A woman betraying her own husband, and making Matthew look like a fool in the process?*

I stopped typing for a moment, trying to decide whether or not to write to him about my suspicion that pages had been pulled out of Frances's diary. Although I wanted to contribute something more to our conversation, that piece seemed best saved for when I could show him the book again in person.

> *By the way, I meant to show you this* New York Times *editorial when you came to my house. (Link below.) I've struggled to understand why Frances Barnett was so obsessed with the Herbert Hayden case, but seeing it in this context helps. Still doesn't answer any questions about her final days in Haverton, but maybe before that she was just following the zeitgeist?*

"SCIENCE IN COURT"

October 26, 1879

The trial of Rev. Mr. Hayden, at New Haven, on a charge of murder, is likely to be placed in the category of celebrated cases, chiefly on account of the original investigation into the peculiarities of arsenic of which it has been made the occasion. It is probable that, at the close of the expert testimony of Prof. Dana, the jury will be better informed in regard to that particular poison than most professional chemists were before. The witness did not rely on his previous knowledge of the subject or the information to be found in the books, but was sent to England at the expense of the prosecution, for the purpose of visiting the principal establishments for the manufacture of the drug and making fresh inquiries. The result will be an actual addition to our knowledge, having a real scientific value . . .

I skimmed the rest of the article for the second time. The writer summed up Dana's testimony—the very same "octahedron" testimony that had Frances Flinch Barnett so up in her diary, and then summed by marveling again at the potential for criminal cases to "extend the borders of scientific knowledge."

My phone rang just as I hit *send*.

It was my neighbor, Patty.

"Abby? I thought you might want to know there's someone

parked in front of your house. Person's been sitting in their car there for a half hour. Can't tell if it's a man or a woman."

Setting Lucy on the carpet, I peeked through the blinds to see an old dark blue sedan. In the driver's seat was a person whose face was not visible—but whose short black hairdo was familiar. "Oh, I know who that is. Thank you."

"Why're they just sitting out there, though?" Patty demanded.

"Umm. I think she doesn't want to wake the baby. Thank you, Patty."

I zipped Lucy into her full-body pink fleece with lamb ears, pulled her onto my hip, and walked outside. Stephanie saw me coming and lowered her window. Her hair was less tidy today—more troll doll than pixie—and she wasn't wearing any makeup.

"I was about to call you," she said. "Thought that might be better than knocking on your door. But I was having a cigarette first. Sorry."

"Did you want to come in?" I asked.

"No," she said quickly. "I just decided I should tell you something."

"Here? I can't really . . . um . . ." I pointed to my daughter's head, hoping she'd understand. "I guess I could go in and get my coat."

"Just sit in the car with me, how about?" Stephanie said. "I'll put the heat on."

I hesitated.

"Come on," said Stephanie. "I just want to talk to you for minute, but I don't want to bother you and I don't want to invade your house."

"You wouldn't be invading—"

"Look. I'm just going to say a couple of things and be on my way, okay? I'm not crazy. I've just got places to be."

I opened the car door and lowered myself in. I figured that Patty was watching with her big all-seeing Liza Minnelli eyes and would take quick action if she saw anything untoward happening.

"Good," Stephanie said as I slammed the door shut. And then she turned the key and turned the heat on, as she'd promised. "I think I want you to know the whole story. It would be one thing if I came after you to tell it. But you came after *me*. So that's different. Isn't it?"

Her breath was yeasty and sour—beer breath, maybe.

"Uh . . . I guess so."

"I went back and forth on this," Stephanie said. She pulled the Christmas tree–shaped air freshener from her rearview mirror, sniffed it, and then tossed it into the cluttered backseat. "No smell left."

"Back and forth on what?" I asked, trying my best to settle Lucy in my lap.

"Whether I should tell you. But as I said. You came to me. You *want* to know. And it's your house. So you have a right. Or at least, *I* have an obligation. Or maybe I don't. But I feel I should, so here I am."

"Okay," I said as patiently as I could. I tried bouncing Lucy on my knee, but it was difficult in such a tight space.

"You want to know exactly what happened to me in that house, then?"

"Yes," I said. "I do."

Stephanie nodded, rubbing the lap of her jeans with her knuckles.

"Okay, then. So, I stayed in that room when I was sixteen. Right up there." Stephanie pointed up to the single window of Lucy's small room. "You want to know why I came here to stay with Shirley and Eddie?"

"Because . . . you weren't getting along with your parents? Is that correct?"

"Correct. But that's only part of it. I had to get away from their house because I couldn't face them. I couldn't look at them. Only Shirley knew the real reason. Not even Eddie. She was going to tell Eddie, eventually. I was pregnant."

I stopped bouncing Lucy. "Oh."

Stephanie seemed to be studying me, waiting for more of a reaction. "I'm not the sort of person who goes around telling strangers this sort of thing. But you asked, remember?"

"Of course," I said.

Stephanie sighed. "Shirley said I should keep the kid. That I could live with her and Eddie and they would help me. I remember saying, 'Aunt Shirley, I don't think Uncle Eddie is going to go for all of this.' And she said, 'Oh, he will. He loves children. Just give me time to talk to him. You'll see.' Thinking back, it was probably a fantasy. Would he have gone for it? I don't know. She just wanted a child around so, so bad. She didn't care where it came from. Some women are like that, right? Poor lady. She could never have any of her own. Not much you could do in those days."

"Uh huh," I murmured.

"So that was the dream scenario. Us all raising that baby here in this house. Middle-aged Shirley and Eddie and fucked-up teenaged me. We'd tell my parents when we got Eddie to agree to it. Shirley kept saying she was waiting for the right night to ask him. And then one night, after they had gone to bed . . . I was lying in my own bed up in that room. I was trying to listen for their voices down the hall, praying that Shirley was finally talking to Eddie, and he was saying yes. And I think I was still praying like that as I was falling asleep, thinking *Please please please*. I knew the plan was a little crazy, but I was young enough to hope anyway."

I stared up at the house as Stephanie spoke. I imagined the cheerful green door opening, and Gerard Barnett emerging, walking a brittle old woman down the stone steps. *Please don't take me away. Who is going to take care of the baby?*

"Here was someone wanting to *help* me," Stephanie continued, "which was better than I'd have gotten from my parents, who already hated me for picking bad boyfriends and smoking too much weed. After a while I felt someone was hearing my *please please please*. And then after a few minutes, they were answering it. They were patting me on the back and saying, *Shhhhh. Shhhhh. Shhhhh.* I was so sleepy I thought it was Shirley, and she'd come to tell me that she'd talked to Eddie, and everything was going to be all right. But I sort of woke up and saw no one was there. And when I fell asleep again, I heard it again. *Shhhhh.* It put me to sleep."

Stephanie's gaze was fixed on her steering wheel. My heart was pounding.

"And when I woke up, I was bleeding."

"Oh." I was stunned for a moment. I watched Lucy notice the change in my face. "Oh, I'm sorry."

"Poor Shirley." Stephanie glanced at the front door of the house, then at me. "She was so sad when I told her."

I nodded. Shirley's final words about the house—*Who is going to take care of the baby?*—were perhaps understandable now in light of this story. An old lady lost in a wish that had almost come true.

Lucy looked from me to Stephanie and released a high-pitched but happy scream.

"Sorry," I said. "She's, uh, exploring the range of her voice, I guess."

"She's fine," Stephanie said, smiling weakly. "So, I went back to my parents. And they never knew. It was the lesser of two evils. My parents' house."

"Two evils?" I repeated, feeling my stomach turn as sour as Stephanie's breath. Her story perhaps explained her late aunt's words upon moving from her house. But it presented a much more troubling question in their place.

"Maybe that's putting it a little harshly. In the end, probably the thing I really couldn't handle was Shirley's sadness. Whatever else was in the house." Lucy squealed again, and Stephanie shrugged. "You can see why I never told my brother the full story. Even my parents didn't know."

"You don't really think that the house had something to do with . . . what happened?"

Stephanie folded her arms. "Look. This is what I know. I know that someone was there with me that night. And I know what happened by the next morning. And I knew that the less I was in the house, the less I had to think about it. And I never would have told anyone about it, except there you suddenly were with your little baby and your questions, so . . . I don't usually tell things like this to strangers. I want you to know that."

"Are you sure you don't want to come in for some tea or something? I really need to—"

"I'm sorry." Stephanie shook her head and stared out the window. Patty was now outside in her yard, calling her cat. "I just don't want to go in that house."

"Okay," I said. "Okay. I just—I need to tell you something, too. Your brother gave me a journal. Of someone who lived in the house in 1879. He thought it was a cookbook, but after the first few pages, it's like a diary. And it was written by someone who eventually went to a mental hospital."

"Are you serious? My brother *found* it?"

"That's what he told me. In a trunk full of old law books."

"So, Matthew Barnett's things. So, the crazy lady that Uncle Eddie would talk about."

"Yeah. Gerard gave it to me for thirty bucks."

Stephanie rolled her eyes. "Thirty bucks? My brother's a moron."

"Do you want it back?" I asked "I'd be happy to give it back. I felt weird taking it. He said you wouldn't want it, but I couldn't be sure unless I asked you myself."

Stephanie was quiet for a moment. "Do I *want* to read it? Will it make me feel better about what happened up there that night?"

Lucy squealed, this time with greater urgency.

"No," I admitted. "Probably the opposite."

"Then I'm going to say no, for now. Maybe I'll feel different after I drive away. I have your number."

I nodded.

"I have to meet someone soon," Stephanie said. "Thanks for being willing to talk outside."

Stephanie pulled away as soon as Lucy and I got out.

After Stephanie left, I plopped Lucy in her bouncer for a little while and went digging in the upstairs storage space. Chad had stored our Pack 'n Play crib up there before Lucy was born. Someone had given it to us as a hand-me-down, but since we hadn't yet traveled with Lucy, we hadn't had much use for it. Now I went poking around behind the wall, hunched over with a flashlight.

When I was a few feet in, I bumped into Florabelle. Off-white, split down her middle and across her waist, she guarded the oldest of our old boxes. A headless but formidable schoolmarm. Her posture indicated that she knew exactly what was in those boxes and quietly disapproved.

I flashed the light behind her, scanning over the piles of cardboard boxes. I'd remembered seeing Chad lug the broken-down Pack 'n Play into the space in its gray nylon storage bag. Then I looked along the opposite wall. The bag was propped there on top of a row of plastic tubs.

As I yanked it out of the storage space's miniature doorway, I heard Lucy start to fuss. Right on time. The sun was going down.

Luckily the Pack 'n Play was a quick assembly job. I set it up a few feet from our bed. I didn't know what to make of what had happened to Stephanie in Lucy's bedroom. But I was pretty sure I wanted Lucy to sleep with me tonight.

Chapter 44

Northampton Lunatic Hospital
Northampton, Massachusetts
December 20, 1885

I bundled Martha up right after breakfast and set out for
Louise's. I didn't have to find a way around Louise's aunt
Dorothy this time, as she was napping.

Louise seemed delighted to see Martha and gave her a little
tin with an acorn in it.

"Julia's littlest enjoys this so much," Louise explained. *"The
sound it makes when she shakes it."*

*I was grateful she'd brought up Julia. I'd thought I might ask
about her, and now Louise made it easy.*

*As the eldest of Louise's sisters, Julia was always fascinating to
us, as she'd married when we were young girls. And now she had
six children. The first to do everything. Even before our Clara.*

"She's very well," said Louise. *"She's very proud of her Charlie.
He's so clever, they've skipped him ahead in school."*

*I did my best to ignore the ache that intensified in my stomach
as I formed my next sentence.*

"I was wondering about that time when she got sick. When we

were girls, about sixteen, I believe? Do you remember telling me about that? After Susan was born?"

Louise frowned. "It was after Sarah was born."

"Oh. Of course."

I should have remembered. It was between the two S babies— that time in Julia's life when Louise and I had discussed her so intimately, so frequently. That was the longest time between Julia's frequent babies. Two years. Sarah was born so quickly after Daniel that Julia's health had seemed to suffer terribly. She spent three months in bed, and Louise and her sisters had spent a great deal of time at her home, helping her. She did not become pregnant again—with Susan—until nearly a year after that. That long respite between babies probably saved her life.

"That was ages ago. Sarah is in school now. Did you know that?"

"Yes, I . . . well, I imagine."

"She recovered quite well, didn't she?"

Louise bounced Martha on her knee.

"Do you like your little tin, my dear?" she asked, tapping the tin and then gripping Martha's hand to help her shake it. "Do you like the tin your Louise gave you?"

"Now, who was that kind doctor who treated her then?" I asked. Martha shook the tin on her own.

"Oh, yes. Martha loves her little tin," Louise continued.

"It wasn't Dr. Graham, was it?"

Louise gazed up at me and murmured, "No, Frances."

"What was his name?"

Louise stood up with Martha and carried her to the window. "Funny to think of it, but you probably don't remember snow, do you, Martha? When we have our first snow of the season, it will *seem like magic to you. That something so soft and white could suddenly fall from the heavens."*

"Louise?" I struggled to say, hearing my voice break despite my effort to keep it from doing so.

"Price," she said, without turning from the window.

"What?" I whispered.

"His name was Price. Dr. Thomas Price. I believe he was in New Haven. East Rock."

"Price," I repeated.

"It was a long time ago, remember."

Louise's voice hardened as she said this—making it clear that she did not wish to say anything more about it.

She took Martha's hand in her own.

"I wish I could be there when it happens, Martha," she said, "to see the delighted look on your dear little face."

I almost argued with her. I almost told her that my sharp little Martha, born in January, surely remembered snow.

My mind was too busy, though—determined to hold on to that word.

Price.

Price.

Price.

Chapter 45

Haverton, Connecticut
December 17, 2014

Ralph Greer folded his *Wall Street Journal* as Wallace and I approached him. He was bald and so extraordinarily obese that it felt like Wallace maybe should have mentioned it to me beforehand. He was wearing a colorful sweater vest and a brown-bag-colored blazer, boxy in the shoulders.

"Wallace!" he roared, apparently oblivious to the bearded reference librarian giving him the sink eye. "Right on time, as usual."

Wallace moved two chairs from the computer area so we could sit across from Ralph, who sat on a long wooden bench that stood alongside the picture window near the periodicals—likely because he was too large for the reference room chairs.

"Ralph, this is Abby," Wallace said, offering me a chair.

"You're the one who found the diary Wallace has been bubbling about?" Ralph asked. "Or—maybe not *bubbling*. Wallace doesn't bubble, of course. But occasionally you'll catch him simmering."

I sat down, positioning Lucy to face Ralph. "Shirley Barnett's nephew found the journal and gave it to me. I live in Shirley's old house."

222 • Emily Arsenault

"Oh. I don't remember all of the parties involved, I guess." Ralph put his hand out for me to shake. "Welcome to Haverton."

"I've lived here about three years," I said.

"And she's becoming rather a Haverton history enthusiast," Wallace added. "Abby teaches history."

"Three years," said Ralph. "That's not very long in Haverton years. It's like dog years in reverse. Where did you move from, hon?"

"Boston area. I was a teacher there but switched schools when my husband got a job in New Haven."

"Aha."

Lucy smiled conspiratorially at Ralph. Despite his size, Ralph had a sort of shapeless baby face. And a bald head.

"And you've got a cutie there."

"Thank you."

"Now Wallace here tells me he's got all of the secrets to my past."

Wallace sighed. "I didn't say that, Ralph."

"The journal," Ralph said. "It mentions my great-grandmother, he says."

"Tessa Cowan." Wallace turned to me. "The maid."

"Tessa Ripley at that time," Ralph added.

Wallace handed Ralph his photocopy of the journal—now dog-eared and marked with several hot-pink Post-its.

"I identified the spots where she's mentioned."

"Thanks, Wallace. Always so organized." Ralph opened the journal for a moment, then looked up. "Hey. While I'm reading, you take a look at *this*."

He reached into his sport coat and took out a folded-up piece of paper, handing it to Wallace.

"Ralph," Wallace said. "You've shown this to me at least a dozen times."

"I know that, Wallace, sir. But let *her* see it. What was your name again, hon? Sarah? Penny? Millicent?"

"Abby," Wallace said, handing me the paper. "It's only a copy. Ralph believes this is the secret to his great-grandfather's fortune."

"He kept it in a safe with his valuables," Ralph said. "That's what my father and grandmother always told me. So it stands to reason. Don't you think?"

Lucy continued to stare at Ralph while I read his little piece of paper.

> *Dear Edward,*
>
> *Regrets and guilt too much to bear. Righteousness is elusive. He was right and I shall follow him for my transgressions. It is all true what I confessed to you. For a pittance, I sold my soul and another's.*
>
> *F*

"Who wrote this?" I asked, eyeing the signed *F*. The handwriting was scrawling and clumsy—nothing like Frances's elegant script.

"We don't know," Wallace intoned.

Ralph grunted and stroked his head without looking up from the journal pages.

"But Ralph is certain that it's the key to the whole land deal question," Wallace explained.

"I've even compared it to most of the letters and things my great-grandfather and great-grandmother kept from those days," Ralph said. "To see if I could find a handwriting match. But they didn't keep *that* many things, so there's not much of a pool."

We both watched Ralph read for a few moments. Lucy lost interest in Ralph, grabbed my hair, and tried to suck on the corner of my cardigan.

"I've got to admit it, Wallace," Ralph said, looking up. "It's news to me. I didn't know my great-grandmother worked for Old Man Barnett when she was a young girl."

"Not Old Man Barnett. His son. Matthew Barnett. The lawyer."

"Oh, right. You said that on the phone."

"So that might explain why Old Man Barnett wanted to be generous."

"It might." Ralph flipped to the next marked page and continued to read. "I'm still holding out for a filthy scandal, Wallace. But in any case. *Very* cool to see my great-grandmother mentioned here. I've got a lot of pictures and letters and things from after her marriage, after she and Edward came into more money. It's interesting to get a glimpse of what life was like for her before that."

"Now, while we're talking about this, I thought it might be useful to our friend Abby here if you could answer a question for us."

"Yeah?" Ralph looked up.

"In all of your knowledge of Haverton history, have you ever heard a story about a Barnett woman—the wife of Matthew Barnett, specifically—doing something so, so terrible and unspeakable that she had to be thrown into a state hospital for it? Does that ring a bell?"

"No, it doesn't. Where do you come up with these grotesque ideas?"

"Shirley Barnett's niece recently told Abby such a story."

Ralph raised his eyebrows, the skin on his head wrinkling into a corrugated appearance. "Is that right?"

"Yes," I said.

"But what exactly was the unspeakable thing?" Ralph asked.

Wallace smiled thinly. "You see, we don't know."

"She didn't know," I offered. "Says her uncle Eddie—Eddie Barnett—didn't know, either."

"Let me guess," Ralph said. "Her uncle Eddie would tell her this story every Halloween, and the specifics became more unspeakable with each passing year."

"You know, Abby," Wallace interrupted. "I liked the theory you suggested in your e-mail yesterday. That it was in fact that silly clock-theft case that in fact drove Matthew Barnett away from criminal law. He was probably embarrassed that he was duped by the accused man's wife. It might've damaged his reputation pretty badly, and that's why he started practicing another type of law. His name only comes up in estate cases after that one. But it might have been easier for the family to blame the previous drama with Frances."

"Frances?" Ralph repeated, raising a eyebrow at Matthew.

"The woman who wrote this journal. Matthew's wife. The handwriting's not at all a match with your little mystery note, you'll notice—if that's what you're getting at."

"Oh." Ralph nodded. "Okay. But I'm not really following you about Matthew Barnett."

"It relates to an article I sent Abby yesterday. It's a long story. I'll send it to you as well."

"I'd like that. But in the meantime, I suppose you've solved the mystery of the land deal. It's a little disappointing, I must admit. I'd always thought there was a little more scandal at its heart."

"Scandal is overrated," Wallace said, holding his hand out for the journal copy.

"And where does this leave me with this thing?" Ralph asked, waving the *Dear Edward* note.

"Nowhere, my friend. Put the original back in your safety-deposit box and show it to me again next year."

At that, Lucy burped and Ralph laughed, returning the note to his blazer pocket.

TING!

A penny fell out of the bed as I got in.

I held my breath for a moment, glancing at Lucy's portable crib. The noise didn't wake her—but it made me feel Chad's absence more sharply.

I propped myself up with some pillows and picked up Dr. Graham's log. It was a plain black-bound book, on the large side, with two thick raised ribs across the binding. I felt devious, somehow, getting to touch it and open it in the privacy of my bedroom—out of Wallace's view. I wondered if he was sleepless tonight, worrying about it. He'd given it to me on our way out of the library—wrapped in brown paper and a Ziploc bag. I'd promised him I'd keep it only for a night—or two at the most.

Wallace had marked for me a note about the pregnancy of Frances Flinch Barnett. I decided to move backward from there to see if there was ever anything else mentioned about the Barnett family, and about Frances in particular. I didn't have to go far back for the first mention:

19 April 1878. Margaret Barnett. Gave birth to daughter Harriet Plainer Barnett. Recovering well.

Matthew's sister or sister-in-law, probably. Likely not relevant, but I marked it anyway.

I flipped back pages and pages, scanning the names. Someone had a shattered knee after being kicked by a horse. Then there were some measles cases. Before I knew it, I was two years back.

If Frances Barnett had had any mental difficulties before she had her child, Dr. Graham either didn't know about it or didn't see fit to note it in his journal.

I flipped back to the entry about her pregnancy and started to read through the entries that followed it. It seemed Dr. Graham never visited the Barnett house until Frances's labor.

10 January 1879. Frances Barnett. Gave birth to Martha Elizabeth Barnett. Heavy bleeding after birth but now appears to be resting comfortably.

A few days later, Frances came up again.

17 January 1879. Frances Barnett. Still very weak. Bed-bound.

Certainly it wasn't unusual to be weak after a long and difficult birth. I wondered if it was customary for a doctor to make a postnatal visit or if Frances's case was more serious.

She must have recovered, as there was no mention of any Barnetts for a couple of months after that. Until:

20 March 1879. Matthew Barnett. Consultation regarding wife's nervous condition.

I sat up straight. Wallace had apparently missed this entry. It was early enough that there might possibly have been a postpartum issue after all. So her institutionalization hadn't happened all at once in December, as it had previously appeared to us. It was a few months in the works.

16 June 1879. Martha Barnett. Emergency visit at my home. Stitches on left temple. Fell from bed.

This gave me pause. I was pretty sure Frances Barnett had never mentioned this in her journal. I picked up the photocopy Wallace had given me. Sure enough, June 16 fell into that long stretch of time in which Frances had written nothing.

I kept skimming until another *Barnett* caught my eye—many pages later.

15 December 1879. Martha Barnett. Vomiting and malaise. Recommend mild diet and prescribed digestive tonic.

I stared at the note. I stared at the date. Just a few weeks before Frances had been dragged away to Northampton.

"Jesus," I whispered. Had Wallace seen this? Why hadn't he told me about it?

My stomach tightened as I turned to the final page of Frances's journal. I didn't want to read it again. And yet—I felt I had to.

December 17, 1879

Reviewing the articles from Harry. Perplexing that Hayden might have given that girl so much arsenic at once. Surely he knew he didn't need nearly so much to kill her?

How much would be enough for someone significantly smaller than Mary Stannard? A mere dusting? Perhaps an amount so small the doctors and scientists would not be able to find it?

Was Frances experimenting with her daughter? Putting trace amounts in her food, perhaps?

It wasn't just the content of this entry that disturbed me. It was the tone—which changed so drastically over the course of the journal. She started out so girlishly, in November of 1878—writing of cakes and pies and her husband's grumbling stomach. By October of 1879, it was all organs and arsenic— analytical and obsessive. And then by this entry—the little white gloves were definitely off. I stared at the word "Hayden." It took me a couple of minutes to figure out what bothered me about it. In previous entries, she'd always given him a formal label—*Rev. Hayden. Mr. Hayden.* Even occasionally *Rev. Mr. Hayden.* She wasn't using complete sentences anymore either. All of the girlish formality was gone, as was the chirpy, deferential tone.

I turned back a couple of pages and read this:

December 10, 1879
   I went to the courthouse today, and saw Mrs. Hayden on the stand.
   Am I a strong wife and mother? Is she?
   Am I asking the most pertinent question?

Why was she being so cryptic about what she had seen in the courtroom, when up until then she had been so detailed? *Am I a strong wife and mother?* After all of the gory details and the scientific testimony, why was she asking *that* of all questions? And what *was* the "pertinent question"?

I took a deep breath and glanced around the bedroom. The monitor was off and silent since I had Lucy with me. The door

230 • Emily Arsenault

was closed. My jeans and sweater lay in a mound on the wood floor, as I'd already slipped into my yoga pants and T-shirt for bed. Everything in the room *looked* as it should, but my heart rate quickened and my ears seemed to prickle. They wanted, they needed, they *knew* they would eventually hear the sound: *shhhhh*.

"Don't fuck with me," I said into the air.

But my heart was unconvinced. It raced a bit faster. It *would* happen. When I fell asleep. *If* I fell asleep.

I took a deep breath. *If.* I had a choice. I did not *need* to sleep. Of course, I needed to sleep *eventually*. But I didn't need to sleep tonight. Not if I thought it best for Lucy if I stayed awake.

I set aside Dr. Graham's journal and pulled my laptop onto my thighs. I opened up Google and typed *Mediums Connecticut*.

I paused after typing it—as if to give the house around me a chance to respond to what I'd just done. It didn't—so I continued.

There were a couple of directories of psychics and mediums. Then there was something called "Bob Olson's 'Tested as Legitimate' List" of psychics and mediums. Bob Olson was apparently a big name in the afterlife business.

I went to one of the more general directories and began to scan through the faces.

There was a woman with spiky dark hair and a jade scarf knotted at her throat. Said she was also a hypnotherapist, grief counselor, and Reiki master. *Nope.* Cross her off the list. Fingers in too many psycho-spiritual pies. I just had a feeling my ghosts wouldn't go for that.

Below her was a good-looking young man with a mop of wavy brown hair. There was a hint of Jim Morrison to him.

Not a plus for me. I didn't think I could trust him. *You deserve answers!* Said his description. *I am a born psychic medium and clairaudient. I connect most effectively with the recently deceased.*

There was a white-haired lady with an exaggerated, pink-cheeked Mrs. Santa Claus smile. Adding to the cute, psychically innocuous little-old-me package was the fact that she specialized in "lost pet connections."

Lucy shifted the position of her head and indulged in a few sucks on her pacifier. I watched her until the sucking stopped, then continued down the list.

Next was a double-chinned lady with bleached hair and a closed-mouth smile that was almost a pout. She was wearing a navy blue T-shirt with a crew neck that looked too tight. Her description said: *I have been a psychic medium since age 6. Specialize in haunted spaces and missing persons. Do not charge except for travel expenses. I only take selected cases in which I believe I can be helpful. Call (203) 555-2223.*

She was from Hamden—very close to Haverton. An added bonus.

Her name gave me pause. Fonda Manning. There was something phony sounding about "Fonda." I wrote it down anyway. Maybe psychics had made-up names, like stage names, to keep their paranormal work separate from their normal lives? I wrote down the phone number, too, then kept looking down the list.

A young woman with a lip ring who did Tarot readings and psychic parties. A bald guy who specialized in "Energy Clearings." Several people had the word "healing" in their descriptions. Only one other person claimed to specialize in "haunted spaces"—a guy who also listed Chakras and "angel readings" as his other services. The more I read, the more I was drawn back to Fonda Manning. There seemed a distinct lack of positivity to her profile. For some reason, that made me feel better about her than the others.

BZZZT!

"Shit!" I practically jumped off the bed.

My cell phone. Next to the bed, by the lamp. It was Chad.

"Hey," he said when I picked up. "I figured the cell was less likely to wake Lucy."

"Thanks," I said. "Yeah, she's fast asleep."

"What're you up to?"

"Just fooling around online. How's your hotel?"

"Good. There are white robes hanging in the closet."

"Great," I said. "You can start a cult while you're there."

"Yup. You watching anything tonight?"

"Old Conan clips," I said.

"Oh. Your boyfriend."

"Well, you *are* about a thousand miles away. It's a little lonely."

"Well. Less than a thousand."

What good would the truth do, in this moment—with Chad so many miles away?

"Did you have a meeting today?" I asked. "Or is the first one tomorrow morning?"

"We had dinner with the client. The guy had a giant steak, so rare he might as well have just taken a bite out of his own arm. I try not to overanalyze these things, but I wonder if he's going to be . . ."

I got up and stood over Lucy's portable crib as Chad spoke. She'd dropped her pacifier, but her lips formed a little circle where it had once been. I smiled to myself and then realized I had no idea what Chad was saying anymore.

Were Lucy's lips the usual perfect pink? Or were they a little blue? Lucy's chest was gently rising and falling, but I wondered if the room was getting colder. I touched her hand. Not warm, but not especially cold.

"So I might be out late tomorrow night," Chad said. "But I can probably call you before dinner if you want."

But *was* the room getting colder? My arms felt cold beneath my long-sleeved T-shirt.

"Sure," I said, opening a dresser drawer for a cardigan.

I tugged on the cardigan as we said good-bye. Once I heard the click of Chad hanging up, I felt the cold in the room even more sharply. I'd forgotten how drafty this house got in midwinter—which was almost upon us. I decided to go downstairs to check the thermostat—and possibly nudge it up a degree or two.

I turned on every light in my path down the hall, down the stairs, and into the living room. I overrode the thermostat's automatic night temperature and set it for an indulgent 67 degrees. Then I stood still for a moment, listening for the basement heater to kick into gear.

THUMP.

I jumped. The sound didn't come from below, as I expected—but above. Upstairs, where Lucy lay by herself.

Upstairs.

My legs couldn't move fast enough to keep up with my heart. Up the stairs. Down the hall. All the lights on. Lucy!

Lucy!

By the time I reached the bedroom, my chest was throbbing.

Lucy was still asleep in the portable crib. I reached out to touch her hand, which twitched and curled itself around my finger. Resisting the urge to pick her up, I slid my hand away. Looking around the room, I couldn't find much explanation for the loud noise: fallen curtain rod or broken blinds. The bedcovers were as I had left them, with the laptop still open to the list of psychics.

Before I had a chance to exhale, I felt the distinct sensation of being watched from behind. For a moment, I pictured Florabelle standing in the doorway—mournfully, headlessly disapproving.

I turned around to look behind me—slowly, still holding my breath, and praying I'd see Monty there in the doorway instead.

The bedroom door was open wide—resting all the way against the opposite wall. As if it had been slammed open. I couldn't remember now if I'd opened it that far. I'd been anxious to get downstairs and back up to Lucy as quickly as possible.

I sat gingerly on the bed, taking a deep breath.

"Houses settle in cold weather," I whispered to myself. It made me feel better, so I whispered it again.

"Houses settle in cold weather."

The sound of my own whispering made a shudder creep up my spine and rattle my shoulders.

Because that's probably what a ghost would sound like. Ghosts talked in whispers. Whispers and shushes. Talking any louder, though, might wake Lucy.

Houses settle in cold weather.

But if I thought this fact was really relevant to my situation, I wouldn't be staring at this picture of Fonda Manning and starting to run her phone number through my head as if it might save my life.

"Two-oh-three, five-five-five . . ."

Don't whisper it. You sound like a ghost.

You sound like a fucking ghost.

I could call Chad, to keep me from calling Fonda Manning.

I really shouldn't call this Fonda person until tomorrow. Or ever?

But I couldn't call Chad because when he worried a lot—really a lot—he started to look like a skeleton.

And what a gruesome pair we would eventually be, with me sounding like a ghost and him looking like a skeleton.

I wrote down Fonda Manning's number on an actual piece of paper—in case my computer froze or the power went out or any of those things that are apt to happen in a haunted house. I'd call her tomorrow, no matter what.

As I resolved to do this, Monty hopped up on the bed, curled up next to Chad's pillow, and set to cleaning at one of his haunches. The licking noise diluted the silence. I didn't know where Monty had come from, but I was grateful he was there. Even if he hated me.

We'd be fine. I pulled up some Lewis Black comedy on my laptop and put an earbud in my left ear so I could keep my right one open for Lucy. We'd be fine as long Lucy slept and I didn't.

Chapter 46

A nd so, despite the dropping temperatures and the threat of snow, I managed to plan another trip to New Haven. I missed my brother, I told Matthew. And I missed Mother, in my own way. And there was shopping to do for Christmas! I explained that to him most exuberantly. I wished to lavish my baby daughter with gifts that could not be had here in Haverton. Oh! How girlishly bubbly I made my needs appear. Matthew had business to attend to in New Haven, so it worked out well for us all to travel and lodge with Mother together. There would be plenty of shopping time in which I could claim to have been searching for just the right doll or dress for Martha, to no avail. When, in fact, I'd be searching for a man named Price.

It is difficult for me now to remember if I felt any guilt for my deception. I suppose I was too determined—and perhaps too desperate—to feel guilt.

The travel with Matthew went smoothly as Martha slept most of the way. I recall Matthew kissing my hand as we came close to the city. Mother served us a stew of beef and potatoes, and perhaps the heaviness and familiarity of it helped me to sleep despite my apprehensions.

I do not know how long I slept. I awoke in the middle of the night, feeling something burst in my middle.

I lay still for a few minutes afterward, thinking the sensation had lingered from a bad dream. Then I felt a distinct ache. I crept out of the bed and down the hall to the room where you used to sleep. There was comfort there, in that place where you and I used to play and conspire.

I peeled off the stained layer of clothes, and wrapped myself in a blanket. Rarely had I ever seen so much blood. Only once before, perhaps.

Blood on my kitchen floor.

Blood in my best cake pan.

"Corpuscles!"

The audacity of that word, coming to my lips at such a time! I was a crazy woman, surely. So crazy that I resolved not to share this pain with anyone. I did not feel I was experiencing it correctly, and therefore decided it best to endure it alone—if I could.

I lay there for an hour or two. I was surprised at how quickly the ache subsided.

I crept back into the room where Matthew lay. I rolled the bloody clothes into a discreet ball, changed into a different nightdress, and lay down with a towel. The ache lessened even more, and became relief. And then, after only an hour or so, decayed into guilt.

I had not such a cruel master after all. *I* was the cruel one. How was it that my heart was so different from those of other women? I'd surely have found my Dr. Price if I'd needed him.

Him or someone like him. That was how dark my heart was. Despite the change in my fate, I couldn't deny that now.

Now I didn't need my Dr. Price. Now I had four days in New Haven with little to do but pretend to care about the most precious of children's dolls, and the most delicious of Christmas cakes. How, now that I didn't need the likes of Price, would I spend those days?

Chapter 47

Haverton, Connecticut
December 18, 2014

Once the sun came up, my body seemed to relax a little—in spite of itself. The feeling was like that of a fever breaking. I could sleep a little, couldn't I? If it was daylight? What else was there to do with Lucy still sleeping, and a couple of hours to go before I could reasonably call Fonda Manning? I leaned back on propped-up pillows and dozed for about an hour—until Lucy woke up with a little moan.

When I got out of bed, another penny fell out. As I lifted Lucy out of the Pack 'n Play, the penny circled the wood floor a couple of times and clattered to a stop beneath Chad's dresser. I ignored the sound while it was happening, but after it stopped, it echoed in my ears for a moment, making me forget what I was about to do next.

Wendy.

Wendy and a circling hubcap.

Wendy came back to our room one night with a shiny hubcap in her hands. She had walked all the way to the outskirts of campus to go to the convenience store with the superior candy selection. Sour watermelon candy, I think, was what she was after. A car had peeled out of the lot while she was standing there with her candy, she reported breathlessly. And its hubcap had flown off and circled her once, twice, three times, before coming to a stop with a loud clatter practically right at her feet.

It was really cinematic, she said. *I'm pretty sure I'm supposed to keep this thing. I just don't know why.*

Maybe you ought to clean it up real nice and start eating from it, I said, and then immediately regretted it. She'd mentioned she'd been anorexic in high school, so eating maybe wasn't a laughing matter.

But she didn't seem to notice. Instead, she nodded.

I'll wash it a couple of times if you make a bag of popcorn.

I had obliged, and we'd eaten the popcorn together while I typed away at my computer and she highlighted several pages of a psychology textbook and then took out her seashell stationary to write more letters to old high school friends. The next day, I came back to the room to find the hubcap hanging on a nail between our desks. Occasionally it would come loose from the nail and startle us both with a CLANG and I'd try not to glare at Wendy because I had to admit the hubcap was kind of cool.

And after her brother and father emptied out her side of the room, I'd wanted to tell them the hubcap was hers. They hadn't been sure, apparently—because they'd left it—and I wasn't around for them to ask. And yet a hubcap didn't seem enough of a reason to bother a bereaved family. Not then. Not now. I still had it somewhere.

Where? I couldn't remember. Did it matter now, with Lucy so hungry and me so in need of coffee?

By the time I was done with baby oatmeal, cleanup, and coffee, it was almost eight-thirty. And what grown-up wasn't up by eight-thirty? I wasn't going to grandstand and wait until nine. I'd waited all night.

Hello. You've reached Fonda Manning and the Happy Highways Driving School. Please leave me your name and number and I'll get right back at ya.

I did as instructed even though the "Happy Highways" threw me—reminding me vaguely of the old show *Highway to Heaven.* Maybe Fonda Manning was more stickily religious than her web profile had implied.

Before I had a chance to worry much about it, Fonda called me back.

"Hi, Abby," she said. "Thanks for calling. Sorry I didn't answer. I never answer if I don't know the number. So, you said you found me through the Connecticut Psychics Resource page. What can I do for you?"

"Well . . ." I took a deep breath. "I live in Haverton, and I have a situation with my home."

"A situation. What kind of a situation?"

I sniffled. "A . . . possible haunting situation, I suppose, is the best way I can put it."

"Sure. Okay. You want to set up an appointment for a home visit then?"

"I think so."

"All right. Well, as long as you understand a couple of things. First and foremost, I'm not an exorcist and I don't associate with anyone who identifies as one."

I hesitated. "Okay."

"Next, I'm not an entertainer. I don't do parties. I prefer that no one else be present but the homeowners—or residents, if you don't own the home—when I visit."

"It'll just be me and my daughter when you come. Um, as-suming you can come soon. My husband is away."

"How old is your daughter?" Fonda wanted to know.

"She's five months old."

"I see. Okay. I ask because I prefer not to have children pres-ent. Not because they affect my reading in any way. I just don't like them to be involved. It can be scary for them. I'm not saying that my eyes roll back in my head or my head spins around—don't get me wrong. I'm just saying I don't like to have to edit what I have to say about the spiritual energy, to keep from scar-ing a kid, or whatever. But in your case . . . well, of course, it's fine for her to be there. I'm sure that would be a lot easier for you. Oh, and the last thing is that I have to ask that you not use any artificial air fresheners or scented candles—or spray any perfumes or whatever—for a few hours before I come. Like, three hours."

"Okay." I wondered if she was allergic or if it interfered with her psychic abilities but thought it might be unwise to ask. "Do you have any availability today?"

"Today? Um, that might be a little rough. *Maybe* around five, since one of my driving appointments said he might have to cancel. Otherwise, we'll have to look at tomorrow or the next day. I'll have to get back to you later in the day. You said you're in Haverton, right? Why don't you give me your address?"

Wallace called while I was gathering a load of laundry—a frus-tratingly slow and awkward task with Lucy strapped to my chest, since I had to reach for everything sideways.

"Did you know that Dr. Graham saw Martha Barnett a few

days before Frances was put away?" I asked. "Because she was having a problem with vomiting?"

Wallace was silent for a moment. "Martha . . . the baby? The Barnett baby?"

"Yes."

Of course *the baby*. It seemed to me Wallace was evading.

"I was rather focused on finding entries with *Frances* in them the one time I looked, and perhaps wasn't being as thorough as you."

"Uh huh." I sorted through the tiny, mostly pastel clothes in the laundry basket, pulling out the few darker clothes for a different load.

"I wouldn't jump to conclusions about that. Babies *do* have a tendency to vomit. As I'm sure you're aware."

"*Jump to conclusions?*" I repeated. "I don't know that I need to do a very big jump here. Frances was probably giving her daughter arsenic."

Another long silence. I thumped down the stairs and opened the washing machine in the pantry.

"Abby."

"Yes?"

"Let's take a step back here, now. Have you always considered yourself a historian?" Wallace asked.

"No. Did I ever say I was a historian?" I pulled down a box of detergent pods.

"Aren't you a history teacher?"

"That's not the same thing."

"It's not?" Wallace asked.

"Let's see now. To answer your question, there was a brief

period in the beginning of college when I thought I wanted be a documentary filmmaker. Historical documentaries. So there was a point when I thought I was a historian, yes."

I stared down into the washer. Then I remembered something. Lucy's pajama bottoms on my bedroom floor this morning. They hadn't made it into the hamper, because I'd changed them late at night when she'd gotten pee on them. With her sleeping in my bedroom, the laundry just wasn't all staying in one place.

"So why didn't you? Become a documentary filmmaker?"

I hated it when one half of something of hers got washed, and the other didn't. I knew it was likely a form of OCD or corporate mind control—this belief that I had to clothe my tiny drooling human in "matching sets." And yet I couldn't shake it. I started to mount the stairs again.

"Well, I transferred out of the small fancy-pants college I was going to and went to a big state school. And there I figured out that I wasn't such hot shit. So I got my teaching certificate."

"Well, teaching is a noble profession, of course."

"Of course. More noble than being another twenty-year-old who thinks she's going to be the next Ken Burns, at least. Now, why were you asking this again?"

"Umm . . . I don't remember now. I was going to make some point about objectivity, I suppose."

"I'm sorry," I said. "I'm a little out of it this morning, too. I didn't sleep much last night. Or the night before, for that matter."

"I'm sorry to hear that. Did Lucy keep you up?"

I snatched the tiny pajama bottoms from the floor. "No. Frances kept me up."

"Oh, dear. Poor Frances. What will she be blamed for next?"

I rolled my eyes. I wanted to tell him about Stephanie's story, but thought better of it. Though she hadn't said so, it felt like it had been told in confidence. It was one thing for her to tell the poor unsuspecting recipient of her aunt's spook house— another for me to turn around and tell a big-time townie familiar with her family.

I tried to sit on the bed for a moment, but Lucy grunted in protest. She hated being on my chest if I wasn't up and moving around. "Wallace, I meant to ask you when you were here last. Do you believe in ghosts?"

"Hmm. Good question. I believe that a house . . . a building . . . can retain certain . . . oh, 'auras' is too woo-woo of a word. Certain feelings, certain tones?"

"Is that a yes or a no?"

"I have no idea, Abby."

"Okay. Great. I was just wondering. Oh! So, the other thing I wanted to tell you is that I think a page or two was ripped out of Frances's journal."

"What? When?"

"I mean, before we ever read it. I was looking at it the other night. There is a bit of paper left behind in the binding. It would've been just a page or two, it looks like. There's not a huge gap from a chunk of it being ripped out, but—"

"Maybe the Barnett fellow who gave it to you . . . ?"

"I doubt it, but I should call him and ask if he knows about it. My feeling is that he really never read past the first couple of pages."

"Of course, there are several possible explanations. Maybe Frances made an error and ripped a page out and started over."

"Or . . . *or* someone . . . over the years . . . saw something they either wanted to keep for themselves or . . . destroy, perhaps."

"The matter of the 'unspeakable act' cropping up again. I see. Hmm. Where are the pages taken out? In just one spot?"

"Yes," I told Wallace. "Right before the end. Around Christmas of 1879. Before her . . . final entry."

"Hmm. Interesting."

I stared around the bedroom, trying to remember why, exactly, I'd come up the stairs when I'd been about to start a load of laundry. "I guess you'll want Dr. Graham's log back soon?"

"Oh. Well, yes. But I suppose you can hold on to it for a day or two more if you guard it with your life."

"I can't meet today anyway," I said. "I have someone coming over."

I was hopeful that Fonda would call me back, and I wanted to leave things open in case she did.

"Oh! Well, good. It's not a priority. Tomorrow might be out of the question, of course, but . . . we'll meet soon, I'm sure."

"Sure," I said.

After we hung up, I glanced down at the item hanging loosely in my hands. Of course. That was what had brought me up the stairs. Tiny peed-on pajama bottoms.

Night fell before suppertime—even before Lucy's suppertime, which was typically around five. Fonda Manning called me when we were halfway through a jar of organic pureed peas.

"Sorry I didn't call you earlier," she said. "My driving appointment didn't cancel. So we're going to have to do tomorrow. Would three work? I could do later, but I don't want to press my luck—"

"Three works," I interrupted.

I thanked her, and we hung up. I pushed more peas into Lucy's mouth and stared out the kitchen window but couldn't see much beyond my own reflection. I turned away from the length of my face and the limpness of my hair. I hated such early darkness. I didn't realize till now how much I had been counting on Fonda Manning coming—and breaking the isolation before I'd have to endure another night alone. I gave Lucy another spoonful of peas, then had one myself. I was hungry but too tired to prepare much dinner.

"Protein," I murmured to myself and got out a spoon and a jar of peanut butter.

We sat in the living room after that—Lucy with her board books and squeaky toys, me with my Comedy Central and CNN. I was too tired for anything else. I turned on the Christmas tree lights, but Lucy seemed more mesmerized by all of the talking heads.

"It's fine," I said to Lucy. "You should've seen how much TV they let babies watch in the eighties, and look how good I turned out."

Lucy said "Mmmmm," as if savoring something delicious. When she seemed to grow annoyed with Anderson Cooper, I brought her upstairs and started to change her diaper. Lately, since she'd been sleeping in my room, I'd been changing her on a towel on my bed instead of on her bedroom changing table. After I laid her down, I discovered that my stash of diapers was depleted. I moved both her and her towel to the floor while I ran to get a few more. From the floor she couldn't fall anywhere.

When I came back and moved her back up to the bed, I

noticed something in her hand. It was a familiar translucent toothpaste-blue.

"Found your binkie down there?" I said, changing her diaper quickly. She smiled playfully and put her hand to her chin, missing her mouth. "Very clever."

I laid her gently on the floor again while I put on my yoga pants and then scooped her back up to cuddle with me on the bed.

Lucy tightened her fist around her pacifier. I positioned her head in the crook of my arm, sat back, and closed my eyes for a moment.

"Ooohh," Lucy said.

When I opened my eyes, a blue liquid was running down Lucy's hand and onto my sweatshirt.

"Oh!" I screamed, and rushed to wipe her hand with my pillowcase. I pried open her hand and found the remains of a detergent pod.

"Jesus!" I jumped off the bed and ran Lucy to the bathroom, holding her hand away from her mouth.

I rinsed her hand and tossed the pod in the toilet.

"Oh, God. Oh, God. Oh, God," I whispered. I held Lucy up to my face and examined her mouth. It was as clean as when I'd wiped it after the peas. "You didn't eat any of that, Lucy, did you?"

I was shaking so badly, I was afraid I'd drop her. She didn't seem to notice. She turned to the bathroom mirror and grinned at her reflection.

"I'm so sorry, Lucy. I thought it was your pacifier. I swear I thought it was your pacifier."

I repositioned us on the bed and wondered if I should call a poison control number or a doctor. But I knew that none of it had made it into her mouth. It had broken in the moment I had closed my eyes.

How had the detergent pod ended up on the floor? I *knew* they were dangerous. I'd even read about a kid dying after eating one. The detergent in them was highly concentrated, the story had said, and I'd vowed to stop using them once Lucy could crawl—or once my giant tub of them from Costco ran out. Whichever came first.

What an idiot. Why hadn't I thrown them all out as soon as I'd read about it? What was wrong with me?

I remembered going up and down the stairs as I gathered laundry and talked on the phone with Wallace. I'd been tired and distracted even then. But enough to drop one of those pods on the *floor?* Maybe I had placed it on the bed and it had fallen off.

Just fallen off? Maybe. But somehow that didn't feel plausible.

Maybe something had moved it.

No. Stop thinking that and call Chad so he can put some normal thoughts into your head.

But I didn't want to talk to Chad. I'd have to tell him how close I had come to letting Lucy poison herself. And then I'd have to try to explain to him that I didn't think it was *me*, exactly, who had almost let it happen.

The house—or something in it—was keeping me awake. It was making me tired and careless. Maybe that was all part of its plan. To make me so exhausted that I'd slip up eventually.

250 • Emily Arsenault

Eventually, Lucy would fall or choke or eat poison—because I couldn't protect her.

I began to sing "Down in the Valley" softly. Not so much to put Lucy to sleep—her eyelids were already drooping—but to keep myself focused on something besides my own fear. Halfway through, I realized I couldn't remember all the lyrics. I switched to "Twinkle Twinkle," then "The Itsy-Bitsy Spider." I held on to Lucy for an hour, switching back and forth between those two songs. Then I held her a little longer—until I was so tired I was afraid I'd drift off and drop her.

I put her into her crib and watched old David Letterman clips until the sun came up. Then I crawled beneath my covers, and slept for an hour until Lucy woke up.

Chapter 48

Northampton Lunatic Hospital
Northampton, Massachusetts
December 20, 1885

There was a sizable crowd outside of the courthouse, and it was buzzing with excitement. Eavesdropping on two women who were discussing the previous day's events, I gathered that the wife of Reverend Herbert Hayden had testified but wasn't finished yet.

According to these women, Mary Stannard had visited the Hayden home a couple of times in the days before her death. Once to borrow a rake and once to borrow a pitchfork. She'd visited with Mrs. Hayden, held the newborn baby, and played with the older Hayden children. The way Mrs. Hayden told it, Mary had never been alone with Mr. Hayden long enough for much private discussion to take place. These ladies noted that this account conflicted with neighbors' claims of seeing Mary and Mr. Hayden entering the Haydens' barn together.

In any case, Mrs. Hayden would be on the stand again today. She would face cross-examination.

And that is what I witnessed that day. The prosecuting attorney, Mr. Waller, questioned her about arsenic. Rosa Hayden and her husband had, in the weeks preceding the murder, discussed the problem of rats and the possibility of purchasing arsenic. She admitted that she did not know of his actual purchase of it until after the murder.

As Mrs. Hayden spoke of these things, I studied her dark eyes and her delicate frown. For a moment, I felt deep pain for her. She was still recovering from the recent birth of a child when her husband was arrested for Mary's murder, leaving her all alone to care for and support her children. Whatever the truth was, her experience was surely agonizing.

Soon after the arsenic questions, the cross-examination took a dramatic turn.

Waller asked a series of questions about Mrs. Hayden's relationship to her husband.

"Now, madam, you stated to the jury that you are the wife of the accused?"

"Yes, sir."

"And that you have been married for eight years?"

"Yes, sir; between eight and nine years."

"And that he is the father of your three children?"

"Yes, sir."

"And that he always treated you well?"

"Yes, sir."

"And that you continue to have affection for him and confidence in him?"

"Yes, sir."

"And that if he suffers ignominious punishment, it will be an unjust punishment?"

"Yes, sir."

"The question comes in now, and it is the only question I have

to ask. *You need not answer this question, madam. Wait and give
the counsel time to object.*

*"As Mr. Hayden, the accused, is your husband, father of your
three children, a devoted husband to a loving wife, and as you have
always, and do now, maintain the pleasantest relations with him,
as you have implicit confidence in his innocence, as you believe
that, if he suffers the ignominious punishment that must befall him
in case he is found guilty, it will be unjust, would you, madam,
under such circumstances and under oath, make a misstatement to
save him, whom you love better than your life, from punishment?"*

Mrs. Hayden's dark eyes glistened, and then, all at once, her
face crumpled, and she wept. Several women in the gallery
began sobbing sympathetic tears. Looking about the room, I
could not see another woman besides myself who wasn't crying.

After a few moments, the defense attorneys burst into action:

"Don't answer the question!"

"It is an insult to the witness!"

As these words were spoken, something froze inside of me.
The sensation from the previous night returned to me—that
there was something distinct and defective about my heart.

The prosecuting attorney, Mr. Waller, began to defend his
question:

*"I heard the counsel for the defense say in an undertone 'It's an
insult to the witness.' I deny that accusation. I would not say an
unkind word to this poor woman under any circumstances. Her
devotion challenges the admiration and respect of all, and that she
would exaggerate, prevaricate, or commit perjury implies no cen-
sure upon her or upon womanhood."*

And on and on he went with his bombastic speech, saying

that he'd expect his own beloved wife, a mother of his six beloved children, to do the very same thing—to be loyal to him under such circumstances. He would expect any good and loving wife to do the same. And was he not wrong to remind the court of that?

Some of the women in the gallery benches continued to sob through this flatulent speech. My heart, however, grew cold. My whole chest grew cold, in fact. I grew so icy and stiff I wondered how I would ever extract myself from that courthouse seat.

As the lawyers bloviated at each other for several minutes, I attempted to understand the other women's tears. They felt for Rosa Hayden as a wife and a mother. They imagined themselves under similar circumstances—trying to maintain the health and happiness of her family with her husband torn away from her by overzealous prosecutors.

Everyone felt such sadness for poor, long-suffering Rosa Hayden. Whether her husband was guilty or innocent, her life was agony.

And yet—I hated her tears.

I hated the tears of the women crying over something they thought they understood.

I hated Waller for his speech about loving wives and mothers.

My heart was frozen with a hatred of all of these things. I feared what vile substance might melt out if I allowed it to do so.

That is why I did not cry like the other women in that courtroom.

Chapter 49

Haverton, Connecticut
December 19, 2014

I was holding Lucy up to the living room window when the cute red hatchback slowed down in front of my house. "Happy Highways Driving School" was written in swirling letters across the side. The driver executed a perfect parallel parking job in front the house. A yellow Baby-on-Board style sign in the back window cautioned: *Student Driver.*

After locking her car door, Fonda glanced into her window and tidied the feathery yellow hair that framed her face. She was wearing jeans, red wellies, and a brown bomber jacket that looked several sizes too large.

I answered the door with Lucy in my arms.

"You must be Abby," Fonda said, extending her arm to me and cocking her head at Lucy. "Hey, pumpkin."

"Ay," Lucy said, stunning me with her imitative tone.

Fonda smiled broadly.

"Hey!" she repeated.

Lucy gasped, laughed, and then buried her head against my shirt.

"Nice little place," Fonda said as she followed me into the kitchen.

"Thank you," I said. "Do you want to sit down? Can I get you something to drink?"

"I'm fine for now. Mind if I walk around a little?"

As we stepped into the living room, Fonda took long, sniffling inward breaths. I wondered if she had a cold and if I should keep Lucy at a safe distance. Then I remembered the whole thing about air fresheners and scented candles. Maybe Fonda was primarily a smell-psychic? What would that be called? A clairolfactant?

Fonda took a miniature package of Kleenex out of her purse, blew her nose, and then turned to me.

"I often find it's better to talk *after* I've had some time to take things in. That way, we don't have to wonder later if we've . . . led each other in some way. Usually I find a room where the energy is strongest—if I feel any energy at all—and then sit for a while."

"So I should take you into every room?"

"That'd be great."

I led her slowly around the downstairs rooms, then said, "Okay to go upstairs?"

She nodded. I watched her carefully when we reached the top of the stairs. She sniffled, stepped into Lucy's room, and said, "Cute nursery. I love giraffes. They have the sweetest faces."

She closed her eyes for a moment, then looked at me expectantly.

"Keep moving?"

Fonda nodded. We went down the hall and stood in the bathroom for a while, then Chad's and my bedroom. Fonda paused at the bedroom door, then walked over to a window and looked out for a moment.

"Hmm," she said softly, turning to me. "I'd like to go back downstairs if that's okay with you."

"Sure," I said.

When we reached the bottom of the stairs, Fonda gave Lucy another toothy smile. Lucy gasped with delight.

"Your living room," Fonda said. "That's where I'd like to sit for a while. Is that okay?"

Once she was settled on the couch and had refused another drink offer, Fonda said, "It's usually best if you leave me. I don't mind if you peek in or whatever. But if you go about your business for about fifteen-twenty minutes, that would work well for me."

As she said this, Fonda pulled a pen and a book of Sudoku puzzles out of her purse.

"Okay," I agreed, and went into the kitchen to feed Lucy pureed sweet potato and empty the dishwasher. Fonda didn't make a sound for twenty minutes.

I chewed over the Sudoku. What was that about? *Ghosts are lurking. Look busy.*

After that, I gave in to my curiosity and stuck my head in.

Fonda's hands were folded across the open Sudoku book. She was squinting down at the carpet, biting her lip.

Lucy, nestled against my hip, said "Nnh . . . nnh . . . nnh."

Fonda looked up, her face momentarily blank before answering Lucy's sounds with another exaggerated smile.

"Hello there," she said. "Why don't we talk now?"

I settled Lucy on the floor with a quilt and some of her favorite toys.

"As you might have guessed," Fonda said, "I'm feeling much more of a presence downstairs."

"Oh?" I said.

"Although 'presence' might not be the right word. Whatever you would call it, it dwells mostly downstairs."

"It?" I repeated.

"I'm not sure if there's much intelligence to it. I feel like it's more of a residual haunting than anything. Do you know what that means? A residual haunting?"

"Uh . . . where a ghost takes up residence?"

"No." Fonda blew her feathery bangs out of her face. " 'Residual' means, like, leftover. An aftereffect, you know? A residual haunting is when there's leftover energy from something that happened in a place. Like, if a traumatic event happened in a house, and there's still leftover . . . tension or stress, shall we say. It might interfere with the electricity. It might replay movements or actions from that time, or make noises. It's not an intelligent spirit doing it to scare the living residents of the place. It's just leftover energy. *Residual* energy. Make sense?"

I nodded. "Yes."

"I'm not saying there's anything really dramatic happening here, like an axe murderer lived here or whatever. People are always jumping to that sort of conclusion when I mention 'traumatic.' There doesn't *necessarily* have to be a history of a really unfortunate event for there to be residual energy. And even if there is, it doesn't mean you, the current, living resident, don't have any tools to deal with it. Okay?"

Tools. Hmm. Like garlic necklace and lit torches sort of tools? Or breathing exercises sort of tools?

"Okay?" I said slowly, hoping for something closer to the former than the latter.

"So. Having said that, I will say that I find the energy in this room a bit oppressive. Here and in the kitchen."

"Oppressive?"

"Yes. There's a heaviness to it. I felt it lift as I went up the stairs."

"Oh."

"Now, this has never happened to me before, but I keep receiving a word."

"A word?"

"Innocent. The word 'innocent.'"

I glanced at Lucy. She was gnawing a board book so hard that the whole corner of the cover was gummy. Spit dripped out of her mouth.

"You've never heard words before? In a haunted place, I mean?"

"Well, I didn't *hear* them exactly, but that's beside the point. Certainly I sense certain words or phrases sometimes, along with the energy. But it's the nature of the repetition of the word here that's unusual. I keep sensing it in increments of four. *Innocent, innocent, innocent, innocent.* Like counting. Or like a mantra."

Lucy coughed and then gagged. I knelt down and pulled the book away from her lips to discover that a small chunk of it had come off in her mouth.

"Lucy, no!" I yelped, and fished it out.

I looked at the purple cardboard in my palm, then at Fonda.

"It's scary," Fonda said. "At that age. Even the smallest things are dangerous."

I nodded. "Do you have kids?"

"Just one. My son. It's his first year at college. Southern."

"Oh." I don't know why this surprised me. I suppose I'd thought of psychics as eccentric, single dramatic-scarf-and-dangly-earrings types. "Congratulations."

"You know . . . to be functional as a mother is essentially to operate in a sort of delusional state. Well . . . maybe not delusional. Self-deceptive, I guess?"

I hesitated—not wanting to be rude, but eager for us to get back to the subject of my residual ghost. "Yeah, I guess."

"One gets to know this in my line of work. Driving school, I mean. You have to have at least a small dose of deluded optimism to give a sixteen-year-old keys to a car."

I was trying to pay attention to what Fonda was saying, but philosophies of adolescent parenting seemed a couple of light-years away from my situation at the moment.

"Are you sure of the word? *Innocent?*" I asked.

"Yes," Fonda said. "Absolutely."

I clasped my hand over the gummed cardboard, unsure what to do with it. "And you didn't have the same experience upstairs?"

Fonda gazed down at my hands and smiled slightly. "Well . . . upstairs . . ."

She seemed to be deciding what to say. While we all waited, Lucy grinned at Fonda and grunted.

"What's up, pumpkin?" Fonda purred at her, then turned to me. "Why don't we all go up there again for a minute or two. Do you mind?"

"Not at all," I said, scooping up Lucy.

Once upstairs, we strolled through the rooms again—slowly, noncommittally, as if in a real estate open house. Once again, Fonda didn't seem particularly affected by Lucy's room.

We finished in the bedroom. Fonda walked all the way across the room, tapped on Chad's dresser, and blew her nose.

"It's different up here," she said. "The energy isn't as heavy. I feel something here, but just fleetingly. It doesn't *reside* here the way the downstairs energy does."

"Okay," I prompted.

"What I'm feeling here has more intelligence to it, more of a consciousness. It's female. I'm not sure what the age. When I say it doesn't *reside* here, I mean that it just flits through, like a breeze comes through when the windows are open. That's why I can't get a firm grasp on her."

I was now grasping Lucy so tightly that I had to take a deep breath and try to relax my hands.

Fonda continued. "I feel like a window was, in a sense, recently opened for this energy to start passing through. There's some new element in the house that invited it in."

"My daughter was born five months ago," I blurted. I'd vowed not to give Fonda material to take advantage of—but then, this piece of information was obvious.

Fonda studied me, then pushed a piece of her hair behind her ear.

"I had that thought, when I first noticed it. But . . . I'm not so sure. I suppose it doesn't matter what *started* it coming through . . . docs it?"

"It does if I want to *close* the window." I tried not to sound like I was pleading.

Fonda sucked in a breath. "Now, I know that that's the knee-jerk reaction . . ."

She motioned for me to follow her and wandered down the hall to Lucy's room. She walked by the crib, sliding her hand along its dark coffee-colored rim. Then she stepped closer to the window and touched one of Lucy's giraffe curtains. She inhaled noisily and then shut her eyes.

When she opened them, she said softly, "I don't think she's all that concerned about the baby."

Her use of the word "she" made my arms prickle. *She.* Not an "energy," as Fonda seemed so fond of saying. An "energy" was vague and invisible and woo-woo, and therefore easily brushed off. But a *she* was different. A *she* was undeniably present. However fleetingly or flittingly or whatever euphemistic way Fonda wanted to put it.

I could feel Fonda's gaze on me. I turned away from her for a moment and kissed Lucy's head.

"Abby," she said.

I turned back to Fonda, surprised to hear her say my name with a tone of such familiarity. "Hmm?"

"I think it's important to remember that none of this can hurt you. It can be hard to remember that when we first hear these things."

I wanted to tell her that I could not *remember* something that I had not necessarily thought or believed. Why would I have bothered to call her if I'd held the belief that *none of this can hurt you?*

"Now, I'm not saying that this is *exactly* what is happening here. But right after I had my son, I found I was more . . . sensitive. And I don't mean, like, hormonal. I mean that I picked up on certain energies more than I even had before. For a while. Just a thought."

"Right," I said. *Energies* somehow wasn't a more satisfactory word than *hormones.*

"Anyway." Fonda exhaled. "You asked about 'closing the window,' so to speak. I've found that the simplest approach is often the best. Just acknowledge the presence. Say, 'I know you're here.' Sometimes that's all that's needed to neutralize it. Or even a simple, 'You can go now.' I think that's all you might need for this presence upstairs."

"And downstairs?"

"That might be a little more complicated. That feels more like just . . . part of the house. I find sometimes it's best to think of the residual stuff that way. Like a refrigerator humming, or the heater turning on when the temperature drops. It's automatic. It doesn't have anything to do with you. Unless you *let* it bother you. Now, I didn't ask you much about your experience with the house when I first arrived, but can I ask now?"

I wasn't sure yet if I wanted to confide in Fonda Manning. Maybe this was her strategy. Scare the pants off a client, and then have her spill. Use garnered information to scare her some more.

"I don't really want to talk about it. I have a lot to think about, for now," I said. "Do you think you might be able to come back another time, though?"

Fonda didn't look surprised. "Certainly I can. If you think that would help you."

I led Fonda back down the stairs. "I'm wondering if you can gather more . . . information. If you come again."

"I can certainly try," Fonda replied.

"So . . ." Fonda zipped her bomber jacket up to her chin. "I don't charge for a first visit at all. But for multiple visits I do ask for help with gas. Does that sound fair to you?"

"Oh. Of course. Any particular amount, or . . ."

"Let's say twenty-five dollars or so. If you decide to have me back. I think you're smart to take a few days to think about it. You may feel that you've learned all you need to . . . or want to."

I nodded. "I'll probably call you soon."

Fonda took out a tissue and dabbed at each nostril. "Don't hesitate. But listen. I'd better get going. I want to get to the store while they still have bread on the shelves. You understand, right?"

"Umm . . . yeah?" I said. I *didn't* quite understand, but I didn't want to appear anxious.

"You can call me anytime. *Any* time. I'm used to getting called at night. But I ought to get home."

I nodded again and led Fonda to the door. Before she opened it, I asked, "Just one more quick question?"

Please don't leave me alone in this house.

Fonda's hand tightened over the doorknob. "Yeah?"

"Did you notice my daughter's bruise at all?"

Fonda squinted at Lucy. "Only a little. Why?"

"Does it look like a seashell to you?"

Fonda's hand dropped from the doorknob as she studied me wordlessly.

"I was just curious," I said quickly. "Someone told me they thought it looked like a spiral seashell, and I was just wondering if they were out of their minds."

"It looks to me like a week-old bruise. Is that about right?"

"About," I managed to say.

Fonda nodded and opened the door. "Stay warm tonight."

Chapter 50

Northampton Lunatic Hospital
Northampton, Massachusetts
December 20, 1885

And so I went home to Haverton.

And there I discovered that my kitchen smelled of blood.

Corpuscles? No. As much as I might have wished to put it that way, I couldn't say that my kitchen smelled of corpuscles—anymore. For how does a corpuscle smell? I don't presume to know. It wasn't as if someone had slaughtered something in my home while I was gone. No. Now I *recognized* a smell that had been there all along.

And so I scrubbed. I had Tessa scrub as well. For as long as I could and still seem sane, and then a little bit more.

I believe it is sparkling, ma'am. I think we have done a good and thorough job.

The smell remained.

As I set about returning to my cooking duties and my hobbyist baking, I thought still of Mrs. Hayden. I thought of her on the stand, struggling not to break her wifely façade. Did she believe her husband guilty? Or did she believe him innocent? The other women in the courtroom seemed to sympathize with her situation regardless of his status.

What I could not help but observe—and can I help it that I am more observant than sentimental?—was that the mind sees what it wishes to see and remembers what it wishes to remember.

Mrs. Hayden's husband *had* perhaps spent a few minutes speaking privately with Mary Stannard in his barn. Even so, it was perhaps only a few minutes. There are fourteen hundred and forty minutes per day. It would be easy to forget a few minutes. If one wished to forget.

And Mrs. Hayden could remember a long-ago discussion with her husband about vermin, but not notice the oddity of him purchasing and hiding in their barn a lethal substance without mentioning it to her, regardless of the potential danger to their children. If she *wished* not to notice it as odd.

It was easy for a woman to refuse to acknowledge a darkness residing in her home, in the interest of maintaining—or attempting to maintain—light.

I understood how easy it might be. Perhaps I understood even more than all of those tiresome weeping women in the courtroom on that December day. Yes. Perhaps I did.

Recognizing this, I had to make a decision. I could continue to try to scrub the blood from my kitchen. I could continue to try to forget Mrs. Hayden's words, and the familiar intricacies of her selective memory. I could collect pudding recipes and sew Martha a green velvet dress and hold on to Christmas as one would a piece of driftwood in a swirling storm at sea. I could hope the aroma of warming cinnamon and cloves could mask that smell in my kitchen.

Or I could endeavor to be quite different from Rosa Hayden—to be a cold and analytical investigator of my own memory, and my own heart.

Oh dear! Do you see that nurse hovering in the doorframe? She is going to tell us that our visiting time is over. The supper bell will be ringing soon. I should have known from the diminishing sunlight and the grumble of my stomach that suppertime was coming. Because I met my shirt quota this week, there will be a piece of fruit with my supper tonight.

What do we do in the evenings?

Once a week, we line up for an ice-cold bath. As for the other nights, you might be surprised, Harry. For those of us who can sit relatively still and silent for an hour, there is sometimes entertainment provided. Dr. Earl believes in stimulating the patients' minds. There are Bible readings and poetry readings and sometimes lectures. Some weeks ago, we had a lecture on astronomy. Some months before that, one on architecture. Every two or three months, we are treated to a show from the oxyhydrogen lantern. There is a man in Northampton named Dr. Meekins—perhaps a friend of Dr. Earl's—who is an expert in optics. Every so often he comes and shows magnified pictures with his oxyhydrogen lantern. The "magic lantern," some of the patients call it. Yes? You've heard of it? Outdated, you say? Well, Harry. Even the most scientifically minded lunatics cannot be particular about technology.

The most recent of Dr. Meekins's showing was insects—though I wonder if he'll dare show *those* again, as a few patients woke up in the night screaming about large eyes and sharp mandibles and hairy antennae. I do not always attend those nights with the oxyhydrogen lantern. They sadden me sometimes—for they make me think of you.

I have, besides, already seen many things up close. Perhaps that is what is wrong with many of us here. Once we have seen things up too close—or too far away—we cannot restore our vision to its proper and conventional function. Perhaps mine is a simplified explanation, but I challenge you to devise a better one.

In any case, the entertainment is always short, and we go to bed early—so we can rise with the sun for a full day's work.

Oh. You are right. I was so engaged in my story that I didn't notice the snow starting to fall. I am glad of it. My easiest days here are when I look out the window and see nothing but white. Those are the days when I feel most separate from the world—as if I died on the day of Martha's birth, after all. As if I am in purgatory and have no choice in the matter any longer.

You must go now? You mean you are going to simply walk out into the snow? Where will you go? And when will you come back? Harry!

Goodness. My heart nearly burst just now. I hadn't realized I had enough heart left to worry about. Oh, that is a relief, Harry. I am so glad to hear that you have taken a room at an inn and that you will return tomorrow. I am not sure what your business is in Northampton, but I am happy it has brought you here. We have more to talk about tomorrow, indeed.

Chapter 51

Haverton, Connecticut
December 19, 2014

The house was definitely getting colder. Too cold. Our thermostat was still on the pre-baby settings of last winter, and the sixty-degree nights were no longer going to fly.

Lucy was sleeping soundly, but her hands were chilly. I cursed myself for not remembering to reset the thermostat before I'd headed up the stairs. Why had it taken me this long to notice how cold it had been getting at night? Had Chad been overriding the settings on particularly cold nights?

I had all the upstairs lights on, and last night's *Tonight Show* practically blasting on my laptop—as much as one could blast with an infant four feet away. The idea was to drown some of Fonda's words out of my brain—at least until Lucy was asleep. Now that she was down, I felt too cold to climb under our feather duvet in good conscience. I'd be warm enough, but Lucy wouldn't. She had on flannel pajamas, but her sleep sack was nothing more than a light blanket, essentially. Her face and hands were going to be freezing.

It dwells downstairs.

"Shut UP!" I growled.

I couldn't think too much about Fonda's opinion about the house—as it was just an opinion—at best—after all. I needed to put the matter aside until morning, when I would be able to consider it more intelligently. For now, Lucy and I both needed rest.

But it was so terribly cold.

Throwing a blanket over Lucy was out of the question. That was maybe what the house wanted me to do. Babies her age often tangled themselves—or worse—with their blankets.

I would just have to run downstairs for a quick few seconds—and keep an eye on Lucy with the video monitor. Yes—I'd set up the monitor on the bureau by the portable crib, and take the receiving end with me while I popped down to adjust the thermostat.

Once I had it set up, I kept my eyes on Lucy as I shuffled down the stairs.

When I got down to the living room, I hit the *override* button and quickly tapped the temperature up to 68 this time.

I turned my gaze back to the monitor.

Something flitted over Lucy. A shadow or a change in the light.

Swish. Right over her. Right over Lucy's bed.

I dropped the monitor and ran.

Up the stairs so quick and clumsy that I tripped over my foot when I got to the top, stepping on it sideways. I ran into the bedroom, feeling but ignoring a sharp pain along the side of my ankle, and swooped over the portable crib, grabbing Lucy and lifting her to my shoulder. She flopped into my upper arm, sucking her pacifier noisily. I took a deep breath.

We couldn't stay up here. Not with the "she" who liked to pass through here. Frances?

A few of Fonda's words flooded my head: *A window was recently opened. I don't think she's all that concerned about the baby.*

That was probably an understatement. How different was *unconcerned* from *spiteful toward*? Not enough for me. Not now. Why hadn't I packed up my and Lucy's things the moment Fonda left?

I clasped Lucy against my chest and headed for the stairs.

Two steps down and my ankle smarted. My socked foot slipped. I wobbled and clutched Lucy tight.

It dwells downstairs.

I took a deep breath, then sat on the third step. Moving farther down the stairs seemed too terrifying—too risky.

Innocent. Innocent. Innocent. Innocent.

Did I hear it? Did I hear that word repeated four times? Or was my brain saying it because it was so scared? *Innocent. Innocent . . .*

Shut up.

Shut up, please.

Should we sleep upstairs or downstairs tonight? I wondered.

Neither. How could I *sleep?*

But I *needed* to. I understood now. The house was keeping me from sleeping. It wanted me to slip and fall down the stairs, or drop Lucy, or worse. Let her poison herself while my eyes were closed.

It wouldn't be the first time, would it? Or—really—the second.

"Shut up. PLEASE."

Or else it *wanted* me to sleep, so it could tend to Lucy.

Shhhhh.

"Shut up!" I screamed.

One way or the other. Upstairs or downstairs. I was trapped. I hugged Lucy to my chest. My eyes stung. With tears? Or just exhaustion? I couldn't tell. It didn't seem to matter. Lucy blurred in front of me, so I gripped her little pajamas tighter.

"I'm tired," I whispered. "I'm so tired."

As soon as I let the words come out of my mouth, I thought of the dummy behind the upstairs wall. What was her name again? Split down the middle and across the waist. A broken and faceless mother, just waiting.

Lucy murmured, then opened her eyes. I stared down at them. They were big and brown—so brown I didn't know where they came from. Darker than Chad's or mine. Almost black, and exquisitely so. As beautiful and as foreign as the day she was born. For a second I thought I saw a sadness in them. It was a sadness that said, *You're really going to give up that easily?*

"No," I whispered to her. "Of course not."

I stared down the stairs. If I went down there and I heard the word "innocent," how badly could that hurt me? It hadn't seemed to hurt Fonda.

How long would it take me to get Lucy's things ready and get out of the house?

There were enough of her clothes in the dryer that I could just stuff those in a bag. I didn't need to go upstairs. Her diaper bag was on the counter by the door. Besides, things like diapers and baby food were available at the all-night CVS.

I took a deep breath and carried Lucy down the remaining stairs. After I'd turned on all the lights in my path, I brought her to her portable car carrier in the kitchen and buckled her in. Opening the dryer, I realized I was holding my breath. I let it out and held it again. I shoved all the onesies and pajamas—

along with Chad's white undershirts and a few of my things, as there was no time to sort—into a black garbage bag. I tossed that in front of the kitchen side door, along with the diaper bag. Then I looked for the keys.

The keys.

"Shit!"

When had I last left the house? It was a couple of days ago. I'd had the habit of leaving them in the ignition in my rush to get Lucy out sometimes—especially if she was crying when we arrived home. My crappy old Ford didn't have any fancy mechanism that screamed at you if you left the keys in, and I always left the doors unlocked for ease of loading Lucy and all of her accoutrements. The car was parked right in view of the kitchen—right next to its door on our narrow driveway. Really just a few steps away. I'd go and check, and while I was there, warm up the car. I slid on the mules I'd left in front of the door.

When I opened the door, I was stunned by the cold and by the bright white. There was an inch of snow already on the ground, and a flurry swirling around the doorstep. As the snow-flakes flew into my face, I remembered Fonda's words: *I want to get to the store while they still have bread on the shelves.* And Wallace saying, *We'll meet soon, I'm sure. Tomorrow might be out of the question, of course, but . . .* I had been too distracted to allow those words to really register. They'd been talking about a snowstorm. I didn't follow the news or the weather much these days. What was the point when I rarely left the baby bubble?

I shivered in my pajamas, then stepped down, careful not to slip. Then three steps to the car door and then opened it—*BANG!*

The door slammed behind me. The wind must have taken it.

Rather than run back up to open it, I sat in the car and reached for the ignition. But the keys weren't there. I ran back up the steps. Lucy was crying now—right behind the door. The slam must've wakened her.

"Damn," I said, and reached for the doorknob. It was freezing cold. And it was locked.

I jiggled it.

"No!" I whispered.

Lucy's screaming grew louder, more urgent. Could she see me through the glass? I pushed all of my weight against the door but knew it wouldn't be enough.

Could she see me through the glass? Or was she screaming for another reason? A reason I could not see from here?

Another reason.

Shhhhh!

"Shut up!" I screamed, realizing now how hard my heart was pounding.

I ran around to the front door even though I knew it was locked. I bounded up the steps and tried it anyway, pushing and pounding. From there, I could still hear Lucy screaming— just at a distance. The sound of it—muffled by the house and the snow—made my whole chest throb. I turned from the door and looked out onto the white street. The white sidewalk. The white lawn and front steps. A light wind blew snow into one of my ears. *Swish*.

White began to close in on me. For a moment, I thought it might blind me. I closed my eyes. In the dark behind my eyelids, the muffled screams went on and on into an aching infinity.

Chapter 52

Northampton Lunatic Hospital
Northampton, Massachusetts
December 21, 1885

How did you sleep, Harry?

Did you find your inn comfortable? Is it very far from here?

I did not sleep so well. One of my roommates was crying, as she tends to do on third or fourth nights. I do not know her well, as her English is poor and she works in the kitchen. But I believe there is someone she misses very deeply. That is what makes her weeping so difficult to bear. When I hear her, I invent ridiculous stories to attach to her tears—a dropped pie, a mouse-nibbled cake, a persistent and unmaskable mustache (and she does have a faint one, by the way). That way I can giggle at her rather than be sympathetic with her—*What a silly woman!*—just long enough to fool myself to sleep.

Occasionally, the trick does not work. Last night was one of those nights. After seeing you, I could not convince myself that there isn't a soul that I miss as painfully as that troubled weeper does.

Because there is such a soul.

And I worried, in the depths of the night, that I had imagined or dreamed your visit. I worried that when morning came, the nurses would deny you had ever been here. And then you would not appear ever again.

I made an agreement with my conscience, and it was this: If your visit proved real in the morning, and if you came again, I would tell you the absolute truth. For yesterday, I was not entirely truthful with you. And I was beginning to worry that my harsh penance might be that your presence had been a dream or delusion.

And so:

The arsenic, Harry. Its purpose was not entirely innocent. My intentions were innocent when I purchased it, I assure you. But in the weeks that it sat in my hope chest, more sinister possibilities grew like a persistent mold in the darkest, deepest folds of my brain.

Chapter 53

Haverton, Connecticut
December 19, 2014

I f I walked to a neighbor's house in my pajamas and got someone to call the police or help me pick my own lock or break down my own door—I might be blind by the time I actually got to Lucy. Blind and broken, as my heart now threatened to thrash itself into a bruised and bloody pulp.

I opened my eyes. I wasn't blind. But Lucy was still crying.

I rushed to the side of the house. I found the right window. The side window to the living room. That would have to be the one. I scanned the driveway and narrowed my gaze on the cheap driveway lights Chad had staked along its length. I pulled one up, slipping with the effort but managing to stay on my feet. It wasn't very long or very heavy, but it was metal and it was better than using my bare fist.

The sound of the glass breaking wasn't as loud as I'd have expected it to be. Maybe the snow muffled everything.

It took only two punches with the lamp to clear a big enough hole to reach up and unlock the window. I took off my sweatshirt and used it to sweep the broken glass from the windowsill. Then I put the sweatshirt onto the sill to protect myself from any leftover shards and hoisted myself over and into the house.

I ran to the kitchen and unbuckled Lucy from her car seat. I nursed her for a few minutes, ignoring the draft quickly coming into the kitchen from the gaping living room window. I felt vaguely aware of its cold, but insensitive—almost impervious—to it.

"I'm here," I whispered. "Mama would tear this whole house down, if she had to, to get to you. You know that, Lucy?"

My forearms seized with goose bumps. I folded the bottom half of my T-shirt over Lucy to give her an extra layer against the cold.

She quieted quickly. I buckled her back into the carrier, then lugged it to the coatrack. I put on my maternity coat, as that was the only winter coat I could find from the previous year. Then I checked the pockets of my fall jacket. The keys were there. It hadn't been as cold the last time I'd taken out the car.

I took the side door out, snapped Lucy's car seat into the backseat, and started the car.

As we backed out of the driveway and started out of our neighborhood, I let the heat run on full blast. Most of the lights on the other houses were out—but for a few doorstep and porch lights that gave the whole street a storybook glow.

"Victorian charm," I mumbled to myself, trying to regulate my breath and steady my grip on the wheel.

Snow flew at the window steadily, though not furiously. Driving into the dark tunnel of flakes—lit only by my high beams—felt like driving to another galaxy. I was glad of the sensation, putting great psychological distance between me and the house.

There wasn't yet enough snow on the ground for it to be treacherously slippery. All that was required was a little care—a little confidence.

"I'll manage," I assured Lucy, shouting over the noisy heater.

We arrived at the STOP sign to the main road. I turned down the heat a notch.

"It feels like everyone in the world is asleep," I said into the backseat. "Except you and me."

I turned right—toward the gas station. I could stop there to think about where to go next—rather than driving aimlessly in the snow.

When we reached it, mine was one of only three cars. A man came out of the gas station clutching a small package—cigarettes or gum, I guessed—and drove off. And then it was just me and Lucy and presumably the person tending the register in the store.

I listened to Lucy's thoughtful sucking on her pacifier. Glancing in the mirror, I saw she was wide awake. Wondering, perhaps, what was going to happen next. Nothing like this had happened in her life so far.

Snowflakes landed gently on the windshield.

I considered the wisdom that *No two are alike* and decided it was bullshit. How could we know that for certain, without looking at them all?

I wished I could stay here all night, turning the heat on and off, allowing the snow to hide Lucy and me from the world.

But it couldn't hide us. We were a mother and an infant

wearing pajamas in an old Ford at a gas station in the snow. We'd be a troubling sight if we lingered here too long. We weren't allowed to be invisible. I was more visible now than I'd been before Lucy, and would be until she was about twenty-one.

I was not allowed to sit here and wonder about the fucking snowflakes. Except maybe to consider their cold, and to calculate how many layers of clothing Lucy needed as a result of their falling.

Lucy's sucking intensified.

"I *do* love you," I said. My hand, however, refused to start the car.

I turned from the windshield and stared out the side window. My own reflection greeted me. Dull eyes sunken into purple shadows, American Gothic sort of hairstyle, ragged pajama T-shirt stretched and sloppy around my collarbones. I was exactly the sort of mother you'd expect to find parked outside of a gas station on a night like this.

As I turned from the window, I thought of Frances's words: *Is all of the light to come from me?*

It stunned me to think of them—as I'd skimmed right over them the first time I'd seen them—looking then for more details about Martha and the attempted murder.

Now they scared me perhaps more than anything in that journal. Now I could relate to them.

I started the car. There was only one motel in Haverton—the Candlelight Inn. It had a reputation of being a bit outdated, a bit dingy. But I'd never heard of anything bad happening there, or any reports of rats or cockroaches. A more reputable chain hotel somewhere out of town would be better, but that would mean more driving in the snow. And I was too tired for that.

Chapter 54

Northampton Lunatic Hospital
Northampton, Massachusetts
December 21, 1885

The purpose that developed was suicide. I will be direct about that now, Harry. The notion grew in my heart and in my hope chest in the weeks after the initial purchase. That was, as you'll remember, the same time I realized I was pregnant. In truth, I wondered if my body and mind could endure another ordeal like the one Martha's birth had caused me. I would, in those weeks, sometimes open the chest and lift the package and consider its possibilities, should I grow more desperate. Probably those thoughts were rarely serious, as there was Martha's future to consider. But occasionally, I must admit, they were most sincere. For what good was a deranged mother to Martha? Another pregnancy—at least so soon—was therefore frightening to think of. Try to understand that, Harry.

This fear dissipated when I lost the pregnancy. And after I observed Rosa Hayden—the very next day—a clarity and resolve took its place. The resolve was the one I spoke of yesterday. Do you remember? Allow me to return to that point. It might help you, ultimately, to understand the despair that preceded it.

That resolve blossomed on my second or third night home from that final December trip to New Haven. I rose after Matthew had fallen asleep. By the gaslight, I hemmed the emerald-green Christmas dress I'd begun for Martha. And as I stitched, I tried to focus my mind on this question: When, precisely, had my own mental weakness begun? If I wished not to be like Rosa Hayden, I had to try to examine this matter in detail. I had always been odd. And I'd always known this but had been relatively skilled at keeping it mostly to myself. When had I lost my skill for that? When, specifically, had I become *confused*?

The green dress was beautiful, with white satin ribbons I'd sewn carefully across the bodice. I do not think I was pretending when I fancied how beautiful Martha would look in it—and anticipated how the color would bring out the sylvan spirit of her eyes.

The beauty of it—and my pride in it and my love for its recipient—belied what my mind could no longer deny. My mind's troubles had begun in the late spring of the previous year. They had begun early in my first pregnancy. That is, in my pregnancy with Martha.

It seemed important to determine whether it was *knowledge* of the pregnancy, or the physical effect of it, that had started all of the difficulty. Had the very physical condition weakened my body and mind? Or had my sullen character simply rebelled against the condition, falling into despair at what should have been my greatest joy?

And what of that summer night when I had thrown that goblet and it had damaged Matthew's leg? What of *that* night?

I had not known yet that I was pregnant on that night. In fact, I believe the unsteadiness I felt that evening was my first sign.

Frances. Frances, did you hear me?

I'd stood by myself in the kitchen, ignoring Matthew's request.

I asked you to come here. I asked you to bring me a glass of water.

I was steadying myself on the sideboard, as I'd never felt so light-headed before. What were these colored lights in front of my face? Was this heaven calling me home? As I righted myself and the colors disappeared, I considered what could make a woman feel this way so suddenly, at my age and station.

Had I calculated my condition in that moment and become immediately enraged? Enraged at myself, or at Matthew, or perhaps at the certainty I would die in childbirth?

Frances! Are you daydreaming in there?

Had I felt enraged, or simply doomed, when that goblet left my hand? One or the other, but leave my hand it did.

Frances! What in God's name!

Later we spoke of how light-headed I had been. And it was true that I felt light-headed that evening. I felt the sensation in the moment in the kitchen just before I threw the goblet. And again in the later moments in the parlor, tending Matthew's cuts. But perhaps not in the moments in between. Perhaps not in the moment the goblet left my grasp. That moment had a fierceness to it that had nothing to do with light-headedness.

The cuts were not so terribly bad. When I suggested that he might need Dr. Graham's attention, Matthew said, *Nonsense. It will heal.*

A week later—or perhaps a bit more—I saw him still favoring one foot. I urged him to reconsider, and he said that he would.

I'll go consult with him tomorrow, so you won't worry. And I won't tell him how I sustained it. I'll tell him I dropped the goblet myself. Is that agreeable to you, my darling?

By then I was fairly certain of my condition. I had told him that very day—and he was treating me delicately.

I wondered much, in those days, and in the days after Martha's accident, if he'd kept his promise. I doubted he had.

Now, in the aftermath of Rosa Hayden's tears, it seemed I ought to determine precisely the significance of my doubt. Whom had he told? What had he told them? And why?

Chapter 55

Haverton, Connecticut
December 19, 2014

I was inside the house. Lucy was safe. There was snow on the ankles of my pajama bottoms, melting into tiny puddles around my feet.

Cold air rushed through the hole in the living room window, so I held Lucy to my chest. I pulled my cardigan around her, but it was too thin to provide much warmth for either of us.

The rest of the window was covered in snow, but through the hole in the glass I could see outside. There it was not snowing at all. In fact, our driveway looked like a beach. And as I stepped closer to the hole in the window, I could hear the sound of its waves.

Swish. Shush. Swish.

There was a woman standing there in the sand. She was wearing a black skirt and cable-knit gray sweater. It didn't matter that she had no face and no legs, or that she was broken down the middle and across the waist. I knew who she was. She'd worn those clothes at the wake.

Swish. A gentle wave of water swept over the driveway, wetting only her pedestal bottom. When it receded, it left a single seashell next to her on the driveway.

I woke up with a gasp and glanced at the clock next to the bed: 2:49.

At least Lucy was still sleeping beside me. I pulled her to the very middle of the bed and curled around her. On her other side, I checked the positioning of two stiff motel pillows I'd rigged to keep her from possibly rolling off, then pulled the spongy nylon blanket halfway up her body to warm her.

As I closed my eyes, my mind went back to the gray cable-knit sweater that Wendy's mother was wearing at the wake.

You might not have known this about Wendy, dear. She almost died from her anorexia before she came to college. Her organs were still very weak—her heart was still weak. She couldn't handle those pills like a stronger girl might have. Even if you'd found her earlier—hours earlier—there's probably nothing that could've been done.

She'd clasped my hand in her cold palms as she'd said it, and I had not been able to move my gaze above her sweater and onto her face. Even if I'd managed it, the memorial service was not the time or the place to confess that Wendy had *told* me that she'd been anorexic. It was, in fact, something Wendy was not at all shy about telling. She'd told me on our second night living in that room together.

Nor was it the time or place to mention that I'd always been a little put off by how much Wendy seemed to enjoy explaining to me how troubled she was. I had had friends like that in high school, who seemed to want to compete about whose parents' divorce was nastier or who'd had sex the earliest, or who was really bulimic and who just threw up occasionally for sport. Probably I was like that, too, if we were going to be completely honest about it. But I was in college now and I was *over* that shit. I was smarter than that, and I expected the same of anyone who wanted to be my friend. And Wendy *could* maybe be my friend if she'd just quit embarrassing herself.

No, the wake had not seemed the right place to confess any of that.

Or that Wendy did talk that last night—rather casually, but not for the first time—about wanting to take a pill or a bullet that would make her disappear.

Or that I'd said, *Maybe you need to talk to someone, Wendy.*

And she'd said, *My parents have already made me talk to lots of someones and lots of no ones. The someones they make you talk to are all no ones, really. Because they don't care about you. Not really. They're paid to care and then they say your time is up and then they go home. You know what it means when a person says, "Maybe you should talk to someone?" It means "Maybe you should talk to someone that's not me."*

Well, what do you want me to say, Wendy?

I don't know, Abby.

I'm just trying to help.

Well, aren't you nice?

Maybe you'll feel better if you get some sleep.

Maybe.

Can I turn out the light now, Wendy?

Sure, I guess.

Nor did the wake seem the right time or place to confess that those were the last words I ever spoke to Wendy—unless you counted the words I'd said to her dead body in the morning.

You'll actually feel better if you get up and get your ass to class.

Or at least take a shower and have a little breakfast and see how you feel.

Not knowing that she was dead, of course. Not knowing till the afternoon, when I opened that door and found her curled in the exact same position, knobby knee sticking out of the lilac afghan.

Turned out she had sleeping pills and painkillers and some peppermint schnapps to wash it all down. I had no idea where a person our age even got pills like that. I had no idea where in the room she kept them.

She was smarter than me. Way smarter. I was not such hot shit after all.

I had been a vile young adult. There was no way around that. My parents had tried to raise me right, and Wendy's parents had presumably tried the same, as they seemed nice people—and still we'd ended up in a room together, one of us dying rather casually and the other ignoring her to death.

It had seemed like there should be a time and place to confess all of that someday. All of that and a thing or two more. But of course the opportunity never presented itself. I never saw Wendy's mother again. Why would I? Unless I sought her out.

Which I hadn't.

And yet—I hadn't demanded much of life after Wendy because I knew little—if anything—was owed to me. I spent my life in the presence of privileged adolescent girls, and I listened as best I could to their endlessly erratic emotions because that was approximately what I deserved.

I wasn't such hot shit. But a decade and a half passed, and I'd started to forget that. And then look what I had gone and done. Who exactly did I think I was? I had birthed a beautiful child who would grow up, and whom I'd send out into a world of young adults no better than the one I had been. And I would deserve nothing better. Lucy might. But I wouldn't—no matter how much I loved her. Loving her could only make my punishment and penance more painful when it finally came.

I traced a gentle circle on the flannel back of Lucy's pajamas and buried my face in my pillow. I cried until my eyes were too sore to produce any more tears. My body screamed for sleep, but I forced my eyes to stay open.

Why had I ever thought I deserved to sleep?

Chapter 56

Northampton Lunatic Hospital
Northampton, Massachusetts
December 21, 1885

I had several stops planned in this investigation of my memory.
A visit to Dr. Graham was easily arranged. I simply requested a consultation about Martha's vomiting. And Martha *did* vomit frequently. During my "rest," my milk had dried up while Clara fed her Mellin's baby food. The substitution never seemed to agree with her stomach—nor did cow's milk, which I had tried recently as an alternative. I wasn't alarmed for Martha's health as she was growing steadily enough despite the occasional problems. Still, it seemed a reasonable excuse for a consultation.

After we discussed the possibility of goat milk, I made strategic small talk as I bundled Martha for the walk home.

"Her scar has healed nicely, hasn't it?"

"Oh. Oh, yes. I wasn't worried about it. It didn't require many stitches. Good to be cautious, though, with a young girl's face."

"Of course. Matthew was certainly more cautious with her than he was with himself."

"With himself?"

"When his leg was so badly cut . . . from that broken goblet."

"I don't recall that."

"Around the same time I asked you to confirm my pregnancy. So, now, some time ago. Quite well over a year."

"I believe Matthew may have seen another doctor for that. Maybe he saw someone in New Haven. That was the time of the McFarlene business, wasn't it?"

"Oh . . . I'm not sure. My memory is so hazy when it comes to things before the birth. But I was fairly certain he saw you. Not right after he got cut, but some days later. That's why it hurt him so much."

"I've never given sutures to your Matthew."

"Oh. Are you sure?"

"My dear, I've known Matthew for nearly his whole life. Why wouldn't I be sure?"

"Of course, Dr. Graham. Excuse me."

"Do try to follow my instructions for Martha. And come for another consultation if she doesn't improve in a week."

"Thank you, Doctor."

You see, Harry—I was afraid to mention it to the doctor before that point. I suspected, from the mess I'd seen on my husband's leg, that he never made it to any doctor—though he had told me he had seen Dr. Graham. But he had not seen him—or probably any doctor—because he did not wish to implicate or embarrass me. That was the harsh truth I'd been avoiding when I'd avoided the question in the past.

My husband was simultaneously ashamed and protective of me, his crazy wife. He spoke of me—and treated me in public—as one would the wife of my journal. The effusive one, who loved cakes.

He knew, though, that I was not that wife.

I knew, too, what I was not.

I was not afraid of the truth.

Chapter 57

Haverton, Connecticut
December 20, 2014

L ucy slept late—through most of the chirpy morning shows I kept on low volume as I huddled under the covers and longed for coffee.

When she finally woke up, she nursed for a good long time. As Lucy sucked, I tried to recall when my last decent meal had been and wondered from where she was drawing her nutrition. Probably the fatty parts of my brain, I decided. A few more days and it would be wizened down to just my lizard brain.

I found a package of banana baby food in my diaper bag, propped Lucy up on some pillows, and started feeding it to her. After two spoonfuls, my cell phone rang.

"Well!" said Wallace after I muttered a lethargic hello. "Since that storm wasn't all they were making it out to be, any chance you'll be out and about today? Any chance you'll stop by the historical society? If it's more convenient for you, I could stop by your place to pick up Dr. Graham's journal. I'm about to get coffee myself."

"I'm not at my house," I mumbled. "I'm at the Candlelight Inn."

"*What?* Is everything okay?" Wallace hesitated. "Where is your husband?"

"He's in Chicago on business this week."

"And that somehow led you to . . . the Candlelight Inn?"

Lucy yelped for more banana.

"No." I kept spooning the puree into Lucy's mouth. "Not exactly. There was an incident with a . . . broken window. Last night. At my house."

"You and Lucy are all right, I hope."

I took a hungry half-spoonful of the banana myself. "Yes."

"What happened?"

"I'm not sure," I said. "I heard the glass breaking in the middle of the night. I wasn't sure if it was something from the storm or . . ."

"There wasn't a terribly strong wind, I didn't think."

"Exactly. So I was worried it might be some intruder, trying to get in . . . someone throwing something. With Chad's car gone, maybe they thought . . ."

"Oh, dear."

"Yeah, so . . . I didn't feel safe staying there alone with Lucy, in any case. I know this isn't the nicest place, but it was between here and driving out of town in the snow."

"How terrible for you! Well, in that case, you *must* let me bring you some coffee. You're just a mile from where I get my morning fix, anyhow. A doughnut or a muffin? Lucy is too small for doughnuts yet, right?"

"Did you find this place comfortable?" Wallace asked, handing me a large coffee. "Sugar? Cream? I got some extras for you since I don't know what you like."

"Thanks," I said, deciding I'd ignore his original question unless he repeated it. I'd tidied up to make the whole setup look less desperate than it was—straightened the bedcovers and shoved the garbage bag full of baby laundry in the closet.

I placed my coffee on the tippy motel table in front of him and poured two sugars into it. After a long sip, I felt my brain shuddering back to life.

"This place has been around since I was in high school," Wallace said. "It wasn't called the Candlelight Inn, then. It was called Sweetly's Motel, and my mother always claimed that only prostitutes stayed here."

"Was it true? Haverton prostitutes?"

"I don't know. I wasn't an enterprising enough young man to verify it for myself."

"Uh huh." I took another sip of coffee.

"But the Candlelight folks cleaned the place up a bit when they bought it twenty some-odd years ago."

I nodded.

"It's a shame you had to leave your house." Wallace arranged a few doughnuts on a couple of napkins on the table. "I hope you called the police—if you really think there was some kind of potential intruder."

I shrugged and drank some more coffee. "Oh, I don't know."

"Don't know what? Don't know if you called the police?"

"I didn't," I admitted. "I think it was something to do with the storm outside—something hitting the window. I was just spooked, is all. I needed to be somewhere Lucy and I could rest."

"Which you couldn't do with a broken hole in your house and snow flying in."

"Exactly." I took a bite of doughnut, staring at his hands, clasped in a neat bridge between his knees. I couldn't read his expression. We both watched Lucy, who was lying on her tummy on a couple of blankets, gnawing on a board book.

"I had a medium come to my house yesterday," I said.

Maybe if I'd managed a few more sips of coffee before this moment, I'd have had the presence of mind *not* to make this confession. But part of me felt compelled to share this with someone.

Wallace stiffened in his chair and put down his coffee cup. "Oh?"

"Yeah," I said.

"Where did you find this medium? Someone you know?"

"No. I found her online."

Wallace looked away, rearranging the position of the napkinful of doughnuts on the table. "Did she have any insights for you?"

"Yes. Several. She seemed to think my house has a ghostly presence. Or maybe two."

"That's what they're paid to do. And two gives you something to choose from, based on your preconceived idea."

"She doesn't charge anything. She does it to help people."

"Do you feel she helped you?"

"Um. Wallace, I really appreciate your concern. But this conversation is getting a little too Socratic for me a little too quickly."

Lucy began to fuss on the floor. I put down my doughnut.

"Why don't you let me pick her up?" Wallace said. "So you can finish your coffee. Would that be agreeable to her, you think?"

"Sure," I said, shrugging. "Try it."

Wallace scooped up Lucy and settled her on his knee, opening the board book for her to look at the first page.

"Why, that's a caterpillar," he informed Lucy. "I have a grand-daughter that's just about a year older than you. How about that?"

"I didn't know that," I said. "What's her name?"

"Scarlet. I don't see her that much. She lives near Phila-delphia."

I nodded.

"So," Wallace said, turning a page of Lucy's book. "Since you brought it up, is there anything this medium said that you wished to talk about?"

"What she said confirmed what I've been experiencing in the house. I'll say that much."

Wallace sighed. Lucy stared at him, then began to cough out brief, uncertain little sobs. I took her from Wallace and gave her a pacifier. She probably wanted milk, but I didn't want to make Wallace any more uncomfortable than he clearly already was.

"How much did you tell her about what you're . . . experiencing?" Wallace asked. "Before she confirmed it?"

"Nothing," I said. "I was very careful."

"I see," Wallace said quietly.

Lucy and I gazed at each other for a minute or two. I loved those black alien eyes. When she was sixteen and spoke to me in full sentences and sentiments, would they seem any less enigmatic?

"You can't stay here with Lucy for long." Wallace paused. "I wouldn't think."

"Of course not," I said. "I just needed to rest."

Wallace stood up with another sigh that I couldn't interpret. I thought for a moment that he might be getting ready to leave.

"Weren't you going to show me Frances's journal?" he asked. "The business about the missing pages?"

"I don't have it with me."

"I don't suppose you have Dr. Graham's log, either."

"No."

"Hmm. Well, do I recall correctly that you said these missing pages were right before that final entry?"

"Yes."

"Shame you don't have it with you. I didn't think much of it at the time, but now that you mention this . . . that last page where she wrote those rather cryptic things about arsenic amounts. Did you notice anything odd about it?"

"Umm . . . aside from the fact that it was flat-out *diabolical* in its tone?"

"Yes. Something more mundane than that. Did you notice anything?"

After a moment's thought, I told Wallace about how, in her final entry, Frances stopped using titles like *Reverend* and *Mr.*

Wallace sucked in his lower lip. "Huh. I hadn't noticed that. But *that's* interesting, too. No, what I noticed was so subtle I hesitate to bring it up. I didn't think much of it until you mentioned on the phone about the missing page. I thought the ink on the final page was just *slightly* darker than on the ones before it. Maybe Frances had gotten a new fountain pen and ink for Christmas? I don't know. Maybe the page before it—she messed up the page, ripped it out, and started over?"

"Or wrote something terrible about her intentions, thought

better of it, ripped it out, and wrote it a little more cryptically,"
I suggested.

"Why on earth would she do that? That assumes she thought
someone was reading her journal. And even if she did, she didn't
do a great job of covering her intentions. She still did, as you
say, sound a tad diabolical."

"At least I've gotten you to admit *that*."

"Have you contacted Gerard Barnett yet?" Wallace asked.
"Asked him if he knows anything of the missing pages?"

"No," I admitted. "I doubt he'll have anything to say about it,
but I'll call him today."

"Hmmph. If I believed more firmly in these things, I'd say
you should ask your psychic about those pages. Maybe she'd
have a theory."

"Fonda and I didn't talk about the journal."

"Fonda? That's her name?"

"Yes."

Wallace rubbed one of his eyes vigorously. "Did you talk to
her about Frances at all?"

I stood up with Lucy and brought her to the mirror at the
back of the room, by the sink. She grinned at her reflection
while I watched Wallace. He kept his hands on his kneecaps,
jouncing them slightly.

"No," I said. "I waited to see if she came up with anything
that sounded like Frances."

"And did she?"

"Vaguely. She said that there was a female presence upstairs.
Sometimes. That she comes in and out."

"Ooh." Wallace reached for his coffee. "At her own bidding?
Like through a sort of ghostly cat flap, or some such?"

"She didn't specify about the exact apparatus at all, no."

"Does she go downstairs?"

"I don't think so. There's a different energy downstairs, she said." I continued to watch Wallace in the mirror. From where I was standing, I couldn't tell if his little smile was amused or nervous. "It just keeps saying the same word four times over."

"Did she say *what* word?"

"Of course she did. *Innocent.*"

"Innocent?"

"*Innocent innocent innocent innocent,*" I said.

Wallace's eyes snapped, studying me more intently. The smile fell from his face.

"What is it, Wallace?"

Wallace crossed his arms. "You're joking."

"Uh . . . no." I whirled around and looked at Wallace directly. Lucy gasped in protest. "If I were joking, I'd have told you a funnier word. Like *carbuncle.*"

Wallace shook his head. "Who is this woman? Is she from Haverton?"

"She's local. But she lives in Hamden."

"She's scamming you. What does she look like?"

"Does it matter? You don't know her, do you? Fonda Manning?"

"No, I don't know her. But . . . Can you come to the society house? I'd like to show you something."

Chapter 58

Northampton Lunatic Hospital
Northampton, Massachusetts
December 21, 1885

I f indeed I was not afraid of the truth, then there was no
sense in delaying my next investigative move.

Frederick Baines. Once-incessant bearer of pumpkins and
cabbages. Why had he stopped? Why did we no longer see him?
It seemed I'd never seen him after Martha's birth, but too often
I used that event as a marker that, in fact, meant nothing to
anyone else. Was it *truly* at that point that we'd stopped seeing
him? Or was that simply, coincidentally, when my memory had
begun to cloud?

I remembered distinctly, however, that in the early sickness
of the pregnancy, I had had to find a purpose for three whole
cabbages that he had brought. How I hated the stink of cabbage boiling, and it made my nausea infinitely worse. I'd cursed
Frederick and his cabbages, and wondered what sense it made
that he brought them to *us*. He was a single man, yes, but a man
of slender means and likely a friend to many families who could
use a spare cabbage. I felt guilty cursing him, and yet, how my
stomach ached! I could scarcely help the gripes spitting from
my mouth.

Confounded cabbage!
Infernal vegetable!
Thankfully, Matthew was not present, so I could holler to my heart's content.

Where was Matthew on that late-autumn evening?

Of course. He was in New Haven. For the hanging. I'd ironed his best suit for him and waved to him from our doorstep, at a loss for what words a good wife says to her husband on the eve of such an occasion.

So yes. That was the last time we saw Frederick—a day or two before Matthew left for the hanging. Frederick had not knocked on the door but simply stood outside by the fence until I noticed him out the window and sent Matthew out to see what he wanted. It seemed to me the exchange over the cabbages was brusque. And I wondered why Matthew had pressed upon Frederick a small amount of money for cabbages for which we most certainly had not asked. Would not this only encourage him to bring more cabbages?

I didn't point this out to Matthew as he was already anxious about his upcoming engagement in New Haven.

Well-meaning fellow. Let's not encourage him, though. Try not to converse with him much if he comes by while I'm gone.

I agreed—simply because I didn't wish for any more cabbage. But Frederick did *not* come by that weekend while Matthew was gone. I don't recall wondering about it for some time after that. After all, I was slowly preparing to die—so of what consequence was the odd little man who used to appear with pumpkins and cabbages?

I could not say of what consequence he was, could I, until I'd spoken to him myself? Rosa Hayden would perhaps turn her head and nurse her babies and her birth wounds and never think of it again. But I was not Rosa Hayden.

On the day following my appointment with Dr. Graham, I wrapped Martha in several blankets, tucked her into the carriage, and headed up Wiggins Hill.

The sky was a menacingly dull white—milky, like a blind man's eye. The hill's many maples creaked their discontent at the cold. I pulled my scarf over my mouth and nose and pushed the carriage forward as fast as I could—as if to outpace the chill.

I had to walk past the McFarlene cabin to get to the place where Frederick and his brother stayed. I knew which was the McFarlene place because Louise had convinced me to come up this way long ago to gawk at the place where a man had died—at its broken-down fence, its worn women, and its notorious woodpile.

One of the yard chickens seemed to stare at me accusingly.

I beg your pardon? I said to her, more to calm my nerves than anything else.

As the chicken shifted her gaze downward and pecked, I noticed that she was not the only one who had heard me. There was movement at the side of the yard. A woman was feeding additional chickens there.

Are you all right, ma'am? the young woman said, coming toward me.

Yes.

I was startled—not only by her presence, but by the red of her hair. She was one of the women who sometimes stared at me in church.

She was equally startled to see my face. I knew then that she knew who I was. She had always known. I was Mrs. Matthew Barnett.

It's a cold day to be out walking with such a small child.

I could not tell if this was a rebuke or a simple statement of fact. Her expression was flat, her eyes unblinking. This was either John McFarlene's young widow, or her sister-in-law. I'd heard through Louise that they lived together now.

Yes.

Can I help you find something? Someone?

I realized that I was reluctant to say I was looking for Frederick Baines. Wouldn't that look strange? Hadn't it always been strange—that Matthew had associated with him at all? Even in the odd and dusky hours that he'd shown up near our house. It had only been two or three times, really. And that perhaps made it even more odd.

Sometimes I like to see unfamiliar parts of town. Simply for the sake of seeing something different from the same old sights.

Your daughter is so small. The sight she loves best is probably still you.

Oh, I don't know . . .

In my surprise, I could think of no response. My feet, instinctually, began to take me away from this woman, even though my heart knew how graceless it was to do so.

Good day to you! I called behind me.

She didn't reply—at least, not audibly.

I quickened my step. I pushed the carriage toward Frederick Baines's place.

Chapter 59

Wallace flipped through a file cabinet while I settled Lucy on the floor on the towels I had borrowed from the motel.

"Abby." Wallace swept the cabinet closed, holding an overstuffed file above his head like a pizza pie. "I'm going to preface what I'm about to show you by saying that my exhibit about the McFarlene murder was *very* popular. I believe I mentioned to you that I did this particular exhibit about two years ago?"

"I think so."

"Here we are." He pulled out a desk chair for me. "This was among the many articles and photos I had on display during that month."

Wallace thrust an old newspaper article—covered in a plastic protector—into my hands.

MCFARLENE HANGED

APPROACHED THE DEATH CHAMBER CALMLY, EXECUTION CARRIED OUT WITHOUT INCIDENT

NEW HAVEN, Nov. 16, 1878–John McFarlene was hanged at the State Prison at 12:15 this morning for the murder of his brother-in-law, Walter Beck, in June in Haverton.

McFarlene maintained a stolid demeanor as four prison guards escorted him to the death chamber. He was also accompanied by his spiritual counsel, Rev. Richard Gilbert.

When asked for his final words, McFarlene said:

"Innocent, innocent, innocent, innocent. What does the word mean, gentlemen? I do not claim to be sinless, but neither can my persecutors. Remember me on the day of your own death, and ask yourself in the presence of God if you are truly more virtuous than me."

The trap was sprung at 12:15. John McFarlene was declared dead at 12:27.

Twenty-one men witnessed the hanging, including the prison wardens, McFarlene's spiritual counsel, three newspapermen, and several lawyers from both the prosecution and defense sides of McFarlene's trial in August.

"He said 'innocent' four times?" I dropped the article and put my hand on my aching middle. I could picture my coffee curdling in my stomach.

"Yes. Indeed he did. It's rather puzzling. He said 'innocent' several times and then essentially admitted he was guilty. Then he added that the people hanging him were guilty as well, just for good measure. Everybody's guilty, really. I've always found that an interesting thought to go out on. A lot of the visitors to my exhibit seemed to feel the same way."

"Oooh," Lucy said. She'd commando-crawled her way to the edge of her towel and was examining the historic dirt between the old wooden floorboards.

"Well . . ." I pulled Lucy back onto a towel and gave her my plastic hair clip to examine. "I suppose I agree . . ."

"I do what I think will be my most popular exhibits in October," Wallace explained. "At the same time as the Pumpkin Harvest Days, and in June, for the Strawberry Festival Fair. I very deliberately did my McFarlene exhibit two Octobers ago. That sort of thing—murder and hanging and such, I mean—draws people in from the town green. Lots of names for the guest book. Justifies the small budget needed to keep the place open."

"I see."

"The McFarlene exhibit was one of the most popular I've ever done."

"Really?" I pushed my hair behind my ears, hoping Wallace didn't notice how greasy it probably looked. I couldn't remember when I'd had my last shower.

"Some of the Haverton High kids came in here and did an extra-credit project for their shop class. Built a sort of gallows on the front lawn to draw people in. I'm not proud of that. I'm really not. But I like to keep this place open, and Pumpkin Harvest Days is my sweeps week, so to speak."

Wallace planted his elbows on his knees and grasped his hands together. "My point is . . . a *lot* of people came in and saw that exhibit. And see this glass display case?"

"Yeah?" I looked where he was pointing. It had a couple of old quilts hanging in it.

"I had 'Innocent, innocent, innocent, innocent' written in big letters across the top."

"Oh," I said. I wondered why Wallace didn't tell me that from the beginning. "You're saying you think Fonda Manning saw your exhibit?"

"Doesn't that seem reasonable?"

I shrugged. "Umm . . . she didn't seem like a historical society kind of lady. I mean, not to be snooty. But if you'd met her—"

"The Pumpkin Harvest crowd is not an academic crowd. It's a candy-apple, caramel-corn, and wool-sweater sort of affair."

"Again," I said. "Not to put anyone in a box, but Fonda didn't seem like the sort who'd even be into *that*."

"Nonsense. Who doesn't like candy apples and caramel corn? Even if she didn't see the actual display, it's quite possible she heard about it."

I wondered which of us was more pathetic—me insisting my psychic was legit, or Wallace wanting his dusty little historical society display to have been so influential that people in surrounding towns were chatting about it in their spare time.

"Possible." I took issue with *quite* possible, but I could give him *possible*. "But how could she know I lived in Matthew Barnett's *house*?"

"You gave her your address when you called her, did you not? And then how long between your first call and her visit?"

"Less than two days."

"But almost two days?"

"Well . . . yes."

"Plenty of time to research the history of a house."

"But where would she have done that besides . . . the Haverton Historical Society? Has anyone been in here in the last week?"

Wallace narrowed his eyes at me. "Zillow, for starters. It wouldn't have been hard to figure out that your house was sold just a few years ago by the Barnett family."

"Wallace . . ." I sighed.

"Yes, Abby?"

He'd been so kind to me, I didn't want to hurt his feelings. "Well . . . including but not limited to people who saw your Pumpkin Harvest display . . . how well known would you say the McFarlene murder is around here?"

Wallace shrugged. "It's hard to say. I know a lot of townies and history buffs. Among the general populace, however . . . I'd guess not very."

I nodded. "Well, in any case, maybe I ought to learn more about it. Can you set me up with more of those McFarlene articles? I'd like to educate myself a little more. I know Matthew Barnett was one of the lawyers, but it might help to get some more details."

"Certainly." Wallace put a careful hand on his desk, close to mine, but not touching it. "But . . . what have we decided about Fonda?"

Lucy grunted at my hair clip, which was just out of her reach now. I pushed it back to her. "Were we deciding something about her?"

"Weren't we?"

"Not yet, I don't think. I'll probably want to see her once more before I decide anything."

Wallace sighed and flipped through his plastic sheet protectors.

"Well. There's a lot of repetition in some of the news coverage. But here is the first article about Walter Beck's death."

BODY FOUND IN HAVERTON WOODS

HAVERTON, June 2, 1878–The body of Walter Beck of Northbury Road was found in the east part of the Haverton woods. It was brought back to his home and there examined by coroner Henry Matson, who determined the cause of death to be murder by bludgeoning. His brother-in-law John McFarlene, with whom Beck recently had a known dispute, has been arrested by constable Robert Young.

"Okay," I said, setting down the article.

"Later articles will reveal, and much was made in the trial, of how McFarlene's sister was probably being beaten by her husband, which is likely why she took refuge with her brother. It seems like the defense didn't know what to do with that information. Because it made McFarlene more sympathetic, but at the same time helped build the case for his guilt. Anyway, before all of that—here's an article about the first hearing."

MCFARLENE TO BE TRIED–PUNISHMENT BY HANGING WILL BE SOUGHT

THE HEARING IN NEW HAVEN–SURPRISE EVIDENCE PRESENTED ON THE THIRD DAY

NEW HAVEN, June 18, 1878–Surprising evidence was brought forth on the final day of the hearing regarding the death of Walter Beck of Haverton, who was found dead on June 2.

Josephine Beck, wife of the deceased and sister of the accused, was lodging with John McFarlene and his wife Victoria the week of the murder. According to the Becks' neighbor Nora Cromwell, of Northbury Road, Josephine confessed to her that very week that her husband had committed a brutal act upon her, and was probably staying with her brother out of fear of further harm. Josephine, however, denied Mrs. Cromwell's claims.

Both Josephine Beck and Victoria McFarlene deny that John McFarlene ever left his home on the night of June 1. George Dover, of Wiggins Hill, however, was walking home from Dickerson's Tavern that night, and says he saw John McFarlene walking home, limping slightly, and with blood on his shirt. He asked John what the trouble was, and John replied that he was chasing a fox away from his chickens–but gave no explanation for the blood or the limp. George's wife Katherine claimed to have heard men yelling in the distance about an hour earlier than her husband's arrival home.

When questioned, Clarence Morris, his wife Sarah, and their two children—all also of Wiggins Hill, and in closer proximity to the McFarlene home—said that they heard no disturbance that night.

Frederick Baines, of Alsbury Road, recently gave the constable three pieces of firewood he said he had received from John McFarlene as barter for vegetables. Mr. Baines noticed several dark red stains on them just four days earlier, when he was setting to burn them.

Constable Young and Coroner Matson suspected the stains were made from blood.

The presence of possible bloodstains on the transported firewood might not have been considered stellar evidence in and of itself—had it not led investigators back to the McFarlenes' woodpile for further investigation. There they found several more stained logs and, crammed between two pieces of wood, a bloodstained shirt.

The wood and shirt were promptly given to a Yale scientist by the name of Benedict Tipley. He examined the stains and determined that they were made by blood—very likely human blood.

"The corpuscles were all between 1/2,800 and 1/3,200. The human range is between 1/2,700 and 1/3,800," he said to the hushed courtroom. "I was able to examine them yesterday evening, in my laboratory. All of the examinable corpuscles were in human range."

This was the first piece of physical evidence in a hearing that has mostly been taken up by conflicting accounts of the night of June 1 by Haverton residents, particularly residents living on or near Wiggins Hill.

Judge Mitchell Dunham determined that the case should go to trial. Proceedings are expected to begin next month.

"Okay," I said. "Wow. This was probably a very big deal for quiet little Haverton."

"Yes. Nothing as big as the Mary Stannard trial. It didn't have quite that level of sex and scandal. But yes . . . for Haverton. And presumably for Matthew Barnett. A young lawyer from town. His first big case. The main counsel was a seasoned New Haven lawyer, of course. But still. Here's a taste of Barnett's prosecutorial duties. He didn't get to question any of the key witnesses."

Wallace handed me another article, titled "McFarlene trial continues. Last two witnesses testify for the prosecution."

Wallace ran his finger down the long article and tapped at the start of a paragraph about halfway down. "Matthew questioned this tavern witness, if memory serves."

I read a few paragraphs of the article:

Robert Carpenter, a Haverton resident and frequenter of Dickerson's tavern, said he spoke with Walter Beck on the very night he was murdered.

Matthew Barnett, assistant to Prosecutor Oliver Knowles, took up the questioning for this witness.

"Approximately what time did you see Walter Beck at the tavern, Mr. Carpenter?"

"I believe it was about ten o'clock."

"And did he socialize with you?"

"Yes, sir. He was quite eager to talk, and I happened to be sitting close to him."

"Why was he eager to talk? About anything in particular?"

"Oh, yes, sir. He was very cross with his wife. He said she'd left him in a lurch—went to stay with her brother when she should have been tending to her duties at home. He said he was going up Wiggins Hill to get her and take her home."

"That very night?"

"Yes. That very night. He said he was headed there after one more beer."

"And then did he leave the tavern, after that last beer?"

"No. After two or three more he did, sir."

Mr. Barnett waited for the quiet laughter to subside before asking his next question.

"Was he intoxicated?"

"Difficult to say. They say Beck had a hollow leg."

"Let me ask a different question, Mr. Carpenter. Do you think Mr. Beck was of sound enough body and mind to make it up Wiggins Hill? To carry through with his plan?"

"Yes, sir. I do."

I looked up at Wallace. "So Matthew got to be part of the show."

"Yes. And right before the prosecution rested its case."

"And then he went and saw the hanging. What date was that again? I wonder if he told Frances about it in detail. I wonder if he knew how delicious she found such dark topics."

"Let's see." Wallace checked the article. "The hanging was on November 16. She was pregnant at the time, right? Interesting.

It's hard to tell how much he told her. It seems in her journal that her internal life was very much her own. Shared it with her brother but not so much Matthew. Maybe Matthew didn't confide much in her, either."

"Maybe," I said. "Can you hand me your journal copy?"

Wallace slid it over to me.

"*November 16*," I read. "*What should a young wife think about, when her husband is so engaged?* So, engaged in watching a man hang. Nice. Either she took it very lightly, or she was trying to distract herself by thinking about her Christmas baking."

I looked through the next few entries. "If she addressed it specifically, I would think I'd remember."

I stopped at December 19. *We haven't so very much pumpkin now that that Frederick fellow does not come to the house anymore.*

"I wonder if this Frederick is the same Frederick in that article? Frederick Baines?"

Wallace sat up. "Which?"

I pointed to the name in the journal. "There."

"Oh. Well, Frederick was a common enough name in those days. But I suppose it's possible. It was a small town."

I considered Frederick Baines for a moment. "You know what's weird about this McFarlene thing?"

"What?" Wallace said.

"Isn't wood, like, some of the easiest evidence to get rid of? Just burn that shit in your fireplace. What gives?"

Wallace smiled at me patiently. "I think the idea is that John McFarlene didn't know there was blood on it."

"Even though he bludgeoned the guy with it? Bludgeon your brother-in-law with a log, then give the log to your neighbor?"

"First of all, I don't think anyone ever said McFarlene

bludgeoned Beck *with* a piece of firewood. More likely a shovel or something else that was *near* the woodpile—though the prosecution never located the actual weapon. Maybe he just beat the hell out of him. In any case, he probably was not even aware of the blood on the wood. There were several blood-stained pieces. It was the cut end of the logs—like some had splattered against the whole side of the woodpile. Maybe he just needed the money or the food his neighbor was paying him for the wood. And aside from all of that . . . we can't hold up the standards of evidence collection and police work to what it is today. People were hanged on a lot less. That's one thing that makes the Herbert Hayden acquittal, by contrast, rather shocking. *They* actually had some decent evidence. Now *that* was a man who deserved to hang. But—alas."

"Right," I said. I wondered if Frances Barnett ever got to hear that the verdict in the Hayden case was not guilty. She'd been dragged off to the loony bin before the trial had ended.

"In any case," Wallace continued, "it's obvious that McFar-lene wasn't the sharpest tack. That's clear in some of the trial details. There were several character witnesses that made him sound like a sweet old oaf. A sort of teddy bear who was per-haps avenging some wrong done to his sister. Again, made him seem sympathetic—but also very guilty. I've never envied the jury in that case. A murder was a hanging offense. The defense never had much clarity about his strategy, I'm afraid."

Wallace handed me another article. "This story covers Fred-erick Baines's testimony. Here the main prosecutor's question-ing him."

I skimmed through the article until I got to Frederick Baines's actual testimony—which was relatively short:

"Do you know what day it was that John McFarlene gave you firewood?" asked Mr. Knowles.

"It was a Thursday, sir," answered Mr. Baines. "Thursday, June 6."

"Did you pay him with money or produce at that time?"

"No, sir. We have a regular agreement. My lettuces and squashes and cabbages for his wood. It's a trade between neighbors. We give these items to each other when we have them. Not always on the same day. Not a formal agreement of payment."

"I see. Now, why did you need wood in the summer?"

"I use a fire-burning stove in my house, sir. I don't have a coal stove for cooking."

"Now, days later, you brought some of this wood to Constable Young. Why was that?"

"I saw that three of the pieces had strange splatters on them. Normally I would not have given it any notice, I reckon. But I knew John was embroiled in this bad business about his brother-in-law. I thought the constable might want to know."

"I see. Did you notice the marks on the wood right away?"

"No, sir."

"When did you notice them?"

"When I was about to use them, sir."

"And when was that?"

"Two weeks after John gave them to me."

"Did you ever have any disagreements with John McFarlene?"

"Disagreements? No. We got on quite well as neighbors.

Not everyone on Wiggins Hill can say that. But I never had any quarrel with John."

"Thank you, Mr. Baines."

I skipped down the cross-examination.

"Mr. Baines, how often would you say that John McFarlene supplies you with wood?"

"It depends, sir. Every couple of weeks in the winter months. Less so in the summer. I don't use as much."

"Is he your only source of firewood? Or do you ever cut your own, or trade with anyone else for it?"

"I don't chop my own because of my bad arm, sir. Hurt it when I was a boy. Sometimes I get some from the Reilly brothers at the bottom of the hill. But only in the winter, when I need more. I wasn't getting it from anyone else in June."

"I understand. Now, before Thursday, June 6—the day you say that John McFarlene gave you the stained wood—before that, when would you say was the last time he supplied you with wood? Before that time?"

"I don't remember that well. Maybe three weeks before."

"Did you have any left over? From that batch? When he generously gave you some more on June 6?"

"I believe I did, sir."

"Where do you store your firewood, Mr. Baines?"

"In a small pile just outside my door."

"So the wood from June 6 was added to the very pile

you had of your previous supply of wood, that had not yet
been used?"

"Yes, sir."

"Now, what makes you certain that the stained wood
comes from the June 6 batch?"

"Well. Because it was at the top of the pile, sir."

I stopped reading.

"It seems like the defense attorney had a decent point here,"
I said, pointing to that portion of the article. "This idea that the
firewood was stained with Walter Beck's blood is kind of . . .
flimsy."

Wallace read it and considered it for a moment. "Well, sure.
He got Baines a bit befuddled. But it didn't amount to much.
Because the prized evidence was the blood on the *existing*
woodpile and shirt hidden inside it. Frederick Baines's wood
was simply what *led* the constable to that. They hadn't inves-
tigated that part of McFarlene's property before that, I don't
believe."

I put down the article. "It kind of reminds me of the 'barn
arsenic' business in the Herbert Hayden case."

"How so?"

"Something that was conveniently found later. In that case,
convenient for the defense—although it seems like the octahedron testimony kind of exposed it for the fraud it probably was.
In this case, convenient for the prosecutor."

Wallace nodded. "Again, evidence collection wasn't anything
like it is today. Things like this happened *all* the time."

"I understand that," I said softly.

But I was distracted by the similarity. The late-in-the-game nature of the discovery of evidence. I wondered if Frances—so familiar with the Stannard case, and presumably quite familiar with the McFarlene case—noticed the similarity as well.

"Can we find out more about Frederick Baines?" I asked.

Wallace steepled his hands and pressed the tips of his middle fingers against his lips. "What do you want to know about him?"

"Wouldn't you be curious if he was a personal friend of Matthew Barnett's? Wouldn't that be . . . interesting?"

Wallace sat back in his chair. "Well . . . Sure. I don't think any of our basic sources—out-of-town newspapers and town records—are going to be able to tell us who was friends with whom. Frederick Baines—like most of the witnesses in the McFarlene trial—lived all the way up on the hill, where the poorer folks like the McFarlenes lived. Matthew came from one of the most moneyed families in town and lived down in the village in a nice little house. Maybe they were civil. But they probably weren't friends."

I glanced down at Frances's journal, reading the Frederick mention again.

"Both the Frederick who testified and the Frederick in Frances's journal traded or sold squashes," I said. "So can't we be pretty confident it's the same guy?"

Wallace raised his eyebrows and took the journal copy from me, rereading again. Lucy let out a frustrated whimper. I bent down and rubbed her back.

"Huh," Wallace murmured.

"Do you think McFarlene was guilty?" I asked.

"Almost certainly. It seems a shame, though, that he was

hanged. Beck was probably not a nice man. Just tragic all around, really."

Lucy's elbows gave out underneath her, and she began to cry. I picked her up.

"John McFarlene's last words don't sound unintelligent to me."

Wallace nodded. "I've often wondered if someone helped him prepare them."

"Why would anyone do that?"

Wallace wrinkled his nose. "Well . . . why not?"

"I really need to feed her," I said. "Maybe I should go back to the motel so she can nap, too. She didn't get enough sleep last night."

Lucy's pitch rose as I said it.

"All right," Wallace said, raising his voice to speak over Lucy. "Later on, then . . . We are certainly free to go looking for this Frederick Baines's birth and death and marriage certificates at the town clerk's if you think that would tell you something. I doubt it will. Maybe we should do a search in the available Connecticut papers."

"Yes, maybe," I shouted, rubbing Lucy's back. "My laptop's at home, though, and I don't even know if the Candlelight has Wi-Fi. We'll see."

I opened the cranberry door, and Wallace stood up. He touched the arm of my coat to stop me from stepping outside.

"Are you going to be needing anything else today? Do you need help with your window?"

Lucy wailed at him and then hid her face in my chest.

"Thanks, Wallace. I'll be okay," I assured him and slammed the door harder than I meant to.

Chapter 60

Frederick Baines's place was a small cabin. I'd heard his cousin sometimes lived there with him. Perhaps when in a different mindset, I'd have hesitated to knock at the door of two bachelors.

But knock I did, and Frederick appeared. He was taller than I remembered him—but thin in the face, with a boyish dewiness to his eyes. His hair was long, slick, and gathered at the back—but his bushy beard was incongruously unkempt.

"Mrs. . . . Barnett?" he said.

"That's correct, Mr. Baines."

Frederick shrugged one shoulder. "Are you wanting some squashes?"

"Well . . ." I hadn't thought of trying to cover the purpose of my visit, but now that I'd been given an opportunity, it seemed a sensible idea. "Yes, if you have any. Two or three. That's what I can fit in the carriage with my girl."

"I have two acorn squashes I can sell you. Don't have a lot to spare. Sold most of what I grew and need to eat myself."

He slipped back into the house and reappeared with two small squashes—the size of baby's heads.

I paid him generously and tucked them at Martha's feet. "Why don't you ever visit our home anymore?"

Frederick's eyelids twitched at the question. "I never came *into* your home, ma'am. I don't recall that I was ever invited."

"True . . . yes. But you would stop by."

"When your husband wanted some of my squashes or cabbages, I remember. Mentioned it in town and I came by with them. Those were the only times I was near your house."

"The last time you ever came was just before McFarlene's hanging."

Frederick stared at me. "Was it?"

"You seemed upset when you spoke to my husband."

Frederick took a step backward into his house. "Ma'am?"

"There's something more to it, isn't there?"

"I don't know what you mean, ma'am. With all due respect."

The next question simply jumped out of my mouth, much as that goblet had sprung out of my hand that time with Matthew: "Are you afraid of me?"

"No, ma'am." Frederick took a deep breath before forcing his mouth into a stiff smile. "I'm not afraid of you."

"What if I told you I knew your secret? Would you be afraid of me in that instance?"

His smile disappeared as his mouth fell open, and his gaze shifted from me to the treetops above our heads. A strong gust blew through us, billowing the bottom of his untucked shirt.

"Your little girl, ma'am. She looks cold. You ought to get her home."

"My girl is hardier than you would think."

"I heard she has to be."

I felt a stab at that response. It occurred to me that his aim was to have me rush off in a paroxysm of indignation. I *was* shocked. *What did he know about me? What did* everyone *know?* And yet I stood my ground. I gripped the handle of the carriage tighter. His words and his expression confirmed nothing of the specifics I'd come here to sniff out—but confirmed something more general. He was far more sly a man up on the hill than the beseeching figure he presented down in town.

"Did my husband convince you to do something you regretted later?" I asked.

The silence that followed my question lasted several moments. A strong gust swept over us. Martha cried in protest. I believe her little fist even emerged from beneath the blankets, punching defiantly at the air.

"I'm afraid we might both know a good deal about regrets soon, ma'am."

Perhaps it was the cold wind that had just blown through me, but in that moment I had a grim sensation that he was correct. Frederick had not said yes or no. It was possible he had not fully understood my question. Maybe it didn't matter.

All three of us were powerless against this chill sweeping through us. There was something malevolent in the coming winter air. I could feel it more keenly up here—far from the comforts and aromas of my home. I had tried for so long to hold it off. Why had I then come up here to meet it?

I stared down at Martha's pink fist. How cold it would grow, and how quickly. I wrapped my palm around it. I began to push the carriage with one hand—as awkward as that arrangement was.

I must bring her home and keep her warm for as long as I can. However long that might be.

"You have a Merry Christmas," I muttered over my shoulder.

He seemed to stare through me as he replied—not threateningly, but with a lost and vapid expression.

"You, too, ma'am," he said.

Chapter 61

Haverton, Connecticut
December 20, 2014

I nursed Lucy in the car and then drove in the direction of our motel. About halfway there, I turned into the Stop & Shop and idled the engine for a while, trying to decide what to do next. I couldn't bear to go back to the room just yet. It would smell of cheap lemon-flavored air freshener and stale coffee. And a salty residue of last night's dream would surely still be in the air.

No—I couldn't go back there yet, and what was the point, now that Lucy had already zonked out in the car anyway?

I drove up and down the length of Haverton's main highway, trailing a morning kindergarten bus for part of the way, and then eventually stopping for a coffee at a drive-through. After Lucy had slept for a solid three-quarters of an hour, I parked in the Haverton Public Library lot.

Once we were inside, I sat at one of the available computers. Wedging the still-dozing Lucy into the crook of my left arm, I fished my wallet out of my purse with my right. It had been a while since I'd used my library card, so that required a bit more digging.

"Can I help you?" Someone was standing behind me, watching me. I tried my best to turn without disturbing Lucy.

There stood a bone-thin woman in an admirably ugly corduroy skirt—dark green and maize floral down to her ankles.

"You look like you've got your hands full," she said.

I pulled out my library card and repositioned Lucy in my arms so I could reach the keyboard.

"I'm fine, thanks," I said.

The woman nodded and returned to the reference desk.

Once logged into the Connecticut historical newspapers database, I hunt-and-peck typed "Frederick Baines" with one hand.

Three articles came up. The first two were the articles Wallace had shown me earlier in the morning—from the McFarlene trial. The third was dated October 14, 1885—several years after the trial. I clicked on it.

SUICIDE IN NORTH CRANBROOK

The body of Frederick Baines of Vine Street was found in his home. He was hanged by his own hand. His cousin Edward Cowan returned from work at approximately 5 P.M. and made the grim discovery. There was no suicide note. The cousins were lodging on Vine Street while working temporarily for Mr. Henry Caldwell, owner of Caldwell Orchard.

My arms must have stiffened because Lucy seemed to sense my surprise. Her eyes opened, immediately alert and alarmed.

I stared down at her, knowing what was coming but praying, for a moment, that I could hypnotize Lucy out of it with my gaze.

"Lucy," I whispered as my stomach dropped.

She'd *warned* me. At the historical society. She hadn't gotten enough sleep. It had been time to go home for a long, long nap. But I had ignored the warning, fed her on caffeinated breast-milk all morning, and cut her nap short—and was now going to get what I deserved.

Her mouth opened and a primal sort of scream came out. The woman typing next to me jumped. The reference librarian cringed. By the picture window, a familiar bald head lifted itself up from behind a *Wall Street Journal*.

The whole library stood still and waited for me to do something. I stood up and put Lucy to my shoulder. When I tried to grab my purse, I noticed that my wallet was still sitting by the keyboard. Attempting to grab it with the same hand, I dropped both. Lucy's cries grew more terrified—perhaps my clumsy movements had scared her even more. I secured her against my shoulder again and closed my eyes for a second.

There was no suicide note.

That feeling of near-blindness—from last night in the snow—was upon me again.

Shhhhh.

If I opened my eyes, each of the books in this library might open, and all of their secrets might fall out, covering me like snowflakes.

Swish. Swish. Swish.

"Hey, Amy!" I heard someone bellowing. "Or—Annie, was it?"

When I opened my eyes, the librarian was by my side, slipping my wallet into my purse and my purse into my open hand.

I could see Ralph Greer putting down his newspaper and struggling to his feet, but I was too rattled to greet him.

"Thanks," I whispered to the librarian before heading for the exit. She walked with me, her earth-mother skirt fluttering around her calves. As she held the door for me, I thought I saw sympathy, rather than disapproval, in her eyes. But of course I couldn't pause long enough to determine that for sure. It was not until we were back in the car—and I was nursing Lucy yet again—that I realized I was still wearing my pajama bottoms.

Chapter 62

Northampton Lunatic Hospital
Northampton, Massachusetts
December 21, 1885

When Martha and I were back home, I held her in the rocking chair and told her a story. I began with a real circumstance from long ago: Father and you and me in the woods, looking at a layered, shell-like fungus that had grown on a tree. I realized, a few sentences into the story, that it was nothing more than a pleasant memory. It did not have a beginning or an end. A child might prefer something more fanciful, no? So in my story I had us walk deep into the woods, where the mushrooms grew more and more numerous. Until we were surrounded by mushrooms, growing ever larger, and ever brighter. None was of a type you or I or even Father could identify. We kept climbing until we reached a precipice. And there the mushrooms were an alluring periwinkle color. Father picked one and offered it to me. And then he picked one and offered it to you. We both ate them because we trusted Father. And we found that they could make us fly. We flew over the hills, admiring the changing color of the leaves, and the close view of birds in flight. We were so far from home, though, that I wasn't confident the effect of the mushroom would last me long enough. So I landed in Haverton, while you and Father kept flying, more confident that you would get home eventually.

And that's how I ended up here, I whispered to Martha. Thankfully, she was asleep. The story had not ended as happily as I had intended. Perhaps I'd tell it differently next time.

I laid her in her bed and took out that old journal you'd given me.

And then I wrote what I had been afraid to write for so long.

I wrote about my memory, of which I was now confident.

Chapter 63

I nursed Lucy in the car until she dozed off. But when I tried to put her in her seat, she woke up and started screaming bloody murder again. So I curled her back onto my chest and let her sleep, closing my eyes and abandoning the idea of leaving the library parking lot any time soon.

I thought about the article I'd read just before I'd left the library.

There was no suicide note.

And yet there was—wasn't there?

Ralph Greer's mystery note. Signed with an F. Frederick Baines. Written by Frederick Baines but kept in Edward Cowan's possession and never brought out into the light of day. Why? To protect the family's reputation? It would seem a suicide would do enough damage that the fact of there being a note wouldn't make a great deal of difference.

Right?

It all depended on the contents. I wished I could remember the exact words of the note. Something about selling one's soul for a pittance? Something about righteousness being folly, or something like that?

Ralph had not come after me once I'd bolted with the screaming Lucy. Should I go back in and tell him what I had discovered?

There was no suicide note.

And yet there was.

It seemed the wrong thought for a woman to have while holding a milk-drunk infant to her chest. I popped in a lullaby CD. After three songs, Lucy was as floppy as a noodle and undeniably dead to the world. I got out of the front seat and buckled her into her car seat in the back.

After I returned to the front, I started up the car and turned up the next lullaby: "All Through the Night."

I pulled out of the library lot. I got on the main road, heading south out of town. It didn't matter exactly where I ended up—as long as it distracted me from the words in my head.

There was no—

"Shut up," I murmured. *"Please."*

Gerard Barnett was hesitant when I suggested I come over, but I employed my authoritative teacher voice and talked fast.

"I'm in the neighborhood. Actually right by the Arby's where we met. And I'm wondering if I could come by and look at the books you have left from Matthew Barnett's collection?"

"Uh. There's only one left that I didn't sell, remember?" Gerard paused. "And it's not for sale."

"But could I still look at it? And the trunk that they were stored in? Do you still have that?"

"Yeah. But it's a smelly old thing, really. Why?"

"Anything you have of his. Or his wife's. Anything. I want to look at it."

"Well. Okay," he said.

When he greeted me at the door of his modest brown ranch house, Gerard said, "The trunk's in the basement. You'd have to go in the basement. Is that going to bother the baby?"

"Why would it?" I asked, closing the storm door behind me.

"I don't know." Gerard waved us through a dim den with a courtroom show playing on the television at full volume. "It's a little dark. It doesn't smell great."

"I think she'll be okay."

Gerard nodded and opened a door between the den and the kitchen.

Lucy and I followed as he clunked down the stairs. The predominant smell was of dryer sheets, and the place was no messier or danker than your average basement. There were two old electric guitars in the darkest corner—one with strings, one without.

In the opposite corner was a pile of white sheets and clothes jiggling on the vibrating washer—an enormous white bra dangling from the pile, swinging slightly.

"Now, what's this about, exactly?" Gerard said, leading me to a small wooden trunk by the dryer. It was about a foot high, with black metal bands and clasp. "Have you been talking to Patty again? Because I think maybe she tends to exaggerate. She probably gave you some idea that this thing was full of all kinds of old letters or antique treasures or whatever. I'm sorry to disappoint you, but—"

"I didn't talk to Patty. It's just that there were pages ripped out of Frances Barnett's journal."

Gerard opened the trunk and motioned for me to look inside. It was empty but for one book.

"Her journal?" He repeated.

"Her cookbook. It was really a journal. If you read past the first few pages, it's not about cooking at all."

"What's it about?"

"Her life. But there's a page missing." I set down Lucy's car seat and reached for the single book in the trunk. "May I?"

Gerard nodded. "You read the whole thing?"

"It wasn't that long, actually."

Bouvier's Law Dictionary, said the gold lettering, difficult to read against the worn black spine. I opened the front cover to see a simple but elegant book plate: *Ex Libris Matthew Barnett*.

"See," said Gerard. "His name right there. Cool, huh?"

"Yeah," I said. I closed the book, turned it over, and opened the back cover. Just simple endpapers, yellowed with age. I opened the front again and flipped the first few pages carefully.

"You know anything about the law?" Gerard asked. "If it wasn't the last of the books, I'd offer it to you. But as I said at the Arby's, I've got a *little* bit of a sentimental streak, you know? Enough to keep the one book."

Beside us, the washing machine was working up a lopsided rhythm. *Tha-THUMP. Tha-THUMP. Tha-THUMP.*

"Uh huh," I murmured.

Any second I'd here a *swish* and there it would be.

The sound of paper sliding against paper. Paper sliding out of a book, and into the open.

"You have a lot of that kind of old family stuff yourself? Your grandmother's wedding dress, or whatever?"

I shook the book.

"Easy, kid. Easy. That thing is worth a little bit of money."

THUNK. THUNK. THUNK.

I gripped the book by both covers, pages hanging downward, and swung it back and forth.

"Hey," Gerard snapped, stepping closer to me. "Honey. Stop that. Is this what you did to the cookbook?"

I backed away from him, gripping the covers tight.

"What's wrong with you?" Gerard demanded. "Didn't you say you were a history teacher? Don't you know this shit is fragile?"

Swish.

I stared at my feet, and at the clouded gray concrete around them.

"Did something fall out?" I whispered.

"No," said Gerard, putting out both of his hands and closing them around the book.

I yanked the book away and shook it again.

"I think something did. Didn't it? She hid it and she wants me to find it."

"Honey. Give that to me."

Gerard reached out and touched my elbow for just a moment. I looked up at his face—perplexed, almost alarmed. His hand was an inch away from my arm, his fingers flexing. He wanted to reach out and grab me and pull the book from my hands, but he was too polite.

"Abby. I don't know what you were expecting to find. I'm sorry to disappoint you, but there's nothing in this book."

Gerard gripped the book with both hands and wriggled it away from me.

"She wants *me* to find it," I said again, but Gerard didn't seem to hear me, since the washing machine was continuing to batter itself into a frenzy. THUNK. THUNK. THUNK.

"There was nothing extra in any of the books I found," Gerard said, raising his voice over the noise. "I promise you, I checked each one for little treasures, like old cash or a deed to an old farmhouse somewhere."

Lucy murmured to herself and then resumed sucking noisily on her pacifier. I watched her for a moment and then met Gerard's concerned gaze.

"And yet you didn't even read the whole cookbook," I said.

"That's different," he said. "I'm just not a big reader."

"Not a big reader," I repeated. I was picking up Wallace's odd conversational habits.

"Right." Gerard went to the washing machine, leaned over the pile of clothes, and shut it off.

The thumping stopped. It was only then that I recognized how fast my heart had been going, outracing the washing machine. For how long, I wasn't sure. Since I'd started shaking Matthew Barnett's one remaining law book, or since I'd gotten to his house. Or since sitting at that computer in the library? How, precisely, had I managed to drive here?

"I'm sorry," I said. "I hope I didn't hurt the book."

Gerard glanced at the book, opening and closing the front cover, and patting it.

"Looks fine."

I picked up Lucy's carrier and held it in front of my knees with both hands, swinging it gently. "I should go. I shouldn't have surprised you like this."

I started for the stairs.

Gerard watched me for a moment, and then said, "Uh . . . you need help carrying that?"

"No," I said. "I'm used to it."

He followed me up the stairs—though at some distance, I noticed. Probably he thought I was nuts. Probably he was right.

As he opened his front door for me, he asked, "Hey, have you tried any of the recipes from the cookbook?"

"Not yet," I said. "If I ever do, I'll bring you some."

Gerard hesitated before closing the door, likely contemplating how to discourage me from doing any such thing.

Just what he needed: arsenic brownies.

"Thanks for letting me look," I said and then lugged Lucy to my car.

Chapter 64

Northampton Lunatic Hospital
Northampton, Massachusetts
December 21, 1885

It was a mild night in the early summer of 1878. Two or three days after the night I'd dropped—or thrown—that goblet at Matthew's feet.

I don't know why I woke up. I probably would have gone promptly back to sleep—or not even awoken fully—had I not noticed that Matthew was no longer beside me. We had retired together, but now he was gone. I sat up to verify his absence and noticed, with that swift movement, that my head ached. I'd forgotten, in my slumber, how ill I'd felt of late. I stood up and felt the full brunt of it. Yes, it was true, still. I'd forgotten the fact of it in deep sleep: I was with child.

There was no escaping that physical fact. In this moment, I had a choice—I could climb back into bed, curl into a ball, and hope sleep would hide my condition from my mind for a few hours more. Or I could creep down to the kitchen, feed this dizzying hunger with a piece of bread, and hope for the blessing of a satisfied sense of optimism.

Perhaps I would see Matthew down there—where *had* he

gone? Perhaps I would even tell him about the child. I would have to soon, after all, and maybe his happiness for it would comfort me? Wasn't that possible? Even if I could not yet muster any gladness at it, perhaps I could be swayed? Matthew was skilled at swaying, if nothing else.

As I started down the stairs, I heard a sigh from the kitchen—and then a slight moan. Was Matthew in pain? I didn't cry out to assist him, though—for the sound felt like something forbidden—something not meant for my ears. At the bottom of the stairs, I lightened my step as I moved through the front room. The kitchen gaslight was lit. I peered in through the crack in the door. Another soft moan.

I stared across the kitchen and could see no one. I wondered about a ghost, or perhaps an exceedingly dramatic mouse. A whimper came from the direction of the floor, and then a sigh—perhaps, it sounded to me, a sigh of relief. I looked down and there was Matthew. His back was to me. Beside him was his hunting knife. Beneath its tip were two red drips. He was hunched over my best cake pan. From where I was standing, I could see the tips of his toes. His leg was naked up to his knee. He was gripping his calf, squeezing and sighing—once, and then again. The wound I'd recently inflicted was widening and bleeding under his knife.

I turned away and inched back toward the stairs. I rushed up them as fast as I could without making noise. When I reached the top, those pink and orange lights appeared behind my eyes again. Was it my hurried movement up the stairs or the scene in the kitchen that made me so dizzy?

I fell back into bed. I shut my eyes. Either way, I was grateful for the softness of the bed and the anesthetic darkness.

I kept my eyes shut but willed my body to stay awake until Matthew returned. My body, I should have known, no longer took cues from my mind. It had a task of its own, and that task required rest. I must have succumbed to sleep because when I opened my eyes, the sun had risen, and Matthew lay beside me.

Chapter 65

Rowan College
Rowan, Vermont
February 27, 1998

A h. Mr. Cromley," Professor Duran was saying to the guy in the dopey brown-and-red stocking cap. "Before we can take issue, or disagree, or object, we must first *understand*. And to *understand* what Wollstonecraft was trying to say, we must first *understand* what Burke said, with which she took issue. And, for that matter, what Thomas Paine said before him. And to *understand* all of that, it might help if we return to our texts."

I feared and loathed Duran in a way I secretly found delicious. He was exactly how I'd imagined a college professor was supposed to be—crabby and derisive and unsympathetic in a way high school teachers were never allowed to be. To endure his contempt felt like a novel form of maturity.

In that particular moment—a week after Wendy's death, and my first day back in class—I craved his disdain. I breathed it in like oxygen, wishing it were me he was humiliating instead of the Cromley kid. I wanted Duran to stare me down and announce to this class—to the world—how very little I knew.

"Let us take out our *Rights of Man* for a moment, shall we? I'd like to read this one portion again."

I picked up my Dover paperback.

Swish.

The paper slid out of the front cover of the book, grazed the little white Formica square of desk in front of me, and landed in my lap. A folded square of white paper, with *Abby* written across it on both sides, in thick pencil.

At first I thought of my friend Kristin, who was always drawing unflattering pictures of people we knew, their worst features exaggerated and grotesque: crooked teeth, limp hair, oversized glasses. She would be just cruel enough to draw a picture of Professor Duran, eyebrows shooting out like porcupine quills, to make me giggle in his class and draw his caustic attention.

When Duran's face was buried in Thomas Paine, I opened the paper. The only picture inside was of a nautilus shell, curled in the top right-hand corner. I recognized the stationary before I did the handwriting. It wasn't Kristin's.

I had spoken to Wendy when she was already dead.

And now her ghost had written back.

Chapter 66

Haverton, Connecticut
December 20, 2014

After I parked at the Candlelight Inn, I turned and stared at Lucy's mirror for a while. I couldn't remember driving back here. The guy in the stocking cap. Duran. *Rights of Man*. That was all as clear as if it had happened this morning, but all I remembered from the trip back from Gerard's was that somewhere along the way I'd been behind a dirty white sedan with Mylar balloons in the back.

My cell phone rang.

"Abby?"

Chad. Chad in Chicago, which might as well have been the moon.

"I've been trying the land line all day," he said. "You're out with Lucy in the snow? I didn't realize till today that you guys have snow out there."

"The snow wasn't that bad, actually."

"That's what I'd heard. But still, I was surprised. What've you two been up to?"

"Well . . . we didn't spend the night at home."

"What?"

"It's a long story." I paused. I didn't want to tell the same lie

I'd told to Wallace. If I was crazy, I'd have to let Chad know eventually. For Lucy's sake. "I had to break a window. In the living room."

"What? Why?"

"There was this issue with the keys, when I ran out to get something. The door locked on me, and Lucy was inside crying. I panicked. I had to get in to her quickly."

"Wow." Chad made a sucking noise. "Sounds rough."

"It was."

"Are you okay? Where did you stay?"

"The Candlelight Inn."

"Ooh. For real? That sounds like an adventure. You'll be back at the house tonight, though, right? Do you want me to call someone to help you with the window?"

"I'll take care of it. Don't worry."

Chad was silent for a moment. "How's Lucy liking the flea-bag motel?"

"It's not so bad."

"When do you have to check out, anyhow?"

"Umm . . ."

"What about Monty?" Chad asked before I could answer.

"Oh . . ." I said softly. "Monty."

"He's still at the house?"

No wonder Monty hated me now. He sensed how easily I could forget about him.

"Listen. I'll go back to the house soon. I'll check on him."

"Well. I hope he's not freezing his little kitty ass off." I could tell that Chad was trying hard to sound nonchalant.

"He's probably fine if he's upstairs," I said. "But I'll check on him. In fact, I'm just headed back to the house now."

"Do you want me to try to come home early, Abby?"

I considered this question. What was he really asking? *Are you crazy, Abby?*

Was I? Or did I just need someone to help me face the house? Probably. But that someone likely wasn't Chad. The house didn't seem to take much notice of Chad, nor he it.

"I don't think that'll be necessary, no. It's not like we don't miss you, but . . . Look. Now that you mention Monty, I'm kind of worried about him. I should go. Love you."

I watched Lucy in the mirror again for a moment. Her delicate eyelids fluttered, opened, and then closed again. She sensed the motionlessness of the car. I picked up my phone and dialed Fonda's number. She didn't answer, but I left her a message asking if she could meet me at my house.

"Monty?" I called.

His kitchen bowl still had some food in it, but I poured more in, hoping he'd hear it. He didn't come running. But Monty had never been that sort of cat. I decided to set to work on patching the window, figuring he'd make himself known when he felt like it.

The living room was freezing, of course. I carried Lucy in with me, and kept on my coat while I swept up all of the glass I'd left. As I finished, Lucy began to wriggle and squawk in her carrier.

"Let's just get the hole in the house fixed, sweet pea," I said, picking her up and carrying her to the kitchen. I strapped her into her high chair and dropped a bunch of amusements on its tray: a washcloth, a squeaky toy, plastic spoons, and a cereal bowl.

I knelt at the recycling bin and selected a large piece of cardboard for covering the hole in the window.

Then, gripping the back of the high chair, I pushed Lucy into the living room. It was colder there, but at least we'd be in the same room.

I plugged in the Christmas tree lights to make us feel cozier, and then duct-taped the cardboard over the window—adding a few extra crisscrosses. The effect was no more secure—just extra derelict-looking. It wasn't much, but it would keep some of the heat in, and keep Monty out of the cold for one more night.

"Nice work, huh?" I said to Lucy.

Before she could reply, there was a knock at the side door in the kitchen.

"I bet that's Fonda!" My voice was high-pitched and overenthusiastic, as if anticipating a hired clown.

I rushed to the door and let Fonda in. She was wearing a fluffy charcoal beret pulled over her ears, covering her feathery hair and giving her a more mysterious look than she'd had the previous day.

"You might not want to take your coat off," I called behind me as I led her into the living room. "It's kind of cold in here. We had a little incident with the window."

Fonda gazed at the duct-taped window, then looked down at Lucy—playing with her colored spoons in her snowsuit and hat.

"Hello, pumpkin," Fonda said.

Lucy was too busy trying to insert a spoon into her mouth to notice Fonda.

"What happened to the window, Abby?" Fonda asked quietly.

"I'm not sure." I shrugged. "It happened during the storm last night. The wind . . . something with the wind?"

This version of the story didn't sound as good as it had when I'd told it to Wallace. Fonda nodded anyway.

"You mentioned on the phone that you didn't spend last night in your house?"

"No," I said.

Fonda stepped closer to the window and put her hand on the duct-taped crisscross. "Replacing a window can be a pain in the ass. You gonna have someone come fix it? Or are you or your husband handy with this sort of thing?"

"We'll figure it out, I'm sure."

"You also said that you had some other questions for me?"

"Yes," I said.

"Bee beeee," Lucy chimed in, and Fonda smiled at her.

"Busy baby," Fonda said, mimicking Lucy's singsong tone.

I waved my hand toward the sofa. "Why don't we sit down?"

Fonda pulled off her hat and joined me on the sofa. I dragged Lucy's high chair over so she'd be close to us.

"What do you think the word 'innocent' means?" I asked.

Fonda shrugged with one shoulder. "I don't have any more insight into the meaning of the word than you do."

"But you said that there was something heavy down here . . . something oppressive. Heavy with what, exactly? 'Heavy' doesn't tell me anything."

"That's a good question," Fonda admitted after a moment's thought.

She sat silently for little while. Lucy said, "Meh meh mah," and I reached over and stroked her hair.

"Guilt," Fonda said. "Does that make sense?"

"Not exactly," I answered. "But . . . does it need to?"

"I guess not. I just thought . . . the feeling doesn't match the word. But there you have it."

"There we have it," I repeated.

I smoothed Lucy's hair across her forehead and behind her ears. There was a bit of banana puree dried on one temple, but her hair still felt silky smooth. It was amazing how well a baby held up without much bathing—compared to an adult.

Fonda squinted into the Christmas lights. "Guilt and fear make a powerful mix."

"Were we talking about fear?"

"Weren't we? Yesterday, I mean? Without saying the word?"

"When was that?"

"The whole conversation. That's why I'm here, isn't it? Because you're afraid of something in the house?"

Lucy lifted her head up slightly so I was now touching her eyebrow. She smiled at me, and in that moment I didn't want to admit to being afraid of anything.

"Is it possible I brought something—or someone—with me into the house?" I asked. "Something that wasn't here before I moved in?"

"Of course . . ." Fonda puckered her lips and bobbed her head, considering. "I have no reason to say no. It's *possible*."

"Because just yesterday you were saying that something sort of opened a window, and let something in. And maybe one of us . . . my husband or I . . . let it in?"

Fonda put her hands in her hat—probably to warm them. "Well . . . that was a metaphor, about the window."

"I understand that, but . . . maybe my moving in . . . or my husband and I moving in . . . let it in?"

"Tell me . . ." Fonda burrowed her hands deeper into her hat. "What is it you think followed you into this house?"

Lucy's attention had strayed from my hand to the Christmas tree, so I pulled my hands into my lap. I was silent. I didn't wish to give Fonda any material.

For a minute or two, we both listened to Lucy murmur, "Nam nam nam."

Fonda leaned closer to Lucy and said, "Can you hand me one of those spoons, pumpkin?"

Lucy didn't oblige. She looked at me, picked up a spoon, put it in her mouth, and smiled beatifically.

"Did she mean to hurt her?" I heard myself say, blinking hard. "I need to know. Did she *want* to hurt her?"

Fonda turned back to me and stared at me for a moment. Then she stood up, paced the room a couple of times, and sniffled.

"Does the smell of the Christmas tree bother you at all?" I asked. "I forgot to ask you that last—"

"Shhhhh," said Fonda and sniffled again—louder this time.

She stood in the middle of the room and stared at me for so long that I wondered if I was supposed to get up and do something. Offer her a drink? Turn off the Christmas lights? Run?

"You are focused so much on a few words on a page," she murmured. "Why so much on that? Don't you know they were written by a phantom hand?"

"What?" I said, and felt my mouth fall open

"Does that mean something to you?" Fonda asked.

"Can you say more? What phantom?"

"I don't know, Abby." Fonda sat on the couch and clutched her hat again. "I can't explain everything I say. It just comes to me that way."

Tears stung me eyes.

"Did she *want* to hurt her?" I asked, my voice nearly breaking. "*Tell* me."

"I don't know." Fonda slid an inch or two away from me. "I don't . . . Who are we talking about here?"

I shook my head. "I shouldn't have to tell you. If you're for real, you should know."

And then I heard a jangle of collar and tags—Monty padding down the stairs. He appeared in the kitchen doorway then angled sideways to rub my calf. He appraised Fonda's leg for a moment, then crept into the kitchen.

We both listened to him crunching his food for a few moments.

"You already know which ghost you have to live with," Fonda said after a while. "Don't you?"

I shook my head but said nothing.

"You can break all the windows you want, Abby. And still you won't let the ghosts out."

Fonda cocked her head and studied me. I hadn't told her I'd broken the window. But anyone with half a brain and half a heart could probably figure out I was crazy enough to do so.

"We have to learn to live with our ghosts," she said. "To some extent, anyway."

"How convenient," I said softly.

I buried my face in my hands. After a moment, I felt Fonda's thick fingers tighten painfully around my elbow. She was silent for a few seconds. Her nails sank into the flesh of my upper arm. I wondered if Lucy was watching us but didn't want to remove my hands from my face and have Fonda see my tears.

"You can allow yourself to be blinded," Fonda said. Her voice was so low now that it might've been at a frequency audible to only the two of us. Lucy babbled obliviously in her high chair.

"Or to see in such sharp focus that you might as well go crazy." Fonda loosened her grip. "The trick is to find the delusional space in between."

I let my hands fall from my face. Fonda's eyes were the bright alien blue of fake contact color, but still fierce and hard.

A sob escaped my lips, but no words.

"Exactly," Fonda whispered.

I snuffled and wiped my eyes with my sleeves, then searched my pockets for tissues and found none. Fonda handed me a wad of them from her jacket pocket.

"Are you all right now?" she asked after a couple of minutes.

I took a breath. "I don't have a choice."

"No." Fonda's lips formed a very slight smile. "No, you don't."

Next to us, in the living room, Lucy was saying, "Ma ma ma," her voice rising with glee and confidence. She was talking to the Christmas lights as if they were old familiar friends.

"Isn't that just the sweetest sound?" Fonda said, her voice returning to the cheerful tenor it had had when she first walked in.

With shaking hands, I unbuckled Lucy from her high chair. I held her to my chest for a moment, patting her warm back. I wanted Fonda to leave now so I could nurse Lucy.

"Thanks for coming out one more time," I said. "What's your gas fee, again?"

"Twenty-five," Fonda said. "Cash, please."

I nodded without looking at her and touched my lips to Lucy's hair.

Chapter 67

Y ou are wondering, aren't you, Harry?
          Did I really see it?
          Did I see blood on my kitchen floor?
Did I see Matthew cut open what was once a small wound and make it large—digging deep into his leg with his hunting knife?

Did I see him collecting a puddle of blood in my best cake pan?

Did I see all of this a mere two days before Frederick Baines noticed the odd thing about his firewood from McFarlene? Three days before they found more stained wood and a stained shirt in the McFarlenes' woodpile?

If I could be certain of it in December of 1879, when I finally wrote of it in my journal, how was I not certain of it when it actually occurred, in the summer of 1878? And if I so often get lost in my memories now, what is to say which are real and which are not? From where I'm sitting, is it even possible to convince you? Here below the white balustrade with the wire covering, to keep us from throwing ourselves over.

I shall have to try.

Let me frame it this way—

In the fall of 1878, I was ill in a way I had never been before. Had I not dropped or thrown a goblet and not been able to remember *which*? Had I not been feeling unsteady and fatigued, seeing colored spots, fearing certain death and perhaps, as a result, not caring what was real and what was not, for it was all the same at the bottom of a cold and lonely grave?

The birth and the early days of Martha's life had clouded the memory into insignificance. My "rest" had made me uncertain of much that had come before it.

But in the months since, I'd grown stronger and more certain. I'd heard the lawyers on the Stannard side and the Hayden side talk of deceptions and planted evidence and corrupt witnesses and bumbling doctors. I'd considered the barn arsenic and the blood on Hayden's knife. I'd considered all of this and then considered my husband's ambition. And John McFarlene swinging at the end of a rope. My mind was now clear enough to consider all of these things in one related category.

And I was not Rosa Hayden. I would not cover up my husband's darkness. I was certain of my own mind, at long last.

I wrote about it, with clarity and certainty. I even wrote of my resolve to tell you about it, Harry. Not to shout it from the mountaintops or tell all of my friends or even a single newspaperman. Just to tell one soul, for now. On Christmas, when I saw you again. What might happen after that, I didn't know. I thought you might advise me. Or at the very least, share the burden of my secret.

But Matthew came to me with Dr. Graham before Christmas. Dr. Graham and two nurses and a strong young man with whom I could not fight. I was stringing popcorn and berries when they all came through the door. The sun was setting, and Christmas was three days away.

We think it is best for you, Frances, to go with Dr. Graham. We think you need another rest.

They let me kiss sweet Martha before guiding me to that carriage with two sturdy and determined brown horses. They came for me in the evening so as not to make a scene in daylight. The trip took two days since we spent that night in Hartford. But I was here by that Christmas Eve.

Merry Christmas to me, Harry. Here you are and now, at last, you know.

Chapter 68

Haverton, Connecticut
December 20, 2014

After Fonda was gone, I went upstairs and laid Lucy in the Pack 'n Play with two board books, two rattles, and a stuffed turtle. She grunted and then squealed at the turtle, so focused on its rainbow shell that she didn't seem to notice when I slipped out of the room with a flashlight.

On my way down the hall, I reached into the bathroom for a towel. Then I opened the storage space by its small door and ducked in. It felt colder than usual inside the space, as it had soaked in much of the cold from downstairs. I shined my light briefly on Florabelle and then quickly threw the towel over her and moved my light beyond her. The U-Haul boxes at her feet were from the most recent move to the house. The ones farther along the space—labeled in blue and green Sharpies—were from our move together before that. Those boxes had moved from our first apartment to our second to here without ever being unpacked.

I knew which box I was looking for. It was a banana box, slightly larger than most of these, with the square opening at the top patched up with duct tape. I remembered closing up my copy of *Rights of Man* inside of there, between a couple of other books and a peacock-embroidered pillow my grandmother had made. I had never opened the box after I'd transferred out of Rowan, but I'd hauled it with me wherever I lived after that.

Chad was as much of a pack rat as I was, so he never asked what was in each box. He simply helped me move them from apartment to apartment to house as he did his own.

I moved farther into the dark, bent over, shining the flashlight across all of the boxes until I reached the one with the bananas on its side. It was on the floor with three boxes stacked on top of it. After moving those boxes, I set down the flashlight and lifted the banana box top.

Rights of Man was three books down, beneath Henry David Thoreau and a smelly paperback of Sophocles' plays. Wendy's note was still wedged inside—where I'd left it. Where she'd left it. I held it close to the floor so I could read it by the slant of light from the flashlight.

Dear Mom,
    There just isn't much left but pain.
    I was never enough for you. Now I'll be nothing for you.

Dear Dad,
    Play those Mamas and Papas one more time for me?

Dear Chris and Davey,
    You know I love you. I am sorry.

Abby,
    Please give this to my family.

The words made my legs wobble. I tried to sit on the floor, but there wasn't enough room. Half-kneeling, I let my knee settle in the banana box and rest on the peacock pillow.

A phantom hand.

Couldn't Fonda have been talking about Wendy's words? And couldn't that make these words bearable?

Back when I'd first discovered the note, I had had to make a decision, and the decision came down to this: Wendy had already caused devastation. She had put into my hands one extra piece of wood for the pyre and instructed me to throw it. I had chosen not to.

It seemed the decent thing to do. I'd hoped. And yet—it was Wendy's pyre. Her one chance at a pyre in all of eternity. Should it not burn exactly as she liked?

But then—there was the issue of her heart being weak, and her dying with a dose that most would've survived. And the fact that she had taken that dose while I was in the room— albeit asleep—instead of waiting until she was alone. Maybe she had not expected to die. Maybe those words were supposed to accompany a rescue, and to be discussed with great emotion by a hospital bed. In which case—they were not meant to devastate—not really. And were rendered moot by her miscalculation.

I would never know which was the case. I only knew that my name was on the note, and so the burden of it was mine alone. And that once the decision was rendered, I really could not change my mind weeks or months or years later.

A phantom hand.

Maybe. Maybe the phantom was anger, or illness, or pain? And she had not meant them? Either way, the note was mine now. A stab in the heart meant for someone else—a burden I could accept because I was numb to it when I was nineteen.

But I was thirty-four now, and Lucy was crying.

I stood up at the sound of it and bumped my head.

"Coming, honey," I called, rubbing my head and hunching over to make my way out. I tripped over the top of the banana box but managed not to fall.

By the time I reached Lucy, her face was a deep red and wet with tears. She'd noticed she was alone, and she was angry about it. I held her close to me and paced the room until her wails turned to gasps and then to sighs and then to silence. We stood together by the window and looked at the snow, the bare trees, and the smoke curling from the chimney of the house behind our yard.

"You'll like winter," I said. "When you're a little older. We'll make snowmen and snow angels."

And then I tried to think of something to add—something to enhance her vocabulary. I considered telling her that I always found the first snow bittersweet, but that seemed a creepy thing to tell an infant.

My cell phone rang, so I shoved Wendy's note into my jeans pocket to free up a hand to answer it.

"Where are you right now?" Wallace wanted to know. "The no-tell motel?"

"No. My house."

"Oh. I'm happy to hear that. But what about the window?"

"I've patched it up with tape for now. I'm going back to the motel in a little bit."

"Bummer. Are you sure you want to do that?"

"Well . . . no."

Wallace was silent for a moment. "Have you had dinner?"

"Lucy has."

"That doesn't answer my question."

I put my hand on my stomach. It had gone numb several hours ago. I'd trained it to be satisfied with coffee and occasional bites of baby food.

"Because I was thinking of ordering in," Wallace was saying. "Chinese. And I have something I want to show you. Something *very* illuminating. *Exciting*, really. I'll go that far."

"And I've got something to show you, actually."

"You had time to do a little research today, then?"

"Yes. Is it possible we're going to show each other the same thing?"

"Why don't you come over here for a bite, and we'll find out? You don't want to go straight back to that sad little room yet, do you?"

Wallace's apartment was a spare and tidy little place. His open kitchen looked out to a living room with a glass table and a beige sofa and loveseat set that smelled like the inside of a new car. There was no television—and a distinct lack of clutter that I wasn't sure should make me jealous or sad.

"Lucy's looking quite well." Wallace sat on the loveseat and made a silly face at her. "Her bruise is pretty much healed."

"Oh . . ." I said, looking at it myself. I hadn't thought about it much all day. Probably because he was right. The bruise was almost gone. "Yeah."

"I don't suppose she'll let me hold her again?"

"Well. She's had a weird day."

"Me, too, Lucy," Wallace said. "I should have known that a day that began at Sweetly's was going to be an unusual one."

"Things got weirder after that?"

"Indeed they did. Ralph called me. He said he saw you and Lucy in the library, and it reminded him that he had something he wanted to show us. So he invited me home for a beer. You'd have been invited, too, if you'd answered your phone. Now, I don't normally have beer at three P.M., but that's Ralph for you."

Wallace leaned over the coffee table and pulled forward a piece of paper that had been sitting there.

"Ralph said that after we all chatted, he couldn't get the name 'Frances' out of his head. He felt he'd seen the name before, in his family's papers. So over the past few days he's been looking. And he found this. It's a copy, of course. He scanned this for me. It's a letter from his great-grandmother's many papers."

October 7, 1886

My Dear Tessa,

My sister mentioned to me in a letter that you are soon to have a child. Although it has been many years since I have seen you, I felt compelled to send my good wishes. I don't much care for sewing these days, but I am making an exception for the child on his way—or her way—to you and Edward. I shall be sending you a baby's nightdress in coming weeks. And I shall pray for a healthy and joyous arrival.

I think of you often, and hope you know how
instrumental you were to my freedom. Your secrets are,
therefore, my secrets.

As ever,
Frances

Lucy noticed the weakness in my grip as I finished the letter and grabbed for the paper.

"Frances" was all I could say as I wrestled the paper out of Lucy's fist.

"It's her handwriting," Wallace said. "Don't you agree?"

"Yes. Amazing."

Lucy grunted in agreement, grabbing at the paper as I held it away from her.

"It was memorable to Ralph, in part, because of its reference to secrets. Now, we might not know exactly what those secrets are. But what I found remarkable about this letter—and what I thought you would appreciate as well—is that it shows that Frances actually got out of the asylum. Eventually. By 1886."

The note should have been a revelation—a relief. I couldn't determine why it made me uneasy.

"Couldn't she have written this from the asylum, though?" I asked.

"And made reference to her freedom? I think not."

I nodded, sliding the letter back onto the coffee table.

"We *might* know what Tessa's secrets are, actually," I said. "I wasn't able to print out what *I* found, but do you have a laptop?"

"Of course," Wallace said, fetching his computer from the kitchen.

I told him to access the Connecticut newspapers database—as I had done at the library—and search for Frederick Baines.

"Third article," I said. "From 1885. Not the two 1878 ones from the McFarlene trial. You've already seen those."

Wallace was silent for a moment, reading the article.

"Oh my," he said.

"It makes me think the *F* in Ralph's note—the one he showed us last time—has got to be Frederick."

"And you think that was a suicide note."

"Something like it. Now, I don't remember the exact words, but—"

" '*Righteousness is elusive. He was right and I shall follow him for my transgressions. It is all true what I confessed to you. For a pittance, I sold my soul and another's.*' Ralph's persistence has burned the whole thing into my memory."

"And doesn't that sound to you like—"

"Yes," Wallace said. "Like Frederick is feeling some guilt about the McFarlene trial. Oh, my."

"So Edward Cowan—by then Tessa's husband, right?"

"I'm not sure of the exact dates, but yes, probably."

"So Edward Cowan had something on the Barnetts after all. Not on the old man. But on his son. On Matthew."

Lucy wriggled and whimpered uncomfortably. I began to circle around the room but found few distractions. On one wall, there was a mural of Wallace's family pictures.

"See the baby?" I whispered, holding her up to a photo of a cherubic toddler in red overalls, sucking on the handle of a hairbrush. "So Edward Cowan maybe blackmailed Matthew Barnett with this note."

"Maybe. And maybe it wasn't the *note* itself that Edward

used to blackmail the Barnetts," Wallace continued. "Maybe it was just information he had. If we believe, based on the note, that Frederick was feeling depressed and remorseful about helping to hang McFarlene. Perhaps he gave his cousin an earful before he did himself in. And then we see that two months later Edward Cowan got that wildly cheap land deal from the Barnetts. And Matthew Barnett was the only person in that family involved in the McFarlene case. So it stands to reason . . . The 'pittance' came from Matthew—the young lawyer eager for his first big prosecutorial win. Doesn't it?"

Lucy put her wet little hand on my nose, then slid it down to my chin.

"Absolutely," I said, still bouncing Lucy slightly. "The 'pittance' might be money given to him to help falsify that firewood evidence in some way. Maybe put his own blood on it, who knows?"

"Hmm. A possibility."

An electric *ding-dong* sounded, making Lucy's eyes pop.

"Ah!" said Wallace. "That will be our dinner."

While Wallace answered the door, I thought about the possibility of Matthew Barnett and Frederick Baines falsifying evidence together. And then I considered the date of Frederick's death. November 1885. Not long after Matthew Barnett lost his "Coin and Clock" case.

A case in which a forged letter *almost* helped him. Had it not been exposed as a likely forgery.

Don't you know they were written by a phantom hand?

"Abby?" Wallace said, plunking the take-out bag onto his kitchen counter. "You seem deep in thought. What are you thinking?"

"It seems to me that fakery shadowed Matthew Barnett wherever he went," I said slowly. "Did you ever think that *he* was the one who forged that letter in the case with the old lady and the stolen coins and stuff? And not the accused man's wife? That either he did it, or he got someone to do it for him?"

"I'd never thought about it that much. It seemed rather a silly case to begin with. Though I suppose I've felt sorry for that poor old lady."

"And probably I'm not the first person to think that Matthew was responsible for the forgery," I continued. "Maybe people were whispering about that around town. That maybe Matthew Barnett wasn't exactly a man of justice. Maybe that's why he switched to another form of law. But maybe, meanwhile, it was all too much for Frederick Baines."

"Maybe," said Wallace. "Maybe it was a trigger for him. Am I using that word right? I hear all of this talk of 'triggering' these days, and I'm never quite—"

"And if Matthew Barnett was willing to forge something for a case like that, a theft case, he might've forged other things as well?"

Wallace ripped open the take-out bag. "Like what, Abby?"

"Like a journal entry that makes her look like she's capable of something terrible. Something that would justify putting her away."

Wallace abandoned the paper bag and stepped into the living room with me. "Something unspeakable."

"Yeah," I said.

Wallace sank onto the loveseat. I sat next to him. We were both quiet. Even Lucy observed the silence for a few moments, glancing from me to Wallace and smiling vaguely, as if anticipating a punch line.

"What a creep," Wallace said after a while.

"I wonder if she got a divorce?"

Wallace shrugged. "Well. That wasn't easy in those days. But perhaps she managed it. It doesn't appear she returned to Haverton."

I considered this—and realized what unsettled me about Frances's note to Tessa. It didn't mention Martha at all.

Lucy's lips twitched as her eyes began to close. She hadn't really gotten enough sleep today, and she was giving up on us. We had grown silent and boring.

"You know," I said. "I think it was easier to think Frances was crazy and homicidal than to consider the other possibilities. Because if she wasn't, then . . ."

I didn't finish my sentence for fear my chin might start wobbling.

Please don't take me away! Who is going to take care of the baby?

Wallace nodded. "I know what you mean."

I was eager to change the subject slightly—to keep from spontaneously blubbering as I had with Fonda. "If Tessa was 'instrumental' to her freedom . . . I wonder what that's about."

"Perhaps she told someone about something she had observed while in Matthew's employ," Wallace said. "Something that brought his story—or at least his reasons for institutionalizing his wife—into question. Perhaps she used the information she had from her husband—Edward—to help leverage some kind of release for Frances. Perhaps they were closer than her journal indicates. Or perhaps Tessa simply had a conscience."

"Is there any other correspondence from Frances to Tessa Cowan?"

"I asked Ralph that, of course. He said not that he knew of. Not that he could find."

"Uh huh." I steadied Lucy's head, which was flopping onto my chest as she dozed.

"Would you like to lay her down somewhere? In the bedroom, where it's quiet? So you can eat?" Wallace asked.

"That would be nice," I admitted.

Wallace led me to the apartment's one bedroom. Across from the queen-size bed, there was a single dresser that might've been an antique—with a television sitting on top of it. The only other furniture in the room was a little table by the bed with a lamp and a single book—a Tony Hillerman mystery with a bookmark stuck in the very beginning.

"Shall we put pillows on the floor?" Wallace asked as I positioned Lucy right in the middle. "In case she rolls?"

I hesitated. I didn't want to impose, and Lucy rarely moved much once she was deep in sleep. On the other hand—

"Yes," Wallace answered for me. "Let's."

Wallace arranged the pillows around the bed and then cushioned the remaining space with a blanket from his closet.

"You are welcome to my couch tonight," he said, "if you don't want to go to the trouble of getting her in the car and whatnot. You said you have Lucy's portable crib in your trunk, right?"

"Yes," I said. "And I appreciate the offer. But—"

The invitation was tempting. Wallace's place felt so warm and tidy.

But there was no hiding in warm and tidy places. I would dream of Wendy again eventually. Wherever I slept, or whenever I woke, or however long it had been since the last time I'd thought of her, she would always, ultimately, be waiting for me—in small, dark rooms with twisted bedsheets. In motel rooms and hospital rooms. In the dorm room where I'd drop Lucy off for college. She simply *would* be.

"But what?" Wallace asked.

"But I've already paid for that room," I said. "I may as well sleep in it."

Chapter 69

Yes, Harry. I *did* write about that. I wrote every moment of that memory that I could manage to describe. A year and a few months separated the experiencing of it from the writing of it, but I did my best—to lift the more definite details from the fog of memory.

You say that he showed you my journal? Well, he did not show you the entire thing, then. Or he was selective about what he showed you—if you didn't see this memory described. Aside from that, was there anything more that Matthew could accuse me of other than eccentricity? And perhaps a peculiar lack of certain elements of femininity? Both were unsettling to Matthew, always, but were either of those characteristics a crime?

What? *What?* What else did you read in that journal? Of what could you have suspected me? To think me deserving of this fate? To leave me here for more than a thousand lonely days.

You, Harry? You who are made of such similar substance as your sister? How could you have believed it? Clara was blinded by her wish to mother a child—any child, perhaps. But you?

Matthew made such a compelling case, did he? Martha's vomiting, and arsenic in my hope chest, and a conversation I had
with Louise, even? Did you offer that to him yourself? Or did
Louise betray me as well? Believe me, Brother, she was not as
shocked by that conversation as she might have pretended to be
for your sake.

And now you are not so convinced of Matthew's claims, because why? Because my old house girl came to you and told you
a secret? Told you that in light of that secret—her husband's
secret, come by way of his cousin Frederick—she thought you
should consider your sister's fate more thoroughly?

You needed that mousy little maid to tell you to think again,
think more carefully, about your dear sister?

You poor dear. What agony it must have been, to think such
things of your sister, for five long years.

You poor dear.

Get me out of this place in the name of all that is holy, Harry.

You will say you are my keeper, and you will have them release me to your care. Brother, husband, cousin—they don't
care—as long as you are a man. You'll see. Wave down a nurse
and say whatever you wish. Your words will be like magic to
them—as Matthew's were the bitter day we arrived. Go ahead
now, Harry. There shall be no talk of forgiveness until after it
is done.

Chapter 70

Haverton, Connecticut
December 21, 2014

I must have slept, even though I did not sleep well. It was one of those nights when you see the hours and minutes ticking away slowly on the digital clock, but when the sun rises, and you look back on it, it didn't feel like six hours, so you must've slept for part of it, or maybe even for several very brief and unsatisfying parts.

The sun—but not Lucy—was up when Chad called. He was at the airport, he said. Where was I? He'd called the land line twice already. He'd convinced his boss to let him come home a day early. He'd be home in an hour.

I'd check out and meet him at the house when Lucy woke up, I told him. And I did.

He was already in the living room when I arrived.

"You left the tree lights on," he said.

"Oh. Well, that probably made things cozy for Monty, at least."

Chad didn't say anything about wasted electricity or fire hazards. Nor did we say much about the window—just stood together in front of the duct tape crisscross for a minute or two.

"They say some mothers get superhuman strength if their

child is in danger. Like, they can lift a car up to get a trapped kid, or whatever."

"This didn't require superhuman strength," I admitted. "Just plain old-fashioned crazy."

"Well. I think it was probably in the same sort of category, though."

"If you say so."

"I wasn't sure I should mention this," Chad said. "But Patty called me yesterday and said she was worried. She saw the broken window. Luckily, that was after you and I talked. Or I would've freaked out."

"Luckily," I repeated.

"You know what I was thinking I might like to do?" Chad said, turning from the window as if to dismiss it and lifting Lucy out of the car seat. "Get Lucy's picture with Santa Claus."

"Uh . . . I don't think I can handle the mall today."

"I'll bring her. Then swing by the Home Depot for glass on the way home. Get some new hinges for that door while I'm there, maybe? Give you a chance to rest."

"Okay." I shrugged.

I couldn't visualize what this rest was to look like, but I was happy enough not to be a part of this phonily seminal moment in Lucy's life—her first time in the sweaty lap of a department store Santa. Maybe this could be—officially and forever—Chad's parental territory.

Back before we had Lucy, Chad and I discussed Santa a great deal. We'd discussed it with the same intensity that some might religious upbringing, or public versus private school.

Is it appropriate for parents to trick their children into believing something that would ultimately be revealed as a big fat fake? Was that the kind of relationship one wanted with one's child?

Well, if that's how you feel about it, then why do anything nice with the kid at all? Chad had said. *Why give them a night-light, when eventually they're going to have to get used to the dark? Why let a kid have a dog or a cat, if you knew it was eventually going to die one day or another?*

That is totally not *the same thing,* I had argued.

Now I remembered the discussion as a comical sort of black hole from which I'd since been mercifully released.

"What's so funny?" Chad wanted to know.

I smiled. "Just be sure to get pictures. I'm sure all the grandparents will want one."

I climbed straight up the stairs the moment after I heard the car pull away from the driveway.

The house felt cold—even gutted, somehow—without Lucy in it. I did not wish to wander its untidy rooms and recall the troubled moments of the last few days, or speculate about what Lucy's infant mind made of them.

Still, on my way to the bedroom, I stepped into Lucy's room and gazed into the crib for a moment. Scattered across the rosebudded sheet were a few rattles and stuffed animals I'd dropped in there for her a few days ago—before I'd set her up in our bedroom.

I was glad that the room had no mirror. I could think of no more terrifying specter than that of myself—so disheveled and depleted, and staring at an empty crib.

"Frances?" I whispered. "How do I endure this?"

I turned from the crib, stumbled down the hall, and fell onto my bed. I closed my eyes. I had no choice now. It was sleep or death. My body was shutting down on animal instinct. As I curled up on the bed, I felt a little corner stick into my hipbone. Wendy's note, still folded up in yesterday's jeans. I made myself a silent promise not to forget it and run it through the washer by mistake. I'd find a place for it. But where? Back in the banana box, buried in *Rights of Man*? Under my pillow? In my bra? My wallet? Would there ever be a right place for it?

Shhhhh.

My ears heard it, but my eyes didn't have the energy to open. I felt fear deep in my chest, but since Lucy was out of the house, it didn't seem significant enough.

Shhhhh.

It didn't matter that Lucy wasn't here.

I don't think she's all that concerned about the baby.

Of course. I understood now.

Shhhhh.

This voice would always be here, gusting in my ears—offering me its uneasy comfort—the only kind of comfort I would ever have again. Even after Lucy—and whoever came after her—was grown and gone from my arms, gone from my sight. Long after we were both gone from this house.

Neither my brain nor my body could lift itself out of the exhaustion that had overtaken both.

And then there was one last hushing, so soft it might've just been my mind repeating something it had already heard some time ago, and wanted to hear again. Either way, it drowned in the sound of my own breath, surrendering itself to sleep.

Chapter 71

Windsor, Connecticut
September 13, 1886

They are coming to see us on Saturday? They will stay a night, I presume? Or two? Or three?

Shall I cook up a goose? Or a turkey? I caught a large trout in the river the other day. I wonder if there's a chance I could catch one again? Does Martha like fish?

And might you know what sweet things she enjoys best? Does Clara ever make her ginger snaps? Hers never did have enough snap to them, in my opinion. Neither in flavor or consistency.

Yes. Of course I'm perfectly well. I'm joyous, in fact. I've said it many times already. You may as well put me back in the asylum if you are going to ask me to live without seeing her—to live completely outside the light of her spirit.

So I understand the conditions you put forth to Clara in your letter. It is for the best. Martha now knows another mother—and perhaps Clara was always destined to be a better one than I. I would have liked to have had more of a chance at it, but—no. I won't dwell on that. And no, Harry, I do not need your soggy handkerchief. I never cry. I never engage in any behavior that might be mistaken for womanly hysteria. I know better than that.

And what shall we have Martha call me? Frances Winter is how the locals know me. But for Martha—perhaps Aunt Franny? Aunt Frances? Mrs. Winter? Whatever you think fitting, I suppose. I will be anything you and Clara want me to be. It doesn't matter, as long as Martha comes.

I will be fine.

I will even be well, Harry, as long I can once again—and again—see the evergreen of her eyes.

Author's Note

Mary Stannard was brutally murdered in Rockland, Connecticut, on September 3, 1878. The Reverend Herbert Hayden, a local minister, was tried for the murder in late 1879. The *New York Times* articles quoted herein are real, as are accounts of the words spoken in the courtroom, including the scientific testimony of Dr. Samuel Johnson, Edward Salisbury Dana, and the other Yale professors. Dr. Johnson, however, had unnamed assistants working with him on his stomach experiments—and there I inserted the fictional Harry Flinch, Frances's twin brother.

Arsenic under the Elms: Murder in Victorian New Haven, by Virginia A. McConnell, is an excellent resource for readers who wish to read more about the case.

The Northampton Lunatic Hospital was a real institution that opened in 1858. Between 1864 and 1885, the superintendent was Dr. Pliny Earle, who instituted a program of intensive work therapy (considered by some to be slave labor, as under Earle's leadership the institution's farm turned a profit). My fictional Frances Flinch Barnett would have been a patient during his term as superintendent. Dr. Earle kept very detailed records of the management of the hospital, and I have tried my best to make the details about the conditions of that hospital as accurate as possible. According to most sources, conditions steadily worsened after Earle's departure, due in part to overcrowding. The hospital was renamed Northampton State Hospital in the early twentieth century, and remained open until 1993. It was demolished in 2006.

Haverton, Connecticut, however, is not a real place. The McFarlene murder trial is also fictional.

Acknowledgments

Many thanks to: Ross Grant, Lisa Walker, Laura Langlie, Carrie Feron, Nicole Fischer, Elise Bernier-Feeley, and Nicole Moore.

About the author

Read on

Insights,
Interviews
& More . . .

Meet Emily Arsenault

EMILY ARSENAULT is also the author of *The Broken Teaglass*, *In Search of the Rose Notes*, *Miss Me When I'm Gone*, and *What Strange Creatures*. She lives in Shelburne Falls, Massachusetts, with her husband and daughter. ∾

Q&A with Emily Arsenault

Your previous novels are mysteries, and this is more of a ghost story. Why the change of genre?

I never really considered myself a mystery writer. My first few novels just happened to have murders or mysterious deaths in them. *The Evening Spider* is a book that happens to have a ghost in it. I wanted a little change of pace, but still wanted to stay generally within the "suspense" category. I believe ghost stories were what really made me a reader when I was a kid, so it's my first literary love, in a sense. I always wanted to try writing one eventually.

Do you believe in ghosts?

Sometimes. I believe in them when I am alone in my house at night. Then the next morning I always talk myself out of it. I think that's a pretty common experience. There is a personal element of this story because I believed there was a ghost in my house when my daughter was a baby. It started when she was a few months old. Like Abby, I would hear a very human-sounding shushing sound on her monitor sometimes just as I was waking up to the sound of her crying. My house is relatively old (built in 1900), but I hadn't really gotten a "haunted" feeling from it before my daughter was born. The creepy experiences tapered off around her first birthday. Maybe ▶

our ghost just likes babies and doesn't care much for toddlers.

How did you learn of the Mary Stannard murder, and why did you want to write about it?

My maternal grandmother was a Stannard, and her family hailed from the same part of southern Connecticut as Mary Stannard. I didn't know about the Mary Stannard murder until recently, however. Oddly, I grew up hearing that an ancestor of my grandmother's had been hanged in New Haven for poisoning her husband in colonial times. A few years ago, I asked my mother for specifics. She said she thought the woman's name was Mary Stannard. I casually Googled something like "Mary Stannard New Haven poison," and all of this information came up about a very different case—in which a Mary Stannard was the victim, not the murderer. It was in the late nineteenth century, rather than the seventeenth or eighteenth. I asked my mother if the story could have gotten mixed up over the years. She said no—she'd also heard of the nineteenth-century Mary Stannard murder over the years and had probably just confused the names in her head. I'm still not sure of the veracity of the colonial-era story—but in any case, I got hooked on the Stannard-Hayden case pretty quickly. I found the *New York Times* and *New Haven Register* accounts fascinating. It is a very sad and disturbing case.

Of course, I still wonder if there is a family connection. A second cousin of mine who has done some genealogy research claims not to have found a direct connection between Mary's family and ours. But I think there is some connection. I hope this is not too creepy a thing to say, as my mother will surely read this—but there is a picture of Mary Stannard that was often in the newspapers, and I think it looks a great deal like pictures of my mother at the same age.

How did you research the Northampton Lunatic Hospital?

I went to Mount Holyoke College in South Hadley, Massachusetts, which isn't too far from Northampton. At the time, the hospital was still standing, and I heard of students sometimes going to the site to get their Halloween jollies. Though I never visited the place myself, I'd hear about it often both then and when I moved back to western Massachusetts later. I was curious about it but didn't have much reason to research it until after I started this novel. I did most of my research in Forbes Library (Northampton's public library, where they have a wonderful collection and a librarian devoted to local history). The most helpful resource I used was *Psychiatry in the Nineteenth Century: The Early Years of Northampton State* ▶

Q & A with Emily Arsenault *(continued)*

Hospital. I also read many of the annual reports of Pliny Earl—the superintendent of the hospital from 1864 to 1885.

This is a ghost story and a half-historical novel—but it is also a book about new motherhood. Did your own experiences as a mother inform the novel?

To a point, yes. I do think that early motherhood did some interesting things to my brain—some positive and some negative. My postpartum experience wasn't as dramatic as Abby's. Ghost notwithstanding, I never took doors off hinges or hired a medium or fled my home in the middle of the night. But I think that something that happens to Abby—and that I experienced as well—is that once you become a parent, your perspective changes. I know it is a cliché, but I was surprised that it turned out to be true! Moments from your childhood and adolescence are seen in relief, in a sense. You suddenly see everything through the protective parental lens, and it can be terrifying. ∽

Have You Read?
More by
Emily Arsenault

For more books by Emily Arsenault check out

WHAT STRANGE CREATURES

The Battle siblings are used to disappointment. Seven years after starting her PhD program—one marriage, one divorce, three cats, and a dog later—Theresa Battle still hasn't finished her dissertation. Instead of a degree, she's got a houseful of adoring pets and a dead-end copywriting job for a local candle company.

Jeff, her so-called genius older brother, doesn't have it together, either. Creative and loyal, he's also aimless, in both work and love. But his new girlfriend, Kim, a pretty waitress in her twenties, appears smitten. When Theresa agrees to dog-sit Kim's puggle for a weekend, she has no idea it will be the beginning of a terrifying nightmare that will shatter her quiet academic world.

Soon Kim's body is found in the woods, and Jeff becomes the prime suspect.

Though the evidence is overwhelming, Theresa knows that her brother is not a murderer. As she investigates Kim's past, she uncovers a treacherous secret involving politics, murder, and scandal—and becomes entangled in a potentially dangerous romance. But the deeper she falls into this troubling case, the more it becomes clear that, in trying to save her brother's life, she may be sacrificing her own.

MISS ME WHEN I'M GONE

Author Gretchen Waters made a name for herself with her bestseller *Tammyland*—a memoir about her divorce and her admiration for country music icons Tammy Wynette, Loretta Lynn, and Dolly Parton that was praised as a "honky-tonk *Eat, Pray, Love*." But her writing career is abruptly cut short when she dies from a fall down a set of stone library steps. It is a tragic accident, and no one suspects foul play, certainly not Gretchen's best friend from college, Jamie, who's been named the late author's literary executor.

But there's an unfinished manuscript Gretchen left behind that is much darker than *Tammyland*: a book ostensibly about male country musicians yet centered on a murder in Gretchen's family that haunted her childhood. In its pages, Gretchen seems to be speaking to Jamie from beyond the grave—suggesting that her death was no accident—and that Jamie must piece together the story someone would kill to keep untold.

Eleven-year-olds Nora and Charlotte were best friends. When their teenage babysitter, Rose, disappeared under mysterious circumstances, the girls decided to "investigate." But their search—aided by paranormal theories and techniques gleaned from old Time-Life books—went nowhere.

Years later, Nora, now in her late twenties, is drawn back to her old neighborhood—and to her estranged friend—when Rose's remains are finally discovered. Upset over their earlier failure to solve the possible murder, Charlotte is adamant that they join forces and try again. But Nora was the last known person to see Rose alive, and she's not ready to revisit her troubled adolescence and the events surrounding the disappearance—or face the disturbing secrets that are already beginning to reemerge.